JAGUARS

Georgina Garrastazu

STORY MERCHANT BOOKS
BEVERLY HILLS
2014

THE STORY MERCHANT

Jaguars

Story Merchant Books
400 S. Burnside Avenue #11B,
Los Angeles, CA 90036
http://www.storymerchant.com/books.html

ISBN: 978-8-9897154-5-4

Cover Design: David Angsten & Buffalo Creative Group
Interior Design: Lisa Cerasoli

Jaguars

For Olga and Alexander

"Jesus said, 'When you make the two into one, you will become children of humanity, and when you say, 'Mountain, move from here,' it will move away.'"

Gospel of Thomas, Verse 106

P r o l o g u e

As the wheel turns in the stone calendar, so also do our collective definitions of truth and humanity. My interest lies in what is beyond the wheel, in what is the origin and finality of our essence. Time does not itself change, but times do. I can attest to it because having retained my awareness for thousands of years, I enjoyed and suffered countless lifetimes. Due to a confluence of events, and more than one deal, the miracle of a new body was granted to me through the vehicle of incarnation.

My previous existence was spent as a seer in the Golden Age of my people, the Toltecs. There, a rare art rendered me nearly immortal. Since man first learned that death lurked, waiting for us all, he has contrived to avoid its touch. My people unraveled the mysteries of longevity and I became the recipient of the secrets of how to prolong my life.

Only one problem confounded me. Immortality is worthless without apotheosis. Man must evolve himself into a power before reaching for immortality. My master, the great Lord Quitzalcuat, understood the timing of such a feat. In my haste, I reached for the prize prematurely. This time within the wheel, I will temper my ambition and pluck the fruit of my labors when it is ripe.

My season upon this earth opened when humans knew the secrets of perception, shape shifting, and the fluidity of time. When pyramids were the storehouses of knowledge and scant wisdom, I danced around, upon and in them. In those days, my people were not savages, but one would not truly call us civilized, either.

Portents and the paths we walked upon determined what our names would be. Strong omens dictated the name that I would be given. I am Zaki Raxa Palo, named for the white churning waters of a sea chilled green by the hurricane that blew through my land at the time of my birth. I refer to myself as Zaki, Raxa, Palo, or other names that I give myself now and again. The names are not important, but the missive is.

Even today, my chosen names must always have meaning and significance, even if it is only personal. To do otherwise would be to sever myself completely from my origins and symbolically repudiate them, to lose myself truly in time. Such modernity is too progressive for an old-fashioned thing as me. I could not bear it.

Ask me who I am and I will tell you that I am a dreamer who knows the exultation of being the enemy of the creatures of the abyss. As a dreamer, I released my stare upon this world and saw wonders beyond the curtain of my eyes. I have lasted to this day because of my resolve and because I entered the eternal order of those who wage war against the enemies of humankind. Those enemies are called the Xibalbans:

They turn man against man, they use owls as messengers,
They foment sin, wickedness, and cruelty,
They are lords of falseness and hypocrisy,
Their true flesh is black and white,
Lords of folly, lords of confusion,
As it is stated. They disguise themselves as what we most fear
To despair us, to separate us from hope.

Popol Vuh, Part Three

They are indeed black and white. I know because I have seen them. Their realm is the underworld. Once again they are in our midst and active. They are abominations. The story of how they can be battled must be told. That battle was, eons ago, only capable of being waged by a player on the grand ball court. Times have changed. The arenas are many.

Now, it is the duty of every member of mankind to fight those beings. The game has already begun. The stone markers are mounted and the ball is in motion. The stands are filled with the fans of the opposing team and few of ours are there to wish our side well.

We are currently losing. We must change that.

We must fear.

The man who fears nothing has never seen Xibalba, and he loves nothing.

Part One

Beginnings

Up in the banyan tree, the jaguar climbed. Silently pacing the wild peccary that lingered beneath the shade, she maintained her position out of its sight.

The peccary sensed danger and pawed the ground with its hooves, tasting the air for predators with its snout. Every few feet, it changed the direction of its path. Beady eyes scanned the jungle beyond the clearing of the banyan, searching to discover the reason for the stillness in the wood.

Undeterred by the peccary's erratic path, Chahal walked along the massive tree's limbs. Fluid and sinuous, she flowed through the canopy like ocean water past anemones. Her careful steps did not warn the beast of her approach. Only the atmosphere noted the passing of menace. A careful huntress, she had taken time to rub herself against trunks and branches that the peccary left its scent upon, a hunter's camouflage.

The banyan she was on possessed seven trunks. Thick lattices of branches connected the differing trunks with a network of walkways up in the air. The clearing they were in bordered the jungle.

Outside of a dense wood, a banyan would ravage and strangle weaker plants. Our banyans were sacred and often their growth was guided to create sanctified earth. Those places abhorred the hunt. This glade, having seven trunks, could only be natural. No priest would fashion a septenary temple. Here, blood could be spilled freely.

Blowgun in hand, I looked up to where I last saw Chahal and could not see her. After having spent a long time looking at the green in the jungle around me as I tracked the peccary, the sun filtering through the leaves distorted my vision and rendered the jaguar invisible. Giving my eyes time to adjust, I saw her perched a man's length away from the animal, above him. Her yellow fur and black rosettes became discernible only when I focused on them.

Chahal caught my gaze and looked to my left, indicating that I should circle around to cut off the beast's escape.

The peccary snuffled the ground, using its snout to sniff underneath the fallen leaves.

I waited for the wind before moving beyond the bush where I crouched. Soon the wind would envelope everything in the clearing under the banyan tree. Shadows ghosted among the greenery as I watched it approach the peccary.

Gusts stirred the large dry leaves around the beast, giving me audible cover. Hunched low, my feet touched bare ground instead of leaves as I ran watchful of my path. Almost parallel to the peccary's position, I found myself in mid-stride when the wind died.

"Craaack," the dry branch, under my foot, sounded.

I grimaced as my extra step disturbed the silence of the jungle.

The peccary took off. Grunting and wild-eyed, it ran my way.

Chahal pounced, missing the beast by two man lengths.

Flustered, I dropped my blowgun. The peccary did not change direction and I realized it was charging me. Hooves pounded the earth in its efforts to escape Chahal. I scrambled up a trunk of the banyan moments before it could gore me to leave me wounded behind for its enemy.

The jaguar growled as she barreled past me after the fleeing swine.

Staying up in the tree, I waited for my heart to calm. A short time later, I spotted my blowgun and various darts on the ground and climbed down to pick them up. After I retrieved them, I glanced around and turned to look behind me.

The jaguar sat among the bromeliads, watching me. Calmly she sat, as if the chase had never occurred.

I walked towards her and she stood. Turning her back on me, she led me to the edge of the jungle, where cultivated fields lay nearby. When I stepped on to the plain that marked the boundary between the wild and the domesticated, she left me and returned to her hunts.

I tried to follow her back into the jungle and pushed aside foliage to peer back in, but could not see my cat and sole friend. Skilled though I was with the blowgun in the privacy of our home, the hunt revealed my deficiencies in stealth and action.

She had given me the chance to hunt with her and I spoiled the hunt. Many suns would pass before she allowed me to hunt with her again.

I turned to the west, towards my tribe's lands, and saw our temples glistening beneath the late afternoon sun and made my way alone.

Not yet was I a man. I carried no bounty home.

Among my people, a boy became a man when he could survive alone in the jungles or when his body was capable of producing semen. Girls became women when they had their first menses. Manhood and womanhood depended upon the potentiality to reproduce. Every child looked forward to the day when he could enter the fellowship of adults. I was not the exception.

How they precisely knew when a boy became a man is unknown to me. I suspect it was the duty of the matrons, who cleaned my quarters, to check my mat, bedding, and clothing for moisture. They needn't have bothered. I was so proud of my issue that I took my proof, a soiled loincloth, to my father Naualalom, our king.

"Father. Father. Look. X el nu puz nu naval pa nu varam (*I had a wet dream*). I'm a man," I yelled as I ran into the throne room. He was there with his advisors and a common man who had come in for assistance or judgment. The men backed away and grimaced when I passed by them, holding out before me the brown cloth I had worn to sleep, which was still shining with wetness.

The throne room was in an underground cavern, lit by resin torches and perfumed with incense. Various natural shafts led to open air, which allowed fumes to escape. It was a coveted room in the cavern system. Some of the other smaller caves smelled dank with stagnant air. Here, though, the air was fresh, easily supporting the flames of torches and incense.

Ornate murals covered the walls. At various paces, large niches were carved into the walls. Some led to passageways and others were solely recesses without any escape. Woven tapestries and large painted cloths blended with the murals. The walls without openings had benches carved into the walls. In the farthest region from the main entrance, my father's throne stood flush with the wall. The benches stopped two man lengths from the throne, so that its back did not have a recess behind it.

My father sent everyone away, even the guards. When we were alone, he told me, "Ah, you have finally become a man." Glancing down at the cloth I still held, he laughed. "What a fine thing." Ruffling my hair, he rejoiced and congratulated me some more.

I loved his laugh. Never was it reticent or restrained. Instead, it was full and rumbled out of him like thunder, causing his belly to shake. He was not an overweight man, but he was stout and had a bit of a paunch. I had not inherited his bones. Instead, I was skinny and slight. His thick hand could wrap both of my wrists easily.

How different we were. Full lips lent color to his round red face. My mouth was smaller and my weight caused my cheekbones to jut out. His brows were straight, lending him a cruel look unless one noticed the playful glint in his eyes. We dressed alike and both wore our hair in long braids that went past our waists. That was typical of the men in my tribe, though, I could not claim it as a true trait that we shared. If I looked more like my father, I would not feel as strange as I did. How I envied the russet skins of my siblings.

"My son has entered manhood overnight. As your father and the first man you told, I am obligated to teach you two things before you go back to your quarters. Are you ready for your first lesson, my son? Here it is. When I am holding counsel, you are not to burst in again as you did today. From now on, you must carry yourself as a man would."

This was not what I expected. I was crestfallen. Immediate celebration had been what I envisioned. Apparently, that was not to be.

He moved his head back to peer at me. "You are how I was when I was your age. It was a fine thing you did. I would not have had it any other way than for you to be yourself, Zaki. Now you are a man and have been declared as such by the king of your tribe. No, as my son and future heir, you will not be allowed to burst in again as a child would. You will enter as an adult and will observe the customs of conduct, which are used in the places of authority. You will learn all of these things. It is time."

He stood and seated me upon the throne, a large stone platform cushioned with the symbol of his authority, his ceremonial mat. He knelt on one knee and looked up into my face. "There is a promise you must make me now."

"What is it, father? Anything you ask, I will do." I was apprehensive about his solemn demeanor and felt that I would do anything possible to make him smile or feel pleased again.

"You must learn as much as you can and you must come to me whenever there are questions you are too shy to ask others. Do you understand? There will be times when your heart will not allow you to approach or bother another living being. I know this because I was only a bit older than you are now when I first sat upon the grand mat of kingship. My own father passed away soon after I became a man and now all that I have of him are memories of being his child. Few memories do I have of him after I became a man. We are fortunate that I am still here with you. You must come to me whenever you need to discuss what you have learned and seen. Let conversation bind us, as father and son. Allow me this."

"You will have what you ask, father. You shall be my confessor."

"I do not need to be your confessor. There are others who will supply that need as they braid your hair. No, I need to be with you as my own father was not with me. It is enough that I can hear from you about everything you learn."

"Why do you speak of such horrible things, father?" His words about my grandfather pained me; I did not want to think about becoming an orphan. In addition, the superstitious part of me believed that to speak of death was to invite it. My mother died giving birth to me and my only full blood relative was my father. My half-sister, Maricua, raised me and was a mother to me. I had other half-siblings, whom I rarely saw.

"Nonsense. You are now a man. I am telling you to cherish it. Time has the curious quality of forever flowing on, regardless of our presence."

"Why must we speak of this?" I asked.

"I speak of this because today I have been reminded of how little time we have. I want you to learn and be aware of everything that goes on among our tribe. One day, you will sit upon my mat and rule our people."

"What happened today?"

"When you ran in here, you reminded me of how I was when I was your age. This led to thoughts of my father." He paused for a moment, as if weighing his words. "To speak the full truth to you, today my oldest advisor left his body behind. He was the last of my father's counselors and now he has gone," he said.

The man he spoke of was an elderly man whom I had seen accompanying him many times. He was kind to me and always produced a sweet treat for me whenever I ran to my father and he was around. I didn't know his name and regretted never having learned it. It shamed me to ask my father what it was, so I didn't.

"Now," he said looking intently at me, "It is customary for me to ask if you have a question for me. My only requirement is that I answer you as if you are truly a man... who you now are, unless you have collected sap from a tree and tried to pass it off as something else." He winked at me and grinned. "Well?"

His question caught me by surprise. I didn't know what to ask him, so I asked the first question that floated through my mind. "Why don't we wear leaves as clothing?"

He looked at me for a few moments and chewed his upper lip. I soon realized that he was trying to keep himself from laughing.

"I don't know," he finally said. "If humans were alone in the matter and although I wasn't there, I would guess that too many people got rashes from the plants. Since man did not know, at first, which ones were bad for wearing, they probably took them haphazardly and experimented with different leaves. Some of those must have been poisonous, of course. Then, we need to broach the subject of dry leaves. They tend to crumble and make great homes for insects. Clothes that cause itching have never tended to be too popular. They aren't often stylish, either."

We laughed, he with heartiness and me with embarrassment.

"So?" he asked. "Were you serious when you asked me that question?"

I shook my head and admitted that I hadn't actually been interested in learning about that, but had not been able to come up with a better question. He laughed until he was hoarse.

Back then, a part of me wanted to be the noble man of rhetoric, but I was far from eloquent. Many days, I would sit anywhere where men congregated, in order to watch them speak. In court, I watched the men argue the merits of certain courses of action or the fates of other people. I admired those who were able to speak well and answer rapidly. Sometimes, I would merely delight in the cadences of their voices without listening attentively to what they said. Their rapidity of speech dazzled me. I yearned for the ability to answer questions and converse without having to mull everything in my mind before I said it. My quickness to answer my father was the result of this wish. I had spoken without the requisite thought that must accompany speech.

He watched me with soft curious eyes. We sat in silence until one of the guards approached to advise my father that he had a visitor.

"Go on, Zaki. Go see your sister, Maricua. Tell her that I will be by later to speak with her. Also, think of another question that you would rather ask of me. It isn't right that your first question should be without relevance."

I left. Chahal waited for me at the cavern entrance. People were accustomed to seeing her, yet they gave her a wide berth whenever they had to pass her.

We walked home, side by side.

A festival, celebrating the boys who had become men, occurred once every year. My father would announce to the court that I had reached manhood and they would allow me to attend. It was to take place eight days after I stormed into my father's court with my dirty undergarments.

There was no end to the relief I felt from not having to wait another year for the festivities. No one of minor age could take part or attend, or so I believed.

Once, when I was younger, I sneaked out to try to see what went on at the festival, but Maricua caught me as I reached the outskirts of the crowd. Well, soon I was to see the whole thing. A sense of exhilaration filled me whenever I imagined being a part of those throngs of tall people celebrating.

In the late afternoons, it was my custom to sit in the walled garden outside of my sleeping quarters. Lush plants, fruit trees, and flowers of intoxicating fragrances were in bloom. The seclusion and quietude of my little orderly wilderness often put me to sleep or led me to reverie.

Chahal lazed under a citrus tree.

The garden led to a larger enclosed area, which ended near the river. Since it was not the rainy season, the water ran warm and sluggish. I took a swim to cool off, but it did not ease my discomfort. It was very hot outside and as soon as I dressed myself again, I was sweating.

When I reached my quarters, twilight was near. Calling Chahal to me, I parted the curtains leading to my rooms and allowed her to enter before me. She seemed to love these little courtesies. How I knew that, I didn't know, but I was certain of it. It pleased me to pamper her.

Servants had already lit the torches beside the entry-ways. Somehow, I preferred the evening's false lights to the sunlight. When the shadows danced along the walls, I would often sit for hours and watch them. That night, I didn't watch shadows on the wall or play with Chahal. I tried to imagine what the festival would be like, when I heard footsteps in the hall.

Maricua and my father came in and sat down in front of me. Her face was flushed and she would not meet my eyes. I had no idea why she was upset. It was rare for her to pout or frown. Her face was alien without her customary grin. Her face was formed for smiles and laughs, only. She held her hands clasped and stared down at them, while my father grinned from ear to ear.

"So, how is our little man?" he asked.

"I am fine. What is happening? Maricua? What is it?"

She would not look at me. Something was definitely wrong and I felt a horrendous sensation of expectancy in the pit of my stomach.

"Oh, Maricua is simply worried about you, dear boy. Don't worry. She expects that you will stay her little brother forever, but we all know that such things are not to be. It is the natural order that we all grow up and come to have responsibilities. She will get used to it," my father told me. "I have arranged everything."

"Arranged what?"

"Your schooling."

Maricua began to cry. She was certainly not one to cry gracefully. Her body was racked with sobs and her delicate bronze face soon became red and swollen. If I had not seen it happen, I would have not believed that she could change so rapidly. Never had I seen her cry before. Seeing her, that way, put me into a near state of panic.

I leaned forward to brush tears from her face. She grabbed my hands and held them to her face. Hot tears soaked my hands. After a time, she began to calm and let go of me. I looked over at my father.

He did not look upset or worried about her and merely shrugged. "She will be fine, Zaki," he said as he stood up. "Come with me, we have things to discuss."

I hugged her and then went to him. He smiled and put his arm around me to lead me to the hallway. I looked back. Maricua was watching me with a sad face. When my eyes met hers, she grimaced horribly yet nodded and motioned for me to go with my father with a wave of her hand. Only then did I feel comfortable leaving with him. I saw her lie back and close her eyes.

My father shrugged again and said, "She'll be fine, I assure you."

As we walked, my father said, "Today is the burial day for my eldest personal advisor. You have never been old enough to come with me to attend a funeral procession, so watch what I do and learn from it. Let us take our time walking there, though, because there are a few things I want to tell you."

I nodded my head. I felt guilty about leaving Maricua distraught. We reached the main entryway of the estate Maricua and I shared and began walking towards the temple grounds. Four guards surrounded us, two beside us and two behind us. They were unobtrusive and I was used to having them near whenever I walked with my father outside.

"Not tomorrow, but the next day, you will begin learning under the Cabicacmotz."

"Who is that?"

"Remember all of the times that you have tried to get my attention, but my guards would not let you through to talk to me?"

Many times, I had sought him out, only to be rebuffed by the guards. Most of the time, they let me through with impunity, but every once in a while they would stop me. I told my father that I believed it was a joke they played on me occasionally to amuse themselves when they didn't see Chahal with me. Since it did not happen often or regularly, I didn't pay much attention to it.

"Well, that was because I was with my special advisor, the Cabicacmotz. He is the lead teacher of wisdom as well as my closest friend. He is one of the few people I trust implicitly. He and I studied together. His understanding and knowledge are the meat of legends. He has invited you to be his pupil, after I made it known to him that you had become a man. It is a great honor. Tell me, what do you think of that?"

He was guaranteeing me entrance into a world that I knew nothing about but had heard whispers of. I was intrigued with the possibility of becoming a great man like my father and those around him.

One thing made me pause. I thought of Maricua. Perhaps she knew better than I did what was happening. She was sad or, worse yet, horrified about this. As my surrogate mother, she was unparalleled as my protector. It was a joke between us that every victory of mine was equally hers since she felt pride whenever I accomplished anything worthwhile. She had taken the responsibility of raising me after my mother died while giving birth to me. She took care of me and dried my tears. My father's wives did not even glance in my direction.

I decided that there might be reason for caution. Maricua's love for me was evident in everything she did. Knowing that she was not given to emotional outbursts or fits of crying, I suspected that there were valid reasons for her concern. This tempered my joy and I began to ask my father questions pertaining to what I would be doing and what I could expect from going through with it. There was really no question as to whether I would go, of course. I knew I would, if only to please my father. Still, I had to uncover information that I could use to placate Maricua and put her at ease with the situation.

"You will be given the keys to unlock power and knowledge," he told me. "There is not much to tell, really. Once you go, it is self-explanatory. I will be here to answer your questions at the end of the day, but no words of mine could prepare you for what is ahead. It is an adventure. Remember that you are there as my son. As such, you are expected to behave yourself with the utmost diplomacy and discipline."

"That's all that you can tell me? You have made me even more curious, but I still don't know what to expect."

He laughed and put his arm around my shoulder. "Then expect what you don't expect, because it is what will happen. Don't be surprised by the feats of other humans," he cautioned. "Whatever you see, remain calm at all costs. There is more to people than meets the eye, or there could be if they trained themselves properly. We are fortunate to have the means to better ourselves."

We walked in silence along the dirt path until we reached the base of one of the larger stone temples and sat down on the steps. Twilight was almost over and many people held torches. The guards positioned themselves before us in a fan arrangement.

"Let's stay here until the crowd leaves," he said as he indicated the people walking in single file towards one of the smaller pyramids. "Let us allow them to give their tribute in peace."

A grand procession of the tribe was paying homage to the memory of my father's friend. Up they went, laden with gifts that properly showed their respect. They came down empty handed. Many cried. Others were calm or did not know him well enough to cry tears for his absence.

"Have you thought about the question you would like to make me answer?" he asked.

For once, I was prepared. "Yes," I told him. "I would like to know how you met my mother and where she came from, since she was not of our tribe."

He looked at the ground with a sad smile on his face and said, "Ah, the eternal gap in the one-question rule. Make the question complex." He took a while to compose his thoughts and finally spoke. "She came from beyond the sea. She and her brother were found shipwrecked on the little atoll west of here."

"What? She had a brother? I had an uncle?"

"Yes, you have an uncle."

"He's still alive? He survived?"

"Yes, he's still around. You will meet him soon, I promise."

My mind reeled. "Why has he never wanted to come and see me? Does he understand that, other than you, he is my only full-blooded relative?"

"He spent a lot of time with you when you were a baby. The rest is considerably more complicated. He has been away for quite some time and has only recently returned completely. Perhaps he will tell you the story of what happened to him. I assure you that there are valid reasons as to why you have not seen him for such a long time."

I didn't know how to respond to his words. Clearly, he didn't want to disclose to me why I hadn't seen my uncle for a decade. I wanted to question him further on that, but instead I asked, "Where were they from?"

"I honestly don't know. I did not recognize their descriptions of their land. From what I gathered, they were from a place beyond the sea, on the other side of the world."

Although modern Western man has experienced the embarrassment of knowing that in their recent history their ancestors forgot that the world was round, my people always knew it. We were foolish in other ways, but nothing could have made us ignore the obviousness of that one fact.

"Did they look like our people?"

He smiled broadly and shook his head as he ran his hand over my head. "No."

Was he indirectly telling me that I also looked foreign? Could it be? Was that why no one wanted to claim me as his or her brother, except for Maricua? Foreigners were welcomed, in my tribe, but they were not trusted implicitly, either. The thought that I might be considered an outsider in my own land, worried me. "Do I look foreign?"

He tilted his head and pursed his lips as he looked at me. "Perhaps. Your hair is a bit different. Instead of red highlights, you sometimes have yellow highlights when the sun touches your hair. You are also a great deal lighter than most of our people. You don't notice that because you have spent years allowing the sun to kiss your body. I know that you are not this dark naturally; I saw you when you came into this world. Your skin was the shade in between your mother's and mine. You are a mix of the two of us. You do not look foreign to most people because the features are a blend, but I see her in you."

"Was she pretty?"

"Son, she was the most beautiful woman I have ever seen. Her hair was a silk of brown and gold. And her eyes! Her eyes were gold. Never have I seen eyes like that. Oh, every once in a while, a green or a blue eyed one lands on our shores, but never a one with golden eyes. Her brother has told me that it was not a common thing from where they came from, either. I cannot properly convey to you her beauty. I will have to take you to my private home one of these days because one of the plasterers captured the exact likeness of her face as she looked when asleep. It does not give one a good idea as to what she actually looked like, with her beauty, but you will at least be able to see her features."

"I would like that very much," I said.

"We can talk more about her some other time, Zaki. In fact, it is not right that you should use your first question in manhood on things that I should have told you about before. Please think of another question. We will talk about this again, so do not worry that the subject is closed. If I were you, I would spend a little time with the Cabicacmotz before I asked my question. Your question should concern the subject of being a man, not wasted asking me about things that you have a right to know, such as your heritage."

I nodded.

The crowds of people were now only a trickle. My father and I sat on the steps, in a comfortable silence, and waited until everyone left. The moon was low on the horizon, and it was in no shape to illuminate much.

The guards were now carrying torches and I noticed that the darkest man wore a bundle on his back, making him look like a hunchback. I wondered where it came from, since I had not noticed it earlier. Could he have had it the whole time or did I simply fail to notice when he picked it up?

The guards were solemn men and took their post seriously. They were ever alert, yet they were in repose, never seeming to make sudden movements unless they detected a threat to my father's safety. When they needed to move, they were like wind. One could also ignore them easily for they kept to the background. They were like gliding statues, gracefully moving, yet never expressing sound.

My ruminations about the mystery stopped when my father stood and indicated that it was time to make our way towards the temple.

As we walked, we conversed and reminisced about the entombed man. I was only able to mention that the sweets the man gave me were the best I had ever tasted and that I appreciated his kindness. My father explained that it was customary to approach a grave while speaking well about the life that the person had led. Naturally, this led to the subject of his succession.

"You do not yet know whom he chose to sit on his mat after him, do you, Zaki?" my father asked me as we reached the base of the stepped temple.

I was at a loss for words. While I could identify some of the people in my father's court, I was never a fixture there and knew only a few names and faces. I didn't want to let him know that I had not bothered to learn who was in his court and said, "No, I don't. Who is it? Do I know him?"

Father laughed. "How is it that you do not wait to have your first question answered before you ask another and another? It is like the little boy who grabs at sweets and reaches for more before he has even swallowed one. You are a glutton. Except that, you won't become obese. Rather, perhaps, you will become engorged with information. At least I can console myself that my son does not have one of the more difficult vices to contend with."

"No, he doesn't," a man spoke from behind us.

My first reaction was to look at the guards. They did not react to the newcomer among us.

I turned around and saw the man who spoke. He wore a dark hooded cloak that concealed his facial features. My father did not look back at him and kept facing forward. It annoyed me that someone had intruded into what I considered a time meant solely for my father and me. It was private and I felt, somehow, cheated. "Who are you? And do you often butt into conversations that don't concern you?" I asked as I walked towards him.

Still facing the temple, Naualalom whispered to me that I should shut my mouth. The man raised his head and laughed. The sound of his laughter made me want to hit him. I knew that he was having fun at my expense. I could have sworn, at that moment, that he had rudely insulted me. My mind raged and I cherished the thought of having the guards seize him and whip him for his insolence. How dare he insult me in front of my own father?

"No. Pride and violent thoughts are his vices. They intoxicate him," the man said.

Red fury filled my eyes and I moved to strike him, confident that my father's guards would help. My fist moved through the air and struck only empty space. Where was he? I looked around. The man had only been an arm's length away from me and now he was gone.

I turned to look at my father for an answer and was surprised to find that he also was not there. All of the guards were looking up at the temple. I looked upwards to see what they were seeing. My father and the hooded man were almost to the top of the pyramid, looking down at me. Oddly, the guards were there as well. When I glanced to where the guards had stood a moment before, they were gone. What was happening? It was impossible. Determined to find out, I ran up to them.

When I neared, I saw the look on my father's face. He glared at me with eyes that were cold and fierce. They were not the kind eyes of my father. Never had I seen him look at me like that. I knew that my father had no compassion towards me, at that moment. I felt his desire to kick me down the steps. I realized that I had embarrassed him before someone very important to him and that he was ashamed of my behavior. I knelt. "Forgive me, father."

"It is not me whom you should be apologizing to, Zaki."

I turned to the man at his side. "Please forgive me my irreverence; I did not realize who you were." I didn't know who he was, but it sounded good to my ears.

The man glided towards me, over the steps, as I stood up. My eyes widened with surprise and my mouth hung open. His movements were unnatural and I became very frightened. I stepped back before he reached me. My fear that he would touch me was so great that I felt that I would vomit.

"You still don't know who I am, but don't be frightened, little one," the man said. "I am not going to touch you or strike you as you intended to do to me. Your apology has been accepted."

He then became a blur and was gone.

Father looked at me and said, "The next time I tell you to shut your mouth, do it. If that was your best effort at diplomacy, then you are going to have a very difficult time of it with the Cabicacmotz. It is he whom you just insulted."

There were no words to express my regret. I sat down. "What have I done?"

"Unfortunate as it is, the ugly truth is that you insulted the man who has offered to teach you all that he knows and who could, quite literally, squash you like a beetle under his foot, if he so desired it."

My regret was complete. I began to retch. I would have fallen down the side of the temple if my father had not grabbed me by my braid. When I was finished, I looked up at my father and saw him grinning down at me.

"Don't worry too much. I happen to know that he won't step on you like a bug. He's my friend. He will do everything he can to turn you into a man of wisdom. When a man reaches the stage that the Cabicacmotz is at, he has overcome his anger at others. He reins himself in. He's probably having a good laugh about you right now." He began to snicker. A few moments later, he was fully laughing at my predicament.

I was in the throes of desperation and he tried to console me. I had to banish any remembrances of how the man glided over the steps like a phantom or else I would get sick again.

"He probably saw a lot of me in you, Zaki. Oh, I was once unruly and incorrigible, so I was quite capable of making our teacher pull his hair out of his head. But, like you, I was the son of the ruler, so he took my best interests upon himself and wound up scaring me half to death."

"He has come into my dreams and will not give me a moment of peace," my father said in a ridiculous falsetto, like a woman's voice. "I told my father, 'He is haunting me. What am I to do?'"

"What did he say?"

"Nothing, of course. He knew that I had to bring myself to order and that my teacher was merely doing what I needed to have done to me."

"Is that supposed to cheer me?"

"Don't be so dour. Either you never act like the brat you are, as you did back there, or you get the crap scared out of you. I am sorry. Perhaps I did not spend enough time with you while you were still a boy. It is clear you need outside disciplining. The basis of your view on life should not be based solely on what Maricua and I have told you. Someone else will now demand your attendance and attention.

I have given the Cabicacmotz permission to teach you and to do whatever is necessary to mold you into a man of genius. Try not to act like a complete fool, please."

I was aghast. There was my father, telling me that I behaved like an idiot child and that he was leaving me in the care of a man who terrified me. "What have you gotten me into, father?"

'The adventure of a lifetime. It is not easy for the teacher when the student does not make the necessary effort, though, so strive to learn how to command all of your energy," he said. "Let's get along now to Zotabah's tomb."

We climbed down and went to another temple, the smaller one where the people had gone into.

Instead of climbing the outer steps, we entered through a small opening at the base of the structure that led to a steep inner stairwell. This was the eeriest temple we had and its sole purpose was for the dead. None of the other pyramids, to my knowledge, contained inner chambers.

It took us a while to climb the steep stairs. Normally, I would run up the steps, but that would have been unseemly for a funeral. Finally, we reached the place where the mourners had ascended to, upon the roof of the temple.

A short distance away, on top of the temple, stood another structure. There, a large room awaited us. Two guards were posted inside the entrance. They stood alongside the largest torches, which stood at the portal. Several smaller torches were arrayed throughout, illuminating every corner and suffusing the room with a golden glow.

My father told the guards to wait outside to prevent any who might have entered the subterranean route behind us. After my father's personal guards satisfied themselves that no one else was in the room with us, two kept watch with the others over the passageway while the other two protected the entrance into the room.

Flowers, pottery, and jewelry filled the chamber. A long sarcophagus, adorned with shiny stones, was in the center upon a platform. The walls of the room were formed from large square blocks of stone, which had been carved to show scenes of warriors engaging in various endeavors. One of the blocks had been removed. I looked for it and did not see it around.

"Why is this missing?" I asked as I traced the edges of the hole.

"Tomorrow, he will be placed in there."

I looked at the sarcophagus. It did not look as if it could fit in the hole. "How?"

"Yes, it doesn't seem as if it could fit in there, but I assure you that it will. It has been perfectly measured. The sarcophagus will reside in the temple, with his body, for a period of seven days. Thereafter, it will be placed inside the earth."

"Where is the stone that covers the hole, though?"

"One of the stone workers is carving the inside of it to include an image of him. Don't bother with worrying about that, Zaki. Look around."

I examined the articles that people had left behind.

My father was pleased. "Look at how revered he was. Tomorrow when his wife comes, she will see the testaments telling her how much people loved him."

"Then, these are gifts for her?"

"In practicality, yes. She may take them home if she so desires it. I doubt that she will, though. She already has many possessions. Among the people who have no wealth, the wife takes what is left for him. Our customs take into consideration the fact that the widow may need assistance, but she, as I said, is already wealthy and may decide to have many things placed inside with him or she may even give it to the poor."

"Everything will stay here, for now, then?"

"Certainly, unless some buffoon tries to steal something. I would feel very sorry for that person." He looked around, smiling with satisfaction. "Burial rituals are strange, are they not? People leave things for him, but no one is stupid enough to believe that Zotabah could take these things with him. There is a chance that his spirit will become curious about his burial and may come back to look it all over. Then he will see what those people who loved him left. That is a possibility. Who knows? Either way, the practical result is that he is no longer here and no amount of riches or keepsakes could entice him to come back to life. I am happy for him. My feeling is that he has accomplished what he needed to do here and is now enjoying himself every moment. He certainly deserves that. He was a wise and good man."

I noticed several ornate pieces of jewelry and was surprised that mourners had left such costly objects. "Why do some people leave such valuable things?"

"Perhaps that person has wealth and is not bothered with leaving it or they may have given it from their heart regardless of its value. Or both, maybe. Whether a person has truly given or pretended to is often hidden. Some people may leave an arrangement of art showing what the person meant to him, others leave things that held special significance to the two of them. Their reasons for doing so are as varied as the number of people. Notice the flowers, Zaki."

"Why?"

"It is evidence that he was revered even among those of our tribe who do not have riches. The widow might even see this display and decide to donate the valuable articles to the poor." He thought for a moment before continuing, "The poor, when they walk to the grave of those whom they loved, pick the most beautiful flower that they can find and leave it as a token of their respect. It is a custom among them. They have little upon this earth, which is why they are often the ones who leave the most appropriate and beautiful of articles in a grave. It finely echoes the transitory nature of life… Anyway, I tell you that when a man can earn the respect of the poor, we know his true worth."

"How is that? I don't understand what you mean."

"It means that the man did not treat them as if they were unimportant or worthless. He saw them as people. If only those with riches visit a man's tomb, we can conclude that he never learned where the true wealth of our tribe lies. These flowers mean to me that he affected those who did not have our advantages, and that they knew him as a friend. He made progress into making their lives more manageable or easier. The exact circumstances, I don't know, but I see that he did not confine his interactions to those who hold court. That impresses me and it should impress you as well."

I looked into a clay jar that sat near the base of the sarcophagus. Oval stones of many colors filled it. Some had intricate designs carved into them. Many were polished, while others were rough. The only thing similar about them was their size. "How curious, father. What are these?"

He came over to where I was and peered into the jar. "Those are probably from his students. He was the man who knew how to use stones and taught others how to use them. His knowledge was formidable."

"Yes, but what are they for? They're all rounded and about the same size."

"They fit into the navel."

"Really?" I took a blue one out and tried to place it in my belly button. My father slapped my hand and sent the stone rolling to the floor.

"Don't ever do anything like that again!" he yelled.

His reaction stunned me. Why would he care that I had tried on someone else's jewelry? I asked, "Why not?"

"Because it's dangerous. These stones were on another person and are not toys. They are not mere decorations. They were devices to focus the attention of warriors and men of power."

I had no idea what he was talking about, but I did not want to argue with him. Tonight had been strange enough and here I was adding to my problems because of my ignorance. I vowed to keep my hands at my sides and not touch anything else.

My father removed a strange cylinder from under his robes and placed it upon the sarcophagus. I did not know what it was and did not ask. I removed one of my bracelets and placed it next to my father's gift. We left and walked in silence back to our home, the home he most often stayed in, in any case.

In general, the men in my tribe only had one wife per man. Tradition demanded that the king have four wives.

They represented the east, the west, the north, and the south. Each woman represented a cardinal point. Certain familial lineages belonged to different directions and each direction demanded that the king take a wife from one of their houses.

My father, much to everyone's chagrin, once had an extra wife. That wife was my mother. I would have been considered a bastard except for two very important reasons. I was the first son and he married my mother in a ceremony before the whole tribe where he declared her the wife of his spirit. She was the only one that he had truly chosen for himself. Being a foreigner, she had not been in the line of women who would marry him.

The marriage was a renegade maneuver. One that would cause me untold grief, but I had no standing to complain since I would not otherwise have been born.

None of the other wives had been able to bear him a son before she came into his life. To their horror, she became pregnant with me three years after my father married her.

I had six older sisters when I was born. Maricua was father's first-born child. She was the daughter of his first wife of the east. The current easterly woman married my father after Maricua's mother died. My mother was the only wife who was glad to have Maricua around and who was willing to share a home with her. When my father married my mother, she, reportedly, was happy to move into the home occupied by one of my father's former wives. Maricua became a daughter to her. When my mother died while giving birth to me, Maricua took over my care. Therefore, the home I lived in was once the first eastern woman's home.

Sadly, the wives of my father were touchy and selfish. For three years, Maricua was alone after her mother passed. Since none of the other women wanted to care for another woman's child, my father was forced to keep the east estate solely for Maricua, her maids, and guards. He quickly had the workers prepare and build the new east wife's home to the east of Maricua's home.

As to the physical locations, my father's home was in the middle ground, a place of solitude. The women were only allowed to enter the outer courtyards. Why this was so, I have no idea, but that was the tradition. Adjacent to the masculine home were the private homes of the women. These were sprawling estates, surrounded by gardens.

Because the current east wife's estate was to the east of our home, it was called the East-East. We lived in the West-East. The East-East was not as pleasant as ours was. I'm sure the east wife was not pleased to be relegated to the outskirts of my father's private properties, especially considering that we had the choicest land. Being unwilling to compromise, sometimes works to one's detriment. She was such an unpleasant woman, that I was quite pleased to imagine her jealousy whenever she looked towards the west, towards us.

A hastily built home is never as durable as one that has been there for many generations. For a few years, the other wives were envious of her home. It looked new and pristine. Over the years, the lack of time spent in planning and building it became apparent. Many walls failed and had to be repaired. Something was always wrong with it and the woman came to regret her inflexible stand towards my eldest sister.

One of my father's duties was to have as many children as possible, it seemed. He was always spending his evenings at the women's homes. These homes were considered his, of course, and he kept a private suite at each estate. Curiously, though, he always slept at his own estate or in the suite he kept at our home.

Apprehension filled me when I anticipated the first day of lessons. No longer did I daydream about the fun I would have at the festival. My mind reeled with memories of how I behaved poorly towards my new teacher.

Maricua told me awful tales of boys who had not pleased the lead instructor and the punishments that he had inflicted upon them. Although I had already experienced a scare from him, I became concerned anew when she told me of various powers that the Cabicacmotz had. To hear Maricua tell it, he had no compunction in using them to make his students behave.

"If I were you, Zaki, I would train my mind to only hold proper thoughts, because once the Cabicacmotz gets a hold of you, he'll read the thoughts in your mind and judge you," Maricua told me. "He may like you or dislike you, as the case may be, but either way it will be very uncomfortable for you if one day he catches you thinking he's mean, rotten, or an idiot. I'm telling you, he's very scary to be around."

"One day," she continued, "I was in the place of court and two men were in dispute over whether one of the men had done some thing or another. I'm not sure what it was about because I couldn't hear very well and they didn't talk very loud. All of a sudden, the Cabicacmotz entered the court. He had never walked in like that. Usually, it is known if he is going to be there or not. He came in and stood in front of the men, looking at them. I don't know how, but he waved his arm in front of them and a flaming wall appeared before each man. The Cabicacmotz looked at the men through the walls of flame and then waved his arm again and the fires disappeared. He accused one of the men and turned to leave when the man foolishly denied what he had said. Oh, the Cabicacmotz got into a terrible rage. Terrible. He sent fire into that man's hair and he would not extinguish it until the man confessed. That man was in agony. Oh Zaki, it was horrible to watch. I thought that I would pass out. Never have I seen anyone in such pain."

I swallowed hard and tried not to act as horrified and scared as I was. I asked her, "Did he kill him?"

"Did who kill who?"

"The man with the fire on his head. Did the Cabicacmotz kill him?"

"Oh, no. He's still here. He's bald now and his head has hideous scars all over it. Sometimes I see him when I venture into the market. He keeps a turban over his head, but the children tease him a lot and pull his turban off. You know how mean kids can be. He must be embarrassed every day. Even though he lied, I feel sorry for him."

"That is appalling, Maricua. Why would you tell me a story like that?"

"It's no story, Zaki. I'm telling you, you'd better control your thinking. I doubt that he would do anything like that to you because you are the son of Naualalom, but he can still make your life miserable. In case you haven't caught on, our father will not intervene in your instruction. It is considered a privilege to learn what you are going to be learning."

"What is it that I am going to learn?"

"How to command power like the Cabicacmotz."

"I don't want to set people on fire!"

"That's not all the Cabicacmotz does, Zaki. Haven't you noticed that some men in this society are different from others? Some men are more men than others are. Power infuses them. Those are the men who are priests or other men of might and energy. They are called the lords of the life force. You will learn their secrets. You should be proud that you were chosen. Father told me that the Cabicacmotz chose you the first day that you arrived with Chahal."

"Really?"

"Yes. But I'd be scared if I were you."

"Why?"

"You will be like the Cabicacmotz. He is the most powerful man in this place. It is he who wields the real power here, not our father. Yet he has no interest in being in power." Maricua's eyes glazed over as she gazed absently into space. "He is the man behind the king who everyone is frightened of. He is stronger than any man here is. They all know that they cannot beat him, so they acquiesce to his authority. Yes, he is a true lord of the life force. He could subdue everyone, yet he chooses to teach instead. The way he lives is perfect. His life is simple. He has few belongings, yet he lives in luxury." At that point, her voice acquired a dreamy quality. "The soft grass is his bed mat. The trilling of birds and the humming of insects is his music. He lives alone in a strange place, an encased forest. It is an existence of solitude, yet it is not lonely for him because he has all of the companionship one could ever need, the birds, the trees, and the stones...Yes, he is wise, but he is also capable of moral umbrage. He is the best man in this city, in many ways. He is also quite a fine man for a woman to look at."

"Weren't you telling me about what a scary man he was a moment ago? Now, you sound like you admire him."

"Well, I admire him too, even though I find him frightening. There is more to people than one aspect. People are not only one way."

I knew that she was hiding something and I suspected she secretly liked the man. Despite the story she told me of the horrid thing he did, there was awe and veneration in her tone when she spoke of him.

"But to get back to why it is a difficult time for you right now," Maricua quickly said when she caught me smirking at her. "You will not be like other people any longer. Those people don't care about the things that normal people care about, anymore. The boys who go to the Cabicacmotz are there to learn, but most of them have not been chosen as you were. You are commanded to attend these lessons because of your standing as the son of the king, but there was also an important omen about you. Something besides your birthright pointed you out and demanded that you go, also. Don't you see? Your destiny has already been determined for you. All you can do is to go along with it. It is a tremendously difficult path and one that you must take whether or not you like it. You can't get out of it. Therefore, if you are going to be around that man, the best thing you can do is to keep your thoughts clean and wholesome. Don't go around thinking badly of other people, especially him."

"How can I learn to do that?" What she was talking about seemed to be a very difficult thing. I sometimes noticed my thoughts and there were times when I enjoyed thinking of people in less than kind ways. Sometimes, even, I would imagine them engaging in all sorts of unsavory things, like stealing or spitting in the community water wells, especially if they seemed like proper upstanding citizens.

"Simple. Wish others well. Treat others as you would like to be treated. The trick lies in treating others in your thoughts that way, as well. Do you think that you can manage to do that?"

I told her I would, but in truth was not at all confident that it was even possible for me to do so. I was going to try, though. I didn't want anyone setting my head on fire. I wasn't even sure that I could ever like anyone who was capable of doing something like that to someone else. Naualalom was my father and wanted me to follow in his steps, however, and I was determined not to bring shame to him. I had to try my best, particularly if I wanted to undo the damage I had already done.

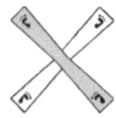

Father asked that I see him before I left for my first lesson. I took care to dress well, as it was a special day, and donned my finest dressings and jewelry.

Chahal accompanied me.

When I walked in to see my father, he was alone, except for his guards. He praised me for looking handsome. I felt a surge of pride.

"Unfortunately, it is not proper for you to begin your instruction looking like the son of a king. Please remove your jewelry, armbands, and any other finery."

I was puzzled that he wanted me to dress like a commoner. I thought that he would be pleased with my preparations.

"Come here, my son," he commanded me. "I am not saying this to you in order to make you unhappy. I am saying this to you because it is your first day with the Cabicacmotz. It is imperative that you go before him without any petty concerns about your appearance. What will make you look good to him is the absence of thoughts about yourself. Trust me. If I had not told you to dispense with those things, he would have himself. Moreover, he would have done it in front of his other students. I am merely trying to save you the embarrassment that I went through myself when I had my first lesson with the Cabicacmotz."

"You also were taught by him, father?"

"Well, I was taught by his predecessor, the previous Cabicacmotz."

"You mean that is not his name?"

"It is now. The Cabicacmotz is not addressed by the name given to him by his parents. It is a title, which has become a name. The title or name, if you will, is handed down from one Cabicacmotz to the next. Much as my title, Naualalom is used."

Although I was peripherally aware of these things, I had not pondered them or made the necessary connections, which would ordinarily lead one to logical conclusions about life and how it worked in our culture. The actual mechanics of our society eluded me since I was essentially a spoiled child that was not accustomed to thinking. I merely accepted things the way they were without pondering their origins or history. Life was simply the way it was.

"Behave yourself today. Be alert and think before you speak. I have every confidence in you. Now you don't have to worry about the Cabicacmotz shaming you in front of the other boys. You will go as every other boy goes. That is why everyone is expected to wear the minimum. By looking at those boys, you would never be able to guess which social rank they belong. Most of those boys are from the noble classes, but there are some exceptional cases where students are taken from the ranks of even the lowest hous-es. This is a good thing and I am proud that our tribe allows genius to be recognized in anyone and not merely in people who have been fortunate enough to be born into certain circumstances. Those boys will be the ones who really have initiative to learn. They will be tough competition for you," he said as he slapped me on the back jovially. "Should you ever be lucky enough to have to compete against any of them, that is. Treat your classmates with kindness. Respect and listen closely to everything the Cabicacmotz says. Pay special attention to what he does. Agreed? Everything he does is pertinent to the lessons. Remember that."

I nodded and my father embraced me. He sent me on my way, but changed his mind a moment later when I turned to leave. Chahal would stay with him, rather than go with me. It seemed to me that the day was getting worse. He tried to make me feel better by telling me that she would be the talk of the court. His words were no consolation, but I did not argue. I left.

When I was close to the place of instruction, I paused to collect my wits and to clean myself up a bit. Sweat dripped in my eyes from the heat and the rag I used to wipe my brow was already fully soaked. The day was sweltering. A wind blew from the south, but it was a warm wind. I was glad that soon I would be in the shade of the jungle.

The previous day, Maricua walked me there so I would know where to go. When we got there, I tried to get a sense of the place, but felt nothing. I found it strange that a place where so many things probably happened would not feel different from other places. I felt that it should have a presence, that indefinable something, which filled the air with the past moods of whoever had been there, or what had occurred. Instead, what I sensed was silence, nothing else.

I finally reached the shadowy jungle canopy. The place of instruction was in a grotto bordering a tranquil waterfall.

As I walked closer, I heard the sounds of boys yelling and a great deal of splashing. Peeking through the foliage, I saw that there was a group of boys. A few seemed younger than I was. They were all swimming and playing. The larger boys frequently pulled the smaller ones up and threw them into the water. They looked like they were having a tremendously good time. I was in awe.

Besides Chahal, I had never had playmates or friends. For some reason, other than Maricua, my other siblings wanted nothing to do with me. They would leave abruptly whenever I came around. There were six which were around my age, but younger, five girls and one boy. At first, their mothers would shepherd them away when I came around, but the children had quickly adopted the practice.

When I questioned Maricua about it, she would avoid my queries by telling me that I was imagining things, but I knew that it was not my imagination. Unfortunately, due to the locations and the isolation of the estates, no other children lived nearby.

Occasionally, I would strike up a conversation with someone around my age that I found in the town or in the market area, but it was always short lived. Almost invariably, the youths I met were the children of traveling merchants, the pochtecas. They had little use for friendships that were doomed to last only one day. They preferred the company of children like themselves, who belonged to families who traveled with theirs from town to town for trade.

If it weren't for Chahal, I would have always been alone. Therefore, to see a bunch of kids, laughing and having fun, enthralled me. I wanted to join them, but I had become shy from my years of solitude and merely watched from behind the shrubbery.

Suddenly, the group grew quiet. My first thought was that perhaps they had seen me looking through the bushes, so I came out and joined them.

The reason they calmed down I quickly realized was not that they had noticed me, but that they had seen a man who entered the clearing. He was slim with light brown hair, which fell in soft waves to his shoulders. If that was not unusual enough, what made him even more of an anomaly was the fact that he was light of skin and had a short beard trimmed close to his face. The people of my tribe had reddish skin similar to that of the soil where we lived and never did the men have hair upon their faces. Even the man's eyes were remarkable. They were not black or brown; they were a curious shade of brown and green. He wore simple clothes, like a commoner. No jewelry adorned him, yet he carried himself like one from the great houses, the nobility. The man was serene and poised.

"Who is that?" I asked a small boy near me.

"That is the Cabicacmotz," he answered with a fearful look.

I was confused. Although I had only seen him last night, albeit in the darkness, I had doubts that this was the Cabicacmotz. My mind had already imagined his facial features and this man looked nothing at all like what I had thought. For one thing, I expected him to look like us. The man from last night appeared to be a tribesman. My father himself told me that they had been classmates. My father had no hairs of white, but he appeared much older than this man, who moved with the athletic easy grace of a panther.

The strange young man before us could not be a genuine child of the tribe. How could he have been initiated into our customs? Foreigners were not taught our secret arts, ever. Yet, he was to be our teacher. How could this be? Since I had been prevented from disturbing my father when he was receiving counsel from the Cabicacmotz, I had never seen him. This man was not what I had expected, at all. I wondered if the man from last night was someone else and whether this was a joke being played on me by my father. My mind was in turmoil.

"You will learn the art of stealth," the Cabicacmotz informed us when everyone had gathered in front of him. "You will first begin with tackling the nighttime. I can assure you that it is, most times, easier to exercise the principles of stealth at night rather than during the day. In daytime, you must learn how to hide within the light. An infinitely harder task, since it involves fooling the eyes of others, if one desires to remain undetected. More will be said on that later and I will…"

"But what if one deems it more advantageous to reveal oneself?" a boy interrupted. "What if the situation demands that one should allow one's presence to be known?"

The young man was in the very back of the group. I had chosen to sit in the front, at the extreme right of the Cabicacmotz, so I would not miss anything. I knew that my father would demand a precise account of my first day.

The Cabicacmotz suddenly disappeared from where he stood and reappeared before the young man. He moved there quicker than the wind. "I told you that more will be said on that later," he shouted as he loomed over the boy.

A young boy sitting next to me had knelt to see who had asked the question. He stared wide-eyed as the Cabicacmotz moved thirty paces from his place before the class to materialize in front of the young man to yell at him. The next instant the Cabicacmotz again stood in front of us. The young boy fainted when he saw this. Gently, I tried to wake him up. No one seemed to notice that he had passed out. When the boy woke up, a few moments later, he still seemed scared and moved to sit closer to me.

"The path of learning will not be free from troubles," the Cabicacmotz said as he looked with disdain at the boy who fainted. "It is an arduous path, but it will bring you joy when you unite with it. Do any of you have any questions?" he asked us. "There is a time for everything in this class and it is, at this time, your destiny to have me determine the time for what you will do. This is the time to ask questions. The proper time to ask questions is when I tell you that you may, not when I am in the middle of speaking. I repeat, it is an arduous path, that will bring you joy when you unite with it. Ask your questions now," the Cabicacmotz demanded.

Although I was petrified, I stood up.

"Zakiraxa, you may ask your question."

"I would like to understand your last statement, esteemed Cabicacmotz."

"Continue."

"When we unite with the path, it will be joyful, even in the face of trouble? How can such a thing be?"

"I tell you that even within trouble, you will be joyful. If you do not struggle against learning, if you regard it as the purpose of your life, you will know that times of trouble and great difficulty are valuable lessons that can reveal extraordinary things about life, others and yourself. Plus, they are usually free," he answered.

"Thank you." I slightly bowed my head in reverence. I had been shown that this was a customary gesture of respect. His response had not cleared the matter up for me. The stress of embarrassment was dissolving my concentration and I struggled to remind myself of what he had told me. That night, I resolved, I would ask my father to explain it to me.

"Are there any more questions?" the Cabicacmotz asked the group. No one spoke. "Since there are no more questions, we will continue. We now return to the topic of stealth and moving within the night. Tonight you will listen to what the night tells you. Please go to your homes and eat your evening meal. Then go out to a quiet place and listen to the sounds of the night. Sit, walk around, or both, but listen to what the night tells you. If you listen carefully, you will learn a great deal about the darkness."

"There is a matter which I must take care of today. The rest of our lesson will be suspended until tomorrow, after you have tried on your own to discover what you must learn about the nighttime. You will report back here tomorrow night and share what you learned by yourselves. Depending on what you learn, if anything, we will discuss it. The moment the sun hides behind the earth, you are to be here." The Cabicacmotz turned away from us and disappeared into the trees.

The students walked calmly away in silence. After they were a proper distance from the grotto, they began chatting amiably and roughhousing. I didn't know anyone and no one talked to me. I looked to see where the boy who had fainted was and saw him walking in the other direction with an older boy, the one who had interrupted the Cabicacmotz. I went on my way to see my father and to get Chahal.

When I neared the palatial grounds, I saw a great deal of people gathered around. Some came to look, others walked away shaking their heads in dismay. "What can be going on?" I wondered.

Making my way through the crowd gathered at the southeastern gate, I listened in on the many conversations going on around me. From the bits and pieces I heard, I inferred that a woman had injured a young prince who was visiting from another tribe. Some spoke about how a situation like this could cause a war with the tribe to the east of the city. The people were visibly upset. Guards came and dispersed the crowd.

The estate was silent. No one spoke. I questioned every servant I saw, but they all refused to meet my eyes or answer me. They lowered their eyes and rushed away from me. I became more and more worried. Could it be that we were really preparing for war because of a silly quarrel? After all, what woman could possibly beat a man?

Unable to find anyone at home to answer my questions, I walked to my father's court. Usually the path to court was bustling with people, but no one was about. It was eerily silent.

I walked through the hall leading to the throne room to see if, perhaps, I could receive some answers from my father. The throne room was still and empty. As I walked to the back of the cavern, I heard footsteps echoing through the hall and two male voices speaking softly. I caught a glimpse of my father and the Cabicacmotz.

Maricua had confirmed that it was common knowledge in the household that the Cabicacmotz was the advisor of our father and that when they spoke they were not to be disturbed. Everyone had known this, except for me. Somehow, the fact had eluded me all of those years.

My curiosity was piqued. I wondered what they discussed when they were together and knew that I should not be listening in. The temptation was too much for me. Unable to contain my curiosity, I ducked in behind the decorative cloths that adorned the walls and concealed myself there.

"She beat him with a stick, Cabi. A stick. Can you imagine that?" my father said to the Cabicacmotz. "What am I to do with Maricua?"

"Did the young man do anything to displease her?"

"He showed up and that was enough. One of the princes of the eastern city. The oldest, in fact. Luckily, they don't know what's happened to him, yet."

"Where is he now?"

"He's with Saralel, the resident healer. We'll have to let him leave after he is well, though, and he's bound to tell. What will we do? Troublesome neighbors are problematic, but when the cause of the strife is due to a member of the royal family, it is even worse. What am I to do with that girl? Her temper is as uncontrollable as wildfire and her tongue is sharper than arrow points."

My surprise was beyond measure. I could not imagine Maricua doing anything cruel to another person. Yesterday, she had been telling me to be kind to others, even in my thoughts.

"She is the oldest daughter, as you know," Naualalom continued. "It is customary that she marries first. I am afraid that her younger sisters will kill her if this continues. She has chased off every man who has tried to court her and refuses to marry. The others complain that they will wind up as spinsters. It is turning me into a crazy man. The problems running the kingdom are nothing in comparison to the problems running my households. I am at a loss as to what to do."

"First, we must tend to the young man," the Cabicac-motz advised. "Who is the second oldest daughter?"

"Marilya."

"Is she beautiful?"

"Oh, yes. Very," Naualalom answered.

"Do you have any objection to the young man becoming your son in law?"

"No. I have heard that he is a fine lad. That is another reason why I find this whole thing distressing."

"Good, then this is what we must do. We begin by sending Marilya to tend to the young man's wounds. She must be kind and patient with him. She must apologize for her sister's actions by telling him that Maricua is, well, a bit crazy. With luck, he will become infatuated with her and her with him. When he is almost well, we send in Maricua to apologize to him. Tell her to tell him that the reason she beat him was that she did not want him to fall in love with her because she knew that her sister Marilya was already taken with him and wanted him to herself. She is also to disclose to him that she is in love with a man, but is keeping it secret for the time being, and that he is the only one whom she has confided in. She is to extract a promise from him that he will not tell anyone that she is carrying on a love affair. He becomes her willing confederate. It would also help if she befriends him and advises him on how to go about winning the love of Marilya. She will come across as the kindly, but slightly odd, sister who did not want to estrange her other sister and who is unavailable because she loves another. It is a plausible explanation and one that could work. Of course, his attendants must be treated lavishly and kept away from him until he is better and our plan has had a chance to work."

My father roared with delight. "I love the plan, Cabi. Thank you. What is wrong with me?"

"Nothing, Naualalom. It happens to all of us. The situation was too close to you for you to be detached from it. Remember what our own Cabicacmotz taught us? If we hold our hands to our faces, we cannot distinguish the lines in our palms. Only by holding it away from ourselves can we see the lines clearly. This is why it is good to seek outside counsel. It provides the means for viewing a situation from another perspective. In addition, we all need to talk. Providing, of course, that who we talk to can be trusted. We both know how difficult that can be to find. That is why I speak to you about my problems and why you speak to me of yours. You are and have always been my most cherished friend, Alomi, and I am always available for you."

I peeked out from behind my hiding place, carefully keeping the curtain from moving, and saw the Cabicacmotz and my father embrace for a moment and pat each other on the back. My father again thanked him for his help. They walked out of my field of vision and I did not dare move to see where they were. My fear of discovery overpowered my nosiness.

The Cabicacmotz laughed and loudly said, "Now what in the world are we to do about that foul-tempered daughter of yours?"

My father laughed and said, "Maybe we can sell her to the cannibals."

"They wouldn't stand a chance, Alomi."

They hooted and laughed for a good while. Their laughter began to grow softer, to lessen. It sounded to me as if they were walking away. I hid for a while longer and strained to listen. The room was utterly quiet. Silent.

Believing that they had left, I poked my head out from behind the curtain, saw no one and ventured out completely.

I came face to face with the Cabicacmotz. My father sat on the throne, smiling at me. I swallowed hard, then yawned and stretched my arms as if I had been sleeping.

"Were you sleeping?" my father asked.

I shrugged and forced another yawn.

"Do you always sleep standing up? Next to the wall? Behind curtains and without even a bench? What an unusual way to sleep," the Cabicacmotz dryly said.

I did not know what to say, so I decided that it would be best to tell as much of the truth as possible. "I apologize for pretending not to have been listening. It's that I wanted to find out what had happened and no one would tell me anything. Then I came to see father and when I saw that you were both together, I didn't know what to do," I lied. "So I hid back here."

The Cabicacmotz patted me on the back, put his hand on my shoulder and gently walked me towards father. "It is good that you told the truth, or most of it, Zaki. Not right away, but at least you quickly calculated your options and decided to do the best thing. In this case, the best thing was to tell the truth. In other circumstances, the truth may not always be the best choice. One of the things you will learn from my instruction will be the quick discernment of what should be done in any given situation."

"Do you mean that it is sometimes necessary to tell lies?" I asked.

"Ah, that is a good question. Well, Zakiraxa, it is imperative that you speak the truth diplomatically, but there are some circumstances where it will bring dire consequences. These, of course, are not to be found in your average daily communications with others."

"Give him a scenario, Cabi. He is obviously not grasping even a word of what you are telling him," my father told him.

The Cabicacmotz looked at me and apparently saw the truth of what my father said because he nodded and continued speaking. "Imagine that the security of your tribe is at stake. It becomes necessary to enter the territory of your enemy to determine whether they are preparing for war against you. You discover that they are most certainly planning to invade the land of the people you hold most dear. You are discovered and someone asks you what you are doing there. Do you think that it is wise to tell them why you are there?"

I shook my head.

"No, you are most correct. Only a fool is a willing inform-
ant to the enemy. It is more advantageous to hide your
intentions and get away in time to warn your people of the
danger they are in. There are times, though, when truth is
the best course of action. This is the case, most of the time.
Especially in one's everyday interactions with others. We
shall leave that topic for another day."

"Did you hear everything we spoke of, Zaki?" my father
asked.

"Yes, father, I believe I did."

"What do you think about what Maricua has done?"

It took a moment for me to reply. "I do not believe she
could have done that."

"You do not believe she beat a young man who called
upon her with a wooden stick?" the Cabicacmotz asked
laughing. "Why not? What's not to believe?"

I was flustered. I had not expected them to press me to
answer their questions and focus on me in this way.

"Zaki is embarrassed, Cabi. He feels that he is betraying
Maricua's trust. Besides Chahal, she is the only person that
Zaki spends most of his time with. They are great friends. She
is the one who raised him when his mother passed away,
but of course you already knew that."

"Is that so, Zaki?"

"Yes. Maricua is a wonderful person. She has been most
kind to me and she always has time for me. That is why I
cannot imagine her beating anyone. Her heart is gentle
and so is she."

The Cabicacmotz peered at me with a questioning
look.

"She is helpful and gives her time without expecting anything in return. She is not mean and I have found her to be most patient. Maybe that man did something bad to her. I admit she has a temper, but it takes a great deal to anger her. A great deal," I stressed. One thing I knew was that I did not want the Cabicacmotz to punish her. My sister had beautiful jet-black hair, with braids down to her waist.

The Cabicacmotz continued to gaze at me. After a few moments of silence, he asked me, "Has your sister ever expressed a liking for a boy? Any boy?"

"No boy, sir." I didn't want to mention that she obviously, to me, liked him.

"Does your sister hate boys?"

"No. She is nice to me and I am a boy, or I was, so she must like boys."

"That is not entirely correct, Zaki," the Cabicacmotz answered. "You are her brother and she, most likely, considers you as a mother would. Perhaps you are the exception."

"Has she talked with you about anything concerning her future plans for marriage or, at least, romance, Zaki?" my father asked.

"No, father."

"Why do you think that she beat on that poor boy, then?" the Cabicacmotz asked as he looked down at the floor.

"I do not believe that she did such a thing. She is not like that."

"I can assure you that she did indeed do such a thing, Zaki. Now please answer the question."

"May I think on that for a moment?"

"Of course, take your time," replied the Cabicacmotz.

I sat down on the floor, leaned my back against one of the walls, and began to go over, in my mind, the things that Maricua had said. At that moment, it seemed that she and I had never conversed about anything important and I could not remember anything that was even remotely worthwhile to mention. Suddenly a thought dawned on me. "Maybe Maricua does not like the lifestyle of a wife very much."

"What do you mean?" my father asked.

"Well, she was telling me the other day that the way the Cabicacmotz lives is the proper way to live. Maybe she did not like the way the young man pictured life for her when he asked her to bind herself with him."

"What?" the Cabicacmotz asked.

"She said that your bed was the velvet grass and that your music was the song of nature and that she liked that you lived life in a simple manner. She said that ....," I stopped talking when I realized that I was on the verge of completely disclosing what Maricua had confided to me.

My father demanded that I tell them the rest of what she had told me.

"I cannot tell you that in front of him," I said pointing to the Cabicacmotz who had an expression of horror and disbelief on his face.

"Then come over here and tell me," my father commanded me.

I stood up and walked to where he sat. I bent over and whispered in his ear. "She said that the Cabicacmotz was the best man around and that she found him beautiful to look at. Don't tell him, though."

Naualalom grinned from ear to ear. "She said that, eh?"

"Yes." I smiled and felt my face blush. I glanced over at the Cabicacmotz who also looked rather embarrassed, but couldn't hide his smile. I thought that he looked younger right then, but I could not fathom why I felt that way.

"I think that you had best leave for now, Zaki," my father told me. "The Cabicacmotz and I have very official business to attend to," he said and laughed.

As I walked down the corridor leading away from the throne room, I strained to hear what they were discussing, but the sound of my steps did not allow me to discern what they were saying.

That night, I had no other recourse than to complete my assignment for the Cabicacmotz. Maricua had barricaded herself in her quarters and refused to come out, even for me.

The next day, Maricua was no longer hiding in her room. She pretended that nothing unusual had happened.

When I tried to bring up the subject, she pointed her finger at me and said, "Don't you dare mention yesterday to me. I don't want to hear one word about it."

I shut my mouth and pretended along with her. She acted like her cheery self. It was unnerving, but I was glad not to have to think about things. I still couldn't believe that she had taken a stick to anyone. She was always sweet and kind. It was unthinkable to imagine her being hurtful or violent.

In the late afternoon, Maricua and I were playing a game when our father walked in with a smile on his face. Maricua became noticeably flustered, probably believing that he had come in to scold her for the events of yesterday.

"Hello, father," she said.

"Hello. What are you two doing?" he asked as if nothing was wrong in the world.

"We are playing a game that we bought from the merchants when they came to the marketplace last week. Zaki is winning, as usual. He has an uncanny luck for this game and already has two of my jade pieces to show for it."

I held up the jade for our father to see.

Naualalom smiled and ruffled my hair. "Well done, Zaki. Do you think that you can give up the game even though you are winning? I have something I need to discuss with your sister."

A look of panic was immediately on Maricua's face. She mouthed the words telling me not to go. Father noticed what was going on and quickly spoke, "Don't worry. I am not here to reprimand you about yesterday's very ugly events. I am merely here to talk with you about another matter."

Maricua lowered her eyes and mumbled, "Yes, father."

My father motioned me to leave. I quietly handed Maricua her jade pieces and walked out. The Cabicacmotz stood in the passageway, leaning against the wall and staring at the ground. When he saw me, he turned a deep red and his frown turned into a sheepish look.

"Hello, Zaki."

"Hello, Cabicacmotz. Are you waiting for my father? I'm afraid that you will have to wait quite a while. He is talking to Maricua."

"Yes, I am. Your father would like me to talk with your sister. So here I am."

All sorts of thoughts filled my head. I became very afraid that my father had brought the Cabicacmotz to punish Maricua. "Please don't set my sister's hair on fire, sir," I pleaded.

The Cabicacmotz looked bewildered. "Why on earth would I do such a thing?"

"Because she was bad. Please don't."

"I can assure you, Zaki, that I will not harm your sister in any way."

"Really?"

My father then peered out of the entrance to Maricua's quarters. "Zaki," he said when he saw me. "Didn't I tell you to leave? Go now and prepare yourself for your lesson. The Cabicacmotz will be there on time and you had better be, as well. Get out of here. And no staying around and eavesdropping, like yesterday," he warned me. He motioned with his hand as if to shoo me away.

"I am leaving now, father." I quickly began to walk down the hall.

"I promise, Zaki," the Cabicacmotz called after me.

I turned around in time to see the Cabicacmotz and my father disappear into Maricua's rooms. "What was that about?" I wondered.

There was no time for me to ponder the event because the time was indeed approaching for me to begin my second lesson with the Cabicacmotz. It was common knowledge that one should be well rested and well fed before attending any sort of lessons. I had to eat and take a short nap. I had time, but not time for idling.

The prior night, I went out with Chahal and sat in the garden. There had been no chance to ask my father about it, since he was busy, so I tried my best. I attempted to listen to the night, but was not sure that I had correctly determined what it was that I was supposed to be discovering. My mind wandered a great deal and I had trouble figuring out what to do. I really tried to listen to what the night had to say, but I was only able to make simple observations about it. If the night was able to communicate in some way, it found me quite deaf. I finally fell asleep in the hammock.

I went ahead to the servant's dining area. Whenever I did not want to eat in solitude, I went there. The servants were always kind and I felt comfortable around them. Only they, my father, and Maricua ever made me feel welcome. In addition, they usually gave me a meal of hearty proportions. That day was no exception. They laughed when I wolfed it all down. After I ate, I took a little nap in order to refresh myself for the evening's lesson.

When I woke up, I looked at the sky and knew that I should immediately head off. On my way, I did not see any of the other boys. Fortunately, I arrived in time.

Many came late. The Cabicacmotz was visibly annoyed and chastised them. "I told all of you to come back when the sun hid behind the earth. The sun falls in the west. For most of you, your quarters are west of here. That means that the sun hides behind the earth later there, than here. It disgusts me to see that you have not noticed that it is a minimal difference of time when darkness falls here than when it does at your homes. How could you not be aware of such simple matters? It is pure logic. Are you all pampered fools? This grotto, not your homes, will be the gauge of the time for my lessons. You must be ever mindful of the topics of time and distance. Your very survival may be at stake one day over these very things that seem so trivial to you now. Don't you realize what you are here for?" He stared at us and shook his head. "If you are unable to calculate the time when the sun will dawn, you may be in an enemy camp and be discovered if you foolishly wait too long to escape or find a good hiding spot. Do not allow this to happen again."

"The night is here, though, so we will make use of it now. Gather around, everyone. Sit on the ground. We must now relax for a while. Put yourselves at ease. Feel free to chat quietly with each other until full darkness envelops us."

At once, the other boys began to whisper and laugh among themselves. I did not know anyone, so I did not do more than smile when my eyes met another's. I heard someone come and stand beside me. When I looked up, I saw that it was the boy who had been upbraided by the Cabicacmotz yesterday. He appeared to be my age, but I could not tell for sure. We greeted one another. He sat down next to me.

"I am Cham," he told me.

I told him my name.

"Do I have to call you such a long name? My real name is Chamanyol. There is more to my name, but I don't want to waste my breath saying it. We might be here for days if I do. Call me Cham, it's easier."

I immediately liked him and was quite impressed with his lack of shyness. He had a mischievous grin and shiny eyes that darted around, seldom settling on anything. His hair was cut short around his ears and the nape of his neck; the rest hung in a long braid down to his buttocks.

At once, I felt at ease. This was unusual for me, I always pretended to act as if I was comfortable and confident, but I seldom was. "My family calls me Zaki. That should be all right."

A moment later, another boy showed up and sat near us. I saw that it was the boy who had fainted. "This is my younger brother," Cham informed me.

"My name is Hac," the young boy said.

I greeted him and introduced myself. I noticed that he wore his hair like his brother and that they were almost identical, despite the difference in their ages. Cham appeared to be a few years older than his brother was. I found myself wondering why Hac was in the class, since he was clearly younger than we were. He seemed shy, especially in comparison with his brother. Cham was obviously quite daring, considering his lack of compunction in interrupting the Cabicacmotz during his lesson yesterday.

Cham turned to me and said, "Hac's real name is Hacutya-Cuitlacoya."

I burst out laughing. The term "cuitlacoya" referred to a person who was covered in feces or filth. It was a foreign term that children often used in order to say vulgarities while in the presence of unsuspecting parents or other adults. I had certainly not expected Cham to say that.

Hac frowned at his brother and then looked down at the ground, sulking. I felt bad for him. My own experience with the word had occurred with my brothers and sisters and I remember being quite upset when I learned what it meant.

"I apologize for laughing, Hac. It's because I didn't expect him to say it."

"Don't you worry yourself about that," he replied and smiled. "I remember you from yesterday and I remember that you were the only one who helped me," he said as he gave his brother a dirty look.

"How was I supposed to help you, Hac? I was way in the back and you were up front. Besides it's not my fault that you are such a sissy that you faint at the sight of our teacher."

The brothers began to argue. It was clear that soon they would come to blows and I would be in the middle of it.

Trying to change the subject, I asked them about how they had begun their schooling with the Cabicacmotz.

They told me that they had been in the fields one day when the Cabicacmotz had found them. Their parents were of the class that tended to the crops. That day, they were supposed to be helping, but instead, they had found a subterranean cave and were playing in the water.

They described the cave as being a narrow opening between some rocks at the side of a large hill. On the opposite side of the hill, there were rows of crops, but they had wandered off instead of picking the vegetables they were supposed to.

The Cabicacmotz came across their empty baskets and then began to look around for them. He knew that children had been carrying the baskets because of their footprints, but he became alarmed when he could not find them. He called in many helpers to search for them. Everyone was alerted and they quickly determined that the two lost children were Hac and Cham. Their parents became frightened when the sun began to set and they had not yet been found.

The day passed into night. The Cabicacmotz was about to give them up for lost, when he came near to the small opening in the hill. It was merely a crawl space, obscured by brush. It was a wonder that he found it. With a torch, he entered the cave and found the two boys asleep near the water's edge. He gave them quite a scare when he woke them up. He brought them out of the cave and delivered them to their worried parents.

Normally, the boys would have gotten a beating from their father, but he was too relieved to do that. He had thought that jaguars had taken his sons. As punishment, the boys were sent to bed without any dinner. They pretended to sleep and saw the Cabicacmotz speaking to their parents for a long time that night.

"And that's how we came to be here," Hac said, as if that explained it.

"What did the Cabicacmotz say to your parents?"

"Oh, we don't know. They spoke too softly for us to hear, but we did see that our parents were very happy. After awhile, we fell asleep anyway. Swimming does that to you, you should know," Cham said.

I saw no connection between their story and why they were here, but I did not want to seem too nosy. I decided to try another tactic to discover what I really wanted to know. I doubted that Hac was old enough to be in the class, since I had been led to believe that only those boys who were 'men' were allowed to attend. "Are you going to the festival," I asked them.

"Of course we are," Cham answered. "Are you?"

I told them that I was going and was very excited to, finally, be included among the adults. Cham rolled his eyes and said, "I assume that you are one of the boys from the noble classes, then."

Feeling self-conscious, I shrugged. "So what?" I asked.

"That means, Zaki, that you are not considered an adult until you wet your panties." He used the word to imply women's undergarments and said it in such a derogatory way that I had to laugh. He snickered for a moment and then became serious. "That doesn't apply to the kids who aren't wealthy. We require a sign to be here, and that's a lot less likely to happen."

He looked at me and realized that I did not understand what he was trying to tell me. He told me that the Cabicacmotz had been very perplexed for a large part of the day with their disappearance. Ordinarily, the Cabicacmotz would have quickly found them, due to his special abilities. The fact that they had somehow eluded his efforts to locate them was a very important omen and the Cabicacmotz interpreted it to mean that they were special in some way and that they would benefit from his training. "You see," he said. "If a boy isn't a noble, he isn't allowed to learn what the Cabicacmotz and others teach. We are taught only if there is an omen about us. You, on the other hand, are guaranteed a place here, but only if and when you muss your panties."

We all began to laugh. We didn't stop until we noticed that everyone around us had quieted down and was looking at the Cabicacmotz.

"Certain creatures are at home in the darkness," he began. "These can be classified into animals, insects, reptiles and other beings." He paused for a moment to look at the group of boys sitting in front of him. Seemingly satisfied, he continued, "It should have been apparent to you last night, if you did what I asked you to do, that the sounds of night are quite different from those of the day. Their mood is different, their speed is different and their contents are vastly different. We shall begin with the obvious, the mood. You," he said as he pointed to a boy seated near the back of the group. "Tell us about the mood of the night. Stand up, so that everyone can hear you."

The boy stood. Keeping his chin up, I noticed that his eyes were drawn down to the ground in front of him every few seconds. "The mood of the night," he intoned, as if it would spark his thoughts to order. "The mood of the night is mysterious. It is dreamy, like sorrow, yet harsh. Peaceful, yet it is as if power..." He searched for the proper words to describe what he felt. "It is as if power was like a hot liquid that was ready to burst forth and melt anything in its path. I apologize, but I can't find the precise words to describe the joy and anguish that I felt the night contained." The boy appeared truly embarrassed and quickly sat down.

The Cabicacmotz smiled at the boy. "He is quite right," he told us.

The boy, who had spoken, breathed a sigh of relief.

"He was especially right when he described the power underneath the night. It, indeed, is as a volcano that is ready to erupt, yet doesn't. It keeps us waiting. What ever will we do when it bursts forth? Will we get burned, run, or will we walk on top of it and follow the path it makes?" He stood quiet and still for quite a while, as if giving us time to ponder what we would do.

I did not have to think long about it, I knew that I would rather run than be burned. I was not a stone colossus that was incapable of being hurt. He looked at me and knitted his brow. Then, he looked at each boy in the group as if to assess what they would do. It shamed me to think that he was able to know what I thought and knew that I would be scared. Remembering what Maricua told me, I resolved to make a better effort to have more appropriate thoughts.

"If anyone thinks that they are a coward because they would run from a volcano's red hot fluids, let me remind them that only a complete fool wouldn't run." He laughed. "Believe me, only an idiot would think that they stood a chance against lava. I know. I have seen lava run. My question, rather, was aimed to prompt you to consider what you would do if power and the acquisition of it were presented. Would you not recognize it and be caught off guard, thus getting burned? Would you decide that you weren't ready for it and run? Would you run forever from it or only until you felt it was time? Or would you be as arrogant and stupid as to think that you could play with it as you like?" Again he laughed, only now it had an edge of bitterness around it. "The only intelligent option would be to run. How long you run until you decide to face fate, only you can decide. Keep your eyes open and know what goes on around you, or else you will get burned."

He walked around the group, watching us intently and said, "It will soon be time for you to go to the festival marking your achievement of adulthood. What you will witness there are things that I cannot adequately describe to you with words. Things will happen that you will have a difficult time comprehending. You need to be extremely alert and you need to brace yourselves for both frights and delights. If you succumb to fear, you will miss many of the activities while your guide fans your face to coax you back into consciousness. If you spend too much time with the delights, you will fail to pay proper attention to what you should be noticing. For this reason, you are designated a guardian for the day who will lead you to the correct places for your attention. We will discuss who will be your assigned guides later."

Every boy in the class involuntarily groaned when the Cabicacmotz informed us that we would have a guide. Everyone knew what that meant. A mature male would be chaperoning each of us. This was a proclamation that we would not be allowed to have fun at the festival. What had promised to be a day of frivolous enjoyment was now to be a day of dreary duty.

"Let us return to our lesson concerning the subject of night. Who here can tell me about the speed of the night? Meaning how it differs from that of the day in its tempo."

He looked us over and finally settled his gaze on a boy sitting in the middle.

The boy rose and said, "The day is faster than the night. The insects move more quickly during the day. At night, they move lazily. At least it so seemed to me. Birds stay in their resting spots and I did not notice any of the larger lizards, so I suspect that they also rest at night. It is strange, but it was very difficult for me to gauge time while I was in the darkness. I could not tell how long I sat there. It may have been moments or half the night. I do not know. Everything seemed slower. Am I wrong?"

"No, you were not wrong. It is difficult to tell how quickly time flows unless one notices the movements of the moon or stars overhead. Did anyone here watch the moon or stars during the night?" No one indicated that they had, which was odd since all of us were certainly aware that the moon was swiftly moving towards full. "If you had done so, you would have been able to determine the length of time that passed. You will learn those things as you progress in your lessons. It is not immediately expected of you. During the day, the sun is a constant reminder of time as it progresses through the sky. The stars are also indicators of time, but they are so numerous that few attract our attention. In any case, it is not something that you must know right now. You will learn it soon, but not quite yet."

"My question, regarding the speed of the night, was a bit deceptive," he said to the boy who had answered. "You may sit down now. The trick lies in knowing that the content of the night determines its speed and the content is given by how beings act in the night. Your answer correctly relied upon the creatures around us. Certain living things belong to the night. They are less noticeable to us. From now on, you must take special notice of those creatures. Look around you. Watch what wakes up at night and what lives only for the day. Animals, birds, insects, reptiles, and people. Allow nothing to escape your observation. You should begin a written account of what belongs to the night. Take a scroll or a piece of cloth and adorn it with drawings of the beings that pertain to the night. It will serve as a reminder to you. You must add everything to it that you find. After you leave tonight, you are to begin your observations. Once you are home, make a record of what you saw. Everyone is expected to do this."

The Cabicacmotz then asked us to form pairs and observe the night for what he had told us to become aware of and note. Hac and Cham went together and I soon found myself alone while everyone else paired off. I approached the Cabicacmotz to tell him about my problem.

"I guess you will be paired with me then, Zaki. Unfortunately for you, this initial pairing up is also a long-term pairing. There are an uneven number of students here, so one of you was bound to be stuck with me. The problem is that it is a device used to provide a small measure of safety to the boys from falling into conflicts with bullies. Bullying is prohibited, but it occurs nonetheless. Make sure that from now on you bring Chahal along with you to all of your lessons. She will not be able to stay with you, but she may wait for you at the edge of the clearing."

"Does that mean that I will not be able to make any friends here?" I asked, fearing what he would say.

"No, Zaki, it does not mean that. Between the levels, the rule is that no other contact is allowed between my students. The boys that started these lessons a year ago are not allowed to interact with your group. For a week, your class will not speak to each other, except on certain occasions. The rest of the time they may speak only to their own partners."

"That is what I am concerned with, Cabicacmotz. I do not want to be always alone. I want to have friends and enjoy their company. I have never found friends who were my age. Why must that be taken away from me when I am so close to it?"

"I understand your concerns, Zaki. It may seem that you will not be able to form friendships, but that is not the case here. While you are the one who will not immediately have a sure partner that does not mean that you will not find friends. Only you will be permitted to interact with any of these young men. They are bound to speak only with their partners, until the time of festival, but you are outside of that rule. At times, I will need to pair up with the boys individually. That way you will get to meet all of the boys who are left without a partner. When that happens, they may talk with you. During the lessons, you will usually be with me. And many other times," he added after reflecting for a moment.

"I may mention, though, that it can be an ideal situation." He leant in close to me and whispered, "No bullies with me around."

I had to smile. The way his eyes squinted and his mouth puckered made me laugh. It was a mockery of a bully. Maybe this was not going to be so bad after all.

"I'll bet I'll learn more this way, sir. Thank you," I told him. I was relieved that I would be able to talk to the other boys and that the Cabicacmotz was joking with me rather than setting my hair on fire.

Turning away, he said to the class, "Let us observe the properties of shadows. Look around. They are everywhere. The night is here and this clearing we are in is awash with the light of the firmament while the shadows amass themselves in the jungle. The moon allows each of us only one shadow. Observe each other's shadows, please."

I looked around. There was a boulder in the middle of the clearing. I commented on its shadow's elongated shape.

"We joined it in the field. It stood here alone waiting patiently for us," he told me. "We, each of us, are merely other items."

I wondered at his odd words for a moment and then I was unable to recall what he had told me. At a loss, I changed the subject. "Do you think that I will be able to find friends here?" I asked.

He looked at me with curiosity. "You lost my words back there. Don't worry. It is something people do when they are not accustomed to concentrating and learning new things. It also happens when they are not used to dealing with other people."

I must have had a chagrined look on my face because he assured me again not to worry when I seemed to step into a feeling or state of what he referred to as 'non-thought.' He told me that was a good thing and that it could be used to my benefit.

I asked him how I could profit from such a thing, since it did not appear to be conducive to anything except looking like a fool.

He laughed and told me that later he would teach me about that and that it would be better for me if he answered my questions in the proper order. "Yes. I believe you will find some friends here. Already you have met Hac and Cham. We shall see. You are in the unique position to observe every one of them. Watch them," he said, indicating all of the boys around us. "People are not as simple as they appear. Often, their actions do not match their feelings." He said a few more things. Some of them saddened me.

I worried even more that I would not find friends when he began to tell me that people were very curious beings and that what they did was often at odds with what they felt was the right way of acting. I asked him to tell me an example.

"Well, by now, most of the boys have observed us for a while. When we first paired off, they felt pity for you for being stuck with me, yet they did not have pity on you when they could have prevented your situation. Then, when they observed camaraderie between us, they wished that they had been paired with me. Students often hold those who are in the teacher's graces in disdain. They all, though, know that they should not harbor those feelings and silently chide themselves for feeling in contradiction to what they know to be the proper way to think of others. Yet those feelings and thoughts attack them and they give in to them even when they know it's not the right way to be. If you don't think that is weird, then you are not paying close enough attention."

"I don't know what to think." Fearing that everyone hated me, I asked, "Are you sure that they all thought those things?"

He told me that many had, but also said that there were some exceptional students whose minds did not run into such internal quandaries. I asked him whom he was referring to and he refused to tell me.

It dawned on me to notice what the other students were doing. I looked at them and did not catch any of them paying attention to us.

"Even though you didn't notice them watching us does not mean that they weren't. Remind me to train you how to feel the eyes of others. Some other time, of course. As for right now, they made an effort to tackle the subject of shadows for a while and then observed us to determine whether they were going about it in the right way. Some of them do not yet know that there is more than one way to tackle the problem. Let us return to the subject of observing shadows. We don't want to fall behind. Do we?"

He informed me that each light source produced a shadow and that when people walked among torches their shadows reflected the number of torches used. We sat down and he asked me to observe my shadow for a while and to contemplate about whether the amount of shadow corresponded to the amount of area illuminated or to the areas of my body that were hidden from the moon's glow. He urged me to stand up and walk around him to look at his shadow.

I watched his shadow for a long time, but I was unable to answer him. It was a mystery to me. He did not seem disappointed that I had not solved the problem.

"Don't you see, Zaki, that when you turn away from the light, you are confronted with your own shadow? Face it now."

I did what he asked. I looked down and stared at the shadow stemming from my feet and extending out, elongating my form.

"Now, turn towards the light." He came and stood next to me. "Close your eyes and feel the moon upon your face and try to feel your shadow behind you." He took hold of my head and lifted my chin up, reminding me to keep my eyes shut.

Through my eyelids, I noticed the light from the moon. Soon, I began to feel a soft glow on my cheeks. It was delicate and intangible, but it could be felt. I then tried to sense my shadow behind me and experienced a sensation of vertigo. I immediately opened my eyes to get my bearings.

The Cabicacmotz asked me to describe what I had seen and chuckled when I told him that I felt as if I was blindfolded while on a raft in a storm. He told me that he had hoped that I would be able to accomplish what he asked on my first try, but that I should not be worried.

"It takes awhile to come to grips with all of this. It is my fault to expect too much, too soon. We had better try something else for now," he said and began walking towards the boulder in the clearing. "I would like you to practice that movement on your own when you are home. You can lessen the danger of dizziness if you sit facing a light source and close your eyes. Then try to feel your shadow behind you. Remember to sit," he said. "But come now, we are almost at the stone."

As we neared it, I saw that it was a natural rock that had been carved upon.

"What have we allowed ourselves to become?" he said as he pointed to the boulder decorated with inscriptions and bas-reliefs. The inscriptions were on the east and west sides. The images were on the north and south. "Does man imagine that the Creator can only see to the east and west? Man is a fool if he believes such a thing. His vision is never impaired."

I could not understand what he was talking about. He noticed my stare and told me not to concern myself with his words. Then he began to speak of other things. He told me to look at the images and to pay particular attention to the shadows that surrounded each image. I began to watch the shadows around the figures. I noticed that if I only focused on the shadows, I could see the actual figures better than I could if I looked at them directly. The shadows enhanced them and gave them definition.

"This gazing is always the same, but never the same," he whispered.

I kept my eyes on the shadows as I pondered his cryptic remark. The shadows jumped out at me the moment I realized that it was a confusing statement. I sprung backwards quickly and wound up falling on my rear end, but I kept my eyes upon the shadows. They were alive, undulating with movement.

I heard the loud braying of laughter and looked away. When I looked back, the dancing shadows were no longer there. The Cabicacmotz looked sternly down upon me. The other boys stopped their laughter when they noticed the mean look on his face.

"Go back to your work. There is nothing here to watch. Do as I say unless you are willing to share in whatever is going to happen to Zaki," he yelled.

I saw the horrified looks upon the faces of Hac and Cham as he grabbed me by my arm and pulled me across the clearing. My thoughts were disjointed and my embarrassment was mixed with the maddening thought that a prince should not be treated in such a degrading manner. I was bewildered and wondered what I had done to anger him. All of these ideas, though, ceased to matter to me when I finally realized where he was taking me. He was taking me to the edge of the jungle, beyond the moonlit clearing.

I felt a tremendous fear of the eclipsed woods that he was roughly dragging me to, but my mind told me that I was being stupid and that only children were afraid of shadows and the dark. My body disagreed with my reasoning and was in a state of alarm. Shaking with fear at both the mass of shadows that we were about to enter and the wrath of the Cabicacmotz, I meekly asked him why we were going into the jungle.

"You'll see," he softly said.

He propped me up at the edge, right where the shadows began to grow thickest and stood behind me, holding me by my braid as if it were a leash. I looked into the inky darkness and shuddered. I was about to close my eyes, when he pushed me out of the clearing. In my surprise, my eyes opened wide. It didn't matter, then, whether my eyes were open or closed. The effect was the same. I was surrounded by impenetrable blackness. My eyes strained to become acclimated to the dark. I couldn't even make out the outlines of the trees around me. I moved my hands around me to get my bearings and to make sure that I was not about to bump into anything. Nothing was around me. A sharp tug at the nape of my neck reminded me that the Cabicacmotz was right behind me.

Slowly, I began to see dim shapes. Something was wrong with them, though.

They were moving.

I screamed.

The Cabicacmotz yanked on my braid and I was back in the clearing. I was still screaming because I saw the shadows lunge towards me and then recede back into the jungle.

I passed out for what I thought was a moment and only came back into consciousness when I felt drops of water splash on my face.

"You are lucky that I had a gourd of water with me," the Cabicacmotz said. "Otherwise I would have had to piss on you to wake you up. I'd advise you not to pass out again, I'm afraid I'm out of water and I never learned how to piss perfume."

"What the hell was that?" I asked.

"Why? What did you see?"

"I saw living shadows. The jungle was filled with them. Then when you pulled me out they followed me and then went back into the trees."

"Were the shadows still attached to the darkness of the forest?"

"Yes. They were like tar when it's liquid. It stretches and then gets sucked back into the larger mass." I shook my head to get the image of those things out of my head. "What were they?"

He looked back at the jungle and became very still. After a while, he turned to me and said, "Never mind. They are gone. They were your lesson for tonight, but I'm disappointed that you were not able to guess what they were. In any case, I have no intention of telling you. You will have to make an effort to discover what they were yourself. Few make use of knowledge they have not had to sweat to learn."

It occurred to me that he was only interested in playing cruel jokes on me. It was clear that he was a trickster who was only amusing himself at my expense. I was about to tell him that was unfair when I saw him sigh and shake his head as if he knew what I was thinking. Crap, only then did I remember what Maricua said. He had been listening in to my thoughts. Why wasn't I able to control myself better? I forgot the shadows completely with this new worry.

The Cabicacmotz began to shake his finger at me in a menacing manner. His voice and words did not match his expression and his chiding movements. "The other boys are about to come over and see what happened to you, Zaki. It will be better for you if they believe I am scolding you. When they get here, don't take my words to heart, they are only for show."

I looked over at the other students and saw they were looking at us, but not coming over.

"They're not coming over here," I commented.

"Look again."

I looked. They began to walk over.

"See? I'm not about to lie to you, Zaki. I have no reason to. Let me tell you a few quick things. Don't worry about not being able to govern your thoughts right away. That takes time and work, a lot of work. I am not interested in playing jokes on you, but I am interested in showing you things that are exciting enough to ignite a spark within you. Something that will hold your attention enough that you will put in the necessary work to strive to understand it."

His words went by me without any comprehension on my part. I couldn't understand his point at all. It was too many subjects touched on in too little time for me.

He sighed exaggeratedly, as if I was a hopeless imbecile. Still wagging his finger at me, he softly said, "Knowledge is power. The force behind it is understanding. Every being on this earth must seek understanding. Passive knowledge is useless; otherwise, everything would require mere memory. I presume you know how to add simple numbers?"

I nodded dumbly, still not understanding his point.

"Imagine if you did not understand the reasoning be-hind addition and only knew that two plus two equaled four or that three plus five equaled eight... You would have to store many permutations in your head. If you understand the reasoning behind it, you do not need to memorize anything. Your understanding of the numbers is more powerful than a memorized list. It will enable you to add any numbers, no matter how large they are. One option is limited; the other is endlessly useful. Do you see? I don't want you to memorize details; I want you to understand them. Only then will they have force behind them. If you have to work to discover and acquire knowledge, the time it takes you and the will to get it often has the subtle con-comitant partner called understanding." He glanced to the side. The group of boys was almost upon us. "Remember not to take the words I yell at you in front of them to heart. Watch closely. If they think that you are not the teacher's pet, they will be more likely to feel that you are their comrade. Play along with that and use it to your advantage."

He stood up then and yelled at me, "On your feet, you have rested enough."

The boys were now all around us. Addressing us all, he said, "Apparently you all think that we are here merely to play and pass the time. Well, sometimes playing can be useful. Since most of you aren't in the mood to be serious and mindful of the exercises, let's start a new one. I'm sure you have all heard of it, shadow-stepping. The object is to get close enough to your opponent's shadow and step on it. Pair off."

A boy, I thought it was Cham by his insolent tone, complained, "Ahhh, that's a kid's game."

I expected that the Cabicacmotz would get angry, but he only said, "Not when warriors play at it. You'll see. Now pair off because the next imbecile who talks will get me as his partner. Off with you! Go now."

The boys ran off yipping, happily trying to outrun each other.

The Cabicacmotz turned to me and said, "Let's begin. First, I will go."

I attempted to dodge the Cabicacmotz' steps. The longest I was able to dodge him was for a short time. When I was able to keep him at bay for a bit longer, he told me that I was improving.

Then we switched off and it was my turn to try to step on his shadow. What followed was the most infuriating game of evasion that I've ever had. It was maddening. The worst part of it was that I would almost be upon him when his shadow would nimbly jump away, as if it was humoring my clumsy attempts to step on it and only allowing me to come close in order to tease me.

Finally, after a long time, I was able to nick his shadow with my foot. It was not a certain and decisive step, but it counted and that was all that mattered to me.

"Very good, Zaki. You are catching on," he said when he saw me glance up at him. "For this exercise to work, though, keep your eyes on my shadow."

I was about to ask him what his goal was with this game, but in a gruff tone he said, "Don't worry about what the exercise is for, keep your eyes on my shadow and don't let your eyes wander. Only see my shadow."

For a while after, I was unable to catch his shadow. Then I caught him again. I figured that I would be unable to catch him with a full stomp and, once more, I had to satisfy myself with catching his shadow with a light quick step.

Our last session was particularly protracted. We were all over that clearing, he evading me while I chased his shadow. He would allow me to come close and then he would dart away like a fleeing serpent. I was only peripherally aware of the others around us; they were only sensed, not focused on.

So intent was I on the Cabicacmotz' shadow, that soon I could see nothing else. As I snuck towards his shadow, certain that I was about to catch him, his shadow leaped away such a distance that I was unable to follow it. My eye's vision extended to follow it, but it was gone. I lifted my head, shifting my focus from the ground in order to catch sight of it. The Cabicacmotz stood before me with a huge grin on his face. I could see him as if daylight was all around us, so clear was he. Then I noticed that he had no shadow.

Suddenly, I was no longer able to see him clearly. Everything darkened. I felt fear. "What are you?" I asked in a whisper as I noticed that he was again accompanied by his shadow.

He seemed disappointed by my question, yet answered me, "One of my tasks is to make you aware of the stupendous possibilities of man. To answer your question, I am a man, the same as you."

"No," I said quietly. "You are not like me. I cannot banish my shadow and separate myself from it. Mine stays. Yours does not. Are you a ghost?"

"Of course not. That is a very foolish question," he said as he came to my side and put his arm around my shoulder. He felt real. "I am flesh and blood like you are. Although I can do things that you yet cannot is no reason to believe that I am not a man." He dropped his arm away from me. "As I told you, my task is to enlarge your view of what man is capable of. I can assure you that to be a man is an incredible thing. We are neither meant nor designed to toil like bees in the hive. What we can do is nothing less than astounding. I am to teach you how to do everything I can do. Do you understand?"

I was able to concentrate on his words and comprehend everything he said. Again, the light seemed to brighten. Everything around me was clear and vivid.

This all was so unusual to my normal state of mind that it jolted me. I was accustomed to living life with hazy understanding, as if I were constantly dreaming.

The Cabicacmotz smiled. "Yes," he said. "That is right, and that way of interacting and viewing the world is the way most of mankind lives. Imagine how much stronger and vibrant your life can be if you reject the world of muddled thinking and embrace the immediacy and intensity of the view I wish you to hold."

My mind reeled with the possibility of keeping this extraordinary sharpness of attention. I saw myself as a walking and talking somnambulist that only sees life through a haze that renders the world indistinct, boring, and commonplace. Then I thought of how aware I felt right then. Everything was in vivid focus. I was even aware of the ground underneath my feet. I could feel the hardness of it and the contours of the earth beneath my sandals. I could feel the night breeze caressing my skin and the glow of the moon upon it. Right then, I knew that I wanted what the Cabicacmotz offered. No longer was it merely something to do that was expected of me because of my position. I wanted it. Even though I had an enviable position in the social order, I realized that it was nothing compared to this. I still didn't have anything, to be sure, but I had momentary clarity and the ambition to pursue a more permanent state of clear-headedness. Those two things had made their first true appearance in my life.

The Cabicacmotz smiled kindly. "It is better to be a slave of knowledge than to be the emperor of stupidity. It makes life more interesting." He motioned with his head towards where the other boys were playing. "It is time to join the others and end our lesson. Tomorrow night, you will again have me as your partner, but I will have to spend a few rounds with each boy on this exercise. You will pair off with the boy who is left alone. That should give you adequate time to make friends and acquaintances. Bring Chahal with you from now on, Zaki."

He began walking towards the boys. I followed. When we came into their midst, the boys stopped playing and gathered around the Cabicacmotz. Then he dismissed us, telling us that we had to arrive at twilight's beginning the next night.

When I arrived at home, Maricua was in fine spirits. She was eating a small snack and cracking jokes, asking me whether the Cabicacmotz had set fire to anyone and things like that. We laughed for a bit.

I asked her if father had made her meet with the Cabicacmotz in order to have her marry him.

She blushed. Even in the torchlight, her color darkened visibly. She was about to answer me when one of the servants entered the room and announced that we had a visitor.

The Cabicacmotz entered. The servant, a spindly elder man, stammered a convoluted apology about his having asked the Cabicacmotz to stay outside until he called, but Maricua waved it away and told him that the Cabicacmotz was allowed to visit whenever he pleased. The man-servant seemed scandalized about this new development, but he caught himself before he said anything about such impropriety and quickly left.

I looked at Maricua, who was smiling like a little girl. Then I looked at him, his smile matched hers. I had guessed right. A marriage was in the works.

I had been able to entertain such thoughts with amusement, but when faced with the inevitability of that union, I was dismayed. He and I got along, but he was my teacher and a very frightening figure. Not really a person, in my mind, he was more of a personage. Would I have to watch my thoughts every moment of every day? Judging by my inability to control my thoughts, I knew that having to do that for every moment was burdensome and seemed daunting. All this was accompanied with the fear that I would be left in the house by myself and that I would no longer be allowed to spend time with Maricua whenever I wanted. Chahal was good company, but I sometimes desired human interaction. I felt that life was victimizing me.

"What is happening here, Maricua?" I asked her. "Are you two getting married?"

She grinned and told me that they were marrying. "Isn't that splendid?

I wasn't able to match her enthusiasm, yet I was able to nod. I was sure that the Cabicacmotz was fully cognizant of my discomfort.

"Well, aren't you going to say that you're happy for me, at least?" she asked.

"Um, yes. What is going to happen with me, Maricua? Are you going to leave me here at home alone while you go off with him and live in the woods?" No matter how civilized he appeared, I was certain that he lived like a vagrant animal in the jungle because of how Maricua had described his life the other day.

His laughter rang in the air. "Of course not, Zaki. Your sister is not a wild creature like a deer. She is a woman and a woman needs shelter. The two of you can come to my home or else I will have to live here with the two of you. Can you think of a better alternative? Your wishes will, to be certain, be taken into consideration."

They both looked at me expectantly. I could not think of anything to say other than to ask, "Where do you live, Cabicacmotz?"

"I have an extensive estate in the outskirts, bordering the jungle."

That did not sound like an ideal place to live. We lived in the prettiest area; at least, it seemed so to me. It was perfect. It was large enough to afford us privacy, yet it was within a quick walk to the city center. To live on the farthest edges of the city sounded like the worst place to live. It would feel almost like being exiled. It was primitive and quiet. I was sure I didn't want to live there. The Cabicacmotz didn't need to read my mind; my face betrayed me. I was in wide-eyed horror.

He grinned. "Very well. We will live here, then."

That would be better, but then I was stuck with having him around all of the time. Sharing a house with a new couple did not sound very comfortable to me. I had seen people in love. They were ridiculous. They would kiss and coo things to each other with the cheerful idiocy that is characteristic of those who are madly in love. I wanted to vomit.

"I will have to spend a great deal of time in my own house. It is there that I conduct the bulk of my activities. Also, I will have to carry out the duties of my office."

"What is that?" I asked.

"I am the principal advisor to your father, Zaki."

I knew that, but had merely forgotten it for a moment. "Well, if you have so much to do, how will you find the time to be a husband?"

"I'm sure we'll find the time," he said. The Cabicacmotz and Maricua looked into each other's eyes with such affection that it was tangible. I had to stop my gag reflex. "Why don't we all take a walk? Your sister and I will walk you over to your father's home; he wanted to talk with you tonight."

"So late?"

"It's not that late, Zaki. He is up and awake. He will not sleep for a few hours, yet. I was there a short time ago."

I was game for anything that would afford me time away from them, so I agreed readily. Chahal accompanied us. The Cabicacmotz and my sister walked hand in hand. I would be glad to be away from them.

When we entered my father's grounds, I expected that the guards would stop us. They did not even glance in our direction. They were never derelict in their duties, to my knowledge, so they must have known we were coming.

Maricua sat down in one of the outer courtyards to await the Cabicacmotz.

Large trees canopied the walkways. Everything looked orderly. I had peeked over the walls of his estate many times, but this was the first time I had been allowed to enter. I imagined my father lounging on one of the many benches that were about.

True to his word, my father was awake and greeted us with enthusiasm. Shortly after, the Cabicacmotz left my father and me to continue his walk with my sister.

"We should be very glad for Maricua, don't you think, Zaki?" my father asked me after they had left. We stood in what would, in modern times, be called a living room. It seemed to be a place to receive guests. I briefly wondered what sort of guests would be allowed to come in, since his wives were not permitted to set foot in the place. I privately believed that he was better off having a sanctity of his own where the shrill nagging of his wives could not be heard.

"It is what she desired, I suppose," I said.

He did not push the topic. Instead, he told me that he had something he wanted to show me.

I wanted to complain about the unfortunate circumstance of the Cabicacmotz and Maricua, but something told me not to upset him needlessly, particularly because he seemed so pleased with the arrangement. I looked around since I had never been in my father's home. It never occurred to me to complain about not being able to set foot within his private home. That was how things were typically done.

He lived opulently for the times. Murals of the jungle adorned the walls. The low ceilings gave one the impression of being in caverns of trees. As I stepped close to them, I could see the minutiae of the life that makes jungles thrive. Insects crawled on leaves. Snakes slithered and birds flew to escape danger. It was stylized, to a certain extent, but it was amazing nonetheless. At the time, most of the artwork was in a certain busy style. There was occasional accuracy, but never like the subtle realism before me. Captivated by what I saw, I told him that I loved his home.

"Well, you can thank the artist for that," he said. "Every once in a while, a student shows promise and will paint my walls."

I was astonished. I found it inexplicable that anyone would ever cover up these magnificent walls. "Do you mean that someone will cover this up some day?"

"Certainly. What makes you think things last forever? Besides, the young man is still perfecting his paint mixtures. Perhaps these will not last long in our humid place."

He began walking away, towards the back of the room. "But come," he said. "There is more to see."

He showed me all of the rooms in his home. Most of them were narrow. That was a common feature of our homes. Roofs were more easily placed upon narrow structures. Otherwise, beams had to be placed in order for the palms to be secure.

Each room had murals. It was apparent that the artist who painted the living room was different. These all had different styles and no two resembled each other. The only thing they had in common was the attention to small details. Some depicted war and hunting scenes while others were of bizarre and outlandish creatures. Some of them had a feeling of darkness to them, others of purity and light.

The thing that surprised me the most was where my father slept. He slept in a hammock, as a commoner would. It was the custom for those of noble lineage to sleep on soft cushioned mats. Only peons slept in hammocks. Hammocks were less likely to harbor insects and only a crew of servants could maintain a clean bed. The bedding was occasionally changed and affording such luxuries was beyond the means of the lower classes. After I questioned him about it, he told me that he liked it and that it was good for his back.

When I thought that I had seen the entirety of his home, he said, "Would you like to see where you are to sleep?"

"I'm going to be allowed to sleep here?" I asked, incredulous.

"Yes. You are now in training to become a warrior. It is imperative that you have several places in which to sleep," he said as he walked towards the far end of a long open courtyard.

"Why?"

"You will see. You'll see that it helps certain things. There is nothing I can tell you right now, so you will have to take my word for it."

Once we reached the end of the courtyard, he entered a dimly lit entryway that led to a hall. He walked a few paces and pulled a curtain aside, revealing a small room that had walls painted like the living room. Torchlight, agitated by the wind, caused the scene to flicker and dance. In the far left corner was what appeared to be a soft mat, sumptuous for the times.

He looked down towards the floor at Chahal who always stayed by my side. He shook his head. "That is the strangest jaguar I've ever seen. After a while, one fails to notice her. You have been here with me for a long time tonight and this is the first that I've noticed her." He continued shaking his head as if he was dumbfounded. "That is her art, you know. Being inconspicuous. That is what makes her into an excellent huntress."

After that, he told me that I should get some sleep and left us in the room. The bed was the softest I had ever felt, I instantly fell asleep.

I had forgotten to ask him if I could see the carving of my mother's face.

In the morning, I was awakened by the sound of men shouting. I could see Chahal sitting calmly while peeking out from the curtain, half in and half out of the room. Her tail flicked from side to side in calm agitation.

"What the hell goes on here?" I yelled. It was not uncommon for me to speak to Chahal, but my words were not for her. They were for the world, particularly for the men who were creating a ruckus outside of my room.

She looked back at me and then turned back towards the source of the noise.

I went outside and came face to face with the most amazing sight I had ever seen in all of my young life.

Twelve men were playing the ballgame, bateh, in the courtyard. It was, apparently, an impromptu game. There were no stone markers. Instead, they had removed two torches from their perches on the wall and aimed towards the brackets. It seemed to be an unachievable goal. Yet as I sat there, on a long bench, I saw the impossible. Someone made a goal. The men from the winning team hollered in triumph, the opposing team groaned in disappointment.

I shook my head and blinked my eyes in disbelief. I could have sworn that the ball had behaved strangely. There was no way that the ball could have hovered in the air, vacillating as if deciding which way to go and then decisively lodging itself in the curving metal sconce. It was unfeasible.

Someone loudly calling my name interrupted my deliberations. I saw the Cabicacmotz run over to my side, an exultant expression on his face. He was drenched in sweat and panting loudly when he crouched beside me; he was unable to join me on the bench because of the thick wooden yoke he wore around his waist.

"How did you like my goal?" he asked breathlessly.

"That was you?"

"Yes, and I had a hard time of it, I can tell you."

"But how... why did the ball move in the air like that?"

He asked me to describe what I saw. When I told him, he said, "That is the way the game is played, Zaki. The ball doesn't go in the goal merely because of physical prowess and luck. Great intent is what causes a point to be scored."

"What do you mean? I see that you have obviously been exercising," I said. I looked around and saw that all of the men were equally wrung out and covered in sweat. "All of you were playing hard. Your team simply had more skill. To say that wishing it is what makes a goal happen is an insult to both team's efforts, not to mention the insult to my intelligence."

"Yes, your intelligence," he dryly said. "It is most keen, is it not? When I use the word intent, I can assure you that I do not use it as a synonym for wishing and idle hoping. Those are merely the fantasies of lazy people. I use the term in a very specific way. Intent is a command from within oneself that can change the world around us concretely. It is not a powerless affair, like a wish or a hope. Those are actions without power behind them. Intent is not. Power backs it and causes one's will to come to fruition."

"Then why do you bother to run around and kick or chase the ball?" If it was all as he had said, a game for the mind, I could not comprehend why one's physical body had to be engaged.

"You don't know anything about the game of bateh, do you?" he accused.

I mumbled that I had seen a few games. I had seen them, but those were informal games played by amateurs. The stone markers never came into play.

He explained to me the rules of bateh. It was a game for the body as well as for the mind.

He stood and walked me towards the closest end of the courtyard. Two sacks of grain had been set in the middle, approximately four long paces apart. Indicating that I should look to the other end of the courtyard, he called my attention to the matching sacks at the far end.

"There are two ways to win in bateh," he told me. "The common way is the way of the body. Score is kept for the goals made with our bodies. If no ultimate goal can be accomplished with intent, the game is ruled by the goals of the body. If the goal is made with the use of intent, the game is won. Intent only can use the stone markers at the middle points of the field. Intent is not allowed to come into use when it comes to the goals at the far ends of the field. Do you see what I mean?"

"What prevents you from using this intent to score a long goal?"

"Honor, of course. We are warriors; we give oaths to abide by the rules of the game. Any idiot would know if one of us attempted to cheat in such a manner."

"How would you know?"

"We would know because we see."

"Oh, you mean the way the ball hung in the air and trembled before it went in?"

"That is the only way a normal person would be able to see that something unusual has occurred. I don't mean it that way. A warrior is a man who knows. To view the physical world is called looking. To see means something else entirely and it is not confined to the visual. To see means that the warrior knows things that he could not possibly know from regular channels. He sees into the hidden, his vision is perfect. He can even see into intentions of others. It is not entirely a matter for the eyes. One's whole body knows. That is called seeing. When he advances in power, he can even see energy itself. That is when things get really interesting."

"When will I be able to see?"

"That is up to you and how much power you have."

"Then I will probably never get it in time to see a game. I am only a boy who has recently become a man right now."

"Power is not status in the world; it is something that does not depend on the social order. It is a personal matter. No one can give it to you. No one is going to mutter strange words over your head and confer it upon you. It must be earned."

"How?"

"You are now on the road to that goal, Zaki. Your lessons with me will eventually bring you to it."

We stood there for a short while. His words only stuck to me for a short time. His explanations were the explanations of adults and essentially meaningless to me, a boy with the attention span of a gnat. I could not have known that his words were absolutely true, yet. My thoughts returned to the ballgame.

"So a regular game has two avenues for victory," I said. "The common way is for the goals to be made at the far ends. Then there is the other way, the goals of the sides, right?"

He nodded. "Yes, but remember that the goals at the ends of the fields are protected by the goal keepers. They prevent the opposing team from scoring."

"That I understand. Where do the goal keepers stand to prevent the side goals from being made, though? The goals that supersede the end goals, I mean."

"Everybody on that team is the goal keeper at that moment. The side who wants to prevent it is intending that the ball not enter the hole or goal. The team that is trying to make the goal is intending that it be made. There is no physical interference from anyone trying to keep the ball from entering." He pursed his lips and grimaced for a few seconds. "To be absolutely correct, physical interference against those intending is often allowed. If you see one of your opponents intending, you may jostle them to distract their attention. That is why you see that the game becomes rough for a time. We are trying to distract each other. When it is a decisive bout of intent, you will see everyone become still and focused. At that point, we are all mind and drop our attention away from our bodies."

He had succeeded in confusing me. I complained that his use of the word "see" was inconsistent and that he needed to differentiate between the two versions of seeing that he meant.

He told me that he had explained it properly, that I was being argumentative and difficult, and that there was no importance to which word was used. "One thing is one thing, no matter what name it is given. What you need to do, Zaki, is pay more attention when I speak. If you would, you would notice that the context is different when I speak of different types of seeing. One is the seeing that seers do and the other is the seeing that the public does, which is really viewing. The seeing of seers is beyond you. When I talk about you seeing, I mean the regular normal seeing that every plebeian does."

That was less than flattering. I would have to talk less in order to avoid his insults. I figured that I was safe in asking questions about the ballgame. I asked him, "Why did you refer to the goal as yours when you say that everybody pitches in on that thing called intent?"

"Ah, good catch, Zaki. I see why you were confused. That was my mistake. I was the initiator of the side goal. Here... Well, not here per se because the rules are subject to negotiation. The rules are not set in stone. They are subject to change. Here in the courtyard, the Jaguars..."

"Wait. Wait," I said. "You mean that you are 'The Jaguars'? The royal team?"

"Yes. I thought you knew."

"You are all famous. They talk about you everywhere."

"And yet you have never been to any of our games..."

"No. Maricua never let me go."

"You will have to begin attending our games, then. It is mandatory for all of the students. Don't worry about Maricua. The problem with her is that she dislikes violent games and is uneasy in crowds," he said. "Anyway, before each game, negotiations are conducted to determine the rules of the game. They are lengthy and serious affairs. If we know that one of the opposing team members has a special talent, we will negotiate against it. Anything to mitigate any of their number from scoring the point."

"What kind of talents are you talking about?"

"Do you know why they call me the Cabicacmotz?"

"Father told me that it was actually a title that you earned."

'That is technically correct, but the real reason has escaped you. I know that you know this; you have simply not bothered to reason it out. Our language is an agglutinating one. Concepts in the form of words are clumped together to form new words and, especially, names and titles. Look to your own name and think about it."

He had me there. I knew what my name meant. "Why do we call ourselves such names? Shouldn't a name be a name and nothing more?"

"Do you mean why don't we have meaningless names?"

I nodded.

"There are some of our tribe who do that, but among the noble houses that is usually not done. If it is done anyway, it will generally only happen with the female children. Names have power. Your name reflects the destructive and life-renewing aspects of the hurricane that came through here on the night you were born. That is a good thing. It ceases to be a good thing if you cling to that name throughout your life."

"What do you mean?"

"Take me, for instance, Zaki. Imagine if I had refused to become the Cabicacmotz because I was so tied to my previous name. I would not have had the flexibility needed to be who I am now. Perhaps I would not even have been able to ever be the meteor from the Pleiades, which is what my name means."

"Why do they call you that?"

"Because I can move through the world and the cosmos at incredible speed. A meteor is merely a symbol, a way of saying things; I can move much more rapidly than an actual meteor. You've seen me move."

"Not really. I've never been able to catch sight of you when you're in motion. I only get to see that you end up quicker than a blink in another place. I know what meteors are, but I don't know what Pleiades are."

"It is a constellation that is precious to our people. We are said to ascend there by our astronomer-priests. I will show it to you one night. No one should be unaware of its beauty. But we are straying off course of our original conversation, you wanted to know about the talents that the team members had and how we negotiate bateh rules." He looked to me to make sure that I was following his words. My attention was completely on what he said. Satisfied, he continued, "The opposing team will always take into account my ability to move from place to place. If we know that the opposition has a player that can create phantom objects, such as the ball, we will sacrifice my abilities for his. Thus, you have a game where no trickery of the ball can occur and I will not move like lightning across the field. The only surprises in such a game are when the players acquire new abilities during the actual game. Many times, if a player develops new abilities that the opposing team is unaware of, they will hide it until the actual game. This is not considered trickery; it is the other team's responsibility to gather intelligence on the other team's abilities. Then the negotiations occur. You have not been to a true game, so you don't know, but at the beginning of each game, a scribe reads the particular rules of a game. Then the games commence."

"That sounds very complicated," I said. "I don't remember anyone reading specific rules at the start of the games I've seen."

"That is because you have probably only seen informal games that focus on physical prowess, not games where intent is used. In those games, there are constants in the rules. The game lasts a certain length of time, there are a certain number of players, and the side goals are only made by chance. They are flukes. Those players don't stand a chance upon the royal bateh courts."

"I will add that it is not always necessary to win with side goals. Sometimes the games are so evenly matched that no team makes a side goal and the score for the end goals determines the winner. Otherwise the game might last for years."

"Do you ever go into a game using only the side goals?"

His face clouded over and he became grim, "Yes."

"When?"

"When we play against the Xibalbans."

"The Xibalbans? Who are they? Are they another tribe?"

He stood up abruptly. "That's more than enough for one day, Zaki. Be in the clearing at twilight. I have to go now and bathe. Excuse me."

He did not even look at me. I watched him go, certain that I had said something wrong, but not knowing what.

Although I searched and searched for my father before I left, I could not find him. Hardly anyone was around. Every one of the players was gone. Eventually, I located one of his manservants. He asked me if I wanted him to fetch for a cook, but I declined.

Chahal began her strange raspy purr and I knew that it was time to send her to hunt in the jungle. Over the years, I had learned her language and could tell by her sounds what she wanted. She had many of them. I could mimic them to perfection. Whenever I did it as amusement, she would look over at me and then proceed to ignore me. When she purred first and I mimicked it back at her, she would rub her body against my legs as if to reward me for learning her language or to confirm that I had guessed her intent correctly.

We walked to the edge of the jungle. She looked up at me and I scratched her behind the ear and under her chin. Then she took off like the wind. How she was able to run at such speeds, yet remain silent, was always a mystery to me. I watched her until she disappeared into the trees.

She would return to our home after she was satisfied. That was not entirely accurate; she would come to wherever I was after she was done. Many times, she had found me in the marketplace or wandering around, instead. Sometimes she was gone for days. At other times, she was only gone for an eighth of a day. It varied.

One time, many years ago, I was curious about her hunting activities and accompanied her. She seemed pleased, at first, to have me around, but it soon became apparent to both of us that I was too slow, clumsy, and loud to be an effective hunting partner. People who have never befriended a wild animal have trouble believing that they can express their feelings in very real and obvious ways. She let me know her viewpoint on my hunting with her; it was utter disdain. For a long time, she did not allow me to go with her into the jungle when she needed to hunt. Lately, since I had been working on my technique and practicing with the blowgun, she had relented and tolerated me in her realm, up to a point.

Eventually I went home and had a meal in the servant's kitchen. Maricua was also out for the day. She must have gone to the marketplace to be gone for such a long time, I surmised. Then the awful thought that she was spending time with the Cabicacmotz came to me. I resolved not to think about that. Before, it was funny to imagine them together. Now, it was a certainty and that made it no longer amusing.

Towards the end of the meal, I remembered that I had forgotten to perform the exercise the Cabicacmotz had assigned me. I had not sat down and attempted to feel my shadow. Last night had been stressful with the Cabicacmotz coming over and announcing that he and my sister would marry and me going over to my father's house to sleep. I was still amazed at how natural it felt to sleep in a strange place.

For most of the afternoon, I sat in my garden trying to feel my shadow.

I tried to feel it behind me, when I faced the sun, with no success.

When I shifted position, I was able to lose myself in my shadow. My back was to the sun, so I faced it. For a long time, I stared at it. Curiously, I began to sense depth to it. My eyes moved over its surface, occasionally feeling a thickness to it, especially where it covered the short grass.

Then it began to acquire hues; I was able to see them within it. The hues were not proper colors as they shifted and moved about. They were like the eldritch shades that play on the scales of a fish in the sun or like flames when different sands are deliberately thrown on them to make them change colors.

I was there for a long time looking into my shadow. There was a sense of peace and lassitude to the shades that made me drowsy. I closed my eyes.

The next thing I knew was that Chahal was licking my face. Her breath was fishy and pungent. It annoyed me because it meant that I would have to go to the stream to wash my face.

When I opened my eyes, I got the fright of my life. I was in my room on my mat. Maricua, my father, and the Cabicacmotz were standing looking down at me with worried expressions on their faces. Even Chahal looked concerned.

I wanted to slap myself for my stupidity. I fell asleep, like a bum, and missed the Cabicacmotz' lesson. I sat up and my father gently pushed me back down.

"You must not rise yet, Zaki," he said.

"Why am I in here? Did something happen to me?"

Maricua mumbled that she was going to get me something to drink and left. No one said anything for a while; they simply traded meaningful glances that filled me with apprehension.

"Is anyone going to explain why I am in here?"

The Cabicacmotz sighed and said, "I carried you in here, Zaki."

"Why didn't you wake me?"

"Because he couldn't," my father snapped. "What the hell were you doing?"

I blinked my eyes and shook my head to dispel the grogginess. "I was doing the exercises the Cabicacmotz assigned. I fell asleep, that's all. Am I in trouble for being late to the lesson?"

"No, Zaki," the Cabicacmotz said. "These things happen. Were you doing your exercises in your garden?"

"Yes. Why?"

The Cabicacmotz and my father exchanged a knowing look. Something was going on that I was unaware of.

My father asked me if I had fallen asleep in the garden or elsewhere.

"In the garden, of course. Didn't you find me there?"

"That's the problem, Zaki," my father said. "When you didn't arrive for the Cabicacmotz' lesson, we searched for you. We looked in the garden and you weren't there. When we looked in there again, hours later, you were asleep on the grass. Where were you?"

"That's impossible."

"Impossible it is not because it is a common occurrence among the priests. You are not a priest. You are still a boy with no training in the forces that priests or warriors interact with, yet this has happened to you. Have you received any training from our priests without my approval?" he angrily asked. He looked at Maricua, who came in with a cup of water for me, and asked her, "Have any priests been around here?"

She shook her head.

"Then have you ever noticed that he has been missing? Have you ever found him hanging around the temples?"

Again, she shook her head.

"Then would you mind telling me how he knows how to displace his body?" he said as he pointed at me.

Maricua shrugged, a fearful and confused look was on her face. My father was livid.

I did not believe that my body was displaced or anything of the sort. I thought he was speaking nonsense to cover up the fact that they hadn't conducted a proper search.

My father went into a tirade about cheeky priests and how he was going to kill them when he discovered who they were when the Cabicacmotz interrupted him and asked, "Exactly how were you performing the exercise of feeling your shadow, Zaki?"

Maricua handed me the halved gourd and I took a long swallow. I was thirsty and my mouth felt as if it was full of sand. The water helped me considerably, especially since it gave me a chance to compose my thoughts. "At first I tried to feel it behind me, but I had no luck. Then I figured out that I would be facing my shadow if I turned my back to the sun. Then I looked at it and looked at it until I began to see the colors in it. I felt it; it felt connected to me, a part of me. Then the colors began moving slower than before and it made me drowsy. I must have fallen asleep."

"Do you remember the last color you focused on?"

I told him that I didn't focus on any color, but rather watched them inattentively as they moved about.

He raised his eyebrows at my father.

My father pursed his lips and shook his head. "Are you sure that you have not been learning from any itinerant priests?"

I told him I wouldn't know a priest from anyone else. He replied that he would remedy my ignorance.

He asked the Cabicacmotz if I was telling the truth.

My own father thought I was a liar. That was an awful feeling.

The Cabicacmotz narrowed his eyes and gazed at me, he looked angry. After a few moments, he pronounced me honest. My body relaxed with relief.

"Of course I'm telling the truth. Why would I lie?"

My father locked eyes with the Cabicacmotz and gestured with his head to the archway, indicating that he wanted to speak to him in private.

"No," I said. "Whatever you have to say about me, please say it here. I want to know what's happening. Don't I have a right to know, now that I'm a man?"

"Very well," my father said as he sat cross-legged on the floor. The Cabicacmotz joined him and sat to his right. "We have a strange situation here. A boy with no training has been able to unwittingly do what experienced warriors struggle to accomplish. He has disappeared from this earth and reappeared as if nothing at all happened. What do you think about that?"

I thought they were either having a grand joke at my expense or else they had not looked carefully when they looked in my garden. I told them that they had probably been careless in their search and that, perhaps, one of the trees had hidden me.

"We looked all over that garden, Zaki," the Cabicacmotz said. "You were not in there. It is not a simple case of our glancing at the garden from the entryway. We went in and even inspected the bushes. Also, when we found you, you were in the middle of the grass. I suspect that you were in the same spot where you performed the shadow exercises. Or am I wrong?"

I told him that I had been where he said I was. I asked them whether someone could have transported me from there while I slept and delivered me back to where they had found me.

The Cabicacmotz looked at my father and swallowed nervously.

"What? What aren't you telling me?"

They both looked sheepish.

My father said to the Cabicacmotz, "Let's inspect him and see if he stinks of the pit." Then they narrowed their eyes and watched me.

I was at my wits end with their mystifying remarks. I tried to question them, but they shushed me.

Since they would not let me talk or answer my questions, I decided to watch them. They narrowed their eyes and moved them over my body. Curiously, it seemed that they were not looking at me directly. It was an oblique, yet frontal gaze. It sounds unfeasible, but they looked at me and didn't look at me. It was rather unnerving, especially when they began to rock back and forth like wobbly statues. When they were finished rocking and looking at me, they shrugged at each other. I asked them what they had done.

"Well, Zaki, you were not spirited away by demons, it seems," my father told me.

"Of course not. They don't exist," I complained as I rolled my eyes. Did they really think that I was so superstitious, a gullible child who could be frightened by ghost stories and imaginary monsters?

My father seemed taken aback by my beliefs and called me a fool who didn't know the first thing about what was out there.

"Then what is out there?"

"Everything and nothing," he said.

That was a meaningless description to me. I didn't have the slightest clue about what he was speaking of.

The Cabicacmotz asked me why I had not followed his instructions for the exercise. I told him that I had no success with his exercise and didn't see what all of the fuss was about.

"When I gave you that exercise, it was one for your spirit, not one for your eyes. You have jumped to shadow gazing and that is beyond your abilities right now. The trouble is that, apparently, it is something you have an affinity for."

"No. The trouble is that I was not able to feel my shadow at all and didn't want to suffer the embarrassment of being the only one in the class with nothing to report."

"No one expects you to have success every time, especially at the beginning. What was important was for you to grow accustomed to freeing your thoughts. When the thoughts are not confined to what the senses dictate, we exercise a sense that we have not used since we were infants. To free up the body's rule over what we sense and experience is one of the first steps to the knowledge I am guiding you to acquire. It was an exercise to put you in touch with that mysterious sense which is not dependent upon the eyes."

"I didn't feel my shadow, Cabicacmotz."

"That is because it was only one of your first days with me. What I am teaching you is very difficult. It might take you years to accomplish it. I bet that you were imagining your shadow behind you and immediately discarded it as your imagination. I have news for you; that's exactly what you should have been doing. That tiny spark of imagination is a portal, of sorts, that leads to an awareness that you are unaccustomed to having. Right now, it only feels like imaginings that you yourself have conjured up, but that is only because that sense is still weak and you don't have control over it. You can't even get to it yet. My aim is to get you to that door. You must hone that sense."

"Why was what I did so bad?"

"It is not that you did something wicked or wrong, Zaki. The problem is that gazing is something that should only be done with a watcher when the warrior begins his training. Later on, he can gaze by himself because he has learned to rein himself in and control himself. Right now, you need to take the small steps of an infant. Instead, you took giant leaps that might have landed you in the fire, so to speak. What you did was like installing a roof on a house that doesn't even have walls yet. We must build those walls, Zaki. Please, the next time I assign you an exercise to per-form, please follow it literally. Also, I want you to have someone around to keep watch over you. Any of the guards will do; they will be pleased to watch over a training warrior. If none is available, and you can't find anyone else, have Chahal by your side. She is perfectly able to keep you grounded to this earth." He looked at her for a moment, knitting his brow. "Actually, I believe it best if you make sure that Chahal is there regardless of whom else is there."

"Why?"

"Because it was she who alerted me to the fact that you were in danger."

"Not that I believe I was in danger, but how did she do that?"

"She came to the class and sat down right in front of me and stared at me. I can tell you that she scared the crap out of the other students. Then she would walk forward and look back at me to make sure that I was following her. She led me here. When Maricua and I couldn't find you, I brought your father here. No one, guards included, was able to find you. Chahal stayed in the garden watching the grassy area."

Our conversation ended there.

I did not want to mention the strange dream that I had while sleeping in the garden. It would have been very unwise on my part to reveal my dream, I thought, because I had dreamt that I was a woman. A female, rather. Such a thing would not be looked upon favorably in our culture.

In the dream, I was a goddess and other gods sur-rounded me. Gods I didn't know, yet in the dream I did. Foreign gods. Our thrones were lined around a room, which overlooked an arena. I was in charge of the jaguars and all of the great cats. My throne was wooden and carved with the image of a strange creature. I saw the real animal in a flash. It had large floppy ears and a long nose that reached the floor and swept it. It also had tusks. Its legs were like the trunks of trees and its flesh was gray. Truly, it was hideous and I could not imagine such an animal ever living upon this earth. It must have been an alien animal, peculiar to the world or reality I was in. The animal did not seem bizarre to me in my dream. I remember being very jealous of another goddess who was the one in charge of dogs. I wanted to trade my post with hers because her animals loved me also. I also didn't want to be a goddess any longer because all of those gods were watching executions of humans. They pronounced that they were the just pun-ishments that people deserved because of the acts they had performed in the world. The whole thing sickened me terribly. If anything else happened in the dream, I could not recall.

No, I would never tell anyone about that dream.

The three remaining days of lessons were uneventful. I did not have my night of shadow play with the Cabicacmotz. Instead, he would spend the larger portion of the lesson with one of the other boys. As he promised, I would spend the rest of the evening playing the shadow-stepping game with the boys who were left without a partner.

Because of that, I was able to talk and get to know a few of my classmates. They were pleasant enough, but the time we had did not evolve into invitations to spend our free hours together.

I would have extended an invitation myself, perhaps, but I was reticent to have them know who I was. For some reason, I imagined that they were unaware that I was the son of our tribe's king. This was pure foolishness on my part because they knew exactly who I was the moment Chahal arrived with me at our classes.

The day of the festival approached. I would find myself getting excited about going until I remembered that the Cabicacmotz would accompany me. While the other boys would be with their partners and a chaperone, I would be saddled with only our teacher for company. Chahal would be with me, but it felt lonely to me. Being the twenty-fifth boy in the class was my fate.

A strange thing happened the day before the festival. It was a day where we did not have to attend class with the Cabicacmotz.

I was returning to my garden after a swim in the river when I saw Maricua walking in the larger garden with a young man. At first, I mistook him for a slave because of his peculiar and plain hair.

In my tribe, everyone had long hair, except for slaves, the stricken, or sometimes the pochtecas, the traveling merchants. Almost invariably, the men wore theirs in one long braid down their backs. The men who tended farms would often keep the areas around their ears and the napes of their necks shaved, but that was solely a utilitarian reason, not one done for aesthetics.

The women's hairstyles varied. Every so often, a particular style would become popular among the women. A few weeks later, another style replaced it. It was something I noticed because frequently the hairstyles would be quite elaborate. Despite my pleas to be told the secret of the women's hair, the attendants who braided my hair never revealed the reasons for the new hairstyles to me. Perhaps even they did not know what dictated the whims of the women and their hair. In any case, even Maricua refused to divulge why she wore her hair up one week and a week later would only wear her hair in two long braids.

This young man had short hair. His bangs were above his eyebrows; the rest of his hair was tapered right below his ears. What changed my mind about his social status was that he wore ornate armbands of hammered gold and he had a manservant following them carrying an ungainly tray of fruits that seemed as if they would topple over at any moment. It looked comical, but the man was so focused on keeping the fruit on the tray that none fell off. Maricua and the young man were oblivious to the manservant's plight and didn't even once glance back, so involved in conversation were they. I observed them from afar. I was close enough to see their facial expressions, but not close enough to hear their conversation. They merely walked around the garden repeatedly.

Crafty imaginings took hold of my mind. Perhaps this was a possible suitor for Maricua. I was enjoying the thought of the Cabicacmotz being shut out of our lives when he showed up.

He came up behind them and grabbed a piece of fruit from the manservant's tray, took a bite, and then went up to the young man and put his arm casually around his shoulder. The strange man was startled at first. He must have recognized the Cabicacmotz because he laughed and put his arm around his waist in a friendly gesture.

I was incredibly disappointed. I had looked forward to a confrontation, or perhaps even a scuffle, between the two and there they were, acting like old friends. I knew that I was not thinking good thoughts. My self-examination revealed three things to me. One, I was unkind. I experienced an unsettling sensation of self-loathing upon discovering this ugly side of myself. Two, I feared, yet liked the

Cabicacmotz as a teacher, but I had mixed feelings about having him as a brother-in-law. Moreover, three, I might have wanted the young man to win Maricua's heart for a moment, but I knew I would resent him even more than I resented the Cabicacmotz if Maricua married him. In other words, I was confused and carried conflicting thoughts in my head.

Then I saw something that robbed me of all breath. Maricua looked at the Cabicacmotz. That look contained every good thing that life can consist of. It sounds like the worst sentimental drivel, but it was the look of love. There was hope, trust, joy, and affection within it. My heart pounded within my ribs and I could feel what she felt. It was a universal human feeling of finding completeness within another person. I knew that when she looked at the sky that the sky was a brighter blue for her. The knowledge devastated me. It was a longing so pure and encompassing that I knew that I needed to find that one person who could make me feel how Maricua felt at that moment. I also knew that that look and that feeling was why my father had defied all customs of our society in order to be with my mother. I also knew that it did not allow plurality. It was unique and could only be found in one other soul.

At that moment, the Cabicacmotz patted the young man on the back and took Maricua in his arms, hugging her as they twirled and laughed. Then he placed her back on the ground and took her face in his hands. With incredible tenderness, he lightly kissed her lips. Then he pulled her into another hug and kissed the top of her head. His expression was that of a man who has finally reached the end of a long journey. My fate was sealed when I saw him reciprocate her feelings so completely. As I felt Maricua's feelings, so also did I feel his. They were even stronger than hers were. I felt my heart leap upwards and out of my chest. Of course, this did not happen literally, but I felt it and knew it as the exultation one feels when one loves. Even secondhand, it was an overwhelming and exquisite feeling. My whole body knew what it meant.

That was when I knew that I did not want to be the king. I would sacrifice every luxury and advantage if it meant I would find my counterpart. I refused to surrender my happiness to four shrews merely to have the approval of the tribe. How empty such a life must be. I felt sorrow for my father's path, yet proud for him that he once had his own happiness with my mother.

Then my thoughts returned to the present. Almost immediately, I felt a blow to my sense of goodness, I was ashamed of how I had resented the Cabicacmotz' plans to marry Maricua. I felt villainous and unworthy of the kindness he had shown me. No longer would I allow myself to deprive Maricua of her joy, even in my thoughts, merely because I was jealous of sharing my time with her. Instead, I resolved to be happy for her.

In retrospect, these were certainly simple resolutions and goals that I made for myself. They were groundbreaking only because I had never examined myself or my life before. To be able to imagine plans for my life was unprecedented because I was a thoughtless boy who was used to simply accepting the world around me without realizing that it was meant to be understood. Although I didn't understand my life, I was jaded and bored already with it.

To make decisions, about what I wanted to do in life, renewed me and made me feel the wonder of existence.

That night I slept fitfully, thinking of all the things I had come to realize.

Part Two

The Festival

On the day of the festival, I woke to Maricua's laughter. The Cabicacmotz' voice was a low rumble in the background.

My resolution to be glad for her had not been diminished by the night. I smiled when I heard her laughs and jumped out of my mat. After I had dunked my head in a basin to clear my eyes of sleep, I headed to where they were.

They were locked in an embrace when I entered the room they were in. They were at the doorway to the garden, limned in morning's light. At that moment, my resolutions were no help to me. It embarrassed me terribly to see them holding each other. They were not doing anything immoral, but it made me uncomfortable nonetheless.

The Cabicacmotz noticed me a moment after I arrived and came and patted me on the back as if he was glad to see me. Maricua asked me if I wanted something to eat before we left for the festival. I told her I was very hungry and she went to summon the cook. The Cabicacmotz and I were left in the room, but I felt at ease again.

Confident, I asked him, "Why can't I go to the festival on my own and have fun there?"

He raised an eyebrow and cocked his head as he looked at me. "There is something different about you this morning, Zaki, and I can't quite figure out what it is. Can you tell me what it is?" he asked.

He was right; I felt different. I knew what it was and told him that I was glad that he and Maricua had found each other.

He wagged a finger at me as he said, "That is it. You are lighter somehow. Today you are not gloomy, pessimistic, or only thinking about yourself. For a moment there, I thought we had an impostor on our hands. You learned something important, how to put aside your own wants and desires. Putting aside the self is one of the first moves one makes when one chases freedom. This is an auspicious sign, indeed, on this of all days."

I, of course, was not grasping all of his words, but I really did feel lighter and freer. I couldn't argue with that and shrugged with a big smile on my face.

"To answer your question, though, I'll have to tell you what to expect today. You might have time to have fun and enjoy the festival, but there are several things we have to accomplish before you are allowed to go off on your own."

"Like what?" I asked.

"Well, you have to discover who your teachers are."

"What? Why don't you introduce them to me when I go to their classes? Why don't you teach me yourself? Aren't you supposed to be my teacher?"

"I am your lead teacher, but I don't know what you are supposed to learn yet myself without a sign. We will approach many groups of men and women..."

I interrupted him because this was going too far. I had no intention of learning tasks that were the responsibility of women and I told him so.

"Boy, you have a lot to learn. If you think that women are beneath us or inferior to men, you are quite mistaken. Except for fathering children, and even that is only applicable to mundane human women, women can be expert in any field that you now believe is the sole domain of men. You have been led to believe that women are frail weak-willed creatures whose only ability in life is to bear and nurture children. Isn't that so? Banish that set of beliefs from your mind right now. If you don't, you will have a most trying day today. Women can be the most vicious and implacable warriors of all. They forget nothing, they can be merciless, they sense fear and weakness, and they will mow you down faster than you can think if you are unwary. Do not underestimate them. They are a citadel's final warriors."

"Final warriors? What is that supposed to mean?"

"What it means is that women are hardly ever killed by invaders. They are a city's last defense and means of revenge. They all know this. If all of the men and male children are exterminated, they will be kept for use as wives and mothers. When they are installed under a new rule of law, they will take their revenge for the lives of their sons, brothers, uncles, and fathers. They are avengers. To know that one's fate might be harder to accept than death makes women ruthless survivors who live in the full knowledge of what life might hold. Take them seriously; their defenselessness is only an outward mask."

I didn't want to think about such terrible things, so I changed the subject. I was willing to believe that some women were masculine, but to believe that someone as sweet as Maricua was capable of killing strange men while they slept was inconceivable to me.

The Cabicacmotz grabbed me by the shoulders and shook me. "Believe it, Zaki. That man she beat with a stick would have died if a healer had not attended to him. Some might be vain and coquettish, but even they are granite underneath it all."

"What in the world is going on here?" Maricua cried when she saw him shaking me like a rag doll.

He released me with a sheepish look on his face and said, "I am only advising Zaki to not treat women like weak and inferior citizens. You know the women he will meet today, Maricua. I even had to remind him of the young man who was here yesterday."

"Did you have to bring that up?"

"I most certainly did have to. He seems to think that all women are sweet mothers and kind sisters, even though he knows his other half-sisters and the wives of your father. He really only has you as an example, but he has extended your beautiful qualities to all women, apparently. He cannot go there today thinking that women are like shy does in the fields. The men will not raise a hand to him since he is the son of Naualalom, but the women will have no compunction in doing so." He went to her and lightly touched her cheek. "I had to remind him that sweet Maricua almost beat a man to death with a stick," he said with a sly grin.

She pursed her lips to stifle a laugh, but it escaped. Then she laughed with abandon.

I was amazed that someone as sweet as her could beat a man. I asked them if the young man whom they had walked with in the garden yesterday was really the man she beat.

"Yes, Zaki. That was he. He looks all right now, but that is only because four healers attended to him. Even the principal healer needed help with the healing. Your sister was brutal. Luckily, we smoothed things over with him and he is now going to be marrying your other sister, Marilya."

I knew Marilya. Already I felt sorry for him; she was a harridan. First, he got beaten with a stick by a woman and now he was facing a lifetime of being with a woman who would treat him like dirt. Who knew that fate could be so unfair?

Maricua told me, "Keep Chahal with you, at all times, when you have to meet the women warriors, Zaki."

"How is that going to help me if they decide to beat me like you beat that guy with the weird hairdo?"

That made her snicker. She said, "All women understand the mother's protectiveness of her child. Chahal stands as your protector, an adoptive mother of sorts. They know that she will protect you and attack anyone who tries to harm you. They will not risk death for the mere purpose of teaching you a lesson. It is a move that you can only play today, so don't get cocky with those women," she advised me. "If it turns out that they must be your teachers in some art or another, they can demand that Chahal not be beside you during your lessons and then they might beat you if they find that you deserve or need a beating."

How awful. I was horrified to hear that people might treat me like a slave on a whim, the son of a king. I decided that I had best rethink my plan to avoid becoming the king. A king had benefits. One of them had to be that random women did not beat on him. He had guards. Then again, fate could also decree that he wind up with many ill-tempered wives. What if all women were violent creatures, hiding behind the mask of sweetness? Perhaps things I'd rather not think of were going on behind closed doors. I shuddered.

"Ah, that is good thinking, Maricua. We will have to hide your craftiness from your father or I might be out of a job," the Cabicacmotz told her.

His words, thankfully, brought me back to our conversation. I asked him why he did not teach me what the other teachers would and why he did not know who they were yet. It all seemed very casual and careless. I wondered if he was sloppy with the curriculum.

"Zaki. There are so many subjects that you might be destined to learn, I cannot be expected to know the intricacies of all the disciplines. That is why I am taking you around and introducing you to various groups of experts. My group is principally the one of bateh, the ballgame. I have other groups I belong to, but my office is to oversee the educations of our young men, not to teach them everything about every thing. No one could do that, unless he had lived thousands of years. I am not a thousand years old. For instance, I never learned to handle the plants. If I need to, I must rely on someone else's expertise. Also, I do not know which subjects destiny will point out to you. You might learn about the plants, I don't know. That is why I am your guide today. I will keep track of which groups you will learn from."

I had no interest in plants. It sounded stupid to me. I only had one interest at all, bateh. It concerned me that I might not receive the omen to learn bateh and I questioned him about that.

"Your fate was sealed the day you brought an orphaned jaguar into your home, Zaki. Since I belong to the team called the Jaguars, that was a sign that you would one day belong to us. While every student must watch our games, not all are destined to learn the true game. You are. Your omen has already been satisfied."

I complained that I would not get to meet his teammates because the sign was already fulfilled.

"Don't worry. I intend to take you to meet them. We will sit with them after you have seen the dance of the Cranes. Once they begin to dance, your quota of subjects will most likely be filled. In all probability, you will have many subjects to learn."

I inwardly groaned. Learning about a bunch of subjects was not my idea of a good time. I would like to practice bateh all of the time. Why did I have to study anything else?

The servants brought in a large breakfast of cakes and cut fruit. The three of us ate in silence. I wondered how the day would go and contemplated how I could foil any omens from boring groups.

"What kinds of subjects might I be in for?" I asked.

The Cabicacmotz provided me with a long list. There was a subject called the Keeping of Days, where someone would learn how to read the stone calendar. There were courses in astronomy, mathematics, spying, guarding, water, earth, fire, air, night, day. Almost everything had a subject. There were even subjects within subjects. I tried to ask him about what they consisted of, but he told me that I would have to see what I got before he said anything else. He said that we could be there for days if he had to explain every subject's course of study. He also named many animals and birds in his list. He steadfastly refused to entertain any questions regarding those. I wondered if he was simply ignorant about those subjects and that, perhaps, it was like the plants he never studied. I asked him if that was so.

He sighed and placed his head in his hands, leaning on the table. "Oh, nephew, what a long day you will make for me."

"What?" I screeched. "I am your nephew? You are my uncle?"

He groaned loudly. "Yes, Zaki. Of course I am. I thought you knew."

"How could I know?" I pointed back and forth from him to Maricua and said, "And what kind of incest is this? Are you allowed to marry your niece? This is truly disgusting. How can this happen?"

Maricua banged her fist loudly on the table. "You will apologize right now, Zaki. This is not how you were raised," she said as her face reddened with anger. "The Cabicac-motz does not share any blood with me, he is not my uncle. We can rightfully marry. He is your uncle, not mine. My mother was not yours. You know this."

I was getting a good image of what the man she beat received. She was utterly frightening. She did not look sweet and good-natured. She looked as if she would gladly strike me at any moment. I cringed. Even though I knew she was not my full sister, I felt that she was. That was why I had confused myself and accused them of impropriety. I apologized and admitted that I was wrong. I stressed that since she was the only sister I had who cared for me, I always forgot that she was only my half-sister.

She softened when I said that. "I understand," she said.

I looked over at the Cabicacmotz. He was biting his lip and seemed very uncomfortable. I braced myself to continue. "Why have you never visited me? Didn't you know that I was lonely and felt as if I almost had no family?"

"You exaggerate, Zaki. You had your father, Maricua, and Chahal." He glanced toward the doorway and looked as if he realized something. "Get up. We have to leave now or else we'll be late."

We stood up and he continued, "I visited you often when you were young. The problem is that I have been away for a very long time. Sometimes I am here and sometimes I am not."

When we reached the garden gate, we stepped onto the path and began walking towards the temples. Already, there were people heading there.

"What does that mean? During the times you were here, what was keeping you from visiting?"

He stopped in his tracks and faced me. "Just because someone's body is here doesn't mean that they are really here. You can't know this yet, but the path we are on does not always let us do as we wish. Being the Cabicacmotz does not always afford one the opportunity to enjoy a family. Now," he said, motioning with his hands, "I have time to have a real life. I am no longer the emissary to every tribe that we are connected with. I no longer have to spend time in places I'd rather not think of. Do you see what I mean?"

I had no idea what he was speaking of. He made it sound unpleasant when it was known that ambassadors led exciting lives with every comfort. I had heard my father complaining often enough about the costs associated with their maintenance. If he had been in distant lands, why didn't he simply say so? I looked at him as if he were crazy.

He placed his hands on my shoulders and said, "Zaki. If I could have been close to you, I would have. There was nothing I would have preferred doing. Believe me when I tell you that if I had been able to, I would have been there for you. I know that you had a lonely time of it, but I was even more alone than you were."

"Why are you trying to confuse me? You must have been around sometime. I heard my father when he told me that you had chosen me as your student when I came home with Chahal. You told me, but he had told me that before. If you saw that, then that means you must have been around. Don't lie. You owe me that."

"You are wrong, Zaki. No one owes anyone anything. My training will burn that misconception out of you, yet things happen and there are not always other possibilities available to us. Sometimes the things that happen are so horrendous that when we return to life, we savor what we can get even more. I didn't want to not see my only kin."

"Where in the world were you that was so terrible?"

"That is the thing. I wasn't always in this world."

"Then how could you know Chahal was an omen for me?"

"Because that happened before I was taken."

"You were held captive? Where?"

"I will tell you that some other time. It's too awful to speak of on such a good and important day for you. The thing is that when I was taken, I was here only bodily. It took a long while for me to recover. For a long time, I passed from this world to another as if I were dreaming. I spent years like that."

Again, I did not understand him clearly. What he was saying did not make any sense to me and seemed impossible. How possible it was, I was yet to discover.

The thought crossed my mind that he was crazy. He had even admitted to it. I wondered if he was dangerous in any way. Then another part of my mind countered that thought with another; my father would never allow Maricua to marry a deranged man. I clung to his words that he had not wanted to be away from me.

"You didn't want to go away from me?"

He shook his head. "No. You are my only connection to this world, the only one whose blood I share. Perhaps the only reason I survived was because I clutched the memory of you."

"I still don't understand how you were taken or gone," I said. "Was it like what happened when I supposedly disappeared?"

"Someday I will explain it properly, but you do not need such fear in your life right now. Your father and I were unsure whether you remembered me or realized that I was your uncle. Now we know. You did not remember me; you must have been too young. We thought you might realize that I was your uncle because he told you about my sister's eyes and mine are not brown, either. We thought you might have been playing a game with us."

I felt stupid. Days ago, when my father had described my mother to me and told me I had an uncle, I had looked at everyone to see if they might have been him, but it never occurred to me to look at the Cabicacmotz. He felt and looked too alien to me to be my kinsman. It frightened me that half of me was so distinct from my people. I was now unsure about whether they were really my people or not. There was a mysterious place in the world that I might belong to, yet not belong to. I was in genetic limbo, caught between two worlds. Not one or the other.

"I wasn't playing a game with you. It simply didn't enter my mind. Why didn't you tell me that you were my uncle right away?"

"I thought about it, Zaki. I even talked it over with your father. We decided that it would be best to let you figure it out or else take a while to tell you."

"Why is that? That seems sneaky and cruel to me."

"Not really. You are beginning your training. We wanted you to get comfortable with yourself and me before you were told. If you were told right away, you might feel that any accomplishments you made were done not on your own merits, which is only right, but merely because you were my nephew, someone I would favor no matter what. It is information that could negatively affect your confidence. That is something that is not in your best interests, you need to feel secure in your worth. Conversely, you might have felt that you didn't need to try as hard if you thought you had a teacher who would be too lenient with you. That is also detrimental to development of your genius. So we wanted to have you in the position where you would try your best, yet not feel that anything you do correctly is merely because I favor you above any other boy in the class."

I nodded and smiled. "I will do my best. I promise. Can you make me one?"

"What is it?" he asked with a dubious expression.

"Will you promise never to set my hair on fire?"

He barked with laughter and said, "That I can promise. I would rather set my own on fire than do it to you. You can be sure of that."

"May I call you uncle?"

"No! Not even in the house. You might get used to calling me that and accidentally say it in front of the other students. Besides, you need to get accustomed to calling people by their titles. It is the custom here and you need to comply with it. You will see, after a while the people behind the titles grow into their titles to such a degree that they become the title. They are no longer persons, they become personages."

"Are you like the previous Cabicacmotz?"

"Not physically, but he and I were nonetheless exactly alike. I am not as fearsome as he was, but neither am I incompetent in that regard."

If he told me that the former Cabicacmotz was a frightening man, I believed him. He was quite scary himself. I had not forgotten the first night I saw him or him forcing me to encounter the shadows in the jungle. Secretly I was glad he was my teacher and not the one he had. At least I had the security of knowing that he wished me well and would not harm me. I now had the confidence that someone was on my side besides Maricua and my father.

He must have read my thoughts or feelings because he said, "Don't get overconfident with this information, Zaki. You being my nephew will also mean that I will expect more of you and be more demanding. It also has the flipside. Everything does. You will see." He motioned me to continue our walk.

"Is there any way that I can concentrate on bateh?" I asked.

"Ah yes, you mean can you get out of having any other courses besides bateh, don't you?"

I told him that I did not see any reason to saddle myself with learning anything else, since the omens had been so clear with Chahal.

He gave me a look that did not reassure me in the least. "One thing you will learn is that everything applies to bateh. Not always directly, but in some way. Learning is not a stagnant thing, which is confined; it is something that has wide applications to the world around us. Think about what you are now learning with me about the night and stealth. We are only in the beginning stages of my instruction, but you will come to see that it is not only applicable to the night and spying on troublesome neighbors. You will see that some of the concepts and things you learn can be applied to the everyday world around you and how you interact with others."

"Well, what about these signs and omens I am supposed to expect today?"

"You need to pay more attention to my advice, Zaki. Learning is for your benefit. You cannot become an effective player by only playing bateh. You want to do what you like and that is simply not going to happen. Now you wonder if you can defeat these omens in such a way that your wishes will be realized. Trust me; there is no way to vanquish them. One group may require that an omen be portentous, another may notice that something accidentally was spilled on you or was not spilled on you, as the case may be. Another group may simply notice that the wind blew from a certain direction and conclude that you should learn from them. There is no way for you to get out of this, so I advise you to acquiesce yourself to your fate. Besides, the learning you will receive is anything but boring. Would you rather spend your whole life sitting around in your rooms? At least this way, you will have some adventure and excitement." He looked around then and seemed worried. "Zaki? Where is Chahal? She was supposed to come with us today."

I gave him a smug smile. "She has been pacing us in the tall grass off of the path."

"Your father warned me about her. She is inconspicuous when she wants to be, isn't she?"

I nodded.

"That is really creepy," he said with a laugh. "All of my instructions on stealth might not even match up to what you should have learned by now from her if you had been properly noticing her moves. I will have to feature her in one of our classes. Well, we had best hurry along now. I hear flutes."

I had not noticed it before he spoke, but there were some flutes being played in the distance. Not a song being played together, it was more like lone flautists who were playing competing songs, oblivious to one another. As I listened, drums began playing. Their beats were not as inharmonious as the flutes and blended better with the multitude of tootlings I heard.

We continued walking until we reached the edge of the crowd. Chahal was now at our side, as she did not have any cover to camouflage herself with. Even so, she did not seem agitated in any way.

"Will Maricua be with us at all today?" I wondered aloud.

"She will probably be here later. If I know her, she will not be willing to miss the dance of the Cranes. Then, she will leave before the bateh game."

I asked him why. He told me that she liked the beauty of the dance, but was ill at ease with the violence of the ball game.

"Does she belong to any of the groups?"

He didn't seem to be paying much attention to me and appeared distracted. Absentmindedly, he said, "Maybe she will be hanging out with one of the women's groups. Most likely, the warriors. They like to beat people with sticks, particularly men. Actually, they will make use out of any object within their reach if they have to fight."

When he noticed that I was aghast at this information, he told me that he had been joking with me and that Maricua did belong to a few of the women's groups, but that they were groups that generally did not engage in violence and that, in fact, they were more like informal groups. He referred to them as subsets of established groups. I asked him what that meant. He seemed to be a bit chagrined at having to, yet again, explain things to me.

"I apologize, Zaki. I am accustomed to speaking with adults, so I get a bit frustrated when I have to explain things that need no explanation to older people."

"I thought you were used to teaching us boys. Isn't that what you do?"

"It is now. After I escaped, it took me a while to recover my wits. I was sent to a neighboring tribe, one of our allies, and there I taught mundane bateh techniques to boys who were older than you are. I also had to be part of our own ball games and advise your father."

"How could you do all that if you were far away?"

"You forget that I can appear wherever I like, Zaki. Don't forget that. Don't worry that I will interrupt your private moments in the outhouse, though. I would never do that. The point is that it is an important part of any healing process to take the person away from too much reflection over what has happened to them. To focus the mind away from grief and self-pity can be accomplished by refocusing the person's efforts on helping others."

Somehow, his words were clear to me. My eyes were distracted by all of the sights around me, but his voice captured my attention. I guessed that the didactic process he was engaging me in was somehow akin to how he had to concentrate on others in order to heal himself. It was a brief leap of thought and possibly illogical, but it crossed my mind. I questioned him about this.

It took him a few moments to collect his words. Finally, he told me that, at times, when a person is distracted there is another side to man which comes forth that bypasses everything around us and calls our attention to what is necessary and integral to one's growth or interests. Such things seemed extraneous to what we would normally consider important or notable, but they were lapses of attention that had supernatural origins, which cause us to feel distracted. The crucial implication to all this was that the universe, or the masters of fate, refocused our attention in a subtle manner that allowed us to notice things that fate desired us to be aware of or that we should take note of. It was attention within inattention.

"To be aware of everything around us can be a consuming affair. Every once in a while, though, you will find yourself in another state of being. Right now, it has been triggered by the stress of attending your first festival. The other night, I pushed you into that state by using fright. You became aware of the unthinkable; that shadows can be utilized by men to travel and act. Those times, when we seem groggy or unfocused, mean that another part of ourselves is seeing and taking note of what is really significant."

I argued that I had been aware of no such thing as knowing that about the shadows. He patted me on the back and told me that it was a waste of my time to lie to him or to myself.

"Come," he said. "It is time to begin the process of allowing your destiny to determine your other teachers."

I told him that I wanted to learn more about the sense of feeling distracted, but he rebuffed me with the promise that we would talk about it at some other time.

"What happens at the time is called seeing; we merely don't realize what it truly is and convince ourselves that we have not eaten enough or some other nonsense and fail to take advantage of it. From now on, you should notice those moments and try to extend them. Don't waste them on pathetic rationalizations," he said. "Now stop trying to avoid the inevitable, we are at the edge and must enter the crowd to visit the groups."

All around us, crowds of nobles and commoners wandered about. Some pochtecas had set up kiosks and were bartering with customers. I stopped at one of them, one of the finer ones, which had jewelry. Intricate and exceptional examples of women's necklaces were at the front of the table. There was a beautiful piece of smoothed beryl beads interspersed with turquoise that caught my eye.

I looked up at the Cabicacmotz and a thought passed between us; that necklace would look exquisite around Maricua's neck. He asked the merchant how much the piece was. I expected him to barter with the man when he was quoted an outrageous price. He didn't. He paid the fee quickly in gold beads. The man wrapped it up in a cloth and the Cabicacmotz gently placed it in his pouch. I wanted to ask him why he had not haggled over the price, but I knew why he had not. I was a witness and he did not want to appear cheap or stingy when it came to my sister. I felt that it was a bit foolish, but understood his reasons.

Without a word, he led me past the stalls of merchants. Around fifty yards farther, no stalls were in the festival area. There was a large open area that people drifted in and out of, but I could see nothing past the crowd. I noticed that the inner area of the stalls was solely occupied by local merchants, but the outer perimeter was solely for the pochtecas.

I pondered about which group had the best location and decided that the local merchants were at a disadvantage. Their wares were common and mundane compared to what could be acquired from the pochtecas who brought exotic goods from faraway lands. Furthermore, the crowds would have to pass through them before ever getting to the locals. The tribal merchants appeared glum and watched every purchase made at the pochteca's stalls with open hostility. Why would our leaders have disadvantaged our own merchants in such a way?

I asked him about that detail. It was unusual for the tribe to favor another group or foreigners so plainly, unless they were ambassadors. Ambassadors were afforded great respect and honor, but pochtecas were considered to be little better than parasites. He told me that the inner perimeter of local merchants served the dual purpose of keeping the pochtecas from wandering in and to keep gatecrashers or spies out. To my surprise, he referred to ours as the merchant-guards.

"This is your first day celebrating with our tribe as a man, so I will no longer hide anything from you. Keep in mind that my words are not for everyone; you are to share them with no one, not even Maricua. She knows, of course, but it is an exercise in keeping your mouth shut. All of us have to stop the human tendency to blab and chat about everything we notice or learn. Discussions about such things are only to be done in certain places and at certain times," he admonished me. "Our tribe is ever vigilant about spies and war. One never knows when one is being overheard. The majority of eavesdroppers are innocent bystanders. There is another group that hides within it, pretending to be innocent bystanders. They are the people who are always there at the right time to hear juicy tidbits. It is a knack, a talent. They are masters of stealth, whether in the dark or in the light, their presence is always overlooked; they appear innocuous, but they are not. They are scouts and spies sent by other tribes to gauge our weaknesses."

"Don't appear surprised, Zaki. The world is not happiness and frivolity as you have been led to believe. The real world is one of utter harshness and finality. Not only here in the daily world, but elsewhere," he said as he made an expansive gesture towards the sky. "We have few havens of safety."

"What do you mean?"

"Forgive me, I stray from the subject. Anyway, if we in our tribe find a natural eavesdropper who is ours, we train him to continue his work for the good of the tribe. Otherwise, they will become like gossipy women. By the way, women make the best eavesdroppers and spies. Perhaps men are better, sometimes, at convincing others to commit treason, but that is a different talent. Let us speak more about women, Zaki. Every day men are made aware of the ruthlessness and cunning of women, yet they persist in believing in their masks of tenderness and sweetness. It is one of the masterpieces of women. Truly, to destroy man's insistence in believing their charade is one of the most difficult acts to accomplish. Today you will receive your first lessons in that task. Treat all women you see, not as dolls or delicate objects, but as they are, very capable equals."

I was becoming accustomed to how he jumped from subject to subject without warning. To tell me that I should treat women like men was revolutionary to me. I didn't believe that I could do it. I heard him chuckle to himself and resolved to follow his advice. It had been the chuckle of someone in the know who expected the other person to be rudely introduced to a reality he did not believe was possible. Behaving otherwise would be the act of a fool. To change the subject, I told him I would like to learn more about the merchant-guards.

"Certainly," he said and motioned towards the stalls. I started to walk over there, but he placed his arm across my chest to block my path. He pointed with his chin, towards the stalls, advising me to watch what was about to happen.

I heard a man cry, "They're taking all of our business!" One of the merchants, a man in his middle years, threw down a bag and left his stall in the care of an even older man. He lumbered away from the stall, as if his back ailed him. He appeared worn out and gray. He coughed loudly and placed his left hand at the small of his back as he headed towards an outcropping of rocks. It appeared that he was going there to relieve himself. The Cabicacmotz went there and I followed.

Behind the rocks, the man shook himself like a dog and stretched his body like an acrobat. No longer did he seem old and gray. Instead, he was spry and athletic, appearing to be in fine physical condition.

He ignored me and said to the Cabicacmotz, "Can you believe those damned mongrels? I swear, if I had my way, we would mow them down right now. You should see how smug they are."

"But then we wouldn't be able to put ours into play, would we?"

The man said, "There is that. I hear that Parutzya has some information to impart. She should be setting up a meeting sometime soon. The pochtecas she travels with will be leaving in a few days, so I would suggest that you make some purchases at her stall."

The Cabicacmotz turned to me and introduced me to the man, telling him that I was interested in learning about the merchant-guards. He didn't give me the man's name and only introduced him as one of the merchant-guards. It made me uncomfortable that the man knew who I was and I didn't know who he was.

"It is a pleasure to meet you, Prince Zaki," he said as he bowed in an exaggerated parody of a real bow. It made me laugh and I immediately liked the man. A real bow would have embarrassed me. "What would you like to know?"

I asked the Cabicacmotz if I would have to join the man's group merely because I was interested in knowing what they did. He told me that particular path was denied to me because I was too visible and everyone knew me by sight. That surprised me. I had always felt invisible and anonymous.

Instead of questioning him about that, as I would normally have done, I turned to the man and asked him, "What is your role here today?"

"Good, to the point, I like that. It is like this, many tribes have spies who might have infiltrated this particular group of pochtecas. The regular pochtecas are made up of itinerant individuals and families that lead a nomadic life. They are a loosely bound group and they have the advantage of being mobile. We also use this to our advantage. The game for the spy is to hide their affiliation with our tribe and to spy, especially on the other opposing spies and tribes. Today, though, is a special day here. New talent is being displayed and tested. Our bateh players might have new skills they will use and that other tribes should not be allowed to learn about. We want to appear strong in warfare, yet untalented in other matters. Otherwise, we will be seen as a force which has become too strong and which will, most likely, seek to expand in territory. Do you understand? We don't want other tribes to learn our secrets or find out how dangerous we are. If they did, they would want to wipe us from the earth."

He looked in my eyes as if to reassure himself that I was following his words and continued, "Today, we have to keep them from seeing anything that they shouldn't be seeing. They are on the outer band and will have a hard time sneaking through to this side. They have been warned not to go past our stalls. They will try, of course, and we will act like the angry merchants we are supposed to be and stop them. It is childish, but the rules are standard. Be petty and vicious with them while the festival goes on. If one of us has to stop them with force, the fact that we are guards might become apparent. For that reason, others will shy away from the violence to protect their aims from being known and others will act like angry merchants wanting to get an easy piece of pochteca hide. I cannot tell you how many times real merchants have come to my defense when I have fought a fake pochteca who was trying to sneak in."

I asked him how they were able to defend the festival when the stalls only comprised a small part of the areas people could use to enter.

He nodded. "That is true. Our role is limited to the people who try to enter through the merchant's stalls. The other areas are protected by the sentries and the ones who know how to be other things, who are hidden in the surrounding jungle." He turned around then and began peeing on one of the bushes. When he was done, he said, "I hope you don't have any more questions for me because I've been gone longer than a pee and more like I've gone caca. I don't want anybody to get suspicious about me," he said.

The Cabicacmotz dismissed him. I watched the man slump as if his chest had caved in. When he left, he appeared heavy and slow. No longer was he the fast-talking guard I had talked with. He appeared harmless and dull-witted. I smiled. I had liked him and I was very taken with his acting abilities. I told the Cabicacmotz that the man was likeable and an excellent actor.

He cocked an eyebrow when I mentioned the man's superb ability in acting old. "Acting... Yes, I suppose we could call it transformational acting. Oh, look," he said as he pointed to my father who was headed our way with his guards. "Here comes your father now. He told me he was going to be here a bit earlier than usual."

The Cabicacmotz told me to stay where I was. He walked over and stopped my father from walking all the way over to us. They exchanged a few words and then walked my way. I heard the Cabicacmotz telling him about what the guard had told us.

"Parutzya, eh?" my father said with a smile. "I'll have to set something up then. She and her husband have been out in the field for too long. They deserve a respite from their duties."

"I think that within the next couple of days should be soon enough. I have to speak to a few of my student's chaperones. Would it be all right if I left Zaki with you for a short time?" he asked my father.

My father assured him that it would be fine and he left.

"So, how are you liking our festival?" he asked me with a smile.

"It seems nice, but I haven't seen too much since we just got here."

"The Cabicacmotz told me that you have already been introduced to one of our merchant-guards. It's a nice trick. Don't you think?"

"I suppose so. I never guessed that the merchants were guards," I said.

"Well, not all of them are, Zaki. Some are genuine merchants. Most, I would say."

I asked my father if the other tribes were correct in thinking that we would make war against them if they knew of our strengths. Although my question was somewhat incoherent and rambling as it left my mouth, he understood me.

"Absolutely. When a force becomes too great, others will try to contain it. History reveals the painful lesson that strong and talented tribes will grow exponentially. In times of prosperity, people have more children. Shortly after, land that used to sustain them will become strained and that tribe will look around to see where they can expand. We are there and beyond. Our numbers are too great. Right now, the task is to confuse our neighbors and not allow them to know our strengths, lest they over plan and stop us in our tracks. This is very unlikely considering what we know about them, but we cannot allow them to become desperate. Desperate people conspire with others and if they combine forces, we will lose more people than we should. Imagine if we win a war, yet lose so many people that we cannot hold the lands we take over. It would cancel out the very reason for war."

I was horrified at his words. It was unimaginable that we were on the brink of exterminating our neighbors. I had never traveled to those tribes or traveled at all, but I imagined that they must be people very similar to us. Great sadness filled me. Change, violent change, was in the air and I had been oblivious to it. "When would such a thing happen?" I asked him.

He shrugged. "It might be a week from now; it might be years from now. Who knows?"

I couldn't understand how he could be so casual about it. It was not a trivial affair we were talking about, it meant that lives could be lost. I felt sorry for the other tribes, but what really concerned me were the lives that ours could lose. I asked him to tell me about the other tribes.

He seemed confused by my question. "Do you mean the other tribes within our city or the tribes outside of our limits?"

I shook from within. I felt as if I would vomit at any moment. I sat down on the ground and put my head in my hands. I couldn't look at him, so appalled was I.

"Zaki? What's wrong?" he said with concern.

I looked at him with misery, and said, "How can there be other tribes within our lands, father? Such a thing has never been allowed. Foreigners are always forced to live on the outskirts or are driven off. That is one of the first things I ever learned from you; to tell whenever someone new or different from us was around."

He shook his head, with a look on his face that showed how disappointed he was in my stupidity. "We consider ourselves one tribe because we all came from the east, from Tulan, but in actuality we are many tribes who are united because we originated from the same place and traveled together. Nothing more. We marry within the tribes, most commonly, but that is not always the case. Now, we have built a city stronghold of such magnitude that we must extend ourselves. We are a united force, but our city will not hold us for much longer unless we clear the lands around us," he said and then spoke about the prospect of absorbing the people in them into our own.

I clung to that possibility and asked him eagerly why we didn't do that.

"It is a dim possibility that probably won't happen. It won't solve our problems."

"What could make it happen?" I wanted to think that we wouldn't kill our neighbors as if they were mere rats that had invaded a barn house.

"Affection. Only affection and they are already being recalcitrant in their dealings with us. I don't blame them, but it isn't behavior that will win them allies."

I asked him if the young man, that Marilya was going to marry, belonged to a tribe we could possibly war with.

146

"Almost anything is possible, but that particular tribe lives very far away from us. It is unlikely that they will become our enemies in this lifetime."

"Maybe they are not acting right with us out of fear. That is no reason to wipe them out," I protested.

"It is not only that, Zaki. A bigger problem is that it is difficult to have respect for people who don't better themselves. They are not like us. They worship crap and embrace superstition when the wisest course of action is to verify what they believe in."

"What do they worship? What makes their beliefs any less than ours?"

He looked at me with angry incredulity, and then his face softened. "I forget you are still young to what we do here, my son. The answer to your first question is that they mold sculptures and worship them. The answer to your second question is more complex because you don't know what we do here. We are unable to accomplish it in a constant way, but we have verified that there is, indeed, a Creator. We know he is not something that abides in a lump of clay that someone has molded into something aesthetically pleasing. If those people were like us, they would see this and seize the truth. Instead, they have formed a convoluted system of supposed deities to explain what they don't understand."

"There really is a Creator?"

"Of course. Organic matter and reality itself are too complicated to have come about by chance. Did you think that nothing was intended?"

I didn't think that, but being faced with actual confirmation of a Creator was too farfetched to accept. God was an almost mythical being of whom I rarely thought. On the one hand, I believed wholeheartedly that God existed, yet I was dubious that anyone had corroborated such a fact. There was also the problem that people like the Cabicac-motz were able to do things that I used to consider impossible, so I was left in a limbo of belief.

"What did you mean when you said that you are unable to accomplish that verification in a constant way?"

"I don't mean that the verification is done over and over again, I mean that we have not been able to fully bridge the world we are in with His abode or realm."

"Why in the world would we want to do such a thing?"

"You are joking, aren't you? This world is harsh, cruel, and precarious. Death hunts the flesh encased and you wonder why we want to get out of here? We want to leave here and go to a better place without relinquishing our awareness."

"How would we do such a thing?" I asked.

"We have devised a way. By using the intent and awareness of every living person in our tribe with power, we will be able to fully bridge the two worlds and pass over into there. It is similar to how we build tall structures, a wide and firm base provide the support for the upper, lighter, and loftier edifices. A pyramid of sorts, only this one is an abstract one formed from our very energy."

"When would we be able to do that?"

He shrugged and told me that it was up to our energy level. That was why it was such a loss to the tribe when one of the lords of the life force was lost to death, as Zotabah was. I asked him what lords of the life force were and he told me that men and women who knew how to manipulate energy were what he meant. He further explained that energy was our base element. To believe that we were merely meat was a stupidity. He stressed that those who could see saw that men were not mere meat. They were energy or light. Then I asked him why we needed bodies. He told me that I had to learn much more before I understood his explanation. I complained that any explanation would be helpful.

"The problem with explaining more to you, Zaki, is that you always come up with more questions and we will be here until the sun burns out if I allow you to keep questioning me as often as you like. Not only that, but you will not be able to understand my explanations anyway. As soon as the Cabicacmotz gets back, I have to meet with many of my governors."

I didn't want him to stop talking and asked him why we couldn't teach the surrounding tribes a better system of beliefs.

He sighed with impatience. "We have already tried to show them the truth. They are deaf and blind to it. They are as stupid as monkeys. Their outer appearance hints at intelligence, but when you try to talk to them, they don't understand and continue as they have always done. They are idolaters. They worship lies. They don't deserve life. As such, they will be like twigs in the coming conflagration. Don't ask more about it, Zaki. In fact, it would be better if you banished the whole subject from your mind. Don't allow yourself to think about it. The Cabicacmotz isn't the only one who can read minds. Sometimes that ability is granted to our opponents, as well."

His words sickened me. There wasn't a thing I could say. It seemed that the whole affair was already decided, despite what my father had said about taking the other tribes into the fold. That was only an outer possibility that was given voice. Nothing would come of it and they would die like animals at culling periods. No matter what he said, I still felt sorry for them. After all, wasn't the mere fact that God allowed them to live evidence that they had as much right as we to be here?

"Now stand up and compose yourself. I don't want your future subjects to see you on the ground like a beggar," he said as he gently helped me up.

I looked at his guards. None watched me. I knew they had seen me, but it was somehow comforting that they pretended that I was not acting like a fool. The people who walked around us averted their eyes, though. It embarrassed me that I still acted like a child. I was unused to behaving as a man and repeatedly forgot that I even was one.

A few moments later, the Cabicacmotz came back. My father asked him if everything was going well for the other boys.

He nodded with a pleased look on his face and said,

"Indeed. We have a fine batch of boys this year. I have grand hopes for them. Already destiny has put one into the Ocelots of Dawn and another into the Eagle Knights. This will be a fine year."

My father said, "I look forward to seeing how they turn out." He patted me on the back and said to the Cabicac-motz, "Please bring my son to me when the time comes for the ballgame. I have to meet the others now."

The Cabicacmotz promised to and then my father left.

"Sorry to leave you, Zaki. I was very curious about how the others were faring. I knew you would be fine with your father and his guards. Not much of a chance of anything happening with them about."

"No," I agreed with a gloomy voice.

"What is wrong?" he asked.

I sighed. "Did you know that he believes that we must go to war with the surrounding tribes so we can take their land?"

His brows drew together as he said, "I know. He is a terribly practical man when it comes to the tribe. I have offered and offered him solutions, but they have not pleased him. I don't like the idea, either, but it is the most realistic solution to the problem. On the other hand," he said in a chipper tone, "I have set the seers on the problem and they say that there is no chance for it because something will present itself and eliminate the need for such drastic measures."

"Really? Like what?" I liked the sound of that.

"I have no idea. Not even the seers are able to determine what or how the solution will take form. It is most mysterious. We will have to wait and see what it is."

I breathed in relief. I had heard tales of battle from warriors and it sounded like a terrible thing. Usually it was more awful for the defeated, but war also took its price from the victors in some measure. I wondered what the seers had foreseen. It sounded peculiar to me that they could know a future outcome without knowing the particulars. Still, it must be something auspicious if it could avert a war with our neighbors.

I smiled and asked him what we would be doing and where we were going.

"We are going to visit with the sentries next. Your comportment must be humble, yet strong like a man. Watch out because they are tricky to be around. Don't expect them to act like ladies, they are warriors," the Cabicacmotz advised me.

He led me towards one of the platforms that surrounded the temple grounds. There were eight squat structures, which surrounded the area, formed of stone. There were four large platforms, one at each of the cardinal directions, and four slightly smaller ones for the in-between directions. In the middle of each was a heavy stone carving, called the Chakmol, in the likeness of a person reclining.

Many times, I had tried to understand how the Chakmol earned its name. Its name meant a ring of communication. It was a mystery to me because it was a statue. How could a statue communicate anything? Also, I could never figure out whether it was supposed to be a male or a female. Upon reflection, most of our statues failed to reflect gender, the breasts were always planed.

The statue was on its back with its knees up, the elbows resting on the ground while the body curved upward. It looked like the pose one has at the beach when one rests on the sands while looking at the ocean. The only part that didn't fit that scenario was that the hands curved up, over the figure's abdomen. It was as if the hands were carved to support or receive something. I had tried many times to mimic the pose, but it was an impossible pose to attain, at least for me.

"We have to get our information in a certain manner," he said. "We must get it in bits and pieces. We approach the east first and then go on to the other stone platforms in a counterclockwise manner."

"Why do we have to do it in such a way? Isn't counter-clockwise considered inauspicious?"

"Where ever did you get that idea? Perhaps in some cases it is, but not in this one. The Chuchmox are intimately related to the Earth. As such, we are expected to behave like the Earth in our dealings with them. The Earth rotates in a counterclockwise manner. We must do the same."

"Why do we have to get a message in parts?"

"Shut up. We are almost to the first Chuchmox. Do not refer to her as a sentry; call her by her title of Chuchmox."

"What do I call the other ones?"

"You never stop, do you? We call them Chuchmox also. You will see why."

We went towards the square platform. From where we were, I could see a figure dressed in a bright red tunic. Golden yellow, green, and red feathers adorned the headdress and trailed down her back, splayed on the platform's surface. Red leather sandals were fastened with crisscrossing leather straps that went up her calves; similar straps adorned her forearms. A wide circlet of beads, in yellow and red, covered a large portion of her chest up to her neck.

She was arrayed before the stone figure, the Chakmol, facing the jungle. She was in a similar pose, but I noticed it was a slight variation on the statue's pose. Maybe I was not the only one who couldn't achieve that difficult posture. Instead, her hands were flat on the ground, at the small of her back. It seemed to be an uncomfortable pose, but she held it without any apparent discomfort. Her eyes scanned the surrounding jungle. As we watched, she gracefully switched positions and resumed her pose, only now her feet pointed in the opposite direction.

"Naqahob," she commanded.

I walked to where she was. When I was a few yards away, I looked for the Cabicacmotz and realized that he was not with me. He was back where we had been. I tried to call him to me, but he shook his head and indicated that I should keep going. Chahal walked before me, looking back at me as if she wanted me to follow. I could have sworn that she was interested in getting me to the platform.

"Do you need to feel the safety of others in order to function?" the Chuchmox asked me rudely.

I opted for an honest response even though I really wanted to tell her that she was a disrespectful creature. I said, "It's odd for me to talk to you. All of my life, I've been told never to disturb any of you while you work. So to come to you makes me feel nervous, as if I'm doing something wrong." It wasn't the absolute unvarnished truth, but it wasn't a lie either.

Twisting her lips to the side, she looked at me. A moment later, she signaled the Cabicacmotz to us with a hand signal. "We don't want you to be nervous. We actually want you to be relaxed and at your best."

Pleased, I blurted out, "That's great. I was afraid you would beat the crap out of me." As soon as I said it, I wished I hadn't.

She softly snickered. "You, young man, have given me my first laugh of the day." The Cabicacmotz reached us then and she acknowledged him with a crafty grin. "You wicked man. Telling our future students that we might hit them." She clicked her tongue. "What a thing to say."

The Cabicacmotz shrugged and said, "I had to let him know the possibilities. Besides, I remember my own days with the Chuchmox and they were far from pleasant."

"And I remember hearing stories about you; I hear you deserved what you got. Sometimes when you ask for something, you get it, you know." She turned to me and said, "Don't follow this one's example, little one. He was dreadfully unruly. Apparently, my predecessor had to cure him of that. I prefer a less physical approach to teaching manners, lucky you. So what can I tell you about our group?"

It didn't take me long to think of something and I asked, "Have you seen any spies today trying to peek into our festival?"

"Nope, can't say I have."

"Um, well what about the last spy you've seen, can you tell me about him?"

"Her," she said.

"What?"

"The last spy I espied was a she, it was a woman. She sat in a tree and was gazing our way."

What she was saying wasn't clear to me and I asked her to clarify her statement. She replied that the woman was about two miles away and that she was using a technique called gazing that would open up her perception and allow her to learn our tribe's secrets. The Chuchmox watched me try to make sense of her words.

The Cabicacmotz intervened and told me that gazing was how the Chuchmox were able to alert us to any dangers, saying that the distances were not important and that only the gazer's energy determined what could be revealed to them. He informed me that the fact that the woman needed to be within sight of the city was an indication that she was confined to gazing at things she could see, but that it could have been a real problem.

He said, "She was a gifted woman, but substandard if one compares her to our Chuchmox. They only need to gaze in a direction to understand what is going on." Then he reminded me that I had already performed shadow gazing.

The Chuchmox stood up quickly and said, "Really? This is the one who did the shadow gazing and disappeared?" She jumped down from the stone to where we were and asked me if she could smell me.

I looked at her as if she was a madwoman and tried to back away, but the Cabicacmotz held me by the arm.

"Why?" I asked.

"It will help me in my gazing if I ever sense you out there," she said as she waved towards the jungle.

I asked her how she could possibly use my scent from a distance if she was gazing. The Cabicacmotz answered the question for her, telling me that gazing was not confined to the visual and that gazer's other senses often overlapped into their work.

I didn't want to, but I let the woman sniff me. She walked around me and carefully sniffed my back from the waist to my head.

"Yes, I've smelled you before, boy, as you play in the jungle with your familiar."

"Who's my familiar?"

Her laugh chimed in the air as she used the steps to climb back to her post. "Your cat, silly." She sat at the ledge, dangling her legs.

"What's a familiar?"

I thought she would choke from the laughter that caused her. She said, "Oh Cabi. This one is too innocent to be true. How long has he been with you?"

"This is his seventh day with me," he said.

Her eyes widened at that. "And he has already gazed at shadows? Starting him off a little young, aren't you? I thought you merely brought him by to say hello and introduce him to the idea of us, but you have something in mind, don't you?"

He nodded and told her that he did.

"Learning with the Chuchmox is usually a final step, not a primary one. We are the polishing portion of the art, not the grinding one. What makes you think that he should be with us?"

"Three reasons," he replied. "He worries me because he has gazed successfully on his first try alone. Second, he disappeared while doing so and third, he is unused to being around males and for him, I've seen that a woman's touch would be useful."

"Are you trying to get out of spending the necessary time teaching him what he needs to know?" she asked.

"No, to be honest. I'm perfectly happy to teach him, but he already knows what to do naturally. It's almost as if he had been doing it for years."

"Is this so? Have you been doing it for years?" she asked me.

I told her that I had only gazed the one time, but that I was used to watching the shadows play across the walls of my quarters before I fell asleep.

She raised her eyebrows and carefully watched me. "All right," she said. "We agree to teach you how to do what we do. Not many notice shadows at all."

We made chitchat after that. Finally, the Cabicacmotz told her goodbye and began walking off. She indicated that she wanted to say something to me.

She leaned close to me and whispered in my ear, "Don't be upset or misled by my words back there; we definitely wanted you to become a part of us. I had to make it a bit difficult for the Cabicacmotz. We like to keep him humble or else he would be absolutely insufferable."

"Doesn't he know what we're saying right now anyway?" I asked her.

"Of course he does," she said with a laugh. "My words are for you, though. I wanted you to know that we do not consider you a chore that was forced on us. Nothing could be less true." She cocked her head and shrugged. "Besides, I couldn't give a shit what he overhears or doesn't bother to overhear."

We said goodbye and I went over to where the Cabicacmotz waited with Chahal. We wandered aimlessly around for a while watching people. My interest was taken by the flutists and we sat watching them while we ate cakes of corn filled with meat. It was a delicious treat and I ate several of them. The Cabicacmotz also told me that he had some dried fruit, but it didn't sound appetizing to me since I had already gorged myself with the corn cakes so soon after breakfast.

When we were getting up to go towards one of the temples that the Cabicacmotz wanted me to see, I saw a man standing on a pile of rocks. I had no idea why he wanted to be on them. I guessed that he was trying to look over the crowd to find a friend or something like that.

The man's hair was frizzy with humidity and looked like it had been braided a week ago. His muslin robe was filthy from his having obviously used it as a napkin on more than one occasion. He appeared feverish because his squinty eyes were bloodshot and he fidgeted and scratched himself without any care as to who might have been watching. I concluded that he was crazy.

We walked next to where he was. He then turned around on the big rock, but he lost his footing and half fell on top of me. The Cabicacmotz tried to stop his fall without any luck. I got pushed a bit, but that was all. The man landed squarely on his butt.

He looked up stupidly at us and then cried, "Cabi! What are you doing here? It is great to see you."

"Oh crap," said the Cabicacmotz under his breath. He reached a hand out to the man and helped him to his feet. "Evan, how are you?"

"I've been fine, except for right then actually. I was trying to find some of my apprentices, but they appear to have wandered off. I suspect I will find them giggling behind some bushes near the tent where the women change clothes no doubt," he said with a lopsided grin.

He didn't bother to dust the dirt from his clothes. Grass, dirt, and squashed berries stained the back of his robe. The man was a mess, but appeared jovial and good-natured. From his words, I reassessed him and decided that he must be mostly sane, if a bit eccentric and dirty.

"Oh, don't worry," he said to the Cabicacmotz when he noticed the grim expression on his face. "They'll never get near enough to see a breast. Those witches will catch them first and probably give them a couple of slaps, no doubt. But I assure you that they won't feel a thing."

I couldn't believe that any teacher would be as lenient with his students as to allow them to make nuisances of themselves with the women. It was simply not done. For a teacher to allow it was even more bizarre.

"I'm sure they won't, thanks to your ministrations, Evan," the Cabicacmotz dryly said.

The strange man was looking at me. He was asking the Cabicacmotz who I was when he noticed Chahal rub herself against the sides of my legs. He raised his eyebrows at the Cabicacmotz. "Don't you believe an introduction is in order?"

"Etamanel Evan, this is Zakiraxapalo."

"The first prince, eh?"

The Cabicacmotz nodded with an unhappy look on his face.

Evan invited us to sit with him and his group. He told us that they were all a short ways away around a tree.

"How appropriate," the Cabicacmotz remarked.

He led us to a large tree that was a short distance from the temple grounds. Many men and a few women were snoozing or passing the time lazing in the shade. Everyone ignored us as we sat.

"Strange that you would allow any of your students near to us, Cabi," the man said. "This is probably the first time one of the students you personally chaperoned has sat under the tree with us."

The Cabicacmotz ignored him and watched the crowd.

The man turned to me and said, "We are the plant warriors."

The Cabicacmotz chuckled when the man used the term "warriors."

Evan was perturbed by the Cabicacmotz' obvious contempt of him. "Don't listen to him, Zakiraxa. He does not understand what we do here. We are people who have an affinity for plants, especially those of the seven-pronged leaf. We use the term loosely; sometimes it has another number of leaves, but seven prongs are common. Do you know why that particular one is so important to us?" he asked me.

I told him I didn't know anything about plants and that I had no interest in learning how to spice up my meals since I didn't even have to cook for myself.

He laughed when I told him that. "No. No, Zakiraxa. We are not chefs, although, to be fair, we certainly like to enjoy our food, but I am talking about something else. No, we ingest the plant in order to help us commune with the universe." He took some things out of a pouch he wore. He held up the leaf of a plant. It was green and had seven sharp prongs that went upwards. It looked rather festive and it gave me a good feeling until I noticed that each prong had spiky edges. The leaf itself was not sharp; it merely appeared so in silhouette. The spikes upon the prongs were not truly sharp, either. For some reason, that I will never understand, that feature of the leaf made me back away slightly. It seemed ominous. He handed it to me and I gingerly held it.

He also removed a small green spongy mass, the size of my thumb, from the pouch. He held it up for me to see. "Now do you see why it is so important?"

I couldn't see any such thing. I was sure that I had a dubious expression, but I could not wipe it from my face.

"Look at it closely," he insisted as he handed it to me. I held it in my hand. It seemed to be a tangle of fine plant fibers. It also appeared to have an uneven coating of crystal upon the surfaces of the tangled fibers.

"I'm sorry," I said. "I don't understand what you mean, Etamanel Evan."

He waved his hand as if to push something away and said, "Call me Evan. Everybody does anyway." He looked at the Cabicacmotz and said, "How can he not know what I'm talking about? I heard he was a master gazer. Are you now teaching them nothing?"

The Cabicacmotz impatiently answered, "This is his seventh day under my tutelage. Did you expect him to know everything already?"

Evan seemed taken aback with that. "Oh my, and already such an important feat in gazing. Oh my. Well, let's do a simple exercise, shall we?"

He instructed me to lay on my back in the shade and look up at the clouds overhead. The sun was to my back. He told me that was an important point to repeat from then on, if I wanted to protect my eyes. He instructed me to relax and to move my eyes over the clouds.

I did so, but nothing happened. I complained that all I saw were clouds and he told me that he would allow someone to help me. I didn't know what he meant or even what he wanted me to do. He whistled sharply.

One of the women got up then and stood over me. From my place on the ground, she looked gigantic and very pretty. Her long black hair fell in her face as she smiled at me. Then she did the most outlandish act I wouldn't even dare imagine. She straddled me and sat on my stomach. I could feel the coolness of her thighs chilling my sides. She leaned to the side so that my view of the clouds would not be obstructed by her body.

Something weird was happening to me. I felt a sensation of tickling in my loins and knew that it was somehow connected to the woman sitting on me. It was a liquid sensation of rushing. I also knew that I had to stop the tickling sensation or else I would be disgraced in some way, a way I didn't understand, but my body seemed to know that fact. I struggled to get up. Evan held me down by putting his hands on my shoulders.

"I think you are sitting too hard on him, Xik Haa. Keep your weight in your legs, not crushing him like a bug," he told her.

The woman, Xik Haa, lifted herself from my stomach a bit. I still felt the tickling, but it was diminishing, to my relief.

Evan told me to try the exercise of looking at the clouds again. I put all my focus on the clouds in order to free my attention from the maddening thought that an attractive woman was on top of me.

After a while, I was able to block out all thoughts of my body and the clouds seemed to burst with strings of light.

They were dazzling. At first, it was only small, short bursts of tiny lights. Then, I noticed that the bursts were connected to the weaving strings of light. It was strange because the strings did not tangle, they moved in many directions with a gentle force. Periodically, a string would show its end and the burst of light would erupt out of the string's end. Those had been the short and tiny bursts I had first perceived. I could have looked at those lights for hours. They made me feel joyous and exultant.

The moment I had that thought, I was back in the present and Xik Haa was climbing off me. I wanted her to stay, since I wanted to look at the lights some more. I looked back at the clouds and, almost immediately, I was able to see the lights again. I was happy to realize that I no longer needed a woman to sit on me in order to view them.

Evan had let go of me, I know not when. He moved in between the lights and me. It was most disconcerting. I wanted to tell him to get out of the way. "You do have a knack for gazing, boy. You are fortunate. It took this bum," he said as he gently kicked one of the men near us in the ribs, "a year to ever see anything, even with the help of the leaves." He told me to sit up and that I had done enough cloud gazing for one day.

I asked him what those beautiful strings were. The Cabicacmotz answered and told me that they were energy, that they were the basic element of everything, and that they made up the world.

"Why can't I look at them a bit longer?" I protested.

"It's time to go, Zaki," the Cabicacmotz said as he stood up.

"Wait a moment," said Evan. "You need to take a couple of gifts with you." He handed me the leaf and a few of the tangles of plant fibers. "Here, fold it up in the leaf and keep it in your pouch." He also took a little pipe from his sack and handed it to me. It was a crude and ugly thing made out of brown stone. "You will need that."

I looked at him with a dubious expression and asked, "What for?"

"To smoke, of course," he said.

"I've never smoked anything. How do I do it?"

We sat down again. He showed me what I needed to do, instructed me to remove the seeds, let me know how to smoke the tangles, and advised me to hold the smoke in my lungs for as long as I could. He advised me on how to take the fire from a torch and make it small enough to use in the pipe. He would not allow me to smoke anything there, even though he did to show me. Instead, he told me to smoke a tiny bit that night when I was home and alone, stressing that I should be alone. I asked him why I couldn't smoke any right then.

"Because I don't want to be saddled with a moron acting like a monkey for the rest of the day," the Cabicacmotz replied.

"You need to relax, Cabi," Evan told him.

"Oh shut up," he said.

Evan slapped his forehead and said, "I almost forgot. Zaki, do you now know why the plant is so important to us?"

I gave it some thought and wondered aloud whether it was because the plant fibers also moved in a tangled manner, like the lights. The only problem, I said, was that the plant was physical and thus ended up in a real tangle.

Evan clapped and pointed at me. "He's right. He's absolutely right."

"Merely because things are similar doesn't mean they share any real connection", the Cabicacmotz objected. "The palm leaves resemble feathers, but that doesn't mean that palms have anything to do with birds."

"That's not what the Etamanel of the cactuses says," Evan said.

The Cabicacmotz stood up quickly and said, "I'm not listening to any more nonsense. Mark my words, Evan. If you turn Zaki into a weak-willed weed dependent imbecile, I will come and slay you without any regret. Come, Zaki. We are leaving."

He grabbed me by the arm and pulled me away before I could even express my thanks to Evan or look at the pretty Xik Haa again.

"Why do we have to go away so soon?" I whined. "I was learning stuff."

He stopped in the middle of the path and asked me, "Is that what you want to turn into, Zaki? Someone who takes the easy way?"

"Why is that the easy way? I got to see the lights in the sky, Cabicacmotz."

"You don't know that man how I know him, Zaki. You would have seen the lights on your own. You don't need some whore to sit on you."

"That girl wasn't a whore. Was she?"

"Of course not. It was a way to trap your attention, a very sneaky and pathetic way to trap your attention. It's an old technique that lazy teachers and con-men use, tempting you with a pretty woman."

"It made me feel weird when she sat on me."

He looked at me, as if trying to understand what I meant. "Was the feeling of strangeness localized in some area?" he asked with a knowing smile.

I described the tickling and rushing sensation I felt. What followed was a long explanation of what was happening to my body and a description, albeit all too brief, of the female anatomy. The Cabicacmotz' words mesmerized me. I had never seen an unclothed developed woman before. It had never occurred to me that my body had wanted to make a baby inside Xik Haa.

The Cabicacmotz frowned when I told him that and said, "Stay innocent, Zaki, or you will be saddled with a wife before the year is out."

Our conversation about reproduction ended there, since he refused to entertain any more of my questions. Instead, he returned to the subject of the plant warriors.

"I am going to need to put you in touch with someone, involved with plants, who isn't an indulging idiot like that fool, Evan.

I asked him why he thought the man a fool. He told me that Evan held the belief that he could smoke the plant with impunity whenever he liked, even for his own amusement.

"The problem is that plants are not a joke. They are not something that should be played around with. They are sentient beings which can trap or imperil a person." He told me that usually plants that led one to power were so perceptually debilitating that they were ingested only under the watchful care of a guardian. The problem with the plant Evan favored was that its effects were mild in comparison with other plants and that, therefore, it was acceptable for people to smoke it in private. That led to abuse in its use and people indulged in it. The plant trapped people with its appearance of innocuousness. He described the ill effects that plagued people who used the plant too often. The users became indolent in their everyday affairs and their responsibilities often fell on the shoulders of others because they no longer had the necessary will and determination.

"While they enjoy life and indulge in the illusion that all is light and happiness, their world falls down around them. No teacher should look like a bum or allow himself to appear stained and dirty before his students. No teacher should allow his students to harass our tribe's women as if they were common harlots. And no teacher should stoop to the crass manipulation of a new student by tempting him with an attractive girl, especially if the student is a boy who has had no experience with women."

I interrupted his harangue and asked him why he had allowed me to go and sit with Evan if he felt so strongly against him. He replied that it was not up to him when it came to omens about my curriculum. Even he could not disregard the dictates of fate. He asserted that he could impose balance and that he planned to introduce me to a plant warrior who did have the necessary sobriety that Evan lacked.

Looking around, I noticed that the crowd was a bit rowdier than before. The reason soon became apparent when a troupe of acrobats came down the path, dominating the right of way. We jumped out of their path. Truly, they were a marvel. Many were disguised as animals, so it appeared that various types of beasts were somersaulting backwards in the air, balancing objects precariously, or juggling. I saw that they had an entourage of admirers; small children laughed and ran after them. The acrobats seemed to want them to stay with them because they would herd any who strayed or didn't run fast enough.

They piqued my curiosity and I asked him about them. I also wanted to know why children were allowed somewhere that they were not supposed to be. I had never been allowed to attend.

"Many of those children are too young to be aware of what goes on here, anyway. I happen to know the acrobats and they are performing the important function of babysitting. Those are the children of warriors, most likely. Both parents have to be here, so the Council decided that they would be allowed to attend up until their fifth year of age. After that, they are required to stay at home with the servants until they reach adulthood. That rule is very recent and we will have to monitor how well it works out. This is the first time."

I looked around and saw many unchaperoned boys, who were close to my age, meandering around the grounds or otherwise enjoying themselves. I pointed them out to the Cabicacmotz. It annoyed me to think that he was testing how observant I was. Then I had an unnerving thought. What if they had become men before I did? Wasn't it a biological function that showed up at a certain time for every boy? I didn't know and was reticent to ask about it.

"Those are the children of those who are not warriors. They belong to the under classes. Usually their parents work in the fields tending farms for the vassals above them. Or they are servants' children; many houses employ them and use their services. If you have not noticed, the economy is providing them with more than adequate conditions. In any case, they do not have to wait to attend the festival because they are an integral part in the running of our society. Their parents are the ones who watch over the children of the noble houses who are not allowed to attend until they become adults. It would be very bad form to require them to hire someone to watch over their own children. So on this day, everyone in our society watches over those youths."

"Why don't they stay with the children of the nobles?"

'That is simply not done. I realize it is stupid and arbitrary, but it is not the custom here. Have you ever seen any of your father's or your and Maricua's servants bringing their children along to work?"

How I wished they would. There had been times, in the past, when one of the servants would bring in her baby. Those were exciting times for me. I would get to entertain them for a bit while their mothers worked. When the child reached its second year and began walking, no longer would they come to the house. Until the Cabicacmotz mentioned it, I had been unaware that children of servants were not welcome. I always assumed that the children were with another family member because they were more difficult to take care of when one had chores to complete, if they could run around.

"Babies are transportable bundles that are easy to keep around if one is working. A toddler is another matter, entire-ly. You really have to keep a close watch over them. They get into everything. You have to make sure they don't put things they shouldn't into their mouths, lest they choke. You have to make sure they don't run off into a stream and drown. Many things can go wrong with them. That is why every neighborhood in the village, where the servants live, has women that take care of the children for the other parents."

"Why do you say parents?" I said and laughed. "No man would allow his wife to dictate to him that he should rear his children. That is women's work."

"I say it because it is more precise, Zaki. You, yourself, know that women do not always survive childbirth. There is also sickness, for either sex. Sometimes children grow up without one or even both parents. Sometimes men have to raise the children. Many face that reality. If a man or woman loses their spouse to death, they need all of the help they can get from others when it comes to raising and caring for any children they have. Your sister often goes to help those women. Haven't you noticed that she is often away from the home?"

"I thought she was out visiting other women at their estates or at the marketplace."

"No, Zaki. Your sister has few friends in the noble houses. She has many in the servants' sectors, but she is not one to pass the day in idle gossip with other noble women. Also, she is not fond of going to the marketplace alone." He tilted his head to the side as he watched me closely. "How could you have failed to notice those qualities in Maricua that I find so beautiful? Do you realize how extraordinary she is in comparison with other ladies? Nephew, I am the luckiest man in the world."

He was making me feel guilty somehow, even though I loved and adored Maricua. I told him how I felt and that I knew how special she was. I also added that I knew that she often went to sit in the court and that sometimes I went along with her. I may not have known about the good deeds she kept in secret, but I knew more about her than he did and he should not forget that.

"She goes to the court? I have never seen her there," he said.

"Yes. But don't expect her to sit in the front with the nobility," I told him. "She likes to sit with the public. She even saw you on the day you set that man's head on fire!"

He uttered a very bad word then. He hung his head and exhaled loudly. "Really? She saw that?"

I nodded.

"Of all days to come to court," he lamented. "Why that day?"

I shrugged cheerfully, glad to have shaken his confidence. "I don't know. Why do you worry? She's in love with you anyway. That was a pretty awful thing, by the way. Why did you do it?" It delighted me to embarrass him by telling him that she had seen him at his worst.

"You don't know what he did," the Cabicacmotz said. "That man deserved death."

"Then why wasn't he killed? Wouldn't that be better for the tribe?"

"Our tribe also believes in redemption, Zaki. Such a thing is only done when there is no hope for change, when the person has crossed over into pure evil. Let's not talk about that anymore. Some other day, I will tell you the whole of the story."

We had been walking a circuitous path and were now near a long row of open tents. They looked quite beautiful. Reddish cloths had been hung to provide shade and their ends floated gracefully in the breeze. I wanted to stop and rest, but didn't want him to think I was a weakling. At that moment, a small stone lodged itself in my sandal and I had to sit down to remove it. The nearest tent didn't have anyone in the front part of it, so I sat down there. After I removed the pebble, I stayed seated.

The Cabicacmotz watched me with a curious expression on his face. I noticed that he was also paying attention to the men in the adjacent tent. They were watching us. Actually, to be more precise, they were watching Chahal who was sitting next to me and lazily licking her front paws.

"We must stay here, Zaki."

That was exactly what I wanted to hear, but I decided to be difficult and asked him why.

He looked at me with an expression that told me he knew I wanted to sit and only asked why to be annoying. He said, "Getting a pebble in your shoe is an omen for this group."

"What crazy kind of omen is that?"

"A very good one, as it turns out. You got a stone in your shoe that made you walk on the balls of your feet, since it was in the heel."

I told him that I still didn't understand what he meant and he told me that I should notice what group was nearby.

I paid closer attention to the men who were watching us. They did not attempt to hide their curiosity about Chahal and me. They openly watched us. I watched them back. They were all dressed very regally with jaguar skins over their shoulders as capes or used as kilts and loincloths. I became very excited then.

"Those men must be the other ballgame players from your group, the Jaguars," I gushed. I wanted to go straight to where they were, but the next words from the Cabicac-motz' mouth stopped me.

"No, Zaki. These jaguars are not those of my team."

I reasoned that these men must be the acrobatic babysitters we had seen dressed up like animals. "What do you mean? I don't want to spend my days learning how to babysit and entertain children, while I pretend to be Cha-hal." I was chagrined to learn that I was going to have to be taught by men who performed duties more appropriate for women, even if they were acrobats. "What a rotten group to get sucked into! Why didn't you warn me?"

The closest man barked a laugh and covered his mouth as he fled to a nearby tent.

"Are you playing with me, Zaki? Pretending to be dumb?"

"I'm not pretending." I wasn't.

He rolled his eyes. "Zaki. The sign was clear as day. You are supposed to enter this group and learn from them."

"How could a pebble in my shoe mean anything? That's really flimsy."

"Flimsy is a moron on a rock falling on top of you, especially since it was probably on purpose, but it still is an omen. This was very clear. You had to walk on the balls of your feet like a feline. Like Chahal. If the pebble had made you walk on your heels, it would have been a clear sign that this was not a group for you. Accept it and do not anger or otherwise insult these men."

He walked me over to where the men were congregated. They were all very serious and looked at me with a marked intensity. They were fearsome and muscular men. I was sure that any children who were put in their care would not have a very jolly time. They were too somber. It was sobering to realize that acrobats did not act amusing, energetic, or cheerful when no one was watching them. I hoped they would reject me. I might enjoy it when the servant women brought their babies, but it was not something I would like to do every day. Perhaps if they tested me, they would see that I had no acrobatic skill.

"Balam Ch'ab, this is Zakiraxapalo. He is here upon a clear omen."

He had spoken to the man in the group who seemed to be the leader. He was in the corner, lounging on cushions. Unusual for our tribe, his hair was cut extremely short all around, except for a long ponytail at the crown of his head. His small eyes sparkled with intelligence as he looked me over.

"I heard your pupil refer to us a rotten group. We, the Jaguar Knights, are unaccustomed to overlooking insults, even when it is the son of Naualalom. He is rude. Why should we shoulder the burden of teaching him if he has no desire to be here? Many seek us out; we do not want for members. Maybe it would be a better idea to pretend this omen never happened. We are willing to overlook a pebble," he said.

The Cabicacmotz exhaled loudly and said, "A misunderstanding only, I assure you. Zaki, here, is under the misapprehension that you are connected to the festival acrobats that are watching the smaller children," he said.

Upon hearing that, the left side of the Balam Ch'ab's mouth slowly turned up at the corner wickedly. He turned to the other men.

Several of them snickered. One man even smacked his lips and said, "Kids are so sweet." After that, they all laughed. There was something mean-spirited about those laughs, but I did not know if they were directed at children, in general, or me.

The Balam Ch'ab stood up then and came to me, putting his muscular arm around my shoulder. I slumped under the weight and he eased the pressure. He led me to an opening in the tent, which led to a larger tent. He whispered to me that he and his party were not costume-wearing babysitters. He laughed at that. "We are something else, rather."

I looked behind me and saw that the Cabicacmotz and Chahal followed us into the back tent. Chahal's tail was flicking back and forth as she scented the air with her nose held high. She looked at the Balam Ch'ab and let out a sharp growl.

"I have no interest in harming your human, Lady," he told her. She seemed to understand his words and sat, yet still she watched him without taking her eyes off him.

He took his arm away from my shoulder and instructed me to sit in the corner with Chahal to my left and the Cabicacmotz to my right.

We situated ourselves. The others sat partly in front of me. The Cabicacmotz kept his right knee up as he sat on his heel, balancing his weight on the ball of his left foot. He told me to adopt his pose, as there was the chance that we were in danger and might have to back away quickly.

"No matter what you see," he said. "Do not jump up out of fright. Only follow my lead. Do not make quick movements."

My attention was then taken up with the actions of the Balam Ch'ab. He had stripped completely and was standing naked at the opposite corner of the tent from us. He turned away, so that his posterior faced us. He stretched and contorted his body for a few moments. Then he began a curious crawl around and around his corner. For a while, both legs and arms moved normally, but then he began to synchronize his movements so that the left leg and arm moved in the same way. He alternated between the left and the right. His peculiar movements were graceful and mesmerizing.

A moment later, a prowling jaguar was in the tent with us.

Chahal made sounds of agitation and the Cabicacmotz shushed her.

The jaguar paced in a circle for a few moments and suddenly turned into the Balam Ch'ab crawling around. He stopped and stood up slowly, keeping his eyes locked on mine.

I could not turn away. I was thunderstruck by what had occurred.

"I can assure you, boy, that we are hardly fitting persons for the care of little children. To be sure, we would protect one of our tribe's if we found them wandering the jungle alone, but that is not our true role. Do you still find us to be a pathetic group?" he asked me with a lopsided knowing grin.

My eyes must have looked like saucers and I was only able to shake my head to indicate that that was the furthest thing from my mind. My mind was reeling under the impact of what I had witnessed. I was truly speechless; my mouth was incapable of uttering sounds.

"That's what I thought," the Balam Ch'ab said. "Try not to jump to conclusions next time. Our tribe is worthy and full of talent. Holding your tongue until you truly understand who you are dealing with is something I strongly advise," he kindly said as he began redressing himself. "By the way, those acrobats whom you find so laughable and unworthy of your respect are only babysitting today for the festival. The rest of the time, they are our tribe's foremost experts in the art of combat. They are nothing to sneer at. They are so formidable that I, myself, could not be persuaded to fight against them." He adjusted the fastening that held his jaguar pelt in place and came over to us.

We all stood.

He asked the Cabicacmotz about whom else I would be learning from. He was impressed with the Chuchmox and that I would be learning bateh, but he openly mocked the Etamanel Evan when he heard that he had designed to fall on me. He listened intently to the Cabicacmotz when he told him he planned to introduce me to a better teacher from the plant warriors.

"That is a wise choice. I also do not want one of my students to be influenced by that fool. He would like everyone to become like him. I apologize to tell you what you already know, but you should have been more careful with

Zaki. Evan has been making noise, since he has heard that many want to strip him of his office. He is looking for supporters and he is most desperate. Who better than the first prince to tout his cause?"

"Indeed. Who better?" said the Cabicacmotz.

The Balam Ch'ab turned to address me. "What I am going to teach you requires you to have a will of granite. I also will be watching you to make sure you do not fall under the influence of that charlatan. Do not disappoint me."

I was still unable to form words and nodded to him. He seemed to understand my predicament and advised me to drink a bit and have some food, that that would help me to recover my speech. He lightly slapped me in a friendly way on my back and expressed his happiness that he would now be one of my instructors.

He said goodbye as we left the tent area of his group.

"Strange that you will belong to two groups of what are called jaguars," the Cabicacmotz said.

I made hand motions and used facial expressions to convey my curiosity about when we would be meeting his team players. He told me that I still had a few more things to do before we went there and that the first order of business was to get food and drink into me.

We found a stand where a man was cooking meat and vegetables on spits. It was an unsatisfying snack. The meat was tasteless, except for its burnt flavor and it had a leathery texture. The vegetables, at least, provided a bit of moisture that enabled me to swallow the meat. Afterwards, we went to some stands where women were providing boiled water. Although it was cooled, the boiling deprived it of its freshness. I asked the Cabicacmotz why we couldn't find some water at the nearby stream and he gave me an incredulous look.

"I'd rather not get dysentery today," he dryly said. "When large crowds congregate, people will inevitably need to urinate or defecate. Many will go in the most convenient place for them. A stream or a river is handy. Look at the iguanas, their favorite place to go is on a branch over running water so it will be carried off. Humans do the same. They wish to be away from their waste. Unfortunately, we are not at the clean and perfect origin of the stream. Before it gets to this area, it has to pass through many parts adjacent to the temple grounds. Look over there," he said as he pointed to the north.

I saw a group of children playing in the water of the stream.

"Children are notorious for peeing, or more, in the water. For some reason, water activates the urge to urinate. It seems to be something built into the human body. That's why I never go swimming with all of you at the grotto. If you boys were older, you would know to refrain from peeing there, but you're not, so I avoid the grotto. I advise you to keep the grotto's water out of your mouth."

I was disgusted to learn such information. It was very hypocritical of me. I knew that it was important to keep all waters clean, especially fresh water, yet I often peed in the stream behind my garden. I was caught between being ashamed that the Cabicacmotz probably knew I was guilty of an equivalent crime and thinking that my fellow students were dirty monkeys. All I could do was resolve to not pee in the grotto or the stream in my garden. I was very curious, also, to find out who was upstream of me. Could I have been drinking someone else's pee all along?

After we ate our leather strips, we strolled around and watched people. The Cabicacmotz would point out different people to me and tell me their names and things about them. It was not a gossipy activity; it was more in the nature of acquainting me with certain notable people.

He pointed out a very old man to me. He was stooped and had to use a cane to walk. The man was so old that his hair was white. White hair was an anomaly in my tribe. Every so often, a young person would have white hair and they would be singled out by people like the Cabicacmotz. We spoke about that for a bit. He told me that it often signified a person who was adept at something hidden and usually they tried to get that person together with the right teacher as quickly as possible to prevent accidents.

I asked him what kind of accidents he was talking about, but he called my attention back to the old man.

"Why do you want me to know who he is? Is he the oldest man in the tribe or something?"

"No, Zaki," he said with a laugh. "That man is going to be one of your instructors. I merely wanted you to be able to recognize him. He is the Ahtzic Uinac."

"What does he do?"

"He is the master storyteller for our young men. He is also the town crier. That particular function, though, is now often the responsibility of his prized student, the future Ahtzic Uinac, whom he is grooming to sit on his mat."

"Why don't I need to have an omen to learn with him?"

"The stories of our people are a basic. It is not specialized knowledge. The stories are for every student. They are often tailored to the individual student's needs."

"How can they be tailored if they are for everybody? Won't all the students have different teachers and things they learn which are different from everybody else?"

"The Ahtzic Uinac speaks at the behest of the spirit."

"What does that mean?"

"It means that the Creator or the powers which rule life indicate to the Ahtzic Uinac what story is most pertinent to a certain day. The same force, which supplied the omen of the pebble in your sandal, shows him what story to tell. The spirit is the emissary of the Creator or the masters of fate."

"How does that happen?"

"Such a thing is beyond our knowing. To know how the mind of the Creator works is knowledge we cannot ascertain. To know how the intricacies of fate develop can only be known in retrospect. After the fact, one can examine how things occurred and make guesses as to why. To know beforehand or while things are occurring are powers that are usually beyond man, unless the spirit allows man a glimpse into the inner workings. Such glimpses are given only rarely and the person receiving them often cannot distinguish them from his own thoughts, unless he is a genius capable of such discernment," he said.

I believed that I had found a discrepancy in regards to the omens. It occurred to me as he talked about things that mostly went beyond my current understanding. I asked him about the Chuchmox, questioning him about why I did not receive an omen that indicated that I should learn with them.

He replied that an omen does not always have to be evident to the student if the teacher recognizes it. He told me that when I had shadow gazed and disappeared, it was a sign that I had a particular gift, which should be honed as soon as possible. The Chuchmox were the most adept gazers in our society. What I had done was so extraordinary, he said, that it was clear to him that I needed to jump straight to the top when it came to gazing.

"It is now time to meet the next Chuchmox, the one presiding over the North-East," he said. "We are close to where she is."

We went towards the platform where the Chuchmox was. I was beginning to notice certain things. For example, the platforms of the cardinal directions were further away from the temple grounds. The platforms of the mid-directions were one platform length towards the temples. I asked him about this and he told me that those directions needed to be protected by the outer cardinal Chuchmox. He said that it was necessary to cocoon or nestle them within their more important directions. As such, they appeared to be like the regular Chuchmox, but they were actually a hidden facet of them.

"That is something you will find more about once you begin your training with them. It is unwise to speak of it out in the open like this, so cool your mind and disregard that topic for now."

The North-East Chuchmox wore a tunic that was white above the waist and red below. She held a pose perfectly in line with the Chakmol behind her. White feathers adorned her headdress and she wore red sandals similar to the East's. It gave one the impression that two outfits had been separated and reassembled. I wondered where the opposite outfit was and noticed that on the other side of the Chakmol was another Chuchmox wearing such an outfit. The other one was not apparent, at first glance, since she was partially hidden by the statue of the Chakmol.

I began to ask the Cabicacmotz why the women were wearing opposite outfits, but he shushed me, telling me to be quiet.

White headdress spoke to me then, saying, "Naqahob." I did as she commanded and went up to the platform's edge.

"You wish to know why we are two when the East was only one, yes?" she asked.

I nodded and said, "Yes, Chuchmox."

She turned to the Cabicacmotz and said, "He is polite for a prince. You have trained him well."

The Cabicacmotz told her that I had only been with him for seven days and that any politeness was mine and not a result of his instructions.

Red headdress spoke then and said with a smile in her voice, "Maybe we should co-opt him from you before you contaminate him with your insolent ways."

"Never," he said.

Both women laughed. Their laughter blended so well that it seemed rehearsed. They even stopped laughing at the same time.

White headdress said, "Well, boy, the reason we are two is because we are a blend of two directions. We are not confined to one view. We must inhabit and view the two directions. We are the in-between."

I resigned myself to the fact that I would not fully under-stand what she was saying, especially the part about inhabiting directions.

Red headdress somehow sensed my confusion, even though she wasn't looking at me. She said, "Store my sister's words for now, boy. It will take too long for you to compre-hend what we truly mean today. We will see you later at our fortress."

It seemed that we had been dismissed. I looked at white headdress and saw that she was no longer paying attention to us. Instead, her eyes roamed the jungle. Her eyes seemed to be out of focus and I wondered how she could identify any looming threats if she did not view things with precision.

As we walked away, I asked the Cabicacmotz about that. He sighed and urged me to pay closer attention. He said, "They are engaged in gazing, not in picking out mun-dane threats. They are more for the overview and for detecting what is hidden. If there are physical threats in the jungle, the Balam Ch'ab or people like him will pluck them out and dispose of them. The Chuchmox also pick out physical threats if they get too near and send a relay to the other groups advising them of what they have seen, but they are usually used to detect what is not apparent to the actual eyes." He told me that we had to make a circuit of the Chuchmox' platforms and that we should get it out of the way quickly so that we could get a good position for viewing the dance of the Cranes.

We headed to the North platform. Along the way, I saw a curious sight. A grey-haired man was sleeping in the shade of a small pup tent. Across the path from him, and walking almost alongside of us, his twin was walking with a dancing gait. I knew that they were twins because they had the same braids and clothing. They both had three braids, two at the sides and one at the back of the head. It was not a typical style for men in our tribe. Today, I was seeing all sorts of weird hairdos. Both men were dressed all in white, which was also unusual.

The twin that was awake would walk a few feet and then skip for a few paces. Each time he skipped, it seemed that he stayed in the air for an inordinate amount of time. He appeared to be very joyous and glad, but it was a strange scene since he would laugh and talk to someone who was clearly not there. It seemed as if he was in an actual conversation because after he would make a comment, he would wait a few moments before he spoke again, as if he was listening to an actual response.

The Cabicacmotz noticed where my attention was and told me not to point out the man's sleeping twin to him if he spoke to us. I asked him why not and he told me that it was simply not done. I argued that the man should be used to comments about his twin because twins were rare and they were always celebrated in our tribe. To be a twin was considered a very fortunate thing.

"Your argument would normally hold, but in this instance it cannot because those men are not actual physical twins."

"What are they then? You, yourself, called them twins."

"They are the same person, divided."

"That's ridiculous, not to mention impossible," I protested.

He laughed at me then. "Zaki, a short time ago you were in a tent where a man transformed himself into a jaguar. Are you going to lecture me about what is possible and impossible? I should think that you are quite aware of man's possibilities by now."

He had me there. I didn't know why I persisted in thinking that some things weren't possible. Today I had seen marvels and still my mind seemed to disregard them. I had become accustomed to life and what it could contain. It was illogical of me, yet still I found myself forgetting all I had seen and clinging to my habitual version of the world, the one I had for so many years. I wondered if it was possible for me to forget everything.

The awake twin began chuckling softly as if he were sharing a private joke with someone. He said something under his breath and began laughing in earnest.

"Why is he talking with himself? Or is there another person with him, maybe someone invisible?" I snickered as I watched the man.

"That man is nothing to laugh about, Zaki. He is going to be your dreaming teacher. He has so much power that he can will almost anything and it will be so."

Instead of the obvious, my mind latched onto his use of the term 'almost'.

"Not everything is possible," he said when I asked him about it. "Truth cannot be repealed; it will prevail over man's will. One cannot will the Creator to be powerless or evil. Such things are beyond man's authority." He began walking behind the man. I was compelled to follow. "Be careful around him. What you take as a humorous sight is anything but. Don't think that you can insult or laugh at that man as if he were a foolish peon from another city. When I tell you that he has power, believe it. He has so much that you must train yourself to act perfectly when you are around him. Do not annoy him. Place some value upon your own life and behave properly. In addition, he is definitely talking with another being; it is not a figment of his imagination. If you were able to see truly, you would know that he has powerful company. We will approach him when whatever being is with him leaves."

"How will we know when that is? When he stops speaking?"

"I will let you know the right time."

"Why do I have to learn with him if it's so dangerous?"

"The sign occurred the moment you noticed that he was doubled, a twin. Believe it or not, but noticing that someone is double is a sign in itself."

There wasn't anything I could say to that. I knew that I would not be able to get out of learning with the man.

A short while later, the man went into the tall grass off the path and sat down. The Cabicacmotz quickly followed him, pulling me along.

"Hurry up," he said. "We don't want him to fall asleep again out here."

"Why not?" What did he care if the man fell asleep?

"If he falls asleep out here, he will disappear and we will have to return to talk to his body. I want you to get a good idea of what the double can do."

We were almost upon the man, who was now lying down on the ground, prostrate. He looked up and smiled when he saw Chahal approach him.

"Why hello, Chahal," he said. "How good of you to come and see your old friend again. It has been a long time."

His words surprised me. I watched her trot to his side and sit. The man moved to stroke her behind the ears and she shifted away from him, not wanting him to touch her. Yet she was unafraid of him. Apparently, my friend had another life she led when I was not around.

The man said, "Oh, I'm sorry, girl. I forgot that you don't like me as much when I am in this body."

He looked at the Cabicacmotz and me and smiled. "Hello, Cabi. Hello, prince."

The Cabicacmotz introduced him as Ahtoobalvar.

The man, Ahtoobalvar, stood and nodded politely at me. "Are you to be my student?" he asked.

"I believe so, sir."

"When should we start, young prince?"

I was robbed of thought. There was something so innocent and ingenuous about him that I was disarmed. Most people I met were strictly in the here and now. Even the Etamanel Evan was, with his eccentricities and obvious machinations. This man was here, but he seemed far away. He was connected to something I could not see, something I could only dimly sense. I felt that he was ephemeral, evanescent somehow. His manner was childlike; he seemed to be the personification of kindness. Pure.

"Would you like to see me fly?" he asked me with an expectant smile.

I nodded dumbly.

The moment he saw me nod, he began to skip. As before, his time up in the air, between his steps, seemed to last. After a while, he was skipping on air and no longer needed to touch the earth. Then he veered towards the ground and made one more skip, which propelled him up high into the air, and he flew away into the sky. I watched his flight, expecting him to come back, but he flew off into the distance until I could no longer see him. The Cabicacmotz put his arm around my shoulder and led me back onto the path.

"How are these things real, Cabicacmotz? Why is it that I never noticed these things when I was a child?"

"Simple. This aspect of our society is usually kept hidden. Everyone is engaged in a subterfuge. Everyone begins life learning the rules of that part of the world that we share with neighboring tribes, the mundane. The extraordinary is mostly reserved for this day, when our children enter adulthood."

I had a bad taste in my mouth similar to when one wakes up after a long sleep. It was probably from the leather we ate. "Only then? Why even bother then if you can't use it when you want?"

"We can use it whenever we want, Zaki. My words were misleading. It is not only this day. That would be silly. We use it when we need to. If there are good reasons for doing so, or if no one is around, we can do as we please. Also, we do what we can get away with on the ball court. What is acceptable for the ballplayer is not what is acceptable for the merchant. It is a given that the ballplayers will have unusual skills. The safety is that the unusual usually goes unnoticed by the common people and the untalented. Sometimes we will play extremely gifted ballplayers from other tribes, but they are not often skilled in the esoteric. They may even make side goals, at times, if we are caught off guard. Our talents are not used in those games. If we allow ourselves to forget and we do what is the impossible for them, they will oftentimes attribute it to luck or skill. They have no attention for the part of man that has genius. Do you see what I mean? The mysterious weaves itself seamlessly into the fabric of ordinary reality." He made hand motions that mimicked those that weavers performed when they made cloth. "To prove it to you, I ask that you look around."

I glanced around at the people laughing and having a good time around us. No one was paying any attention to us. I asked him what he wanted me to see.

"Did you notice any gasps of people, as if they were surprised to see a man flying and soaring through the sky like a bird?"

I had not.

"That is because this aspect of reality is hidden to those whose eyes are on the regular reality of this world. Most of the people around us are the general public of our tribe. They have not been singled out to learn the marvels and wonders of existence. Neither warriors nor priests were around when Ahtoobalvar was demonstrating his flight. You were the only one who noticed that a man around us was doubled. His flight went unnoticed. Seeing the normal world is a habit that was inculcated in you. Seeing the larger side of reality is a habit I am acquainting you with. What you should consider is that the regular tribesmen and women around us didn't notice anything odd."

"Why not?"

"One of the things you will learn is that perception is very fluid and all-inclusive when it is in the reality of the mundane and when it is in the reality of those who are called 'lords of the life force.' One obscures the other. Right now, you are getting glimpses and viewing with the eyes of genius. Much better than the eyes of the mundane life, isn't it?"

"But how is it that I am able to see these things, Cabicacmotz? I am not a genius. I just started with you and I am only accustomed to seeing the normal side of this world. Wouldn't that make me into a person who can only see what isn't weird?"

"What's weird is that people only train themselves to see one side of the world when there is much more to see. The answer to your question is tricky and I don't know the exact reasons for it. On the one hand, we have a boy who is accustomed to seeing life as a regular person. On the other hand, this boy has spent a lot of time alone with silence and shadows as his companions. This boy is a quick study and is at a stage in his life where he is still fluid and receptive to learning new things and the teacher's presence affects the boy and lends him the confidence or the energy needed to see the extraordinary."

"How is that? Do you mean that I wouldn't notice anything odd was going on if you were not with me?"

"I honestly don't know," he said. "The teacher, especially at the beginning, is required to foster the idea that there is more to us than meets the eye and that almost anything is possible. My feeling is that the teacher provides the student with the assurance that mankind's abilities can be glorious and breathtaking and this knowing enables your eyes to have more confidence and scope in what they see."

I was trying to follow his words, but they were too difficult for me. It was noticeable to me that he would stress certain points and repeat them. My retention of his words was not keen and I immediately forgot what we spoke of. I asked him whether I already had enough teachers in order to change the subject and to cover up the fact that I was not grasping his explanations.

He told me that it was almost time to start our way towards the sinkhole where the dance of the Cranes was to be witnessed.

Along the way, we spoke of many things that seemed inconsequential. We would point things out to each other that seemed interesting. Thankfully, he stopped talking about the two sides of reality. Occasionally, my thoughts would return to it and then my mind would balk and I would experience a lapse in my thinking.

We found Maricua standing near where the dance was to be held. It was a grassy area next to a narrow and deep sinkhole. The crevasse was so long that it seemed to stretch almost to the horizon. Several crude bridges stretched across it at various points. It seemed like a river had once flowed in its passageway. The Cabicacmotz informed me that its depths had never fully contained water. A shallow brook ran along its winding length. The brook originated underground and returned to the ground, contained and finite, yet always fresh. The brook fed the sinkhole, enabling it to be incredibly fertile. As I looked into the passage, I was confronted with the green of trees and large ferns. The floor was so mossy that it seemed like it was covered in vibrant green velvet.

Birds filled the sinkhole. I noticed men dressed up as birds in there also, but the real birds didn't pay any attention to them. In the trees were musicians. Some held drums,

others flutes, and others held instruments I was unacquaint-
ed with.

Those, with drums, beat a long repetitious song that
seemed to fill my chest. It was rhythmical, but it was not a
song proper. After a while, I realized what the song was.
Many times, I had placed my ear against Chahal's chest
and heard her heartbeat. That was what they were playing. For some reason, my own heart felt as if it was pulsing
along with the drumming.

The beats went on for quite a while. Apparently, it was
the call to the tribe to come and see the dance of the
Cranes. The Cabicacmotz sat down on the ground next to
Maricua. I sat to his left and Chahal was next to me. There
was an order to how everyone watched the dance. The
people with the best view sat. Behind them, others sat
behind their shoulders, also sitting. Behind those, people
kneeled in two rows. After them, came those who stood. All
along both sides of the long sinkhole, everyone watched
within one of the six rows. I was glad that I had an unobstructed view.

When the audience was settled, a different beat of the
drums commenced. At first, it was accented with the calls
of birds. I was amazed that the natural birds did not leave
in alarm. In normal situations, they were easily startled.
Instead, they were a part of the song. Soon after, flutes
began to mimic the birds and then the other musicians
joined in. It was an intricate and beautiful song, yet it was
organic and natural. Unobtrusive, yet melodious.

Then the men dressed as cranes began a curious
dance. It consisted of them mimicking the movements and
gates of cranes. Some real cranes were in there and I saw

how well they acted like them. They would lift up their legs while their spines rolled as cranes do when they seemingly tiptoe as they hunt for small prey, rocking their necks forward and back, eyes sharp. This went on for quite a while as they moved languorously through the greenery. There must have been, at least, forty men and women in my field of vision who were imitating cranes. Their walks were in perfect harmony with the song being played. They seemed to be one with the music. That was the visceral feeling their dance gave me.

Then the tempo of the musicians quickened. What I saw next filled me with awe. In synchronicity with the faster drumming, all of them shook themselves as birds do when wet, fluffing the feathers of the costumes they wore. Even some of the real cranes did so. Suddenly, the men in the bird suits were replaced with actual cranes. I must have blinked at the wrong time because some of the actual birds were replaced with crouched nude men and women. Those stopped and hung their heads, cowering as if ashamed of their nakedness. The cranes, which replaced the actors, flew off as if spooked. The music tapered off and the crowd went wild, clapping and hooting. This caused the rest of the birds to fly off.

I turned to the Cabicacmotz and saw a glistening shine in his and Maricua's eyes. I couldn't blame them; the dance was so lifting that I almost cried myself. What stopped me was the exhilaration I felt for those actors. I felt that they were gifted illusionists to change places so quickly with the actual birds that had been in the gully.

When the crowd had quieted down, everyone left. No one spoke. I knew in my heart that that was the only way to honor those fine men and women. In addition, I knew that they would prefer not to have an audience as they looked for clothes in which to cover themselves. I glanced back into the length of the sinkhole and was a bit surprised to see that the realistic crane disguises were nowhere in sight. I surmised that the musicians in the trees were in on the illusion. Perhaps the outfits had strings attached to them that enabled the musicians to pull them up into the trees to hide them.

I caught up with Maricua and the Cabicacmotz a few yards away where they waited for me. I tried to start a conversation, but they shushed me and indicated that it was impolite to speak right then.

When we were a distance from the sinkhole, I gushed about the performance and how they were the best actors I had ever seen and how they really seemed like cranes.

Maricua looked at the Cabicacmotz and rolled her eyes comically. It made me feel like what I was, a sheltered little boy who had never seen a truly professional performance. She was laughing at my inexperience with the arts.

"Please don't laugh at me, Maricua. This is my first time seeing a great show. It's natural for me to be excited."

"I'm not laughing at you really, Zaki. Don't worry," she said as she kissed me on top of the head. "I simply think that what we saw was a bit more involved than mere acting and prestidigitation."

She didn't give me time to ponder her statements because she said that she was off to see some of her friends and would try to see us later.

"Will you be coming to see the ballgame, Maricua?" I asked.

"No. Absolutely not," she said as she walked away.

"Why won't she come?" I asked the Cabicacmotz.

"I told you before. It makes her too nervous to see violent games, Zaki." He didn't say more about her and asked me if I would now like to go and see his fellow teammates. I eagerly let him know that I would love to. "Come then," he said as he walked towards the direction of the bateh court.

I glanced at the crowd and felt uncomfortable. Looking around, I noticed the Balam Ch'ab a distance away watching us. He tipped his head at me as if he was acknowledging or congratulating me on having caught him watching me.

"Yes," the Cabicacmotz said. "You might want to notice the feelings you experience when you suspect that eyes are upon you. It is a skill that can be quite handy to have at certain times."

I told him that I hadn't known that anyone was paying attention to us until I saw the Balam Ch'ab. He argued that I had felt ill at ease and that my body caused me to look around to ascertain the source of my discomfort.

"The Balam Ch'ab was testing you. Now he knows that you are a sensitive."

"A sensitive what?" I asked with belligerence. To me, the word implied weakness and sissiness, qualities that I was loathe to exhibit.

It was not mere vanity on my part. Homosexuals were routinely exterminated like rats. There was the belief that what they had was catching and that they could contaminate others with their proclivities. It was widely believed that they were hosts for demons and that those persons had willingly invoked them or had become possessed by them because of some weakness on their part. Exile was no kindness, but I'm sure that many would have preferred it if given the chance. There were many aspects of our society, which were most brutal and harsh. That was one of them.

Patiently, the Cabicacmotz told me that being a sensitive was no insult. He stressed that it was a very sought after quality in a student. He also cleared up the term's definition to my satisfaction, which pleased me to no end because being the son of the king was no guarantee against being executed.

"To be a sensitive means that you are a person who is not fully in the reality of the daily world. You have one foot in the other place."

"What other place?" I asked, mystified.

"The place of clear knowledge, of perfect vision. You are not entirely there, however, so your vision is still clouded, but you have a part of you that already resides there if you are a sensitive. Our history tells us that once man was able to see everything and know clearly. His vision was so complete that it frightened and scared the ones who made mankind and they took away man's clarity, effectively banishing him to this reality that we are in now." He looked at me and shook his head. "Don't ask me who the makers of mankind are, later we will speak of it, but not now. In any case, now man's ability to see and know is diminished. When we encounter a student whom we can clearly identify as being a sensitive, we rejoice at our good fortune and recognize that harsh techniques to foster that sensitivity in boys who are not sensitives are not required."

"What?" I asked. His explanation was confusing me and I wanted straight answers from him. I found it very unsatisfying that his clarifications only ended up confusing me more and leading to more questions from me.

"If the Balam Ch'ab gets a student who is not a sensitive, his teaching techniques are going to have to be different. He will have to spend an inordinate amount of time leading you along like a baby. Oftentimes, those teaching techniques are frightening and harsh, as I said. Consider when I forced you to peek into the darkness of the jungle that one night where you almost wet yourself with fright. If I had been able to get to know you a little better before that, I would have taken different steps with you that night. You don't need fright to see, you already partially do whether you know it or not. I was mislead, in a way, because of the way you acted like a spoiled brat on the night you first encountered me when you were with your father. The predilection to violence and the belief that one is too good to be laughed at are often signs that the person is fully here in this world. Truly, you have surprised me."

"What do you mean when you say that I already know how to see? I don't see more than anybody else." I was sure of this. While I had had some unusual experiences already with the Cabicacmotz, I was certain that they occurred solely because he was around.

"Although you don't realize what you see and know does not mean that you don't see and know. You may not consciously know it, but your body is not as stupid as your mind. It knows. Think back. You felt uncomfortable and odd. You yourself did not know why, but your body made you turn around and look for the source of your discomfort. It knew that the source was outside of you. That means to me, and to the Balam Ch'ab, that you are a sensitive. You have no idea how many people are unaware that they are being watched and focused upon. The Balam Ch'ab gazed you and you felt his gaze. That's pretty interesting don't you think?" he said with a sly smile.

I had to return his smile. It made me glad that I was able to talk with him. For much of my life, people had made me feel critical about myself. Other children avoided me and I had been told that I was strange when I had described to them certain thoughts or feelings I had. Long ago, I had learned to hide my true thoughts. Unfortunately, it also accompanied a retreat from regular human interaction, even though I craved it. To enter into a part of society where those things were well received gave me the thing I had long wished for, acceptance.

"Uh oh," he said as he slapped his forehead.

"What is it?"

"I forgot that we had to complete the circuit of the Chuchmox. Come, we have to get that out of the way before we can go and see my teammates. I had wished for you to spend a longer time in their company before our game, but that is not to be. Let's hurry."

As we made our way towards the next Chuchmox, I thought back to the beautiful dance of the Cranes. My newfound pleasure at being labeled a sensitive was dashed by the truth. I realized that I had completely misunderstood the whole dance. I knew then that those men and women were not illusionists. I knew that they were like the Balam Ch'ab and that they had actually transformed themselves into cranes. I wondered how I could witness the Balam Ch'ab's change, yet still cling to the idea that men were unable to become other beings. It seemed inconceivable that such duality could exist within me, but I saw that it was so. Another realization accompanied it; my mind was not dependable.

"Why is my mind so unreliable, Cabicacmotz? I saw the Balam Ch'ab transform himself into a jaguar, but I was unable to remember that such things were possible while I watched the dance of the Cranes. Why is it like that? Am I crazy?"

"No, you are not crazy. You are merely unaccustomed to the hidden realities within our tribe. You may not believe it, but you have posed a very difficult question that will require years of training on your part in order to understand. You are only beginning. Today is not the day for it. I will ask you to ponder it on your own. Why does your mind shy away from certain knowledge when it knows differently, when it knows the truth? Why does it cling to a definition of reality that it has seen is not absolutely true? Is it merely habit or something more sinister? Really, Zaki. Think about that."

We went on to see all of the Chuchmox. The women all wore elaborate outfits that were color coordinated, according to the directions they held. In our belief system, different colors signified and were associated with certain directions. Our time with the women was kept to a polite minimum and it was fine with me. None of them spoke of anything that I considered important. It was mostly chit-chat. Also, each woman was delighted to see and meet Chahal. Most of our time was spent while the women rubbed her belly or scratched her under the chin or behind her ears.

By the time we reached the last Chuchmox, Chahal had become accustomed to being adored. I could feel her narcissistic pleasure at being told how lovely she was. If it kept up, I was afraid that I would have an egomaniacal cat on my hands.

Afterwards, the Cabicacmotz let me know that the only thing, which was required, was that I meet a member of each direction. It was a ritual of acquaintanceship.

When we were leaving the last Chuchmox, the women's twins showed up, walking past us. I expected him to comment on the fact that the women had twins, but he did not.

I questioned him about it, asking him if the women were natural twins or if they were like Ahtoobalvar. He told me that the women were not twins at all and that they only appeared so because they were dressed alike. Each direction had a homogeneity to it, which the women fostered and exploited in order to trick onlookers into believing that there were only a few Chuchmox and that they were merely for show.

"They act like decorations because of their colorful dress and their poses, but they are truly fearsome warriors," he said. "You have seen them around all of your life, Zaki. Tell me, how many of them do you think there are?"

"Well, I guess that there must be twenty-four of them. They alternate, obviously, so they can take over when one of them becomes tired. So, one to relieve the other one."

"There are three-hundred-eighty-four women. Forty-eight for each direction. Always. Never more, never less. You didn't think there were so many because everyone has been led to believe that the Chuchmox are only a regional or tribal custom, an artistic ploy to decorate our platforms and temples. If one does not consider those of our tribe who have foresight, one would properly conclude that they are our first line of defense. You thought the Chuchmox replacing the others were their twins. They are not twins and they are not doubled up as Ahtoobalvar was. Consider this, the security of our tribe is in the hands of women, those sweet docile creatures who bring children into this world and feed us from their very breasts. Our nurturers are our protectors."

"People from other tribes visit here," he continued. "They become so enchanted with our Chuchmox that they incorporate the concept of elaborately dressed women to adorn their own temples. It is an embellishment that they like, never realizing the deadly role our own Chuchmox play. Yes, they are introduced to the idea of the directions and the color scheme pertaining to it, but they consider that mere superstition and aesthetic custom. They don't grasp the esoteric intricacies involved. How they dress actually has no real value other than disguising their numbers, Zaki. It is vitally important to veil one's true numbers from one's enemies. If someone who has lived here, all of his life, believes that there are only two or four women for every direction, then we are hiding ourselves very well. That means that we have well over three-hundred hidden warriors."

"How can you be so sure that the other tribe's Chuchmox are not doing the same things ours do?"

"We have spies everywhere. Our older women regularly travel to other tribes and converse with theirs. They will pick up any irregularities. The one thing that is a problem is that stillness and silence lead the human into the left."

I interrupted him at that point because I was confused about his use of the word "left." It didn't have any special meaning for me and it sounded like nonsense, but I knew that the Cabicacmotz never spoke nonsense. I felt that his whole explanation would be meaningless without a clarification and asked for one.

"To call our women the Chuchmox is very important. In our language, many words have variant meanings. To us, their name means women of the left. When we explain it to people of other tribes, we tell them that it means feeble-minded women. We tell them that we put women, who are not too bright, up as ornaments. We tell them we feel that everyone should have a role in the society and that a problem came up when we had a few women who were lovely, but stupid as sand, and that we created pseudo-vocations for them since they had no other skills other than being attractive physically. They come away with the idea that our Chuchmox are pretty morons and those are the women in their tribes that they install as Chuchmox. They actually think that we are humanitarians, and then they take those ideas unto themselves and undermine their own societies."

"Well, that's interesting, but you still haven't explained to me what being of the left means," I complained.

"Zaki, when you look out at the world and see it, where does your perception originate from?" he asked me. "Where is your sense of self?"

I had no idea what he was talking about, but I told him that it came from my eyes.

"No. No," he said as he came up behind me and put his hands on my shoulders and directed me to look towards the Temple of the Sun. "Make an effort to consciously know where the Zaki that is looking at the temple resides. Where is the part that you consider you feeling where it is coming from?"

His convoluted sentence actually made perfect sense to me, somehow. I looked towards the north and watched the sun glinting off the stones of the temple. I followed the line of my sight back into my skull, past my eyes and into my head. I felt that I was a pinpoint of perception and that that pinpoint was on my right cheekbone, where I felt that it jutted out the most. It was a most peculiar sensation of smallness. It surprised me that I did not feel a stronger connection with my eyes, since I had assumed that the sensation of self would be in my eyes. I described what I experienced to him.

"That feeling of where you are can be moved, Zaki. You will have to learn to move it. The Chuchmox have. They've moved that sense of self to the left side of their bodies. You will too. It is a necessary maneuver, at times, when we want to identify those who want to coerce us and when we want to stand away and be unaffected from their undue influence."

"How could someone coerce us merely because our sense of self is on the right?" I asked.

He laughed then and told me, "Zaki, you always trick me into exploring concepts that are beyond your current comprehension. This will definitely have to wait. Besides, the Chuchmox are the proper authorities when it comes to the awareness of the left. Trick them into telling you about it."

"It's not as if I tried to get you to tell me secret stuff," I explained to rid myself of the faint feeling of guilt his words caused in me. "It's that you sometimes use words that confuse me and I want to know what you're talking about." A thought struck me and I forced myself to ask him about it even though he didn't want to answer any more of my questions. "Isn't there the chance that they won't explain it to me? I mean, when do other boys get trained by the Chuchmox normally?"

"It all depends on the student. Some boys go after the first year is done, others more. Sometimes they don't train the student at all and other times students have gone to them after they've been studying for twelve years. That last figure is the longest I've heard about and it was before my time as the Cabicacmotz, by the way."

"What happens when the older Chuchmox travel to other tribes? Don't they get suspicious?"

"What happens is that they pretend to be beautiful, yet dull-witted, women who have married wealthy men. It is not an uncommon scenario. Then they get together with supposedly similar women and trade stories. They talk about how difficult it was to keep a straight face when a person tried to get them to break their blank looks and other such tales. Which leads us into the reason our women check up on the other tribe's women, silence and stillness can lead a person into another awareness that we would prefer other tribes not have. Our Chuchmox can block out clowns and whatnot from their fields of vision to keep their composure. They do it by concentrating or by directing their attention whenever and wherever they want. We don't want the other tribes to learn how to do any such thing. Our women give those pretend Chuchmox valuable lessons in mediocrity. They tell them to laugh themselves silly the day before their duties or they tell them that the best thing to do is to imagine a worm crawling in the sun or that an ugly man is trying to catch their attention. They will tell them anything but the truth. They will never give them the innocuous sounding advice of emptying their minds of all thought. That chore, which sounds so simple and irrelevant, can open up unimaginable vistas of perception. Instead, they reinforce the belief that talking to oneself about inanities is the way to be a good and composed Chuchmox. That's why we send our women out as informal ambassadors and mentors."

"But what would happen if another tribe's Chuchmox started developing new abilities?" I asked.

"We try to prevent or be aware of that, but mistakes happen. Normally what occurs is that the woman is considered touched in the head. When she tells a person in authority what she is experiencing, the authority first considers the source, a pretty imbecile. Such a person is unreliable because a pretty fool is still a fool. They convince her that she needs to take a rest and give her a vacation for a while. The woman forgets what happened after a time. The fact that she was ignored by someone she considers an authority reinforces the belief that what happened to her was unimportant or the first signs of mental derangement and she takes steps to not repeat what she did out of fear of becoming the local crazy lady. If our women find a woman like that, they give them advice on how to prevent that from reoccurring."

I was rather impressed by the report of how well our women understood their enemies. His words were broadening my definition of how women were. They sounded like cunning and crafty adversaries. It was a bit daunting and inspiring at the same time. I was glad that our women were ours and not another tribe's, yet they still scared me. I was mystified about one thing and asked him, "Why is clearing the mind of all thought so important? Why wouldn't reasoning things out in one's mind be better?"

"The reason you were able to disappear when you were gazing," he said, "was because your mind became silent. If you had been talking to yourself about what you were seeing or experiencing, nothing would have happened. You do one or the other with your energy. Save your internal chatter for when you have to keep your mind fully on this world."

"But I didn't see anything." I whined. "I don't remember anything happening to me. All I did was fall asleep."

"Just because you don't remember what happened does not mean that nothing happened."

I felt that he was accusing me of something, but I wasn't sure of what. It made me nervous and I deliberately changed the subject. "Enough of all that. When am I going to see your teammates?"

He gestured to the right and told me that his team was at a tent nearby; they were preparing themselves for the contest. I asked him why he was not there getting ready also. He told me that he was obligated to complete his duties as my guide and that there was still plenty of time for him to get dressed and prepare before the game. He also warned me that the men were likely to be rowdy and a bit crude and that it was typical for athletes to behave like that before a big game.

He led us to a large tent. It was a simple affair of plain muslin, but it kept the men out of the sun and away from the prying eyes of their fans.

When we entered the enclosure, the men hollered wildly at the Cabicacmotz and for Chahal. They greeted him enthusiastically and made optimistic statements about how they were sure to win because of the presence of Chahal.

I must have looked bewildered by their words because one of the men, a lean dark man, told me, "It's a sign, man. Take them when you can get them." Then he slapped me roughly on the back.

The Cabicacmotz introduced me as his student to all of his teammates. They seemed to be a jovial bunch and they treated me with comforting informality.

One man saw me watching him as he applied resin to a terribly long rectangle of leather. My eyes were drawn to one of the longer sides; it was sliced in strips while the other side was plain and straight. The strips were dyed alternately with yellow and black. "Come here, boy," he said. "Do you know what I'm doing?"

I shook my head and he informed me that he was keeping the leather supple, yet non-slippery, because he would soon wrap it around himself to protect his hips and waist from his yoke. He referred to the leather as his kilt. The yoke would rest upon his hips, around his waist. It was used in the ballgame as an instrument for stopping, propelling, or bouncing the ball. It was the most important tool in the game. Every other customary piece of equipment was extraneous and could be dispensed with, except for the yoke.

He pointed to the yoke, which was on the ground. It was an elaborately carved ring of yellow polished stone with an irregular inner opening. The top of the yoke was smooth and polished, but its outer edges were carved to resemble intertwining jaguars. It was lovely. The outer top edge curled up mildly; the slant was barely discernible. From the inner edge to the outer, it was two handbreadths. The thickness of the stone was a handbreadth. He told me that I could touch it and I ran my hands over it, admiring its smooth carvings. I gaped when I tried to lift it. He laughed.

"Now do you see why I need a nice leather kilt between me and that monster?"

I nodded dumbly and questioned him about why the inner opening was so odd. The opening was an oval joined with a small half circle. The half circle was in the middle of the flatter part of the oval.

"Here," he said as he handed me the leather. Feeling as soft as kidskin, it moved like cloth. "Help me wrap up and I'll show you."

He wore a loincloth without any visible ties or wrappings in the cloth. It was unusual because usually loincloths were tied at the sides of the hips. He noticed my attention and confirmed that it was sewn, telling me that he did not need any bulges poking into his skin under the leather, especially with the weight of the yoke upon him.

He directed me to wrap him in a clockwise manner. I tried to place the edge with the cut strips up, but he told me that the strips must point towards the ground and that they would allow him to move his legs without any difficulty. The top edge of the kilt was right underneath his pectoral muscles and went down past the tops of his thighs. When he was wrapped three times, he told me to stop. The remainder of the leather, he bent backwards and curled counterclockwise into a roll. Then he told me to hold the roll of the kilt in place while he stepped into the yoke.

He tried to bend down and the leather stymied him. "Crap, you wrapped me up a bit too good, even with the strips being cut so long. Hold on a moment," he said as he took hold of the roll himself and did a bit of bending to stretch out the binding.

When he was able to move and bend freely, he again directed me to hold on to the roll. He stepped into the yoke and stooped down to pick it up. When it was up to his waist, he held it there and slowly tried to pull himself into position. It was clear to me that he was trying to move the yoke so that the smaller part of the opening would accommodate the thick roll of leather. I asked him if he wanted me to help him hold up the yoke.

"No way, kid. That's a sure step towards mashed up toes."

It was a bit unflattering, but I had to agree with him. He called over a couple of his teammates. I saw that their yokes were similar to his, but were carved from hard wood instead. When they were at either side of him and holding his yoke, he told me to let go of the roll. He held it in place as he shimmied himself into position. Then he fitted the roll to fill the smaller section. After that, he was snug inside his yoke.

"When the hell are you going to get rid of this damned thing?" one of the men who helped him said. "You'll either break your back or end up with flat toes one of these days and where will we be? Safety begins with your gaming equipment. Wood works as well, if not better. It's lighter."

"I refuse to turn into a sissy," the man with the stone yoke said.

"You'll feel like a sissy if you have to be carried everywhere on a palanquin because this thing fell on your toes."

"Oh shut up and thanks for helping me," he muttered.

One of the men with the wooden yokes told me not to turn into a stubborn fool like the man with the stone yoke. "Every one of us, but him, has switched to wood. One of these days he'll be sorry."

A beetle-browed muscular man yelled, "Hey! What about when that guy from the tribe to the south's yoke broke during the game and he cut his ass on the shards? Remember that?"

Everybody howled with laughter at the memory and I laughed with them, imagining such a sight.

When it was quieter, I asked one of the men why he wore a leather kilt like the man with the stone yoke.

"Different materials, different hazards," he said. "Splinters. In case you haven't noticed, all yokes are the same shape inside. See? The roll fits into the smaller part of the oval. The roll of the kilt has the added benefit of keeping the yoke in place." He got a blank look on his face before continuing. "I must call the men. Excuse me." He yelled to all of the men to gather around him. Again, he looked blank for a moment.

"What did you see?" the Cabicacmotz asked him with an expectant look.

"The Pumas have something new, something we haven't seen before. They are very sneaky, those cats. The shortest man on the team has a new trick; his yoke is not secure and immovable. It spins and he uses the spin to propel the ball in unexpected ways. We need to watch him and learn how he can make the ball move. It will seem haphazard to the audience, but he knows exactly what he is doing. All of his moves are planned and deliberate. He is not the type of man who leaves anything, which he himself can control, to chance. They have been planning this in secret and practicing for a long time. Every member of the team knows how the ball will move when he bounces it, depending on how he moves. They wish to become the official royal team."

"What team doesn't? Can you see any more about how the ball moves in relation to his yoke?" a man in the back asked loudly.

The man with foresight shook his head sadly and said, "No. No more do I see."

The men debated for a while about what they could do and what strategy they would use. Finally, one of the men proposed the idea that they should challenge his yoke, before the game began, with the arbiter. They doubted that it would be granted and steeled themselves for a refusal.

They commented on how no negotiations were allowed for the games that took place during the festival. The treat about the festival game was that all special talents of the players would be put into play during the game to display to the tribe the genius of the men. They thought that a challenge about the gaming equipment might be entertained, as it did not necessarily pertain to the abilities of the players.

"In any case, they will feel a moment of uncertainty and they will know that we are on to their tricks. It will deprive them of their sense of surprise."

"What if it's only a trick to get us to concentrate our focus away from something else?" another man asked.

The conclusion about that was that they would not have put so much effort into occulting the short man's yoke for such a long time and that it must truly be their secret strategy.

The Cabicacmotz instructed the men to pay attention to the man to learn his moves so they wouldn't be taken further by surprise. He told them that he would divide his attention between the man and his teammates and that he would relay anything new or important. The men seemed satisfied with that plan.

Right then, a few other people entered the tent. A tall stooped man came in, followed by two boys. I saw that it was Hac and Cham. I smiled when I saw them. They immediately looked over at me and waved. Their guide walked them over to where I was and greeted the men.

Hac and Cham's guide addressed the Cabicacmotz. "I leave them under your care and with their fellow student," he said as he nodded to me. Then he left.

The Cabicacmotz told us to help the men with their gaming equipment, should they ask, and indicated that we should be at ease until we left for the ball court.

Only a couple of the men needed to be rewrapped in their skins. Hac and Cham helped them since I had already performed a wrapping of the kilt.

After that, the placing of the sandals on the men commenced. The sandals were worn and used. Hac asked them why they had such ragged shoes and several men explained that they needed sandals that did not chafe them or cause blisters and that only well-worn shoes would do. All of the shoes were different. Some men preferred padding on the inner part, others the outer part. The men were very patient in their explanations. The men who had padding on the inner part of the shoe were accustomed to using that part of their foot to hit or bounce the ball during games where kicking the ball was allowed. Such a thing would not be permissible for a formal game, such as the one being held today. They wore the shoes because they were comfortable in them. Each shoe was specifically tailored to the man's customary moves. They commented on how they could know another player's moves by how he guarded or left exposed each part of his body. Such observations were vitally important when it came time to assess teams that they were unfamiliar with.

Then the knee and shin guards came. Again, each piece was individual to the player. Short leather wrappings were placed under the actual guards, in order to protect the skin from the rough bindings. A few men had strange wooden pieces, similar to the yokes around their waists, which would stick out from the knee. They snickered with glee when we asked them what the functions of those pieces of wood were. They explained that it was bad form to hit or injure the opposing team's players with their hands or feet, but that no one could fault them if the other team's players ran into certain obstacles. The gaming equipment was outside of those rules that prohibited injury. The personal equipment could be used in whatever form to give them the advantage. It was a sly skirting of the rules.

215

The next piece of the gaming equipment was the hollow knob, which covered the top of the kilt's roll. The men topped their rolls with knobs, made from wood, gold, or stone, which were carved in morbid head shapes. There was a slit on the cylindrical part of the knob, which allowed it to fit over the roll. They filled the concave inner part of the knobs with a gum that would harden once the knobs were placed at the end of the roll. It was decorative, yet functional.

Once all of the knobs were placed, we were directed to help the men with their collars. These were elaborate affairs, which were fastened around the neck. They, often, went all the way down to the tops of the leather wrappings of the kilts. Some were soft and padded. Others were made from gold, beads, or gems. Some were even made from feathers. The only thing, which made them resemble each other, was that they were all in golden yellow and black to reflect the colors of their team icon, the jaguar.

The next step in the vesturing of the men was the headband and panache. All of the men wore headbands or turbans. The sheer choice of materials used to make the headbands was overwhelming. One man's band was made from stucco over wood, while another only used cloth. Many used gold and sported brilliant gemstones. Some were colorful and some were plain, but none was the same.

Once the headband was on, the panache was arranged. The panache consisted of feathers, which adorned the headband. Our help with the panaches was amateurish and clumsy. It must have been sadly apparent to the Jaguars because, finally, one of the men whistled sharply and several matronly women entered the tent. They quickly went to work arranging the feathers on the men.

The panaches were blue-green, yellow, and black. The black was not a pure black. I noticed that it was the iridescent black of crow feathers, which often reflected blue, at certain angles. It was as if the blue was hiding within the black. This blended harmoniously with the brilliant feathers of the quitzal bird. The rest of the feathers were a golden yellow. When the women finished, the men were arrayed magnificently. The edges were of quitzal feathers while the inner portions properly resembled the skins of jaguars, except for the effect of the iridescence of the black crow feathers.

One of the men commented, "Sometimes boys do not have the light artistic hand of women when it comes to the arranging of feathers. A delicate touch is needed. It is something that must be practiced. Don't feel bad, boys, that we had to call in the women, please." Many men nodded their agreement with his words.

We were astounded that any of the men would feel a need to spare our feelings. We were lowly students, after all. The gesture made us very happy. We three exchanged a look loaded with our thoughts; we felt very fortunate to have found ourselves in the company of such honorable and accomplished men.

The final accoutrements to the men's dress were the arm guards. Like the knee and shin guards, we first had to wrap parts of the men's arms with thin leather wrappings. Over that, we fastened the arm guards. These were made from one of two materials: woven reeds or woven palm stalks. Inside, they were filled with padding.

Our roles were finished, but the men were not done with their preparations. A large group of artisans entered and proceeded to paint the bodies of the players and some of their equipment. A few unusual things were painted on the equipment, such as symbols or stylized renderings that I was unfamiliar with, but the bodies of the men and their kilts were invariably painted with the mottled spots of the jaguar.

During that, we three were left to our own devices. We spent the time exchanging stories about what we would be studying. There were some differences in our curriculums. Little Hac would be studying astronomy, healing plants, being an eagle, acrobatic fighting, and the mystery of stones. Cham would learn hunting and skins, poisoning, spying, and being a crow, acrobatic fighting and about the seven-pronged leaf from the Etamanel Evan. Cham complained that he was given a pathetic and sissy bird to learn about and that he was jealous of Hac's bird.

"Why are you both here with the Jaguars?" I asked them.

Hac answered, "We are to learn how to play the game."

Cham quipped that it was so obvious that it didn't occur to them to spell it out for me and that I must have been half asleep to ask so stupid a question.

I rolled my eyes at that and told them that it had sounded like, from their guide's words, that he was only delivering them to the Cabicacmotz because he was sick and tired of babysitting them all day.

"No such luck, Zaki. We will be right here with you to make sure that you don't become the team's little mascot instead of a real player. Imagine that. You'll actually have to put what you learn into practice with us around," Cham said.

Hac looked like he wanted to laugh at his brother's words, but restrained himself. Instead, he asked me what I would be learning. I was a bit embarrassed to tell them that I had so few subjects. I told them that I would learn from the Etamanel Evan, Ahtoobalvar, the Chuchmox, and that I would learn the art of the jaguar.

They didn't seem to think that I had an easy curriculum. They didn't know anything about Ahtoobalvar and I had to explain it to them. When I mentioned the Balam Ch'ab, they were visibly ill at ease and expressed the belief that it was a bit creepy to learn how to become a killing fiend.

I didn't have time to needle Cham about the hypocrisy of his opinion since he was poised to become a poisoner, because Chahal growled her displeasure at that moment. The boys' faces reddened in shame.

"Sorry about that, Chahal," Cham said to her. "We know you aren't like that, we should have remembered how nice you are. Be a good influence on our friend, here." He leaned down to scratch her under the chin and she allowed it.

Cham's words made me very happy. It was, literally, the first time someone had referred to me as his "friend." I became more optimistic than ever about my schooling, already it had granted me some human company.

The Cabicacmotz came over then and placed a hand on my shoulder, saying, "Be more careful with your words, boys. You will also be learning from me." Then he walked a few paces away. He stood with his back to us, facing his team, with his hands resting on his yoke.

The boys blanched at his words and familiarity with me. They looked at me with apprehension. Cham made a comical face of dread behind the Cabicacmotz' back.

Without looking behind, the Cabicacmotz said, "Stop that, Cham."

Cham straightened his bottom lip into a wry expression of remorse and mumbled an apology.

"Well, boys," the Cabicacmotz said as he turned around. "Are you ready to lead us into battle? It's time that we leave for the ball court." He told us that Chahal would walk before all of the team and us and that we should follow her to the courtyard. He told us that they would walk behind us and that it was customary for the team's acolytes or students to precede the actual team. Chahal seemed to know the way and confidently led us out of the tent and towards the ball court.

When I glanced back at them lined up, I noticed that all of the members of the team had adorned themselves in some way with jaguar pelts. The elaborate headdresses they wore accented their armbands and other gaming accouterments. They looked very regal and fearsome. In addition, each man carried a carving in his hand, a totem. There were sections in the carvings, which were hollowed out to allow the men to grasp them, and the forward sections matched the knobs on their rolls.

Fans yelled greetings to the team. Occasionally, some people would merely watch the team without expressing any good wishes to them, but those people hung back. I concluded that they were fans of the opposing team who were too timid to wish the royal team bad luck to their faces.

As I had that thought, a man who was at the edge of the crowd came forward to push the boys and me. Chahal growled viciously as she turned to face him and the Cabicacmotz came out of nowhere and struck the man across the shoulders with the carved totem he carried. He directed us to keep going despite the delay. When the man fell to the ground, Chahal raked him with her claws across his stomach, drawing blood. Then the whole team walked over and past him, paying him no attention. I saw the man's friends pull the man from the path. He stood up with a hurt look of confusion and I saw that Chahal's claws had merely skimmed the surface of his skin. I was glad she had not eviscerated him.

From then on, Chahal would growl at the onlookers to prevent another occurrence of that nature. Everyone was quite impressed. They would shrink back with delighted looks on their faces or in fear. For a long time, it seemed that the only sound from the bystanders was an oohing sound.

When we had passed through the mob and entered the recess of the ball court, I saw that the other team was already there. They looked at Chahal with anger and she roared a growl at them. It was so vicious and menacing that they all swallowed their spit.

The crowd cheered rowdily when they saw Chahal. I noticed many men quicken to place bets on the game and others lifting their children up on their shoulders so they could see. It was a similar set up to how the dance of the Cranes was. The closest people sat, behind them came the kneelers and those in the back had to stand. The ball court had the added convenience of being in between two ridged hills, so that everyone in the audience had an extra bit of elevation between them and the person in front of them. We entered the manmade gully where the game was played. The crowd was above the court looking down. People in the back of the throng would occasionally jump up to peer over the crowd's heads, despite the hill.

The Cabicacmotz joined us where we stood. "Zaki, it's permissible to climb the steps in the ball court to reach where your father is sitting. Climb up there and sit with him now, please." He waved towards the area where my father and his retinue sat.

"What about us?" Cham asked.

"Follow him. What else?" the Cabicacmotz said as he walked off.

"Where's your father, Zaki?" Hac asked me.

I pointed to where he sat and he waved at us from his mat. Hac and Cham's eyes widened and they giggled nervously. I felt somewhat embarrassed that my father was such an important person, but they would have to discover it eventually. I did not feel shame about my father; rather I felt regret that our social classes were so distant. I didn't want them to treat me as a person who could never under-stand them or get along with them. They were complex thoughts that had never occurred to me before.

"Oh, we can't," Hac quietly said.

"Shut up, Hac," Cham said as he elbowed his brother in the ribs. "Go on up, Zaki, and we'll follow you."

The crowd fell silent as we all walked to the middle of the ball court and began climbing the steep steps, with Chahal leading the way.

The field was long and grassy at its base. Beside it, and also included as part of the court, there were a series of seven stone steps at either side. In the middle step, at the midpoint of the field, there was a sculptured stone facade where the final goal was. It was a stone circle and the ball would have to pass through it for the team to score the final goal in the game. It was understood that this would be a game where that goal was utilized. At either end of the court were stone goalposts to indicate where the other goals would have to pass through. The ball court ran from east to west.

My father was sitting above the northern final goal. We climbed up and he stood, greeting us enthusiastically. Hac and Cham were grinning from ear to ear. My father introduced himself to them, correctly identifying each boy despite never having met them. He made a place for us around him, much to the chagrin of the people who had previously been seated beside him. He placed Chahal to his left. The person beside her was visibly annoyed and apprehensive at having to sit next to her, but she only settled herself down and looked down into the ball court. I sat to my father's right. Hac was beside me and Cham sat next to him. It seemed to be the best arrangement since I didn't want Hac to feel left out and Cham was loud enough as it was. My father's guards sat behind him.

"I hear that you had a good show today," my father whispered to me. "But watch out for that moron, the Etamanel Evan."

I nodded and began to ask him why I didn't have more classes, as Hac and Cham did. He held up his hand as he shifted his attention to the ball court. I stopped talking.

Both teams were lined up on the field. The Pumas faced us and the Jaguars stood with their backs to us, facing the other team.

Because they were not the royal team, the Pumas were not permitted to adorn their panaches with the feathers of the quitzal bird. Where the Jaguars had blue-black feathers, the Pumas had white. They were almost uniformly a soft yellow color in their dress.

Suddenly, a flash of light sparked in the middle of the playing field. The smoke from the flash obscured my view of the Pumas' captain and the men around him. When the smoke cleared, a man carrying a hatchet in one hand and a cone in the other appeared in the middle of the field. He was dressed all in red, even to his headdress.

"Tell me everything later, Zaki. The Popol Uinac Pahom Tzalatz, councilor of the ball court, is here. He is the arbiter of the game and we must listen to his announcements. They might be important," he said with a shrug. "I can't see how, though, since this is the one game of the year where we demand that the ball players use all of their talents."

The man in red, the arbiter with the long title, called the captains of the teams forward to where he stood. He held up a cone to his mouth and loudly spoke, "The Jaguars have challenged the gaming equipment of a member of the Pumas. Captain, state your case." He handed the cone to the Cabicacmotz.

The cone he spoke into was brown. It was made of the same material we used for informal scrolls; it was made from shredded and flattened pieces of bark and sap. The making of it was common knowledge among the lower classes, since they produced it. I didn't know how to make

224

it. Soft bark was stripped and mixed with sap, which served as a glue or binding for the bark. The sap was boiled, I believe. It may have had other ingredients, but the knowledge of the process was never spelled out for me, as it was a common and easily available product. Afterwards, it was placed on flat stones, a roller was passed over the paste to flatten it, and it was left to harden. I was accustomed to seeing that part of the process. It was pliable and often used for short-term record keeping. It had the disadvantage of being vulnerable to water. Books were made from agave paper, but they were more expensive and not in common use by the untitled public.

The Cabicacmotz spoke into the cone and said, "The Jaguars challenge the use of a non-regulation yoke on that member of the Pumas." He pointed to the short man at the end of the line for the Pumas. "He does not have a roll of leather upon his navel. We believe that it is an unacceptable adaptation of the gaming equipment and that it will change the dynamics of the game, as it is currently played. We ask that his yoke be excluded from this game." He handed the cone back to the arbiter who announced that the Pumas' captain would rebut the challenge.

The Pumas' captain received the cone and said, "It is a yoke, pure and simple. It could be said that such a yoke was an antecedent to the yokes we wear today and merely because one of our team prefers an antiquated yoke is no reason to disallow it. The Jaguars have a team-member who insists on using a stone yoke which causes the ball to move more rapidly, at times, than the wooden ones all of us use. In any case, the time for negotiations is over and this challenge is improper. The Jaguars had adequate time to gather intelligence on our team's gaming equipment. They have had a whole cycle of the sun to prepare for this day. We ask that the challenge be denied." With that, he handed the cone back to the arbiter.

"Decision," announced the arbiter. "I find for the Pumas. All yokes are as different as the individual players who carve them. It is permissible to alter the form of the yoke, as it is also an expression of the player's spirit. The challenge is proper in that it only concerns the gaming equipment and does not seek to limit the skills of the opposing team's players. I will remind both teams that they should use all of their talents. In this game, the ball is not permitted to bounce upon or touch the earthen floor. Play as you will!"

Both captains returned to their teams. The Cabicacmotz calmly rejoined his team. The captain of the Pumas had a smirk on his face and his team-members nodded to him.

The arbiter announced that the Jaguars would take the eastern and northern goals, while the Pumas would have the western and southern goals. The Pumas did not seem to like their assigned goals and scowled. I didn't understand why and wanted to question my father about it, but the game began before I could ask him about it.

A few men from each team walked off the court, to their respective ends, since they were replacement players. Because the ball court was one for crowded games, the field was able to accommodate more men than the smaller courts, which could be played with only two players per team if desired. Each team had thirteen players on the field. Even so, there was still plenty of room for the men to run in. The field was the size of the informal games I had seen, so it did not seem strange to me. I had seen the smaller courts, but had not watched any games played within them yet. I briefly wondered why they would bother having the smaller courts if people could not watch the games as easily as they could here.

The teams gathered around in a circle. The captains were at opposite midpoints of the circle, facing each other. The arbiter still stood in the center of the field. He held a rubber ball in his hand. After that, the captains left their places in the circle and moved forward into the middle. They knelt facing each other, each with their left knee on the ground and their right knee supporting their yokes. They stared at each other with open hostility.

The arbiter asked them if they were ready. They both nodded. The arbiter tossed the ball into the air and the Cabicacmotz and the Pumas' captain jumped up and tried to bump each other out of the way so that they could catch the ball on their yokes.

The captain of the Pumas won that particular advantage. He bounced the ball on his yoke. I saw him exchange glances with his teammates as he determined the best man to pass the ball to. Without warning, he twisted his body so that one of his hands touched the ground as he jerked his hip to propel the ball towards their goal at the western end.

The Jaguars were unable to intercept the ball and the goal was won because none of our players guarded the goalposts. The lack of planning made me wince with shame. The fans hissed their displeasure while the other's fans cheered. I saw the Cabicacmotz scold a couple of players for not stopping the ball. After that, those two players hung around the goal as if they were stuck in place.

The other team mimicked the move. It surprised me that such an obvious lack of strategy occurred and I wanted to think that the Jaguars were trying to lull the other team into a mindset of overconfidence or into a belief that they were incompetent.

At either end of the field, scorekeepers stood. Now, a scorekeeper at the western end held up a white plaque. The ones at the eastern end held nothing up, but I could see that the plaques they would eventually put up were yellow. They were on the ground as the scorekeepers milled around with nothing to do. The replacement players behind them nervously paced.

Again, the arbiter put the ball into play, but this time instead of beginning at the middle of the field, he threw the ball up in the air a short distance away from the western goal. It seemed a bit unfair that the Jaguars would be penalized after losing the goal, but the game favors the last team with a goal. As in life, it acknowledges winners.

This time, the Cabicacmotz caught the ball on his yoke. He bounced it repeatedly upon his yoke, moving his pelvis to cause the ball to move. He ran bouncing the ball towards the end of the field while teammates yelled at him to pass the ball or urged him to score a goal. When it was clear that he was planning to do it all himself, his teammates ran interference for him, jostling Pumas out of the way. They need not have bothered because there was no man who could match his sheer speed. He darted around men like lightning.

Then when he was near the eastern goal, he slowed and turned around, facing the west. I couldn't help myself; I yelled at him to keep going. My father put his hand on my shoulder to prevent me from standing up in agitation.

The two men from the Pumas, serving as goalkeepers, moved to the center to protect the eastern goal. They focused on the Cabicacmotz and shifted their weight repeatedly from their right feet to their left. They were not in perfect harmony. Occasionally, a gap would appear, leaving a small, yet clear, path to the goal.

Suddenly, the Cabicacmotz performed a back flip. His movements were quick, but I caught them and could see them. When his hands touched the ground, his body was arched backwards, he jerked his pelvis towards the upper part of his torso, and the ball was propelled into the goal, past the goalkeepers. The crowd went nuts.

It amazed me that he was able to know the perfect time to send the ball towards the goal since he could not possibly have seen when the Pumas' goalkeepers left an opening. He had his back turned to them the whole time.

A woman sitting behind Cham commented to her friend, at her left, that the woman who got the Cabicacmotz was a very fortunate woman. I had to agree with her, a woman would be very lucky to marry such a skilled ball player. When I nodded back to her, she gave me a confused and almost horrified look. Her expression changed when I stated that ball players often became wealthy and that their wives did not have to worry about them as much because their jobs required them to spend a lot of time on the field with other men. She laughed shyly and whispered something I could not hear to her friend who began to giggle like a little girl.

Movement pulled my attention back to the field and I saw the short man, the one with the peculiar yoke, take control of the ball. Even though he was at the eastern end of the field, he was able to send it clear across the field and pass it to one of his teammates who promptly sent it through the western goal. His moves had been very rapid although he was not using any unusual powers that I could see.

After that, the game became markedly violent. I saw the Jaguars exchange glances with one another and I felt that they told each other to keep the ball away from the short man. The next toss up went to the Pumas, but a Jaguar intercepted a pass when he crowded the Puma who caught the ball. The Jaguar's roll and knob had come to life. I saw the knob's head, which was shaped like a snake, transform and undulate with life. Then it actually bit the Puma. I heard the man scream in pain as it sunk its teeth into the flesh of his upper arm. The Jaguar with the snake knob passed it along the field to another teammate. There were a few passes and finally the Jaguars scored another goal.

A short timeout was called in order to remove the in-jured Puma and send in a replacement. Two attendants walked him away by placing their shoulders underneath the man's armpits. They delivered him to one of the healers that awaited him behind the western goal.

For the next toss-up, the arbiter threw the ball upwards at the western end. I wondered aloud about why the ball was not tossed up at the eastern end and my father told me that a deliberate injury to an opposing team's player automatically demanded that the injured team receive the advantage as a sort of payment for the harm.

The passes were a bit slower and more predictable when the men wore standard yokes. The short man from the Pumas tried to put his yoke back into play, but the Jaguars were doing anything they could to prevent him from getting near the ball.

Back and forth, goals were made. The players were truly devilish and canny. I lost track of the individual abilities of the players because of the frequency of replacement players and the fact that everything happened so quickly.

One man would bounce the ball against his yoke with his handheld totem and other times its face would transform itself into a snarling animal. Another was able to become invisible; I could only see the ball when it bounced away from his yoke. One man would throw phantom decoys of the ball, much to the chagrin of the arbiter. A particularly nimble player would use both of his feet to bounce the ball against the underside of his yoke, which made everybody laugh because it looked so ridiculous. Unfortunately, for the Pumas, it was virtually impossible to steal the ball away from him.

Several men grew tails like those of their respective teams and used them to grab or snatch the ball out of the air or away from other's yokes. One man turned to flame to discourage anyone else from stealing the ball. A man from the Pumas could walk on air and ran above the heads of many players. One Jaguar was able to turn himself into any member of the Pumas and steal the ball in that manner. Another man was able to surround himself with protective lightning.

The teams were frightening and glorious to watch. One man could plunge everyone into a cloud of darkness, while another could temporarily blind everyone with flashes of white light. It was quite disorienting. Much to the delight of the crowd, and to the irritation of the opposing team, one man was able to become spiny like a cactus.

Two men were evenly matched; a Jaguar could sprout the wings of an eagle and fly, while a Puma suddenly had the wings of a bat. Another could push others away with his mind. Another could stomp on the ground and cause ripples in the earth, which would trip the players up. A few men on either team were able to bring to life the carvings in their yokes; these would chew up the yokes of players that got too close to them, but they were ineffective against the Jaguar with the stone yoke.

One Puma was able to call forth vines from the ground to trip up the Jaguars. Another man was able to blow strong winds that would blow the balls away from the yokes of the opposing team. The crowd gasped when one of the players summoned wasps from the air to surround him. He sent a couple to bite the players of the Pumas, but the arbiter quickly put a stop to that.

It was impossible to guess the abilities beforehand. One man's hand totem could be used to punch or bounce the ball as well as to push a member of the opposing team. At times, the totems would come to life and then, unpredicta-bly to me, they were inanimate once more.

The men's mundane moves were not as dramatic as their special abilities, but the crowd seemed to appreciate them as much. Sometimes the men would place both forearms together to catch and bounce the ball to a more advantageous position. Some men would use their yokes to roll themselves across the field. Other times they would spin the ball around their yokes, around and around their waists.

At times, I would have overlapping versions of scenes in my mind. At one point, a player hopped into the air over the heads of the opposing team. I saw a man hopping, yet I experienced a simultaneous version of the event, which showed the man with the giant feet of a hare. I felt that I was watching a hallucination and could not reconcile the two versions of the man's moves. The same thing occurred to me when one of the men bounced the ball with his panache. I would see the ball bouncing normally and other times I would see a sheer gelatinous mass or a tentacle move the ball upwards. When I would focus on the unusual scenes, I would experience a falling in the pit of my stomach that caused me to feel nauseous. I strained to keep to the more normal images.

Despite the efforts of the Jaguars to keep the ball from the short Puma, he was able to intercept a few passes and made two goals in succession. After that, the Jaguars became even more violent. The Jaguar assigned to guard the ball from getting to him would bump him out of the way, if the ball were passed to him. The Jaguar was taller and he was able to cover the short man's yoke with his own and take balls passed to him in that manner. From then on, the short man was unable to put his yoke into play.

The game went on and on until the Pumas had an advantage of two goals. By then, the crowd was truly wild. Hac and Cham were both nervously moving as they watched. Absorbed as they were in the game, they were unaware that I was even next to them.

There was a distant rumble and I looked up, along with everyone else, into the sky as a large thunderhead passed in front of the sun. The mood and energy of the crowd altered somehow. Now, there was an ominous feeling in the atmosphere. Even the arbiter who was about to toss the ball into the air stopped. Everything seemed to slow down.

I saw the arbiter toss the ball into the air as the air rumbled. The Cabicacmotz jumped, higher than the Pumas' captain did, and caught the ball with his yoke. Instead of moving towards the east, as he had done for the whole game, he passed it to the man with the stone yoke who immediately jumped onto the northern steps. Bouncing the ball on his yoke, he advanced to the middle step and bounced the ball high enough that it went over his head. I thought he had lost control of the ball until I saw it land on the back of his yoke, where he again bounced it repeatedly. With expert timing, he moved forward and landed on his hands and knees as the ball was up in the air. The moment it came down and was about to touch his back, he thrust his butt in the air, causing the yoke to send the ball towards the goal.

Distantly, I heard men on the field shouting, "No!" Then there was a terrible silence as the ball zoomed towards the circular goal. From my vantage point, the ball seemed to be almost the same size as the opening in the stone goal.

It may have been my imagination, but I saw the ball flutter and change speeds before it entered the circle and came out the other side. I immediately realized that intent had sent it charging forth and that when it had slowed it had been because the Pumas were intending that it not go through the hole.

Everyone in the crowd stood up and cheered, except for a few people. It seemed that the goal was so difficult and unusual that even fans of the Pumas felt compelled to cheer such a victory.

The Pumas seemed deflated. Their captain, with his head hung low, approached the arbiter in the field. He pulled the knob from the end of his kilt's roll and tossed it to the side. Then he stepped out of his yoke and let the kilt fall away from him to the ground. He knelt, before the man in red, facing the east.

All of his teammates lined up at the southern steps with depressed looks on their faces. The Jaguars were expressionless as they went and stood at the north.

Everyone was quiet; no one was cheering. I was unable to understand it.

My father whispered to us that we should not be afraid and that what was going to happen next was either going to be a magical feat or a quick death. We quickly understood his meaning and realized that the Pumas' captain was going to be killed on the spot. Our eyes went wide with horror.

Never before had I witnessed the execution of a ball player for having failed on the field. I had heard about such things, believing the stories to be rumors to frighten children, but I had never seen it or even suspected that it really took place. To see it be performed right before my eyes was too much for me, yet something kept me glued where I sat. Hac and Cham must have also been appalled, because they too were frozen in place.

A young man brought a bale of hay onto the field and the arbiter gently helped the captain place his head upon it, facing us in the north.

The arbiter pulled out the hatchet he wore suspended from the sash around his waist. Then he faced the king, with both palms holding the hatchet aloft. Then he walked towards the Cabicacmotz and stood before him as if offering the weapon to him. I saw the Cabicacmotz shake his head in refusal.

The arbiter returned to his place in the field. He spoke to the captain who was about to die. The captain said something back, but we could not hear their words. The arbiter lifted the hatchet high over his head with both hands.

The field became dark with the thunderhead over us, almost making it seem like night. The crowd began chanting, "Tulan. Tulan." Even I began to chant the name of our ancestral home; as if repeating its name could ward off the horror I was about to witness.

The arbiter whipped the axe down. I saw the captain close his eyes the moment before the blade struck him. It severed his head from his body and blood poured out of him like water from a fallen gourd.

The three of us boys looked at each other in disbelief. Hac leaned forward and vomited on the upper steps of the ball court in front of him. People were lucky that he was in the front row. Cham had no smart remarks left in him and it surprised me to see tears in his eyes. We looked at each other and a thought passed between us; if our schooling continued, one day we might end up like the captain of the Pumas.

Incredibly, the crowd kept their chant up. It began to rain lightly and then it began coming down harder. Still the people chanted.

I looked down at the field. The arbiter stood with his hands at his sides with his mouth to the sky. I thought it was in very bad taste for him to catch the rain right after he had killed a man, but then I noticed that he too was chanting along with the crowd.

Suddenly the dead captain's arms moved. The crowd chanted louder then. I thought that they were the movements of the recently dead, a twitching of the body. Then the arms moved again and he actually reached out his arm and began searching for his head. Truly, it was the most grotesque sight I had ever witnessed.

The three of us looked at each other in wonder and fear. When we looked back, the captain had found his head and was placing it upon his neck.

When it was in the right place, he also looked up into the sky and shouted, "Tulan!" The pouring rain washed away some of the blood on him, but he was still covered in his own gore.

Four men ran out onto the field with a long pallet that was suspended between two long poles. They set it down on the grass, and the captain of the Pumas slowly and carefully laid himself down onto it. He appeared pale and weakened. They carried him away. Miraculously, he had the energy to wave to the crowd.

The people rejoiced.

The arbiter took out his cone and loudly announced, "The winners of the day are the Jaguars, but the defeat is not complete. The Pumas have not been vanquished. They live to fight another day!"

Again, the crowd cheered. I even saw the Jaguars celebrating that the Pumas were still intact. I didn't understand that, but I too was glad that no one had died today.

My father turned to me and embraced me. He told me to take the boys home with me and to let them spend the night at our house. I told him that the boys' parents would be worried, but he told me that they already knew they wouldn't be home that night. Hac and Cham politely said goodbye to him.

We were about to leave when the Cabicacmotz peeked out from over the steps of the ball court at us. "Zaki, Hac, and Cham, go to Zaki's house and get warmed up. Be careful not to get struck by lightning, run as fast as you can to the house. The festival is over. The rainy season is upon us." Then he went back to his team.

We did exactly as he told us. We ran the whole way, with Chahal loping alongside of us.

When we got to my home, we were completely wet and filthy from all of the mud puddles we managed to stomp through along the way.

We quickly disrobed as servants brought us dry garments and set a large fire in the hearth of my quarters. They also brought in two soft pallets for Hac and Cham. Sitting before the fire, we talked a bit about what a strange day it had been, but we quickly became sleepy and retired to our beds.

P a r t T h r e e

Dreaming of War Plans

The next day, I awoke before anybody. Hac and Cham were snoring and Chahal was curled up on the rug in the corner. Birds chirped and I felt the optimism of a fresh day. I laid there watching my friends sleep and knew contentment. Although it was the first time anyone had ever slept over, it felt natural.

Chahal opened an eye and saw that I was awake. She came over to make me perform the ritual of the morning rubbing. Soon she would need her own attendants, but for now, I was it. When she stretched before me, her tail passed over Cham's nose and he yelled.

His scream was so loud that I thought the house would fall down.

Little Hac came awake with a start. Disoriented, he asked, "What's happening?"

"It's a room of terrors. I was dreaming that the man in red was going to cut off my nose with his axe. I felt it and she turned into the man in red," Cham shouted as he pointed at Chahal. "Then I woke up and she had her tail in my nose."

I laughed. "What an exaggerator you are, Cham. All she did was stretch and lightly pass her tail over you. She wasn't trying to do anything bad to you."

"And you call me a baby," Hac said.

"At least I don't wet myself in my sleep like you." Cham turned to me and nastily said, "I shouldn't say that to him. He got cured of that after he was made to sleep in a hammock and mop up his mess in the morning."

Someone clicked his tongue as if he had heard something shameful. We all turned to the entryway and saw the Cabicacmotz leaning against the wall.

"What a spiteful thing to say about your own brother, Cham. If I had known that you were liable to wake up in such a nasty mood, I would never have suggested that you come here to sleep. I would have hung you up in a cage from the beams in my roof, instead."

Cham swallowed loudly. "Sorry," he mumbled.

The Cabicacmotz turned to Hac and said, "Many of the greatest dreamers have been bed-wetters in their youth, you know. Do you have any idea why?"

He came over and sat at the foot of my bedding. I cynically thought that he had not chosen Hac's bedding on purpose, but my mat was more convenient as a chair since it was set on a platform.

Hac shook his head and said that he did not even know what dreamers were.

"Dreamers are men and women who have a remarkable control over their attention in their dreams, Hac. One could say that dreams are their doorway into genius," the Cabicacmotz told him. "Dreams are a portal into unimaginable vistas and power. Hearing that you have wet your bed often is an omen to me."

"Please no, not another one," Hac sighed. "I already have many things to learn."

"That's okay, Hac. This is something you will learn during the hours that you sleep. It will not be much of a burden for you. But I asked you a question; can you guess why the great dreamers have also been bed-wetters?"

Hac looked down at the ground and sadly shook his head.

"It is nothing to be ashamed of, little Hac. In fact, it is something to be proud of."

Hac looked up at him with surprise. "Why? Everyone teases me about it."

"What is convenient for typical daily life has no bearing on what leads a man into greatness and genius. Morons," he said as he cast an eye on Cham, "will try to convince you that it is something shameful, when it is a highly coveted sign among the lords of the life force who practice dreaming. The reason they place such value on it is that the bed-wetter has such deep and vivid dreams that his awareness forgets his body and truly lives inside a dream. You are most fortunate, Hac."

Hac's face lit up with happiness. "Really?"

"Yes, really. I will have to acquaint you with the men who practice the art of dreaming. This is surely a sign of things to come."

He asked us how we had slept that night and we told him that we had fallen asleep as soon as we got home.

The Cabicacmotz looked us all over and told us that he would meet us in the breakfast area when we had changed into clothes that were more suitable. He told us that the cooks were already aware that there were more mouths to feed this morning. Then he left.

"How come the Cabicacmotz is at your house in the morning, Zaki?" Cham asked.

I concluded that my best option was the truth. I told them that he and my older sister were to wed and that he was over at our home often lately. I even told them the story about the prince who called on Maricua and what she had done to him.

They hung on my every word and seemed enthralled with the gossip. I told them not to tell anyone and made them promise not to tell. They promised and seemed very solemn and serious about the oath. I expressed the worry that they might let it slip to another of the boys in our class.

"Those boys and us have nothing in common, Zaki," Hac said. "They're all of the noble classes and don't want to have anything to do with us. They think they are better than we are because we cut our hair differently, so they know our parents are farmers. I'm sure they have no problem eating the food our parents provide and grow, though. They're little rich snobs." He caught himself and added, "No offense, Zaki, but they are nothing like you. You're nice."

Cham nodded as if he was in full agreement with his brother's words.

I was glad to hear that and surprised that I also felt the same. The other boys mostly made me feel uncomfortable too. I told them how I felt and we acknowledged the fact that we all felt comfortable in our friendship, as if we three had known each other all of our lives. What an unusual, yet fine feeling. I realized that the feeling was one of camaraderie. It made me feel strong and safe, somehow.

Maricua peeked in the entryway and told us that she was coming in with our clothes. She brought us fresh clothes and immediately won the boys over with her smiles. The boys beamed when she ruffled their hair. I could tell that they were a bit infatuated with her. I sometimes forgot how beautiful she was and their hopeful shyness around her reminded me of it.

She left us and we all dressed in what she had brought. Both boys sniffed the clothes and said that they were the nicest smelling tunics they had ever put on. Cham said that they were fragrant like my sister and I knew the boy was smitten.

At breakfast, we sat around and talked about the day of the festival. A short while later, my sister got up. She told us that she was on her way to the marketplace. Hac and Cham's faces fell with disappointment. All during the meal, they had kept their eyes on her. When she left, they visibly wilted. The Cabicacmotz accompanied her to the road and then came back.

"I see I have a bit of competition for your sister's hand," he said.

Hac and Cham flushed red.

Cham said, "Our apologies, Cabicacmotz. We had no idea the princess was so lovely and charming."

The Cabicacmotz laughed and told them that he felt the same way every time he saw her.

"Will we be having lessons today?" I asked to change the subject.

"No. Today is a day of rest. I suggest that you all go and amuse yourselves by going to the marketplace or find something else to do. Today I have duties to attend to. Then I have to find a suitable teacher for you. I cannot allow the Etamanel Evan to have free reign with you both. There must be a teacher with the requisite sobriety to lead you into that knowledge. Evan is too unstable. I forbid you both to meet with him in private. From now on, the teacher I find for you must accompany you whenever you must meet with that man. Understood?"

We both nodded.

"Also, there is something I must ask you, Cham."

Cham indicated that he was listening.

"When you had the dream of the man in red, was he a dwarf?"

Cham jumped up with a fearful look on his face and asked, "He didn't look like the man in red, but in the dream it was supposed to be him, only he was in silver and a dwarf so I don't know why it was supposed to be him. How did you know that?"

"Don't worry about that now. When he was going to use his axe on you, did he specify that he was going to cut your nose off?"

Cham told him that was so.

"And then Chahal's tail rubbed up against your nose," he said as if he was lost in thought. "Curious. I think I will also have to acquaint you with a dreaming teacher, as well. Only it will have to be one who uses his dreams for fore-sight."

"Oh Maker of the heavens, please don't let it be," Cham prayed.

"No. No," the Cabicacmotz assured him. "The little bit of foresight you had was only an indication that your nose was about to be touched in some way, it does not refer to the possibility of you having your nose chopped off with an axe. Don't worry."

"Are you sure?" Cham whined. "It was terrible."

"I am sure, Cham," he said as he patted him on the arm. "You too had a sign today. The dwarf, the Zaki Coxol, the White Sparkstriker, often appears in dreams about future events. Here it was a small and insignificant piece of the future. Be thankful of that, young Cham."

I was intrigued by his use of my name. "Does this Zaki Coxol have to do with me?" I asked.

"No. It is merely a coincidence of name. We have many Zakis. In the stories of our tribe, the White Sparkstriker is intimately associated with foresight and the animals. He was the one who hid the original animals when the sun first struck them and they turned to stone. It is said that he knew what was to come and had prepared the nets he used to carry them away beforehand. The arbiter in the ballgame is associated with him because if the Pumas' captain had not returned to life, it would have been up to him to carry away his head and take it to a place of safety. Really, though, it is too long a tale to tell you boys now. I must go see your father, Zaki. Please excuse me. Enjoy your day, boys," he said as he left the room.

"Have you noticed that he always leaves one with more questions than before?" asked Hac. "I am usually more confused after he explains something than before I ask."

We all sighed and nodded our heads.

Chahal began rubbing herself against all of our legs, winding around them as if she was trying to tell us something. Then she went and sat looking out of the back entryway. Every once in a while, she would turn around to look at us and then look out again. The boys were bewildered by her actions, but I knew she wanted us to walk her to the jungle. I told Hac and Cham what she wanted and they were agreeable.

We left the estate. Along the way, we exchanged stories about our lives. They wondered where my mother was and I had to reveal that I had never known her. They were sympathetic and told me about their parents.

They described them as humble farmers and that they had been blessed with kind parents. The Cabicacmotz offered them a place closer to the citadel, but they declined his offer, being more at home in the fields and with the caring of livestock. The king had them relocated to a better area and made them proper vassals. Now they had workers who helped them with the farm.

I asked them why that happened and they told me that it had occurred only because they had gone to study with the Cabicacmotz. It was customary, I was informed, for the parents to be granted favors of such kind, especially if two of their children were taken from the home. Typically, the children helped the parents manage the day-to-day activities of a farm and their leaving had created a shortage of help even though they had two older brothers. To be equitable, the king had raised their rank and now their parents were vassals with lands, instead of what they were before, which was peons.

When we reached the edge of the jungle, I tried to turn us back to leave Chahal to her wanderings, but she had other ideas. She would jump out of the jungle and block our path back towards the city. At one point, she even shoved me with her head towards the jungle. I was baffled because she had let me know that I was a poor hunting companion already.

After a while, I gave in and we began following her.

Cham asked me if I knew where she was leading us and I had to let him know that I was as confused as he was.

"She's acting like she did that night with the Cabicac-motz," Hac remarked. "She would go a few paces away and look back to make sure that he was following her. She wants to takes us somewhere."

We all agreed that was her plan and acquiesced to her lead. She stopped looking back at us.

She took us along a narrow footpath, which had become quite overgrown from disuse. We seemed to walk for a long time. After a while, we heard a loud rushing from a nearby cataract. She led us to the water's edge and she began to lap at the water. We did the same. The long walk had made us very thirsty. We even splashed around in the shallows.

Chahal's growl reminded us of her mission. She sat a short distance away and then she got up and began walking again. She took us over a hill and we found a long disused ball court. She walked to the center of it and sat down, looking at us. Then she began preening herself.

The three of us exchanged looks of amazement. What a find. We could begin to practice here away from everyone. No one would witness our pathetic first attempts at becoming ball players.

Chahal was the queen of our day. Each of us went up to her to pet her and express our thanks to her. She seemed very satisfied with herself.

The ball court was small and looked like it was meant for a maximum of six players. Its sides, the ones where the stone circle for the final goal was, did not have any steps. It was placed on a plain wall.

The court was overcome with vegetation as if the jungle had tried to reclaim its land and cover it up with its greenery. We spent several hours clearing the court with our bare hands. We were able to pull away many of the vines, but some of them had grown so thick that we would need axes or knives to trim them back.

Soon, we grew too tired to continue our work and sat down. It was clear that there were no structural defects to the ball court. It would be perfection when we got through with it. We made a pact then to come back and properly clear it of vegetation. We promised to come and play there together.

All of us were hungry, by then, and we decided that we should go to the marketplace to find some food. Chahal led us out of the jungle and all of us tried to memorize the way as best we could.

On the way to the marketplace, we marveled over our good luck and about how Chahal led us there. We made plans on how we would obtain our gaming equipment and associated necessities.

Once we were in the marketplace, each of us got bowls of spicy corn pottage. We sat on some stone benches that were near the stands of the pochtecas. We were enjoying our meal and kidding around when we saw a group of warriors and officials, led by the Cabicacmotz, approach one of the stands where a woman sat with her goods. The woman seemed very alarmed by the large group; her eyes widened in fear and darted around as if looking for an escape, but there was none.

We were too far off to hear their words. Some luck was with us, though, because we had an unobstructed view.

One of the warriors carried a scale, which he set upon her stand. Another warrior unrolled a scroll and read something off it. By then, the woman's fear was making her shake and one of the men had to grab her arm to hold her still.

An official went behind her stand and produced a similar scale to the one they had brought. He also took a square of gold from an area under the front of the stand. He held it up for the woman to see and she gasped in alarm.

Next, the man removed a similar gold square from his pouch. Then he weighed the gold square against the woman's square on the scale they had brought. The woman's square outweighed the one from the official's pouch. Then the official took an obsidian blade from somewhere on his person and scraped at the woman's gold square. After a while, he held it up. There was clearly a silver colored metal underneath the gold. Even from where we were, we could see that the woman had used trickery in her weights. It was a dishonorable thing to do and it was considered a crime in our society.

The warriors bound her and took her away. She was screaming about her innocence, but no one believed her.

Four warriors were left behind to pack up the woman's stand and her things. Once they had dismantled everything, they hauled it away. Some of it they held, while other things were placed in carrying nets. Nothing was left behind.

Many of the pochtecas began to pack up their belongings and take apart their stands, probably in fear that they too would be taken away. The local merchants grinned in satisfaction and swore at the pochtecas, accusing them of similar wrongdoings and of swindling the public. The pochtecas ignored them.

Now, only a few officials and warriors were left. They were questioning the local merchants who had been near the woman's stand. They seemed to be eagerly giving the officials as much gossip as they could. The warriors looked skeptical, but the officials seemed enthusiastic about what they were hearing.

A man came, presumably the woman's husband, and questioned the pochtecas about the woman and her stand. They pointed out the officials to him and he started a scene, pushing the officials and demanding to know where his wife was. The officials nodded to the warriors and then they took him into custody.

The Cabicacmotz came over to where we sat and said, "Zaki, you will be needed in court today. There is something your father would like you to see."

I looked at the brothers and said to him, "What about Hac and Cham?"

He seemed to think that over and said, "Bring them along. They can wait outside while your father speaks with you."

The boys shrugged and nodded. I knew that one was older than the other was, but when they did things in unison, it gave me the feeling they were twins.

The five of us walked to my father's court. Along the way, Cham asked the Cabicacmotz about the pochtecas we had seen being taken away.

"They will be tried in court. If they are guilty, they might receive lashings or be forced to serve punishment as slaves. I don't know what will happen to them."

"Why did that man admit to being with her? He was free. Didn't he know that he would also get taken away if he did so?" Hac asked.

The Cabicacmotz smiled and said, "He was her husband. He must love her and not want her to be alone in this. Chances are that he will assume full blame for everything. That often happens."

"If that's the case," Hac said, "I hope to never fall in love. Apparently it makes people act stupid and do stupid things."

The Cabicacmotz smiled as he looked at Cham and me and said, "I hope both of you are storing Hac's words. Someday you will have the chance to tease him about his hoping never to fall in love."

When we got near to the court, the Cabicacmotz told Hac and Cham to wait outside on the grounds surrounding it. There were some swings and he suggested that they relax there or take a nap under one of the many trees.

"It is time for you to learn the art of governance, Zaki. Your father wishes you to know the duties he performs and the paths kings must choose from in order to lead their people forward wisely. The lesson for today is the role that he plays when spies present their reports. First, the report of the spy is heard and the questions related to the report. Then, there is the presentation of ideas for action or non-action. Then the king must choose the wisest course. Play close attention to everything. If there is a question you feel you must ask or if you think of a possible solution, think before you speak in order to present it in the most cogent way possible. You are his son and must act with dignity and maturity."

I was intrigued that I would get to hear the reports of a spy. It sounded thrilling and glamorous to me. I savored the idea of travel and meeting foreign people, since I had never done so.

The cavern was eerily silent. No petitioners were around and the guards didn't even look at us. We entered the corridor that led to my father's court. I received quite a shock when we arrived at the throne room.

There were my father and the two pochtecas laughing and sipping fruit juice from gourds as they sat on one of the wall benches.

The Cabicacmotz chuckled at my reaction. I couldn't close my mouth.

My father waved to me and said, "Zaki, son. Come over here and meet two of my oldest friends."

I went over there and my father presented them to me. They were called Parutzya and Carumo.

The Cabicacmotz explained that they had chosen those names for their work. They were non-tribal names that would not be associated with the tribe or its language, names that would enable them to meld easily with the pochtecas.

The husband, Carumo, said, "He looks like a fine boy, Alomi. I see a lot of his mother in him. Nevertheless, I see a lot of you in him, too. I feel sorry for his teachers if he behaves like you did." The man turned to me and told me, "You may not know this, but your father spent years in mortal terror because of the old Cabicacmotz who taught us, and he had only himself to blame for that, even though we helped him in many of his pranks." He turned back to my father. "Weren't those great days?"

They reminisced for a short while about their youthful days together. Then the conversation became serious.

Before they became too involved in their words, I interrupted and asked them why they had been arrested.

The laughter from Parutzya echoed through the cavern. "Don't be afraid that your father has been taken in by con-artists, Zaki. What you saw was a performance to ensure our eventual return to the pochtecas, should it be necessary. The official you saw knew that we kept a fake weight in our stand, for exactly such a purpose, and used it to justify our arrest. The metal is not the usual one used to add weight to gold. Everyone saw that we were obvious cheats. There is no doubt in their minds that we were taken into real custody. If your father determines that we should rejoin them, we will spin a tale about our escape to them when we meet up with them again."

"That remains to be seen," my father said. "We must hear your report first."

Carumo cleared his throat and said, "Our news is vital, Alomi. What we have learned is alarming."

They told us a frightening tale of a tribe who lived ninety leagues to the north-west of us. The tribe was conducting mass sacrifices of prisoners. What filled everyone with horror was that the sacrifices were to the lords of the underworld, which they called the Xibalbans. Now I understood the Cabicacmotz' reluctance to tell me about them. They were frightening figures of terror and evil. They were demons and the antithesis of all that was good.

When the four spoke of them, I could tell they used veiled terms for many things. Much was not made clear to me. When they spoke of the evil tribe reverting to the old worship, they refused to answer my questions about it. I wanted to know if our people had ever done such a thing, but they gently rebuffed me, telling me that once we had been tricked by beings who masqueraded as gods when they were no such thing. That was the most I was able to glean from them about that.

The pochteca spies told us that the tribe was expanding at an alarming rate and that they were overtaking the surrounding tribes in brutal attacks. The survivors either were taken as slaves or were taken as victims for sacrifice. The slaves were forced to enter into servitude in the army and were treated moderately well.

The Cabicacmotz surmised that it was the only option for the slaves as they were now only members of a vanquished people and that most people would rather survive and fight tribes that were not even their own than be butchered upon bloody altars to demons. At least, then, they would have a chance.

I asked, "Do these enslaved people have to worship those Xibalbans?"

Parutzya looked at me with sadness and nodded.

"That is monstrous," I said. "That cannot be allowed to continue."

"I agree with my son," Naualalom said. "They must be wiped from the face of this earth. First things first, we must know more about them. I refuse to go to war without proper intelligence. In addition, they are very far away. What numbers, of that tribe, constitute their fighting force? How much of it is composed of enslaved soldiers? Are the enslaved tainted from being forced to worship, as they do, or can they be saved? If they are incorporating the van-quished into their numbers, empire is clearly their goal. How big are their ambitions and how can they hold it together? How long before they reach us? Will we have to hold off our own wars for land? What are the possibilities of acquir-ing land peacefully and through diplomacy? Can we convince the surrounding tribes to band together with us because this larger threat looms? How will we produce enough food to last us if the war is protracted? Remember, the enemy is far away."

They decided that a war council must be assembled and that later they would resolve the question about whether the spies should rejoin the pochtecas. They were instructed to make maps with as much detail as possible. My father spoke about sending runners to recall our am-bassadors of peace and the need to replace them with envoys of war. He said that they were to secure treaties of solidarity with our tribe, to join us with them as allies. These envoys would impart the information to the tribal kings and sell them on the idea of safety in numbers.

"Is there anything else which you have to tell us?" the Cabicacmotz asked.

Parutzya answered, "Yes, there is something else I have thought of and I have the evidence of it. Please return to me the false weight which was concealed in my stand."

The Cabicacmotz left and soon returned with the block of gold. The metal hidden inside it gleamed dully next to the brilliance of the gold.

The woman took a stone blade from under her robes. It alarmed me and I looked around at the guards, but they ignored the threat and my father and the Cabicacmotz did not react to it. That put me at ease.

She used the blade to slowly scrape away at a little more of the gold and said, "I stole this from one of the camps outside of their citadel. The tribe's warriors ran the camp. They were training their slaves in basic weaponry. The interesting thing is that they are using metals in their lances, arrow points, shields, and war axes. We do not have this, Alomi. We use stones forged in the earth. They use manmade forges to make these things. This metal I concealed in gold to hide away from them. Notice that my blade cannot scrape it or even dent it."

I had never seen such a thing. Everyone was accustomed to gold and silver. They were abundant, but they did not have the strength that the hidden metal seemed to have. This was disturbing news.

"Where are they obtaining this metal? Do you know what it is?" my father asked.

Carumo answered, "I am told that it is something called an alloy, it is two metals mixed together. We have watched the making of it from afar, but we believe that we have only seen its making at the end. The metals are mixed, somehow, and then fired up into red and pounded. This process is repeated many times, the heating and the pounding. What metals they are, we have no idea."

Parutzya added, "We have seen slaves being forced into the caves of mountains. Some come back carrying loads of raw metals. The slaves appear sick and weakened after the work. We believe that they are extracting it from inside the mountain."

"How did they know which metals to mix or how to cook them to be so strong?" I wondered aloud.

Parutzya and Carumo exchanged a cheerless look. She said, "We tried to trade our wares for a weapon or a bit of that metal, but they refused us, telling us that only warriors were allowed to possess the weapons with metals. We were lucky to escape with our lives the day when one of their priests told us that their 'gods' had revealed to them the secret of their making."

"How did you get away?" I asked.

"We were disguised as an old and feeble couple of their tribe when he answered our question. He did not think that we would or could leave quickly, but we could tell that he considered our questions suspicious. We ran off after we pretended to go find something to eat. Luckily, the pochtecas we were traveling with had already started away from the city. We caught back up with them. When a team of warriors caught up to us to find the old couple, they only found younger pochtecas with no understanding of their language or examples of their metal. We had already concealed the bit of metal in the gold after we filched it a few days previously."

"How were you able to converse with the priest?" my father asked.

Parutzya and Carumo looked at each other for a long time. Finally, Carumo nodded to his wife.

Parutzya sighed, "They were speaking our own language, Alomi."

"You will speak of this to no one, Zaki," the Cabicacmotz instructed me after he quickly escorted me out of the deliberations. "To no one, do you understand?"

He extracted a promise of silence from me.

I did not want to think of the horrible things I had heard. The thing I wanted most was to go to sleep. I told him of my desire to take a nap, but he reminded me that Hac and Cham were waiting outside for me and that I would have to rejoin them. I didn't feel like pretending that nothing was wrong.

"This is where you will have to behave like a warrior, Zaki. There are many things that a warrior would prefer to be doing than what he must, but his sense of duty and honor demand that he do what is right for that moment. The right thing for you to do is to pretend that you have not heard the worst news of your life. Pretend that nothing is wrong and that you only had to put up with boring court duties. Do not burden your newfound friends with your clouded mood. Be their happy friend once more. Immerse yourself with their moods and banish your own."

He called Chahal to him and stooped down to speak with her. I could not understand it; he was speaking to her as if she were a person who could understand exactly what he was saying. He said, "Help him get out of the gloom he is in, my lovely friend. Be there for him and remind him of his promise to me." Chahal merely yawned in his face. He shrugged and then started to walk back towards the court. He turned around and added, "Have fun with your friends for a while and then return home for a meal. They will be staying with you again tonight."

I found Hac and Cham sleeping under a shady tree. They did not awaken at our return and we joined them. I was relieved that I would not have to pretend. I was shaken by what I had heard. Sleep claimed me.

When I woke up, the boys were nearby climbing a tree to pick its fruit. I was happy to see them until I remembered being in my father's court and what the woman had said. It was like waking into a nightmare. The world around me darkened to my mood. Colors faded and the happiness I felt at seeing my friends vanished. Instead, I felt that they were a weight upon me that I had to endure.

"Zaki. You're awake," Hac called. "Come and eat with us."

I could tell that the tree they were sitting in did not have ready fruit. Sapodillas covered it, but they were still too small for picking. They tested many fruit with no luck. A cynical thought came to me; I thought they were lucky to have been picked by the Cabicacmotz because they were unskilled at knowing the basics of plant life. Their satchels were bulging. They pulled anones out and peeled off a bit of the skins.

Anones were a luscious white fruit, which grew in the gardens and everywhere freely. It was a heart-shaped bulgy fruit. When it was ripe, it was green, brown, and yellow. The pulpy mass inside consisted of white pods where each pod contained a slick seed. It was sweet and tasty, but one had to spit out the seeds.

Cham hit me with one of the seeds. I gave him a dark look.

"Why are you so glum? You'll feel better with a little bit of sweets. Here," he said as he pulled out another anone from his bag and tossed it at me. "Have an anone."

The anone he pelted at me hit me in the chest and exploded all over my tunic.

"You idiot," Hac yelled at his brother. "You shouldn't throw things at people before they're ready to catch it."

I looked down at the mess all over me and knew it wouldn't have made any difference. The fruit was so ripe that it would have broken apart on its own. The same thing would have happened if I had caught it. I was sure Cham had chosen it for that reason. One thing was certain; my dark mood now had a target. I scooped the mass into my hand and popped one of the white pods into my mouth as I walked towards them. I separated the pod from the seed, swallowed the fruit and then spit out the hard seed at Cham. Luck was with me because it caught him on the bridge of his nose.

"Ow," he complained.

"Shut up, Cham," I said as I threw the rest of the anone at him and hit him on the side of the face. White pulp was all over his face and in his hair.

"Good," Hac said. "Now we'll all have to go swimming to make you both presentable again."

I climbed the tree and sat next to Hac. He opened his bag and let me choose an anone. It was the only fruit in there and I didn't doubt that Cham's bag contained the same. Everybody liked the fruit, which was fortunate because the tree ensured its propagation by producing so many seeds.

We sat there and spat seeds at each other until my mood improved. Chahal sat nearby, licking her paws and giving us disdainful looks. When we jumped down, she immediately stood and began walking towards the estate.

"So we're going to your house again?" Cham asked. "If we're going to see Maricua, don't you think we should clean ourselves up a bit? I don't want her to see me looking like this."

I told him that we could wash up in the stream behind my house, but that he didn't have to bother because my sister would probably not even notice the difference.

"Oh, that hurt," he said as he slapped his chest. He quickly puffed himself up and said, "I'm sure she would notice if I was not as good-looking coming back as I was this morning."

Hac snickered as if he thought his brother was delusional, even while he touched his own head to smooth back the flyaway hairs. As far as I was concerned, they were both crazy to think that my sister would ever deign to notice them.

We bathed in the stream, only wearing our loincloths. Both boys loosened their braids and rinsed their hair. For a moment, they looked at each other before they started braiding their hair. It was clear to me that they were accustomed to doing each other's hair, but their looks were loaded with distrust. No doubt, at one time they had sabotaged each other's hair for some reason. I knew each wanted to look better than the other did.

Once the boys, and myself, were fit to be seen, we went to my garden and entered my quarters. I lent them clean yellow tunics and we all went to the kitchen.

Maricua and the servants were carrying platters of food to the table. She smiled when she saw us. "Oh good, you are all here. How nice to have Hac and Cham here again. I can see why mothers want more and more children. You all brighten our home." She placed the platters down. Then she gave us warm kisses of greeting. I thought Hac and Cham would faint in joy.

We all sat down and the servants served us according to our wishes. The boys asked Maricua if she had cooked any of the food. She confessed that she had stewed the meat and vegetables in broth. They ate that first and paid her extravagant compliments about her cooking. She accepted their words with grace and I could feel her gladness at having someone acknowledge her proficiency with blending herbs and spices in her cooking. I decided to be more appreciative of her work, I felt deficient. The boys had exposed me to myself as an ungrateful brother.

Since it was already dusk, the servants were going from room to room lighting torches and candles.

When it was full night, the Cabicacmotz arrived and seated himself as we were finishing up. He looked beaten and tired, but he managed a smile and a kiss for Maricua. Both boys looked down as if ashamed of having witnessed the kiss. No one talked as the Cabicacmotz ate; the rest of us exchanged nervous looks because of the uncomfortable silence his mood pulled us into.

When he was finished, his mood improved and he smiled. He thanked Maricua and the servants for his food. He asked her if she had arranged for each boy to have a private room. She assured him that she had.

They took us first to Hac's room. It was a pleasant room next to hers. He seemed a bit anxious to be left alone. The Cabicacmotz assured him that he would be safe enough and that there were guards that roamed the estate throughout the night guarding against intruders. It did little to appease his anxiety and I realized that his fear was not about being in a strange house, but that it stemmed from being alone and that he was used to sleeping in the same room as Cham. Maricua soothed him with soft words and sat next to him stroking his arm until he fell asleep. Before he fell into sleep, I heard him tell her that her future children were fortunate to have her as a mother.

Cham's room was a few rooms down from mine. Cham thanked Maricua for letting him stay in her home and for the nice bedroom. Then the Cabicacmotz nodded to Maricua and she left the room.

When she was gone, he told us that tonight was the night to smoke the substance that the Etamanel Evan had given us. He told us that scribes would accompany us through the night to record our words after we had smoked the weed. He urged us to feel at ease with the scribes and to describe everything we felt and thought while the weed altered our way of thinking.

A short while into his instructions, Maricua escorted the two men who would serve as our scribes into the room. Then she left again, presumably to her own quarters.

The Cabicacmotz introduced the two men. He told us that we should pay particular attention, as often as we were able to, to where we felt our sense of self resided. I understood his words because of the exercise he had made me perform regarding that at the festival, but Cham needed special instructions and explanations in order to understand it. He quickly grasped the concepts.

"I am performing my duty here, in accordance with the instructions given to me by your new teacher in this subject. Later on, you will meet him," he assured us.

Neither of us was particularly interested in hearing more about the extra teacher, so we did not pepper him with questions about the man.

"For the smoking of the weed, you both will do it in here together. Your scribes will correct any mistakes you do and instruct you should you need it. After that, each of you will sit outside under the stars and begin your descriptions for the scribes. They will sit behind you and record the passage of time as indicated by the moon and stars. Both gardens are enclosed, so you will not disturb each other," he said.

Our sacks, containing the leaves and the pipes that were given to us by the Etamanel Evan, had been brought into Cham's room. We were told to remove the necessary articles.

When we had the leaves unfolded and the tangled bundles were visible, the scribes told us to unpack the small pipes. Next to each of us, they placed gourds with lit flames within them. They also gave us small twigs and gourds filled with sand.

They showed us how to pack a small amount of the tangles into the pipe. We had to hold the pipes to our mouths and use the twigs to convey a flame to the tangles in the pipe as we inhaled. Many times, we had to be reminded to inhale. They told us that we were to inhale as deep as we could and to endeavor to keep the smoke in our lungs for as long as we could. We had to remember to extinguish the fire on the twigs out in the sand.

Both of us had a difficult time holding the smoke. It was pungent, smelling of wet earth and caused us both to cough considerably. It took us many times to smoke properly our bits of tangles. I began to feel weird after the fourth smoking and there was still more to go. Only a small bit of tangle was smoked at a time. The portion I had received from the Etamanel Evan was the same as Cham's, but the scribes told us that the whole amount was too large to smoke in one sitting. They divided the tangles in quarters. The amount we were each to smoke was the size of the tip of my thumb to the first joint.

Once we had finished, we began to laugh like idiots. My mind was rampant with thought and hilarious things occurred to me. I felt that the weed was a wonderful thing that had filled me with ecstatic joy. I also felt that my whole head was emitting a brilliant golden glow. I could feel it engulfing my head and I knew that everyone in the room could see it. I saw the Cabicacmotz look at me and notice it. I was sure of it.

After that, I was led from the room by my scribe. He took me out to the garden and I sat there for a long time. He sat behind me the whole time, as the Cabicacmotz had said he would. Occasionally, he asked me questions, but they felt far away and not being able to see him made him into an unobtrusive disembodied voice. He urged me to describe what I felt and I exploded into a monologue of things I noticed in the night. The trilling of insects became engulfing symphonies to my ears. At other times, the songs of the frogs overcame them and I noticed that the two sounds did not occur at the same time. I voiced the thought that perhaps I was unable to pay attention to both things at the same time; my scribe did not comment on my words and let me speak as my thoughts jumped from subject to subject.

The warmth of the night evaporated and I grew cold. I felt the chill of morning and noticed that my feet and lower legs were covered in dew, but it did not matter to me. Much later, after I had sat motionless for what seemed like a long time, I began to nod off. My scribe walked me back to my room and helped me onto my mat. As soon as my head touched the padding, I was sound asleep.

I did not awake until midday. From the looks of it, Cham woke up even later than I did. When I went out, Hac was playing with Maricua. It was the board game, called patolli, which we had bought from the pochtecas. He had a small pile of jade next to him. He looked incredibly happy. I suspected that Maricua was letting him win by the expression on her face. Hac hadn't caught on to her tricks. Sometimes she would fool me and pretend to play poorly. I knew she only did it to make me feel good about playing, but it would become tiresome after a time. Hac was feeling the exhilaration of being on a winning streak; it would be a while before he noticed that it was not real.

They greeted me as I walked in. Hac told me that Cham was not up yet. Then Maricua said that the Cabicacmotz was coming over soon with a guest and that she would keep Hac company while the four of us talked.

Cham walked in then sniffling. When he spoke, his voice cracked. "Where should I go to pee?"

I took him to the side of the house. A building there was partially open roofed and divided into two sections. One side was for men and the other side was for women. I showed him the part for men and waited for him outside. Afterwards, we walked to the stream so we could wash our faces and rinse our mouths out. It made me remember what the Cabicacmotz told me about people peeing in the waters. I forced the thought from my mind before I vomited.

We saw the Cabicacmotz and another man walk towards us from the house. The other man was elderly and stocky, yet he walked with nimble steps that were as vigorous as those of a young man were. He wore a faded green tunic. It moved as if the cloth was soft from many washings, yet it was clean and he seemed like a man accustomed to being tidy. His round face was lined and weather-beaten. When he smiled, his small white teeth gleamed.

"Boys," the Cabicacmotz said. "This is the Tzuhunik. He will be overseeing your instruction with the Etamanel Evan."

The man nodded to us. He gave the Cabicacmotz a look and the Cabicacmotz left without a word, leaving us with the man who led us to a grouping of anone trees. He sat with his back against the thin trunk of one of the trees. He motioned to the other trees, as if inviting us to do the same. We chose our trees as he removed the satchel he had slung around his shoulder. He placed it on the ground and removed two scrolls from it.

"Do you know what I have here, boys?"

We shook our heads.

"These are the recordings of your work from last night. They are what the scribes recorded of your words. With these," he said as he waved them, "I can see where your minds are at and how they work when you take the weed into yourself. For instance, I can tell that Cham, you have a great fascination with women's breasts, you have a problem dealing with people and have great anger, but are very honest with yourself and become more poetic when you take the weed. I can see why the weed chose you, it will separate you from the anger you carry. One thing it will not do is satisfy or cure you of your lust for women; the weed will actually make you more sensual. I believe that the reason the weed chose you was because of the need to curb your fury."

The Tzuhunik's words were making us both fidget with anxiety. Cham, probably because he felt exposed by the man's words, especially in front of me. I felt uncomfortable because it embarrassed me to hear such personal information about a new friend whom I did not know well enough and because I knew that soon the man would direct his words at me.

"You will both know each other very well and will form a close friendship with each other that will last your whole lives. I realize that you both feel strange hearing about each other's weaknesses, but in this you both walk hand in hand. Overcome your feelings of embarrassment and shyness. You will need to support and help each other in this life. The sooner you begin the better. In the end, you will have no secrets from each other anyway, so it is better to see and know yourselves before anyone else identifies your weaknesses. This talk we are having, which is more of a monologue now, will simply speed up the natural rate of your friendship," he said in a matter of fact tone.

To my mortification, he started in on me. "Zaki," he said, "I cannot say that the weed itself truly chose you because of the situation with the Etamanel Evan. It is possible that he purposely designed to fall on you. In fact, I believe that was the case. This weed might cure you of your weaknesses or it might become your weakness. If the latter is the case, you will have to fight hard against the tendency, which the weed has to suppress the will of the individual. The problem is that fate allowed your guide to be inattentive enough to where an omen occurred. You cannot get out of this, you must learn about the weed. The weaknesses you both have can be fought and overcome using more routine methods, but these omens occurred nonetheless. You are too accustomed to being alone and silent, the weed will have to be directed to show you or make you more vocal and charming. Although you hide it under a mask of shyness, you have great pride, which is useless, and a detriment to your very being. That and your feelings of entitlement lead you into wrath and that is one of the most difficult sins to banish from one's repertoire of personality. Perhaps it was a real omen; if we consider the problems, which wrath might lead you into. You are poised to become the next king of this tribe. It will be a tragedy if you allow wrath to direct your actions. You will have to work harder than anyone I know because it is imperative for the good of the tribe that you bring yourself into a state of perfection."

I looked over at Cham to see what effect the Tzuhunik's words about me were having on him. His eyes were wide and his attention was completely on the man. I felt dreadfully uncomfortable to have been revealed as a person that was prideful and full of wrath. I knew that the man was right. I asked him what other methods I could use to change myself. His words surprised me.

"You do not have the option of only using other methods for the change needed in you. You must use them in addition to allowing the weed to guide you. Every moment of every day, you must engage yourself in the task of examining your feelings and thoughts. It is very easy to act well, but for it to be a real change, you must steer the feelings and thoughts away from pride and wrath." The man sighed loudly. "The trouble is that those two, let us call them what they are: sins, cannot be permanently banished from your personality completely. For the rest of your life, you must guard yourself from them. What is necessary is to ..." He stopped talking as he composed his thoughts.

Then he drew figures in the dirt in front of us. He pointed to one figure and called it pride. Then he pointed to another figure and called it wrath. He drew a line between them and told us that pride was the entryway into wrath. He drew a long line and told us that it was the road of my personality and life. He said that right now the road led directly to pride and that it was necessary to redirect the road. He placed a stone on the line that led to the figure of pride and told us that I needed to place a boulder in the road, which would prevent me from traveling on the pathway to pride. Then he drew a line from the boulder to another new point. "We need to divert your path to a better place. Let us call it the place of humility. There are two necessary junctions to this better place." He drew two smaller figures alongside the path. "One is known as equality with everyone else, where one person has the same value as the next. The other junction is aloofness, unconcern about one's image, the realization that we are small and insignificant beings who stand within infinity and eternity. We, of course, could substitute other junctions if those two don't prevent you from getting to the place of pride and, thereafter, wrath."

Cham asked him if he should use those two junctions also in order to keep himself from the fury within himself. It shocked me that he was paying such close attention and that he was concerned with his own change. I had figured that he would shrug off the Tzuhunik's judgments and forget all about them, but he was taking them to heart and seemed earnest in his interest.

"If my pride leads me to feel anger, can I use the sense of equality and aloofness to divert me from acting in anger?" Cham asked.

The Tzuhunik wrinkled his brow as he scratched his right ear. "First, it is not the acting in anger which is difficult, it is the feelings and emotions that certain situations engender in us that are the problem. One must cut the root of the

271

plantain tree to get rid of it. If we only cut off the manifestation of it, what is above the ground, it returns to life. The
problem with using the alternate pathways of Zaki is that
your case is different. Zaki feels a sense of pride and entitlement because of the situation of his birth status. Many
might contest his true status, though, because his mother
was foreign and was a fifth wife. That is something that this
tribe had never seen happen before. He still has eminence,
though, because his father truly married his mother within
the words of the sacerdotal chief of the tribe and because
he is the firstborn son of Naualalom. You, on the other
hand, were born into a family that did not cultivate its own
lands. It is more the pride of self-worth rather than one
borne of status, one feels worthy of greater respect by
others because one feels that one is special nonetheless. It
is as illogical and foolish as feeling that one is worthy of
respect because one was fortunate enough to be born to
wealthy parents. Neither situation properly reflects the true
worth of the person. The only thing which distinguishes us is
the manifestation of our own naual, our genius."

"What does Zaki's father have to do with that?" Cham
asked with a confused look on his face.

"Zaki's father is known by his title, Naualalom. It means
genius who bears life or sons. You know this. Do not make
me put voice to what you, yourself, know already please. In
any case, your pride is better described as self-importance.
For you, I would recommend other junctions. Acceptance
of what life has granted you, a true weighing of your own
worth that is based on self-determination and how you
bring about your own genius, and wonder at being in this
world. You both will have to decide for yourselves what

junctions work to divert you from the horrid paths you are on. This is a journey of wits, if those junctions only bring you back to your original road, you must find other junctions, which lead you away from pride and self-importance. Work to cut out the roots."

I did not know what any of this had to do with plants and I boldly asked him that.

"We were discussing what other methods you must utilize in your lives to bring about or hasten the changes that the weed will begin in you. Now, we must speak of balance," he said. "Every time that a plant is used to assist a man in changing himself, there is a price to be reckoned with. Here, the price is indolence and laxity. Those are your foes when you partake of the weed. Using the weed too often will stifle the will. Right now, you both are embarking on the paths that will develop and hone your wills, yet the omens have demanded that you utilize a plant which will hinder that very development."

"Does the will mean determination and manliness?" Cham asked.

"That is a very good question, Cham, but no. Will contains those definitions, but it is much more. Will is the aspect of one's genius that commands nature and more to obey its dictates."

"What do you mean by nature and more?" I asked.

"Has the Cabicacmotz explained to you that life and everything in it can be broken down into one base, energy?"

Both of us shrugged, which made him grimace.

"How foolish of me," he said to himself. "The Etamanel Evan always does the same thing. He shows his potential students the energy that flows in the universe. To be blunt, any asshole that is aware can see them. He acts as if he has revealed a great secret that only he can reveal, when that is not the case. Anyway, that energy, those tangles of light are what make up this world. Seers can see that everything is composed of those fibers. Even when they visit other realms, it is so. Understand?"

"No," I said. "I thought it was only visible in the sky. If what you are saying is true, then why weren't we able to see people in that way?"

"Because it takes more energy than you currently have to break down the physical into its base component. When matter is made, the energy is so densely packed that it takes special skill to unwrap it, so to speak. It is an advanced skill that is not yet available to you. Trust me for now when I tell you that those fibers build the world. When I speak of nature and more being commanded, I mean that the physical world can be affected by the will. The fibers of energy that you saw can be affected."

He thought for a long time before adding, "The fibers of light emanate from the Creator; everything in this world is his will. The fibers perpetuate his will and flow from him. We also are made from those fibers, we are part of his will, but he gave us two great gifts: free will and his light. Therefore, we can generate and create those fibers ourselves, although on a much smaller scale, and we can affect the fibers that are around us as long as they do not disturb his will. Do you see?"

Neither of us understood what he was saying.

He told us that he and our other teachers would repeat his words to us until we finally understood. He tried once again to make us understand by saying, "The will of a man is his command over his fibers and those around him that he is entitled to have command over. When we call our fellows 'lords of the life force', we mean that those men have control over their will. They have command over their energy. They have control over their energy. They command their fibers."

It was clear that neither of us was capable of following his words and he sighed. "Well, no one said it was going to be easy, otherwise men would simply be born with genius. We will have to stop for today. I see the Cabicacmotz and Zaki's cat headed this way. You are both forbidden to see the Etamanel Evan without my presence. From now on, I will accompany you when it comes time to see him. You are also not to smoke any more of the weed until I send the scribes to you. When you see them, prepare yourselves to smoke." He handed us our scrolls and told us to look them over and keep them. "You probably do not remember what you said when you were in the smoke."

He got up and went to talk with the Cabicacmotz. We stayed where we were and looked over our scrolls. I was marveling over the inanities I had uttered after smoking the weed when Cham spoke.

"Zaki? Can you tell me what I said?" he asked as he passed me his scroll.

"Stop!" cried the Cabicacmotz. "Zaki, hand Cham's scroll back to him, please."

He had startled us and we both looked up in alarm. I handed Cham his scroll. The Tzuhunik continued walking towards the outer gate, never looking back.

"Why did you give Zaki your scroll, Cham?

"I can't read what scribes have scribed," he answered.

"Can Hac?" the Cabicacmotz asked him.

"Of course not. We never had tutors."

The Cabicacmotz looked perplexed for a moment. Then he said, "We will have to rectify that. I will arrange for one of the scribes to tutor you both. We cannot have illiterate students. There will be times where you must record things so that you can remember them and if you cannot do that, you might not advance at the proper rate. Also, scribes are expensive to keep around. It's cheaper to do it yourself."

"Does that mean that my parents will have to pay a scribe?" Cham asked. "They can't afford that yet. Will I have to give up learning with you?"

"No, Cham, it doesn't mean that. For now, until both of you learn to do it on your own, we will have a scribe on hand and another for teaching you how to do it yourself. The king will provide the scribes until you know how. It is my fault for not realizing that you and Hac didn't know how to record or read writing." He turned to me and asked me if I knew how to read.

"Maricua showed me how." I had learned a long time ago, but didn't want Cham to feel bad about never having been taught. Before he said anything, I had thought that everyone knew how to read and write. It saddened me to realize that not everyone did, especially when I remembered his eager plea for me to read his own words back to him.

"Keep your scroll in a safe place," the Cabicacmotz advised Cham. "One day, you will want to look back on your first journey into the weed. I will recall the scribe who made the record for you tonight so you can remember what it was you said. I would prefer it if both of you kept private from each other what the scribes recorded for you, at least for now."

The Cabicacmotz told us that we should go to the house to retrieve Hac and that he and Chahal would wait for us where they were. Chahal was busy ignoring us all.

As we walked towards the house, Cham said, "Boy, I never realized what a turd I was until the Tzuhunik spelled it out for me."

"Don't worry," I said, "I'm a turd, too, it seems."

We laughed together for a bit and then he said in a serious tone, "My brother, Hac, isn't a turd, though. Somehow, he is better than that. Maybe that's why I tease him so much. He's always so good."

I nodded and agreed that Hac was a good person. I didn't know what else to say that could express my admiration for Hac that would not sound corny or trite.

When we found where he was with Maricua, he was wide-eyed with joy at winning another round in the game. Much must have happened because he literally had a pile of jade droplets that he had won from Maricua. The jade, all together, was almost the size of one of my fists. Cham's mouth dropped when he saw the riches casually scattered beside his brother.

"No more, Hac," Maricua said. "I refuse to play with you any more today. You have the luck of a beginner and soon

I will not have any stones to bet with. You had best go off with the boys while I explain why I am no longer wealthy to my father."

"Oh, Maricua," Hac softly said. "You can have them all back. You lent them to me anyway, so I would have pieces to bet. Don't tell your father such a thing, please. They are yours. They will look beautiful if you wore them as a necklace."

Cham gave me a "see how good my brother is" look. I nodded.

Maricua laughed and ruffled Hac's hair. "I am joking about you cleaning me out of riches, Hac. The jade is yours. You won it fairly. I didn't even let you win. You will notice that the luck that you have when you are a beginner does not last, though. I plan to win those jade drops back from you one day. I refuse to take them today. You will dishonor me if you insist."

"Well, I must repay you the initial pieces you allowed me to play with."

"That, I will allow. There were seventeen, if my memory holds."

Hac gave her seventeen pieces of jade. From where I stood, I could see that he was choosing the largest pieces. Maricua argued with him about that.

She said, "I plan on commissioning a bracelet to be made from these drops, Hac. They must all be around the same size for the bracelet to be balanced. Let me choose the jade pieces or the jeweler will have a terrible time."

Hac seemed befuddled by her words, but he allowed her to choose the jades she felt were most appropriate. My sister shared Hac's goodness because she chose small drops.

After she had picked them out, she said, "This will be a bracelet that will always remind me of you, Hac, and the good company you provided me today. I am pleased that my brother and you two are now friends. Please come over any time you please, our home will always be open to the two of you." She smiled at the brothers and gave us all kisses on our foreheads as she left the room.

Hac had a faraway look in his eyes as he said, "Your sister is as beautiful as a jade goddess, Zaki."

Cham and I got him out of there and walked him over to where the Cabicacmotz and Chahal sat together. They both stood up as we approached. Luckily, Hac no longer looked moony-eyed with infatuation.

"I have consulted with Ahtoobalvar," the Cabicacmotz told us. "He is helping me arrange guides for you in regard to dreaming. Cham will have need of one who is gifted in prophecy. Hac will need one who also dreamt deeply in his youth. Zaki already has Ahtoobalvar. We will go to his home now."

We walked to the most prosperous district of the city center. There were large homes with gardens. Merchants had set up permanent stores that offered every luxury and necessity for the maintenance of a home. Servants walked about carrying on the affairs of their masters. I knew that many who lived here were noble landholders who preferred to live away from their lands and left them in the care of trusted servants. A great number of them were traders who had accumulated wealth and could afford to live there. The rest of the residents were comprised of retired warriors and priests, though their homes were more modest. I was surprised that Ahtoobalvar would live in such an area; he seemed at home in a tent.

We went to the entryway of a large home. Trees lined the stone path and shaded our walk. Not one leaf littered the ground. It was swept clean. Someone had cultivated the front garden with purple and blue flowers. It was atypical because normally plant growth was allowed to thrive unfettered from human design or whim.

A manservant with a wooden look upon his face stood at the front portal. When he saw us approach, he bowed low. Hac and Cham grinned at each other, being bowed to was a new experience for them.

Chahal wound herself around the manservant's legs and he laughed. His face was transformed. His teeth were white and strong, but crooked. His smile was that of a child. He greeted Chahal with great affection.

"How nice to see you again, my friend. Have you come back for fresh fish?" He asked her as he scratched her under the chin.

Her answering rumble was very clear. She liked the man.

"The master is in the garden. He awaits you. I will take Chahal to the kitchen," he said as Chahal ran into the house. The man tilted his head to the side and partially shrugged. "She knows her way there, she is a frequent guest." He stood to the side as we went into Ahtoobalvar's home.

Ahtoobalvar lived like a king. His homed rivaled my father's home. Truly, it was impeccable. Red tiles in patterns covered the floors. Most people only had dirt flooring, which was packed and swept clean every day, so this was uncommon for someone not of the nobility.

Except for the East wife's home, all of my father's homes had stone floors. The East home had expensive rugs covering the floors. It was a source of annoyance to my father that the woman was always buying new rugs, as well as a constant financial drain. I would have to mention Ahtoobalvar's floors to him. He would prefer an alternative. One large expenditure would certainly be preferable to the periodic, but never-ending, purchases of that woman.

Everyone's eyes were drawn to the floors and the walls. One wall was covered with ceramic masks of an exquisite haunting quality. The features truly resembled people. They were realistic and were not stylized except when it came to the headdresses of the faces. On another wall, there were decorated skulls, the majority of which were human, but there were some of other primates and assorted animals. Some of the skulls had been covered with bright mosaic tiles to give them designs and color.

Figurines and vases were placed around the room. I could have stayed there for days examining the artwork, but the Cabicacmotz walked towards the back of the front room and disappeared behind the curtain of a doorway.

We followed him into an open courtyard. It was crowded with unfired clay vessels and other pieces. In the middle of it all was Ahtoobalvar. He wore the same braiding style I had seen him in before. He was at a strange contraption.

"Faster. Faster," he yelled to one of the servants surrounding him. To another he yelled, "More water, you fool."

He had his hands within a pile of clay that rotated, spurting reddish water, upon a wheel. The wheel had a lower wheel under it, which servants spun frantically with their feet. The two were connected by a wooden cylinder that must have been fixed to the ground. Somehow, he was able to keep the clay from flying off the top wheel.

The clay curved evenly and almost instantly became recognizable as a large vase. The servants slowed their spinning of the lower wheel. When it slowed down almost to a stop, Ahtoobalvar removed his arm from the vase.

He looked up with a smile on his face. "Welcome to my workshop, friends," he said as he dipped his hands into a large basin filled with clean water. One of his men immediately handed him a cloth to wipe his hands with.

He came towards us and asked the Cabicacmotz if Hac and Cham were the young men he had spoken of. The Cabicacmotz introduced them.

"Do any of them have any artistic talent?" he asked.

The Cabicacmotz shrugged and said, "I have no idea."

"Well, I intend to find out," Ahtoobalvar said. "I could always use new talent."

"May I remind you that you are here to try to find dreaming instructors for these two, instead of apprentice artisans?"

"All in its time, Cabi. I find that making things helps clear my mind. What better way to enter into dreaming." He looked us all over. Then he asked us, "Are the three of you friends or merely acquaintances from school?"

"Friends," we all said together.

"Nice," he said. "A unit, if you ask me. A unit that might do best together, rather than separated. We'll see. Maybe somebody will show up as we walk over to the new Zotabah's shop."

"I'm not comfortable with them not having individual teachers in this matter. What works with one might not work with the others. Their personalities are very different. I fear that stronger personalities might dominate the conversations and that integral subtleties might not get the attention they need. I also fear that they might be reticent about asking questions, their friendship is new, they still might feel shy with one another," the Cabicacmotz said.

Ahtoobalvar peered at us and then crossed his eyes comically at us, although his face was set in a serious expression. We snickered. He seemed taken aback by our laughter.

"They don't know how some people look like when they gaze, yet, do they?" he asked. "At least when they begin gazing."

"Apparently not. You will have to start from the beginning with these three. They are all new to instruction."

"I see no trouble with teaching them together," Ahtoobalvar said. "These three are, as I said, a unit. Interesting, eh? That they come from such separate parts of society, yet they have the same feeling about them? No, these three are somehow bound. I don't know why, yet, but they are. Maybe the ones in the middle parts of society feel awkward and unworthy next to a prince, yet they raise their noses at those from below them. So, we have the shunned before us. Don't worry, boys. The shunned are the best, always. And future geniuses from the classes without lands shine brighter because of their extra efforts." He chuckled darkly. "Already I feel pity for your classmates. They think they have an edge only because they were born into families that are more fortunate. Let me be clear with all of you. Everybody is a fool at your age, and anyone who thinks they are better off doesn't know that all the jade in the world will not help them bring forth their genius. Don't be surprised if later on in your lives you outstrip the lot of them."

The three of us grinned at each other. We liked his words. I was glad to hear that Hac and Cham could aspire to the heights of our tribe. Technically they were now of the landed class, but it was a recent development.

There was something very different about Ahtoobalvar, I realized. He did not seem as full of innocence as he had the day of the festival. Today, he was earthy and frank. He seemed like everyone else, although I found him more charming and likeable than most people I met. The quality of otherworldliness that he had was gone.

He was looking at me with a smile on his face. "It's like two different people, wouldn't you say, Zaki?" he asked.

He laughed when he saw the look of horror on my face. I was dismayed that I would also have to guard my thoughts against this man. The problem was that I still didn't know how.

"Thoughts have energy, Zaki. They fly across the universe at amazing speeds. Some people can catch them," he said with a wink.

"Oh, Cabi," a small woman cried as she threw her arms around the Cabicacmotz. "How nice of you to visit with us. Have you come to scold this brute, Ahtoo, about making a mess of my courtyard? I could bring my friends over to visit instead of being afraid that they will get hit in their faces with flying clay." She laughed and squeezed him in a big hug before letting him go.

"Don't nag me, woman," Ahtoobalvar said in a deep rough voice as he took her hand and kissed it with great tenderness. "We have to leave. These young pups need some tools before we can begin."

"Oh," the woman said. "Which one of you is the prince?"

"I am, madam," I said.

"I wanted to let you know that your jaguar is the most polite houseguest we have ever entertained," the woman informed me. "She does have a special love of my cooking, the dear girl. She scared me at first when she started visiting, but now I adore her. I think she has a special sense that lets her know when I am preparing fish."

"I'm sorry she scared you. I am only now finding out about her out of home activities. I never realized she had such an active social life."

The woman laughed and hugged me. She also hugged Hac and Cham. "Well, be off, boys, to do your errands. Take care of my boy."

Ahtoobalvar rolled his eyes, but gave her a warm hug and a kiss before we left. The woman playfully pinched his behind when he turned around. He shrugged at us when he saw our eyes widen with embarrassment.

"Always make them happy, boys. That's a sure way to a good home life. And make sure to pick a woman with an easy smile. If you marry a frowner, she'll have you frowning in no time."

"Then the Cabicacmotz is going to have the happiest life, ever," Hac said. "The princess's smile is as bright as a new sun shining on a darkened world."

The Cabicacmotz grinned and nodded. "That is the absolute truth."

We all made chitchat along the way to wherever they were taking us. I suddenly noticed that Chahal was not with us and expressed my alarm.

"No doubt that she is sitting in the corner of my wife's kitchen waiting to eat my portion of our evening meal. She can be quite a glutton. But don't worry about that, she will find us."

I apologized to the man for the impertinence of Chahal.

He waved my apologies away and said, "Don't take my jests so seriously. My wife and I love having her like us enough to visit us."

We arrived at a merchant's storefront. There was a wooden doorway, which we had to knock upon. Doors were an oddity and were only used in treasury houses and other such places where fine goods were held. My own home did not have one door. We relied upon secured tapestries and guards.

After a short while, I heard a beam being displaced to open the entrance. The wide door swung outwards and we had to step aside. A thin faced young man peered at us. When he saw the Cabicacmotz and Ahtoobalvar, he smiled and offered us entry. After we went in, he put the bar back on the door, locking us all in.

The thin young man was tall and walked as if he was stooped. He was not a hunchback, but his neck dropped low, ruining his posture.

Inside the shop, there were shelves of raw stones, polished stones and other items of the like. It was clear that the man was a fine jeweler. I wondered if he was the man whom Maricua was going to commission to make her a bracelet.

There was a courtyard, in the back, that was filled with items. It reminded me of Ahtoobalvar's courtyard, except everything in this one was of stone. I saw several yokes in various stages of carving and polishing. From the looks of it, the back section beyond the courtyard was also the man's home. Several dogs lay around, sunning themselves. I doubted that Chahal would come to this place.

The man introduced himself as the recent Zotabah. He seemed hesitant to use his new title and seemed a bit self-conscious about it. Ahtoobalvar told him that they had brought us here to be fitted for navel stones.

"Yes, that's very important. Thank you for coming to me," Zotabah said.

"You are the authority on stones, Zotabah. You should expect many more such visits. We needed and wanted the foremost authority on stones and you are he," the Cabicacmotz said to the man.

The man sniffled and I could see tears in his eyes, "Oh, Cabi. It has been terrible. How can I fill his mat? He knew everything. Now, I must even take his title and he was so much more than me. How I miss him. I even hear his voice telling me to polish the stones in a certain way."

The Cabicacmotz patted him on the back and told him that time would make his heart ache less for the old man. I realized, with a start, that I had attended the funeral procession of the man's former teacher.

"He taught you everything he knew, Zotabah. He polished you more than any stone he worked upon. He had great faith in you and your abilities and so do we," the Cabicacmotz assured him.

Ahtoobalvar patted the man's back and nodded. He told him that he agreed with what the Cabicacmotz said.

The man composed himself and wiped his eyes. "And who do we have here?"

We told him our names and he reiterated his thanks for visiting his store.

Hac asked him if he remembered him from the festival. "I'm supposed to learn the mystery of stones from you."

"Oh, yes. Of course, Hac. I do. You will have to forgive me. I am not very good at remembering people's faces. I need time to learn them." He pointed with his thumb at his dogs. "I am a dog person. I can remember any dog I have ever met, but people, well, people take me a longer time to recognize. It must be the lack of fur." The man seemed terribly embarrassed not to have remembered his pupil. He was babbling. "I do recall what we spoke of, Hac. I knew that you would make a fine apprentice. I'm sorry that I seem a bit strange now. I am still mourning the passing of my friend and teacher. I hope you understand."

Hac smiled kindly and took the man's hand. "I understand. I lost my uncle and I still miss him. I know that you will make a good teacher, though. I am very interested in you showing me about stones. My guide told me that you knew all of their secrets. I like dogs, too."

The man smiled as if he was about to cry again. I felt sorry for him. "Thank you, Hac. I am sure you will make a most excellent apprentice." He extricated his hand from Hac's and patted him on the head. "I think I was your age when I started my own apprenticeship with Zotabah." The man forced a smile and slapped his hands together. "So, navel stones today, is it?"

Everyone nodded and told him that was so. He led us to a corner of the courtyard and told us that we had to approach a large long-necked vase, reach in with our left hands, and grab one of the stones within it. He told us that the stones were going to be small and that we shouldn't grab a fistful of many. He told us to strive to grab only one.

Zotabah told Hac to go first. Hac tried to look inside the vase, but the man stopped him and pointed out the picture that had been painted on the jar. It showed a man reaching in to the same type of jar and looking off to the side.

"When you approach ritual objects, you should take a look at the instructions first. Always begin by inspecting the picture. That way, you can be sure that you are doing it correctly. Our artists are very precise and capture the particular way that things should be done."

"Does it matter that I'm not wearing the same type of outfit the man is?" Hac asked him.

"No. Only the body positions are important. Now, try again."

Hac looked at the picture before placing his arm within the neck of the vase again. He stood to the left of the jar with his head turned to the left. His arm crossed his body to reach into the vase. The man nodded his approval. Hac pulled out a small round stone of whitish green. "Jade," he screeched happily.

"Don't you have enough of it already?" Cham dryly said.

"It's a sign that one day I'll have my own princess," Hac said.

I didn't comment on the fact that he wasn't making any sense.

"Well, it is a royal stone," Zotabah said. "But that is no reason to make premature conclusions about what it means. It could be associated with waters, or even that you will become so adept at something that you are granted favors by the king. It has many applications, but mainly it is used to develop self-confidence and to remember dreams."

"If it's all the same to you," Hac said, "I think I would prefer a princess."

The man shook his head and said, "Please remember the possibilities."

I looked over at the Cabicacmotz and Ahtoobalvar. They were both trying to keep from laughing. Finally, Ahtoobalvar burst out in a laugh that broke the Cabicacmotz' composure. "That's right, Hac, go for the gusto. A princess usually lasts longer than a king's favor, anyway." He looked at Zotabah and shrugged.

Zotabah shrugged back and said, "At least the youth is honest and knows what he wants. Maybe we are seeing the beginning of his will emerging. If he works hard and determines that such will be, maybe such will be. It has been reported to help people achieve their desires, but who can say..." He shrugged again.

He went into the shop for a short while and came back. He told us that he had to replace whatever stone had been drawn out in order to offer the full cache of possibilities for the next person. True to his words, he tossed a piece of jade down the neck of the vase.

Cham went next, mimicking Hac's motions. A curious thing happened. When he pulled out his hand, he held a shiny black stone, but on his wrist rested a silvery grey one.

"Ooh," whispered Zotabah. "A dual answer from the stones. One is passive and the other active. The black stone, you will have to wear during the day and the grey stone at night while you sleep."

"What kinds of stones are they?" Cham asked. "What do they mean?"

"The black one in your hand is obsidian. It is associated with warfare and, uh, well... warrior things. It is used as a mirror, so it is said to help one see oneself clearly. Very useful for a warrior, you can judge where you need work and fix it. Being black, it also dispels negativity. The grey one is hematite and has to do with healing, peace, and equanimity. This is a very fortunate omen and help to a developing warrior. The stones realized that you needed more peace when you take your rest. More than the average person, in any case. You must use that one at night when you dream. Most auspicious, young man. Healing provides an excellent balance to the acts you will perform as a warrior. On the one hand, you have the power to destroy and in the other, to heal. So perhaps you will become a doctor or a healer or maybe even one of the great men on the ball court who can bring themselves back to life."

Cham liked the sound of that because he smiled with a wide-open mouth.

Again, Zotabah had to retrieve stones to replenish the cache.

It was my turn. I tried to peer into the vase to see if I could also get one of the silvery stones and Zotabah reprimanded me. It was too dark to see anything anyway, yet still he scolded me.

"It is impermissible to try to force the outcome of the stones," he said. He softened when he saw my look of shame. "Let the stones speak. They will select you, not the other way around."

I placed my hand in the vase and blindly felt around. The slick stones rumbled around my hand as I penetrated its depths. Perhaps I imagined it, but a strange thing occurred. I was able to see inside the vase, even though there was no way I could possibly have done so. I saw my hand moving within a pile of small round stones when a golden glow occurred from within one of the stones near my hand. I grasped the glowing stone between my thumb and index finger and pulled it out. Then the vision stopped.

In my hands was a black stone. I thought that I had the same type as Cham, albeit not the one stone I truly wanted. This one was not as shiny as his was. I shouldn't have plunged my hands so far into the stones, I thought; I should have strived to get one that was on the top surface. I looked up and all three men were squinting at me with hard looks. "Is something wrong?" I asked. I couldn't figure out why they were looking at me as if I had done something wrong.

The men exchanged a look. The Cabicacmotz raised his eyebrows and gave a nod to Zotabah who swallowed loudly.

"That is the stone of seers with magical powers," Zotabah said. "It signifies a person who will have spirit helpers or familiars."

"From the looks on your faces, that must be something bad, right?" I asked.

Zotabah shrugged and looked at the ground. "Not necessarily. No, not really."

I could tell he was prevaricating. "Why?" I asked as I peered at the innocent looking black stone in my hand. It didn't appear to be anything special. It looked like a common polished stone. It was slightly irregular and had small holes that the polishing hadn't erased, but it seemed too innocuous to have as much significance as they gave it. I tried to hand the stone back to Zotabah. He quickly jumped back as if he did not want the stone near him.

"Oh, nothing bad, eh? Then why don't you want to touch it?"

Ahtoobalvar answered me, "It's not that he is afraid of the stone because it is harmful. He does not want to touch it because it now has an owner, you."

"Tell me why this stone means that I will have spirit helpers and why it is a bad thing," I demanded.

"Accept it, Zaki," the Cabicacmotz said. "You will have familiars. You will have conversation and traffic with beings of might from other worlds."

"What worlds?"

"Who knows? But if you have that stone, they will be powerful and in need of containment," Zotabah said as he pointed to my hand.

I gave him a disbelieving look. "How could a mere stone hold a spirit?"

"Very easily," he said. "That stone is made for that purpose."

"How is it made? Who made it?"

"The Creator. All we know is that we find it and it is already perfectly formed."

It was an unsatisfying answer, but irrefutable. "How does this little thing hold a spirit in check?"

He grinned and said, "Now that has a very interesting explanation." He told us to follow him back into the shop. The man went to one of the many shelves and pulled out different pieces of black crystals. Some were long, others were broken, and others were flat polished disks. He placed them all on a padded bench and told us to examine them.

He pointed to the long crystals and told us that it was the stone in its natural formation. He then pointed to the broken pieces and said that they had come upon its secrets by accident. I didn't understand what that meant until he continued.

"The crystal is often accompanied by other minerals and components, which weaken the integrity of the structure. If dropped, they easily break. Therefore, we had a bunch of broken shards lying about and experimented with turning them into jewelry, pendants, or something like that. What we discovered makes this into a truly priceless stone that we cannot allow to fall into the hands of just anyone."

He made us wait for more, savoring our expectant looks. Then he pointed to the polished discs and said, "Look at what is inside the stone."

We looked at the flat discs and saw that there were small triangles littered liberally through the body of the disc. It was black and polished to a fine sheen. The triangles appeared to be an anomaly of the crystal as they were composed of lines that were more charcoal rather than black. It seemed that the black went in one direction, but the charcoal lines went in another, somewhat like when ridges of fur form rosettes upon an animal.

"There is your containment device right there," he said. "The triangle is a shape that is used by those who tangle with powerful beings. The triangle holds the spirit. Touch a spirit with this and if you know what you are doing, you can force it in or entice it to live there." His hands fluttered upwards and out as he said, "And that's all I can tell you about that. It's not my particular field. Because it is black, the stone also dispels negativity. Extremely well, I might add. Sometimes I have to use it on someone if they are the victims of sorcerers or jealous people." He gave a large list of situations where people would benefit from the stone, but stressed that its use was still strictly limited to trusted individuals in the kingdom because of its spirit containing aspect.

"Why did it glow, right before I picked it?" I asked.

Even Hac and Cham looked at me strangely, when I asked that.

Hac asked, "How could you have seen it? Your arm was all the way into the vase and you were looking away. I watched you."

I mumbled that it must have been my imagination.

Ahtoobalvar told me to describe what I thought I had imagined.

I explained what I thought I had seen.

Ahtoobalvar said, "Now I see why you must learn the art of the double. They are seeking you out."

"Who's seeking me out?"

"The spirits. The problem is that one can learn a lot from them, but they like to acquire subjects. They try to entice humans into their world and get them to stay. Having a double is the only way I know of to stay out of their grasp.

The trouble is that developing the double or getting to the point where one can command oneself to enter into the awareness of the double is the work of years. First, you will have to learn how to protect yourself from the spirits if they are coming to you of their own accord. You will have to learn how to contain them. Whether you like it or not," he said.

I was miserable. It sounded dangerous and like a lot of difficult work. In addition, I was thoroughly unfamiliar with anything he mentioned. Whatever this was, it sounded perilous and taxing. Then I had a very logical thought, which buoyed my mood.

"If spirits are seeking me out... Let us say they are harmful ones. If they were seeking me out, wouldn't they want me not to have such a stone? That means that the glow must have come from the Creator or something that seeks to help me or protect me in some way. After all, what spirit would point out the prison that you should use to house it?"

"That is a good point, Zaki," the Cabicacmotz said. "However, we don't know the answer to that. We might debate it and bring it to the seers, but it is too complex to examine right now. I do know that when the glow occurred to you, all three of us were drawn to see into you, but we couldn't see anything. Something stymied us. So, I'll wager, the seers aren't going to be able to offer you more than a list of possibilities. Were you able to sense where your sense of self resided when you experienced the glow?"

I told him that it happened too quickly for me to think of noticing.

"The next time it occurs, try to remember to notice. If you notice, you can perform maneuvers to place it into that position again when you need it or desire it."

"Can I try to do it again?"

The Cabicacmotz looked over at Zotabah who shrugged and said, "It's not a proper use of the stones, but I believe it is important enough to warrant an exception. Let me obtain another stone to replace the one he removed."

After Zotabah found another navel stone made out of the black rock, all of us went outside to the courtyard again. He placed the stone into the vase and the Cabicacmotz urged me to perform the same movements I had when choosing my stone.

I placed my hand inside the vase. Nothing happened.

"Well, that is that. I think it would be a good idea to leave. I'm getting hungry," Ahtoobalvar said. "My wife is cooking up my fish and I don't want Zaki's cat to eat it all before I get there."

Zotabah seemed a bit saddened that we would be leaving as he walked us to the front entryway. He instructed us to commission leather belts in order to secure our navel stones and told us to wear them at all times, even while we slept. For now, we had to place them in our pouches and he advised us to wrap cloths around ourselves to keep the stones in place while we slept. When we received our belts, we were to wear them during the day. He told us that we might want to replace the belts with a cloth for sleep, for comfort. He stressed that no one should touch our stones and that if it happened, we should immediately wash the stones under fresh running water.

"Please come back and give me any reports about how the stones have worked out for you, it will help me identify new uses of the stones or limits they have. You will be helping me build my own knowledge, so please don't forget about me."

We told him that we wouldn't forget him and the Cabicacmotz arranged days and times for Hac to return to Zotabah's shop to learn. Then we left.

"That poor man," Ahtoobalvar said quietly the moment we stepped back onto the street and heard Zotabah latch the door behind us. "The old Zotabah was like a father to him. He must feel a great loss. I have a sister-in-law that would be nice for him. She likes dogs. Do you think I should bring her by to meet him?" he asked the Cabicacmotz.

The Cabicacmotz chewed his lip before saying, "I think you should wait a couple of weeks. Sometimes women only have disdain for men, when they first meet them, if they feel that the man is weak and has no confidence. Wait for him to heal a bit before introducing them. That way she won't have the first impression of him in a weakened state. That's what I would do. Or is she especially nurturing and understanding?"

"She's a bit of an oddball, like him. I think they would be good for one another. I can bring her by under the pretext of helping him clean his store. It could use a good sweeping, if you ask me. I'll still wait a while, you may be right. Women can be merciless. I don't think she's like that, but you never know."

The Cabicacmotz told us that when a person had suffered a terrible loss, such as the death of a mentor, sometimes it could be as traumatic as losing one's lifelong mate or companion. He said that it was extremely helpful for the person to be made to feel that they were needed and important for the functioning of society. Normally, he would have afforded the inheritor of a title a period of grieving time before demanding that they fulfill their function, but Zotabah needed to forget his pain and helping others caused him to focus on something other than the loss he had experienced. He told us that Zotabah was very young to fill the mat he had been bequeathed, yet he had perfect faith in him.

"It will help him to have Hac and a few other boys to teach. The more he is made to act like his former master, the faster he will truly become like him. Out of all the boys the Zotabah taught, he was the only one able to store in his mind everything the man said. He is a treasure house of information, we are fortunate to have him. If Zotabah's knowledge were lost, we would have needed to start anew on the experiments to see what worked or quiz everyone about what they remembered about certain stones in order to piece it all together. That would have been quite a setback."

We walked Ahtoobalvar back to his home and went inside to retrieve Chahal. She sat on one of the walls in the courtyard, looking down at us. She refused to come down until Ahtoobalvar walked us back towards the front of the home to leave.

"I have a great and fun idea of what you can all do," Ahtoobalvar said. "Consider it a way to find power and one's genius. This is the first step to developing the double. Let's see how well you all do. It'll be like a race. Find your hands in your dreams. Only look at them for a quick moment. That's all you need to do." He grinned at us with a mad expression.

He was difficult to take seriously with that look. We boys looked at each other and raised our eyebrows; we thought he was crazy.

Hac asked, "What for?"

"You all have to learn dreaming. This is the only way to begin. Don't you want to fly over the mountains or visit suns?" he said with a smile.

Cham let out an exasperated huff. "There's only one sun."

"No, Cham. We see one sun here, but there are plenty more out there," he said as he pointed upwards towards the sky.

"Why can't we see them, then?" Cham asked.

"We sort of can, but to us, they appear as stars. They are very far away. The only way to reach them and see them up close is to travel there with the double or in dreaming," he answered. "Some foolish people think that the earth is flat, but it is not so. Almost everything floats in dark space and is round, mostly. Other people on this earth have arrived at the conclusion that the earth is round because they followed the dictates of logic and reason. We did that too, but we took it further. We have corroborated it through our genius. We have gone out there and taken a look to see what is there. I highly recommend it. But why take my word for it? Wouldn't you prefer to verify personally that mostly every mass in the cosmos is rounded?" He winked at Cham.

Cham seemed deep in thought, yet nodded. "So to see what's in the stars, we must first look at our hands?"

"Exactly," said Ahtoobalvar. "But remember, you are now starting out; only look at them for a long glance and turn away. Once you find success, come and see me so we can decide what you should do after that. For now, consider it a contest where everybody eventually wins."

We, each of us, told the others that we would beat them and pretended that it was a race to see who was able to see their hands first in their dreams.

Hac was the only one with the sobriety to ask, "How do we remember to look at our hands in our dreams? It's difficult to remember them afterwards, even. Mostly I can only react to what happens in dreams, and sometimes I can't even control that."

Ahtoobalvar said, "The manifestation of the will comes about through two actions on our part. One, unrelenting intent, which can be likened to obsession. Two, absolute command. In the first, you must be persistent until you achieve your aim. In the second, you must be pitiless with yourself and accept no deviation from your path. Both are simple, yet both are hard states of mind to enter. It is difficult to sustain one's determination and it is difficult to have the coldness and hardness with oneself that one needs to achieve what you must do. The tendency of almost everyone is to be understanding of one's inabilities. We love to be kind to ourselves. You have to put a stop to that. You must master yourself."

I grimaced. I didn't understand his words well enough to apply it to the situation. I asked, "Can you give us any clues on how exactly to begin?"

"For the rest of the day, whenever you have the presence of mind, tell yourselves that you will," he said, emphasizing the word, "look at your hands in your dreams tonight. Know it. Feel that knowing saturate you. Accept nothing else from yourself. Accept no excuses and weaknesses on your part. Only accept victory over yourself."

"Boys, there is a part of you which is confident and capable of command over all parts of yourself. Let us call that the spirit, the center of command. There is another portion of you, a version of you, which is the you that dreams. Let us call that portion, the dreamer," the Cabicacmotz said. "Enter into the mood to command and rule. From that mood, you control all of the rest of you, the body and the dreamer. Command the dreamer to look at your hands. Do not allow the dreamer to have full rein. The dreamer is a slave to the spirit. Compel it to behave as you want it to behave."

"Zaki told us that Ahtoobalvar was in two places at once. Is the spirit or the dreamer the double?" Hac asked.

"Yes and no," answered Ahtoobalvar. "Let us go back to the courtyard and sit. This might turn out to be a long explanation."

We all went back there and sat down.

"The self is composed of three parts," Ahtoobalvar told us. "There is the physical body, the spirit, and the dreamer. The physical body is easy to understand because it is self-explanatory; we all know what it is made up of, flesh and bones. The dreamer is the awareness we all have that dreams and acts in dreams, it also thinks in dreams. The spirit is a more confusing affair. It is composed of pure energy and its location is in and around the body. It is shaped like a navel stone, oval and a bit flat on the bottom, the part that touches the earth. If we stretch out our arms over our heads and to the sides, we will have an idea about its size. So it is also around us. All three of these parts of us must be independent functioning units. They must be able to stand alone without the others for support. Otherwise, there is no hope for developing the twin."

"I need to make a comment here," the Cabicacmotz said. "When I have asked you to identify where the source of your sense of self is, you have, up till now, only found it within your bodies. There is another possibility. One day, you might find that your sense of self is outside of your physical body. Also, the energy sphere of the spirit can become smaller and denser or it might stretch in many different directions. It is not always an oval. That can be changed. I only wanted you to know that that is not an absolute feature."

"What is this sense of self you speak of?" Hac asked. "Have I missed some lessons here? I have no idea what you are talking about." He looked at Cham and me to see if we had understood the Cabicacmotz' words.

"I apologize, Hac," the Cabicacmotz said. "I spoke to Zaki and Cham about that subject when they were being instructed on what to do with the seven-pronged weed." He went into a detailed explanation of the sense of self.

Hac tried to do it and smiled, "That is so weird. How did you all come up with noticing it?" He held up his finger as if putting off the answer and thought for a few moments. "No, that is not the right way to say what I'm feeling. It is such a simple thing. Where is the self? Yet I know that I would never have asked myself that question if it had not been mentioned. Why is that? Why is something so obvious and simple, so difficult to become aware of?"

"That is the mystery, Hac," Ahtoobalvar said. "They say that the Creator was so confident about man, that he allowed the demons to cast a spell on mankind to only let us think about certain things, things which were pertinent to this world. They gave us the personality traits and minds that they themselves had for the experiment. They were always complaining about the pride God had about humanity and told him that it was unwarranted. Supposedly, he said that his design was of such a caliber that even that would not stop us. He was right, at least about the people in this tribe. Most of humanity is content with the demonic mind and does not challenge it. We have successfully rebelled against it and thrown it away. We have reclaimed the mind which carries the divine spark, the true mind."

The Cabicacmotz interrupted and said, "This is too large a subject to cover in one sitting and Ahtoobalvar must be allowed to eat in peace. His wife is peeking around the corner every few moments to see when he is going to eat. It is rude to keep women waiting when they are doing something nice for us, so let us hurry. Hac asked about whether the dreamer is the double. I think we should tell them exactly how to get to the double."

"Are you insane? Now is no time to tell them about that. They are merely beginning. They won't need that information until later, and besides, a messenger will teach them how to do it when the time comes about or they must figure it out on their own. Now is too soon. It will lack timeliness and work on their part."

"I am not worried about timeliness or work. I want them to have the necessary information, even if they don't understand it yet, should something go wrong. If trouble finds them, they must make an effort to remember the details. Their spirits will record the explanation and hold it."

"They are starting out. What can go wrong?"

The Cabicacmotz gave him a pointed look.

Ahtoobalvar winced and said, "I had forgotten about that. My apologies. Still, that happened to you after many years in training, not your first time."

"When it comes to that realm, I am now extra careful," the Cabicacmotz told him. "The next time they smell my blood, they might not be as well-mannered as to restrain themselves." He gave Ahtoobalvar another loaded stare.

Ahtoobalvar sucked in air through his teeth. "That I had also forgotten. Some blood is sweeter than others when it comes to revenge."

"What are you two talking about? Can you tell us what is happening? We can't understand anything you are saying," Cham complained.

Ahtoobalvar sighed in resignation. "Nothing you need to concern yourselves about, at the moment. Mankind straddles the realms. The realm of the physical body is this earth. The dreamer's realm is the land of dreams and the underworld. The spirit's realm is of the heavens and the divine. It is necessary to pass through the underworld to gather the energy necessary to propel oneself up into the heavens. To reach the higher realms, one must first conquer dreams and the underworld, one could say. One must defeat those places and reject them. The act of defeating the underworld, Xibalba, has a complementary component, the commitment to light and goodness and the rejection of evil. This rejection supplies man with the energy to traverse the realms and enter into the divine. You will see that the overcoming of sin is a powerful aid to gaining surplus energy. Think of the heavens. Man can see it, but he can't get there from here. Instead, he must enter the land of dreams, the darkness. That realm is like a mountain; one must enter the mountain and go up steep steps, which lead to the top. The top has an opening into the heavens. Perhaps that is too poetic a description."

Cham tried to interrupt to ask a question. The Cabicacmotz told him that it was unlikely that we would be able fully to understand Ahtoobalvar's words, but that we must try as best we could. The important thing, he said, was for our spirits to hold the memory of the conversation.

"When the man has to fight against the underworld's influence or the underworld itself, one of the strongest weapons in his arsenal is the double. Nothing can hold the doubled man because the spirit is a vehicle. When we say that the double is developing, that is actually incorrect. The double is actually a potentiality, which the Creator gave us. We always have three components, we were born with them, and the thing is that we must strengthen each part to make it into an independent functioning unit. The body must be treated well and exercised. The dreamer also has to be exercised. When we eliminate evil from our personalities, we free the spirit and strengthen it. That is the exercise of the spirit."

He took a deep breath before continuing. "The double is brought into being when all three are at their peak. Then the warrior divides himself into his three components and places his immediate awareness into his spirit. Then when he is in the spirit, he purposefully places his spirit into his body or into his dreamer. When he places himself into the dreamer, he becomes the double. He is literally doubled up."

"Where is his body?" Cham asked.

"In normal circumstances, it is asleep. We will not talk about any other possibilities for now. The trick is that he must be asleep in order for his dreamer to detach itself away from the body and perform in the realm that it knows best, dreaming. The dreamer is dreaming. The physical body is sleeping and the spirit stands apart. If man chooses, he can stay in his spirit and travel anywhere, but if he needs to perform acts of power, he must double up."

"Why would the dreamer wander away from the body?" I asked.

"The student is led into the custom of having many places in which to sleep. After a while, his dreamer is confused and wanders away unknowingly. This is why you must have many places in which to sleep. As teachers, we ask that the student get into the habit of sleeping in a certain place. Once that habit is built, we demand that the student break it. This is not done for arbitrary purposes; it is done to jolt the dreamer. The dreamer will often return to the habitual place of sleeping. Once it gets there, it becomes confused and believes itself to be the real body of the student. It then falls asleep in the same place. From that second falling asleep, the spirit comes forth. Don't ask me why because no one knows the answer to why the spirit comes out then. The trick is that the body of the dreamer and the physical body must fall asleep in the same position. When the position of the dreamer matches the position the body was in when it fell asleep, we call that performing the twin positions. Then when the spirit comes forth, it is completely aware and clear of vision. At that point, there are no dreamy elements to his vision; he is in a perfect reality with clarity. He can stay and experiment with that new state, but he cannot perform acts of spiritual power. For that, he must enter his dreamer and double up. Or, he can enter into the physical body and from there perform acts of physical power."

"What does it mean to perform acts of spiritual power?" I asked.

"Calling spirits, banishing spirits, banishing illnesses and things like that count as acts of spiritual power."

"Why would he need to do that to banish spirits? Can't the priests do that without having to go through all those steps?"

Ahtoobalvar and the Cabicacmotz chuckled darkly. "Not usually," the Cabicacmotz said. "They would like you to think they can whenever they please, but it is a lie. The only way to have that power is to unite the spirit into the dreamer, purposely. There are special circumstances where the priest has access to those parts of himself, but those men are rare. They are natural men of power who act without knowing why their acts work. Let us not talk of anomalies, though, because none of you fit that definition."

Ahtoobalvar began speaking again, "First, the awareness is in the body. In dreams, the awareness is in the dreamer, then the dreamer falls asleep and the spirit emerges, pulling the awareness into itself. Then he doubles up. Here are the steps: one, you fall asleep, remembering your sleep position. Two, you wake up as the dreamer. Three, you go back to sleep in the original sleeping position. Four, you wake up in the spirit. Five, you enter the dreamer, combining the spirit and the dreamer. Finally, either you ascend or you perform great acts in the world of man. Understand?"

We all nodded and then Cham proposed questions that made me reassess his intelligence; he was smarter than I had thought. "Wouldn't all those parts of the self always be within the spirit anyway? If the spirit is larger than the body and permeates it, wouldn't that be enough? Where is the dreamer when we are awake? Is it with us? If so, then all three are together. Why would they need to be divided and then put back together again?"

"No one knows that," said Ahtoobalvar. "We have arrived at the precise steps necessary through experimentation, but we do not know everything about why and how those parts of us relate. Right now, my dreamer is inoperable and I do not know what it is doing. Some things are hidden. The steps are the only things you need to concern yourselves with for now. Later on, much later, you will put them into operation."

The Cabicacmotz told us that the trick depended upon where our awareness resided, at the moment. It could be in one of three places: the spirit, the dreamer, or in the physical body. Dreaming was a tool to transfer the awareness that we usually kept in the physical body into one of the other two bodies. He intimated that there could be even more permutations possible. When he saw that we were hopelessly confused by his words, he demanded that we recite the necessary steps in the operation of the double. When he was satisfied that each of us knew them, he told us that it was time to leave.

We said goodbye to Ahtoobalvar, much to the relief of his wife.

The Cabicacmotz walked with us towards my father's court.

Before he went off, he expanded the discussion about the double. "This is a tale that you will hear about from the Ahtzic Uinac. There are depths of meaning in the story and the student's level of understanding affects what the Ahtzic Uinac shares and focuses upon. It concerns the ball playing twins, Hunahpu and Xbalanque. By now, you must be aware that the stories of our people are meant to convey deeper truths than the mere outer story. These are tales meant to prepare the man to accomplish the great feats of the heroes, which are in the stories. The goal is always the same: to do what the Creator wills and to defeat Xibalba. Always."

The story of Hunahpu and Xbalanque was a common tale that was told to all children. Everyone knew the story and wanted to be like the hero twins. We were disappointed that he was going to tell us a story that each one of us knew by heart. Everyone revered the twins, yet to hear the tale once again was annoying.

"Why don't you tell us another story? We're bored of that already," Cham complained.

"What you do not know is that the story is very real up to a point. There were probably never two twins. I mean twins who were born naturally from a marriage. That is, most likely, myth and storytelling. That is unimportant. It is meant to tell you about the double and the twin positions. The double is alluded to in the story if you are intelligent enough to realize it. It states that when the father and uncle of

Hunahpu and Xbalanque were brought forth into the world, they were born at night. Xibalba eventually defeated them. When the twins were born, they were born during the day. You will find that if ..." He stopped talking and said that it would be best if he told the story as it was meant to be told and added his commentaries at the moments when they happen during the story.

Cham took the opportunity to ask, "Wouldn't it be better to simply give out the information rather than obscuring small points inside a tale?"

"No, no one would remember them, then. The story is interesting enough that it is memorable. If one had to remember dry facts, one wouldn't recall them as easily. Think of it as a glue that holds together vital truths," he said as he clasped his hands together. "The day will come when the earth is old, when the secrets within the story must come to light, but that day is not already here. Now, the information must be hidden from the eyes of the unworthy. Only he from whom the naual has come forth in may begin to decipher the story, or those whom the Creator wishes to reveal it to. We have a great interest in spreading this story to the other tribes around us."

"Why?" Hac asked. "Wouldn't it be better to keep the whole story hidden then?"

"No. We seek to make alliances with those who are capable of understanding it. This story is known, all around, as coming from us. If someone deciphers it, he knows whom to go to. Knowledge creates brotherhood."

It was one of the famous stories from our tribe. Everyone knew that the words were ours and celebrated the twins along with us. We called them our ancestors. I was entertaining the thought that what was meant was more myste-rious and a lot weirder than actually being related by blood to the twins, which is what I was originally led to believe.

The Cabicacmotz began the tale. He started with the first part of the story, which dealt with the father of the hero twins, One Hunahpu. He advised us that there were layers and layers hidden in the story, which were unnecessary to our current discussion, but he advised us to pay attention to everything in the story because it was significant, no matter how innocuous it seemed. One Hunahpu and Seven Hu-nahpu were brothers who played the ball game. They were born in the night. They were called down into Xibalba, the underworld. Because the Xibalbans were supposedly upset about the noise the brothers made while they played bateh, they challenged them to a game. In Xibalba, they were defeated because they took the wrong crossroad. They took the Black Road, the road to Xibalba.

"Now, though, we must discuss the roads," he continued. "The roads are the directions. The Black Road means the west. The Red Road is the east. The White Road is the north. The Yellow Road corresponds to the south. When you dream, you must become aware of where the directions are. This is elementary. You must always become aware of what direction you are heading in, in your dreams. Re-member that. It is necessary. The directions will be revealed by knowing. When we dream, something in us tells us what is so. This knowing will reveal the directions around you while you dream. Accustom yourselves, during the day, to always know the directions around you; this habit will automatically be carried into your dreaming awareness."

"This is not integral to your understanding, yet I will mention it. Xibalba is at its full power when it is the blackness of the night, when the earth has rotated to where the sun is obscured by the other side of the earth. One must not go down into Xibalba unless one actually sets out to do so. Anyway, this is the first defeat of One and Seven Hunahpu. They did not realize where they were headed and mistakenly took the road to the west, the underworld, when they might have taken a more auspicious direction."

The Cabicacmotz said, "Two things are important thus far. One, they were born in the blackness of the night. The hidden meaning of this is not related to time, it relates to something much more esoteric. One Hunahpu is the dreamer coupled with the physical body. Seven Hunahpu is the dreamer coupled with the spirit. False doubles, doubles without the necessary power to withstand the tests of the underworld. Because their eyes are the eyes of the dreamer, they do not have the clarity that one has when one sees with the eyes of the spirit. If you will remember, to make the true double, one must be in the awareness of the spirit body. One and Seven Hunahpu were formed with the awareness of the dreamer. Let us speak of what you can expect. If you do those two things anyway, your vision will not be clear and perfect. Things will be visionary and mutable, exactly how they are in normal dreams. This is not what you want. Not to have that clarity is what later leads those two into further defeat."

"Once One and Seven Hunahpu were in Xibalba, they were defeated over and over again because they did not have any clarity. Their eyes were the eyes of dreamers; they were not the eyes of the spirit. Their final mistake cost them their lives. They accepted illumination from the lords of the night. We cannot accept anything from those beings and retain our awareness during the trip. When one is dreaming, one cannot accept any gifts or sustenance from the denizens of that realm, or else one loses awareness and control. Remember that, it will become very important to you in your dreaming. One day, you will probably make yourselves conspicuous in dreams because you become aware inside a dream. Immediately, the beings there will offer you things. If you accept, you can kiss your awareness goodbye."

"The first offspring of One Hunahpu were named One Monkey and One Artisan. One Monkey represents the undoubled dreamer; One Artisan represents the undoubled spirit body. To a seer, they both appear unfinished, incomplete. Their faces are pale and their features are unformed, they are just eyes and thin lips. They do not have the completeness and perfection, which the true double has. They are insubstantial bodies. The real double appears as a perfect replica of the human body. Later on, you will discover that the double can alter its shape in any way it likes."

"The next generation, the sons of One Hunahpu: Hunahpu and Xbalanque are said to have been born in the light. Again, this does not refer to the light of day. It refers to the process where the person performs the twin positions and winds up in the awareness of the spirit, the light. While in that awareness, the true doubles are made. The spirit enters the physical body to produce Hunahpu. The spirit enters the dreamer to produce Xbalanque. Those two are capable of defeating Xibalba because they are perfect and they have full clarity. Their eyes are the eyes of light. Their eyes are the eyes of the spirit. Their predecessors used the eyes of the dreamer."

"In the story, the invitation from Xibalba to come and play is truly brought by the falcon. The falcon represents the light and the realm of heaven; it denotes that the spirit is the ultimate victor. The falcon had swallowed a snake. The snake represents darkness and the realm of the underworld; it denotes the dreamer. The original message was hidden in a louse, which represents the earth, denoting the physical body. Anyway, those two boys were capable of defeating Xibalba and defeating death itself."

"I have a question about the forming of the doubles," Hac said.

The Cabicacmotz nodded and indicated that he should ask his question.

"If one needs to fall asleep again as the dreamer to bring the spirit forth, how then can the dreamer enter the spirit to bring forth Seven Hunahpu?" Hac asked.

"Ah," said the Cabicacmotz. "I see the source of your confusion. It is very astute of you to have noticed that. The answer is that the spirit is always somewhere about, but unless our awareness is in it, it is in repose. When you achieve this, one day, you will have to look around for it. Usually it is not far away at all. We will discuss the finer points one day, but not today."

"What kinds of fine points?" Cham asked. "There's more to this?"

"Much more," The Cabicacmotz answered. "Even the particular positions one holds one's body in are important. No more for now, please."

At that point, he reminded us of something that had bypassed each of us. He told us to think of the parents of One and Seven Hunahpu. Xpiyacoc was the father and Xmucane was the mother.

"It should be apparent to you that these are the names of the original seers who perfected these techniques. Xpiyacoc generated One Hunahpu by uniting his dreamer with his physical body. When this doubled being died, so also did Xpiyacoc because his body was part of the material used to build One Hunahpu. Xmucane generated Seven Hunahpu by only doubling her dreamer into her spirit, thus she did not die."

"When it comes time to bring up Hunahpu and Xbalanque in the story, it is unclear at this time what is meant. Blood Woman, the daughter of Blood Gatherer, the Xibalban lord, is said to have given birth to Hunahpu and Xbalanque. There is considerable evidence to say that Blood Woman is actually a representation for the woman's menstrual cycle. Women have more power and prowess at that time. Anyway, it might be a hint to our female dreamers on when the most advantageous time is for bringing out the perfect double. There are some, of course, who argue that part of the boys was composed of Xibalban material because of Blood Woman. You should ponder all possibilities."

Hac asked, "What's a menstrual cycle?"

By the intent look on his face, I could tell that Cham was as glad as I was that Hac had asked the question. We didn't know what it was either.

With reticence, the Cabicacmotz told us what it was. He stressed that it was not a dangerous thing or a sickness that befell women, but that it pertained solely to the reproductive cycle. It was quite shocking to us, but we hid it well.

"Later on, when the subject comes up about the two rivers that man must cross in order to enter Xibalba, you might ponder what the Red River and the White River might mean. Let your imaginations wander. Weigh all potential permutations of possibility." He looked at us and sighed. "Anyway, already I have told you bits of the story which you should take note of when the Ahtzic Uinac tells them to you. There is more to this story, of course, as he will tell you, so I am only mentioning the salient points. Do you see?"

We didn't know what to say. He had succeeded in shocking us. These were the tales of our youth, exposed as tales of unfathomable mystery. How much more was hidden from us, we feared to know. We were all quiet as we contemplated what he told us.

A short while later, after we had recovered from the shock of learning that our favorite childhood stories were mere cloaks for deadly serious matters, he told us that we had done enough and could do as we liked for the rest of the day.

We did. We gathered up tools from my home to clean up the ball court and spent the remainder of the day pruning back the growth and sweeping it out. By the time we finished up at dusk, it was ready to be played in. We were proud of our efforts when we stood to the side and looked at the tidy court.

I asked them when they would be spending the night over at my house again and they told me that the Cabicacmotz told them that they should go home for the night, but that he would let them know when it was time to stay over again. I got the impression that they were a little homesick. I didn't want to insinuate it; lest they think I thought them sissies.

Chahal and I walked home. When we were almost there, one of my father's guards fetched me and told me that my father would like to see me. The guard walked behind me, for some reason. I couldn't figure out why because there was no chance that I would ignore such a summons. I determined that he was crude in his social graces and decided to point out his lack of manners to my father.

Father sat sideways upon a hammock in the back garden. He smiled and waved when he saw us. Chahal and I went over to him and sat down on the grass before him.

The guard joined his fellows in the fan that surrounded my father.

"This has been quite a day, has it not?" he asked me.

I agreed that it had been. It felt like weeks had passed since the day of the festival and the festival had only been the day before yesterday. "Are your guards no longer permitted to converse with me?"

"What do you mean?" he asked.

"Your man did not walk with me to come see you."

"I saw him walking with you, Zaki."

"No. He walked behind me as if he didn't want to speak with me or as if he suspected that I would run off without coming to you. Why?"

He chewed his lip and sighed sadly. "Zaki, we have now received news that a tribe, which speaks our own language, is engaged in great evil. We know who they are. They are the people who left when we refused to pay honor to the false god, Tohil, any longer. We can be certain that they know who we are and probably where we now are. Intruders will not look like foreigners, nor will they sound different from us because they are our brothers. They may be in our midst right now. I will not take chances with my progeny, especially not my eldest son. You are to sit upon my mat and rule. You will advance our lineage. Also, you are precious to me because of your mother." He smiled at me with affection and said, "Truly, you are my favorite child. Well... you and your sister."

"Do you think that's because both of our mothers are gone?"

"Perhaps, but I think it has more to do with something else. Both women were the sweetest women of all. They had nothing of selfishness in them. They were not jealous or mean of spirit and I believe that both of you take after them in many ways. In my other children, I see their mothers who are vain, selfish, jealous, and concerned with acquisitions of wealth and rank. I see bad things in their futures unless they change and I don't know how to force another person to become better. I should have been more selective in my choices because your mothers were the only ones who were true queens. The process we have is terrible. I am expected to fill immediately any vacant places of the four directions with a woman. Instead of allowing me time to grieve and find a suitable wife, I am commanded to place a woman there without knowing her well enough to like her, much less love her. The moment I became king, they showed me the women and I liked their beauty, believing that only a fine soul could have been granted such grace of form. I only had luck with Maricua's mother and yours, though, and both were ripped away from me."

"Why do you have to have four?"

"The perpetuity of the kingly lineage. Then it is disguised in superstition about the directions. Such a thing is sometimes used for esoteric operations, but it is unnecessary in normal life, except for ensuring a brood of children and the unhappiness of kings."

I had never heard him speak of things with such defeat in his voice. I could understand why he was unhappy, but it saddened me that he was. "Will I have to have four wives also?"

He gave me a hard look and said, "Not if I can help it. I will be making new rules for the tribe and abolishing the practice. I don't care if the ministers and governors don't like it. I refuse to be forced to take another wife, unless I want one."

"Why didn't you do that before?"

"When I came to rule, I had never been with a woman. To have four beautiful women presented to me was more than I could resist. They were all lovely to behold. I thought that I had been blessed beyond all measure. Only later, did I come to my senses and realize that Maricua's mother was the only one with any worth. Then when she died, I was grieving and vulnerable and welcomed the hopefulness that only a new experience of a woman can bring. I had also accepted the situation and did not like the idea of having an unfilled direction; it felt unbalanced. That is why I married the second east woman. She proved to be the biggest headache of all. Therefore, when I met your mother, I was so enchanted by her beauty and goodness, that I established the new rule of the fifth wife, and rebelled against tradition. I was desperate for love and marital happiness, Zaki. When she died so also did I. I resigned myself to my fate."

His mention of the witch, the Eastern wife, spurred my memory. "I saw the most curious thing today, father. Did you know that Ahtoobalvar, my dreaming teacher, has hard fired clay floors? It is like walking upon flattened vases. Wouldn't it be better to put in one new floor so that woman can stop buying all of those rugs?"

"That would make her too happy, my son. She would then complain that the floors were too hard on her feet and would insist on buying new rugs anyway. She would probably say that she has grown accustomed to soft floors because I never built her a worthwhile house with proper floors. There is no contentment in that woman. She always wants more. It is good for her to suffer a bit. To tell you the truth, it pleases me when she is made to wait for things. Still, she has not learned to have a happier spirit. Besides, I am hardly ever there. I only go if I feel like having a woman."

"Do you mean when you make new children with her?"

"Yes, but I try not to have any more children with her. They would be more children made without any love or feeling."

"Then why go over there at all? You don't like her. Can't you refuse to visit and go see the other women instead?

"I could, but she has given me some children and I like to visit with them also. They are young enough that they are still a pleasure to talk to and spend time with. Her influence has not already made an appearance within them."

I could have disabused him of that idea. They were all especially nasty to me, despite the fact that I was their brother.

"Find one woman that you love, Zaki. The other way feels very empty at times. I will fix things so that you are allowed to have only one wife, if you choose. If you choose to have more, then that is your option. It will not be forced upon you. Let us go into the house now, though. It is too dark out here and I want to see you more clearly when I talk with you. Right now, you are almost a shadow."

We all walked to the house. When we got there, the guards posted themselves in various positions and Chahal went to the courtyard. My father and I sat on cushions in the room that was painted to resemble a jungle.

A short while later, one of the guards came in carrying a strange sculpture. It was a face in repose. At first, I thought that it was a mask until I noticed my father's grin.

It was the face of my mother. Her eyes were closed and her lips turned up at the corners in a soft smile. She had high cheekbones and a delicate brow. She did not look like the women of my tribe at all. Our tribe boasted many beautiful women, but her beauty was of another kind. Hers was more ethereal. Sunken cheeks were never in vogue, but they were extraordinarily exquisite on her face. I thought I would be embarrassed to see that she did not look like a child of the tribe, but I was wrong. I was proud of her beauty and exotic features.

I touched the contours of her face and then felt my own face to see if her features had carried over to me, hoping every moment that they would. My only experiences with mirrors were in reflecting pools, obsidian, and smoothed metals. They were inferior to true mirrors and did not give one an accurate idea of one's looks.

I gushed to my father about how beautiful she was. I was utterly transfixed by her.

"Yes, she was spectacularly lovely, Zaki. To see her was to see the sun. She had a radiance about her that sharpened every color in my field of vision. She walked like a queen, she was all grace." He smiled in remembrance. "And yet, when she ran, she ran like a little girl, she was all elbows and knees, no grace then. But I wouldn't have asked her to be any other way because she was free and happy when she ran. How she would laugh, you could not imagine. We would take turns trying to catch each other in the fields. Someday, she and I will chase each other through fields again..."

It frightened me to think that he might start crying. To see such a strong and proud man humbled by life was distressing to me, so I changed the subject. "Why did the Cabicacmotz learn our secrets, if he wasn't a tribesman?"

His eyes widened at my question and I felt that it put his mind on other matters. "In Tulan, we built a great edifice, a ziggurat of incredible proportions. What we have now, are nothing in comparison to that place. All of the tribes had come together to share their wisdom and mingle it together to build a body of knowledge that transcended all superstition and myth. We did that and then we reflected our knowing in the ziggurat. We decided that its summit must surpass the clouds to allow us to see the stars whenever we needed to. Every step upwards was a journey of knowledge. The students would climb each step to reach another level in their education. There were intricacies that they had to undergo for each level, which pertained to the cardinal directions. They would learn the applications of knowledge and all things of relevance pertinent to each direction of that level. The training was intense. Only those who reached the top of their education could reach the clouds and finally see beyond the curtain. There was the physical curtain of the clouds and its counterpart was the mysterious curtain of hidden knowledge. We made a great mistake; we did not ask the Creator to bless our undertaking. We did not even expand our knowing of him. We mired ourselves in intricacies and practicalities as we ignored the source of everything. To punish us, he scrambled our speech. No longer could the tribes intermingle and share knowledge easily. Either we had to learn each other's languages or we could not understand each other. We were like foreigners to one another. That effectively put an end to our enterprise. We could point at objects to determine the sounds that each language made to name it, but we couldn't express or convey what we meant when it came time to discuss intangible subjects. Because of that, the tribes dispersed and went in all directions. We lost each other. Since we had to wander to find new homes, much of our knowledge was forgotten. Centuries passed and swallowed us while we were busy with the practicality of moving mass amounts of people together upon our journey. Thankfully, our tribe has pieced together many of the things we knew in that time and recovered them. What we thought were gods came to us after our speech was separated. Actually, that is a subject best left for another time. Anyway, apparently other tribes were also able to piece together or hold on to their knowledge because the Cabicacmotz' people did so."

"Do you mean that tribes from Tulan also went to the other side of the earth?"

"We came from there. At least, that is what our legends tell us. No one really knows anymore. Who can tell?" he said as he shrugged. "The Ahtzic Uinac recounts that we came over to our land from across the sea. The difference between the Cabicacmotz and us is that he came here by a ship. Our people took a bridge made from the ocean's floor, which had risen up to aid us in our journey. But that is unimportant. When he and your mother arrived here, we were very curious about them. We saw the wreckage of their boat. We only use canoes, but they had an actual ship that could accommodate many people. The master of the ship and the other children on board with them had perished during a storm. For a long time, your mother and he survived who knows how. They finally landed on one of the atolls that are visible from shore. Our people found them and they were brought here to safety. They were very frightened because your mother was already a young woman and was bleeding. If we had not found them, they might have starved or been eaten by sharks, since they didn't even have a raft. Yet they were brought here alive and well. It took them many years to learn our language enough to properly convey to us their story."

"Why were they allowed to stay at all?"

He gave me a look of complete disdain. "We are not savages, Zaki. We do not expel orphans from our borders merely because they are not tribesmen. They were defenseless and had no adult to protect them or care for them. In such a case, there is only one humane thing to do. Adopt them into families of the tribe. Often such individuals are given plots far away from the citadel proper to cultivate. An odd thing happened, though. When they were able to communicate with us, at last, they told us things which identified them as coming from the tribes of Tulan."

"That is incredible. How could it be?" I asked.

"Your mother was only beginning her training with the priestesses of her tribe upon an island. Your uncle had already learned quite a bit and had spent many years upon that island dutifully learning all he could for being such a young child. He knew the story of Hunahpu and Xbalanque, albeit under different and foreign names."

"What were they called in his land?"

"That is too hard to remember or even to pronounce," he said with a laugh. "Suffice it to say that one of the twin boys was called a name which means 'many twins'. Also, his teachers were called a name which used the beginning of the Cabicacmotz' title. The name only used the Cabi' part. The rest I forget. The previous Cabicacmotz was very struck by that one coincidence. He decided to finish their education in honor of them being from Tulan. It was only right."

"Why were they on an island? Couldn't they learn at home?"

"It was the custom among the aristocracy to have their children trained in the arts upon that island. It seems that the female children went at a later time than the boys."

"Why do you think that is so?" I asked him.

He guffawed with great pleasure, as if he savored my question. "Oh, Zaki. What can I say? Women need less training than men do. They learn with surprising ease any-thing, which is put to them. The only subjects they find difficult to learn at first are those involving the calendar, the stars, and the subject of numbers. After they get the hang of it, they are unstoppable. They have a raw talent, which we, who are mere males, do not have. It is no surprise that they are brought to learning the moment they become imbued with power. Starting them off earlier will not ac-complish much more and might even harm them. It is better to allow them an unfettered childhood. "

"What does becoming imbued with power mean? When does that happen to them?"

"When women become capable of reproducing, their time is announced by a flow of blood from between their legs. No one knows why, but females turn into power at that time. What a thing. Boys receive power in a similar manner, but it is not as potent as that of the women."

I didn't want to talk about distasteful biological matters. I wanted to hear more about the youth of the Cabicacmotz. I asked, "Couldn't you have been mistaken about them having been learning about the twins?"

"No, absolutely not," he said with a shake to his head. "Besides, it wasn't me that made the determination. It was the former Cabicacmotz. He took the two of them in and gave them a home, when they first arrived. He had a team of scribes and tutors instruct them in our language and writings. Those two were marvelous. We have taken other foreigners in, but their command of our language cannot compete with the result those tutors accomplished in those two within a few years. To tell you about the significance of the twins, though, the Cabicacmotz told me that it was the only thing that the tribes could agree upon, after they lost their power of communication. With that sign, tribes could identify each other as coming from Tulan. Without it, they are impostors.

"But couldn't the story have been told to them and they adopted it, somehow?"

"Certainly, but the knowledge of the underlying truths in the story cannot be feigned; nor can those truths be guessed at. Only one whose naual has emerged can decipher it correctly."

There was no arguing with that. "Can you tell me more about the tribe of my mother?" I asked.

'The only things I know are what I have told you. The children of nobles were sent to the island to learn." He stopped and chewed his lip in thought for a few moments before continuing. "Actually, I do remember one thing about those people. The general populace was allowed to think that the beings in the stories were true gods when they were not the Creator. I don't understand that part. Their teachings were enshrouded in myth. It seems that the masses were given mythical stories of gods, small and great, but only the learned were allowed to know their real meanings. We have not done that, we give stories, but we do not try to pass them off as gods. In fact, only after Hunahpu and Xbalanque resurrect themselves and defeat Xibalba do they achieve apotheosis, godhood. Then they were given their place among the great stars..."

"Your questions have stirred my memory, Zaki, because I remember something else. In the story about the twins, among Cabi's people, there was an addition, which has perplexed us all. Many people are working to understand it and verify it through practical methods. In that story, the mother of the twins had four children. Two boys and two girls were in eggs, the boys in one and the girls in another. Only two were considered the children of the male god: one boy and one girl. We are trying to determine why they used the imagery of eggs and other finer points, since we love deciphering such mysteries. Right now, many of us prefer to think that they used the imagery of the females to reinforce the idea that women are as adept as men are. That, I believe, is unwarranted and overly positive. From what your mother told me about the society, I have reason to believe that women were undervalued to a certain extent. The rest of us theorize that the women who were twins represent the first twinning, when the person performs a doubling from the awareness of the dreamer. In the story they tell, the two women are most corrupt. One is an adulteress and the other a murderess. Thus, they were base. If you will examine your dreams, you will find that they are not as moral as they should be. They belong to the realm of the underworld. You will have achieved a great victory when your dreams are pure and just. To continue the conversation now, the males had no such stains. The women are in one set. One is a child of the god, representing the dreamer combining itself with the spirit. The other woman is considered mortal; she would be the dreamer combining itself with the human body. Same scenario with the males in one egg. One is the awareness of the spirit combining with the dreamer and the other would be a combining with the meat of the person. Do you see?"

"How did you know that I had learned about this already, father?" I asked him. It truly bewildered me because he was carrying forward topics and conversations that I had only had today with two other people.

"I hear about everything you learn, my son. Runners report to me as to your whereabouts and carry messages from your instructors letting me know about what subjects you are being introduced to and things like that. Don't be upset," he said when he saw my shocked expression. "You are a priority for me. I have many things I must take care of in my position, but none is more important to me than your wellbeing and safety. You cannot blame me. After all, I did ask you to come and tell me about your days, on the morning you became a man. You have not come to me, so I am forced to hear secondhand reports about your education."

I was utterly chagrined to have failed him in that. I apologized to him repeatedly and finally said, "I feel that you are so busy that you will not want to hear about the trivial and unimportant things that happen to me, father. I never feel that I should intrude upon you and add to your burdens by making you take the time to speak with me. What can I say that will be more important than running a kingdom and keeping so many people in peace and prosperity?"

"Neither of us can be more important than such a thing, Zaki. A king must be ready to lay down his life for his people, but more crucially, he must be willing to live for them. It is easy to die for people and causes, but it is much harder to live for them. One day, when you sit upon my mat, you will realize that there must be balance in the life of a king. He cannot be always working. There will be times when he must relax and take his rest. If he does not take care of himself, he will fail his people. He cannot work constantly and not exercise, take in the sun, or sleep. He must have a measure of happiness in his home life that is personal and outside of the sphere of his rule. You and Maricua are my happiness. You do not disturb me when you come to my side. I want you there. In fact, it is an essential part of your training that you spend time in my court. You must become more acquainted with governance. The principles you will learn about governing people can also be used to govern yourself. When you finish lessons, please come and see me. In addition, we should establish convenient times to discuss your progress. Perhaps during the evening meal would be the best time. From now on, I will be at the house for dinner. I will advise the cooks about having an extra guest. Should there be a day when I am unable to attend, I will expect you to come to my home after you finish your lessons."

"Sometimes they end very late, father. The Cabicac-motz will probably continue teaching us about moving in the night and shadows."

"That is unimportant. Those nights will be like tonight, where you are expected to stay the night. That way, if neither of us is too tired, we may talk. Or else we might talk at the morning meal instead. Is that acceptable to you?"

I nodded with a big grin on my face.

He ruffled my hair, messing it up.

"I must bathe in the stream before I go to sleep, father. Also, I don't have anything to put on afterwards."

He sniffed the air comically, wrinkling up his nose in disgust. "Whatever have you been doing, boy? You smell like wild animals."

"Chahal led us to a wonderful place, father," I gushed. "It is a ball court in the jungle. It was tangled and wild when we found it, but today we cleaned it up. It will be perfect for us to practice in. You should see it. It's small, but fine for us since we are only beginners."

With a dubious expression, he asked, "Is it behind a cataract?"

"Yes, it is. How did you know?"

"I believe it is the court I used to play in when I was a boy. The Cabicacmotz and I played in there ourselves. How strange. This is unexpected. What could it mean? And you say that Chahal led you?"

I nodded and asked, "Why is that strange? It was abandoned. It has become overgrown from neglect."

"You do not see what I am saying, Zaki. There is a symmetry here, whose meaning escapes me. I will have to ask the Cabicacmotz to help me figure it out. Let us talk of something else. You will not need to bathe in the stream because the servants are preparing a bath for you."

"I don't want servants to bathe me," I protested.

"No, no, Zaki. You have it wrong. You will have your privacy. Here, I will show you," he said as he stood. "You will be using my private bath. It will be very different from what you are accustomed to, but I think you will like it."

He led me to an enclosed courtyard where a deep basin stood. Servants were filling it up with water they had boiled at a stone grill. I could see the steam rise from it despite the hot and humid night. It looked a bit frightening to me. Boiled water always scared me since it could scald the incautious. I saw a woman shredding leaves into the water. A pleasant odor of mint permeated the air.

"Am I to be cooked?" I asked.

My father chuckled and said, "No, Zaki. You are merely being given a treat that your mother introduced me to. She used to have a hot bath every day. I always wondered how she could stand it until she made me try it. Nowadays, I try to have one twice a week, at least. It is especially soothing if one has tired muscles from exercise. I am sure you will enjoy it." He pointed out a sea sponge and told me to use it to wash the grime and sweat away. After that, I was to rub the mint leaves over my body. He told me to disrobe after everyone was gone and to get in. He also said that I should undo my braid and rinse out my hair and that a woman would come in to braid my hair in a short while.

I took off my tunic and loincloth. The steam was still rising, so I dipped my hand into the basin to make sure that I wouldn't suffer burns. It felt hot, but not scalding, so I stepped into it. When the water reached my upper thighs, I felt some discomfort, but my body quickly adjusted to the temperature. I sat down and undid my braid in the water. I could feel my hair swishing around me as I ducked under water. Truly, it was heavenly. Who could have imagined that sitting in a pot of almost boiling water could be so delicious?

Chahal came up to the basin, sniffing it and the water in it. She dipped her tongue in the water and wrinkled her nose in distaste. She kept on sticking her tongue out and licking air. I could feel her displeasure at having the taste of mint in her mouth. I was glad for it, though, since she had eaten fish today. After a while, the taste must not have bothered her as much because she quieted down and went to sleep on the stone floor.

A house matron came in, a proper confessor, coughing to alert me to her presence. She told me that she would be braiding my hair. She directed me to lie in the water and tilt my head back so that my scalp was under the water. Reaching in, she lightly scratched her nails against my scalp and massaged it. What a wonderful sensation. Then she ran her fingers through my hair to undo any tangles. She took my hair and hung it outside of the basin, advising me to lean back and relax as she groomed my hair.

"Is there anything you wish to tell me?" she asked.

"Not really. I can't think of anything that I have done since my last confession that weighs upon me." I thought for a few moments and said, "Except for one thing and it's more in the nature of seeking advice. Sometimes I find that my thoughts are not controlled. Sometimes they are unkind thoughts and I cannot stop myself from thinking them. I now have teachers who can read my thoughts as if I spoke them aloud to the wind. It is most disconcerting and I wish to be better. What should I do?"

"You are young, but that is a wise wish. I will tell you how I did such a thing. Perhaps that will help you. Have you learned where the dreamer and the spirit reside when one is in this world?"

"No. No one has told me. It has been alluded to, but their actual locations are a mystery to me." It amazed me that even my confessor would comment about the dreamer and the spirit.

"Yes, it is an advanced observation."

"Why do you call it that? An observation."

"Because many things we know, we know because we have placed ourselves in the moment and actually observed how things are. It is important to notice where the self is at any moment. When you are feeling angry, cruel, or unkind, check to see where your self is. Then, determine where the thought originates from. The dreamer belongs to the realm of the underworld, the spirit from the heavens. In me, my spirit is behind my left shoulder blade. My dreamer is behind my right shoulder blade. Then, from the position of the self, I sever the thoughts that originate from the dreamer, if they are unwholesome and unworthy of a being that houses the spirit. When I was younger, it took me a while to catch the thoughts and I could only sever them when they had grown in me. They are like plants, those thoughts. They grow quickly like weeds. Later on, I became adept at the exercise and was able to sever them the moment they sprouted."

"But how did you sever them? Does one use a physical tool, like a flint blade?"

She laughed softly and said, "No, young one. This severing is done with the mind. It seems imaginary, but it is nothing of the sort. It is very effective. There is movement in it. You can perform many actions of this kind with the power of the mind and intent. You intend to sever the ugly thought. You cut from left to right and then you return to the place where your self resides. There is nothing more I can say of it. Notice where the thoughts come from and sever them. The locations are sometimes different for different people. In fact, you do not actually need to observe where your self actually is in this exercise. That comes naturally. You will see that when you strike to cut off the sprouts of bad thought, that your spirit moves into position naturally and without thought. That is the part of you that moves and acts in this maneuver. Later on, you should observe everything about the exercise, but for now, that will help you."

Somehow, her words penetrated my thick mind and I thanked her for her advice. She told me that she was glad to be of help.

"What kind of leaves are these in the water?" I asked. "Are they mint?"

She told me they were and told me that my father enjoyed those leaves the most during the summer months because they left one with a cool feeling after bathing. She finished braiding my hair and tying it.

"Be careful, young prince, not to fall asleep in the tub. It is tempting to because it is so soothing, but you must not drown," she said before she left.

As soon as she left, I used the sponge my father gave me. Its roughness was an interesting sensation. After that, I took handfuls of leaves and rubbed them on my body. It was a bit unusual at first, but pleasant. Then, I laid back and thought as I enjoyed the water. It made me a little drowsy, but the scent of the leaves seemed to invigorate me at the same time. Once the water cooled, I felt chilled even though the night was hot.

Servants must have been watching out for me because a manservant came in with clothes and suede slippers for me as I was thinking about getting out. He placed them on a nearby bench and then handed me a cloth to dry myself with.

My father waited for me outside of the entryway to the bath. He was reclining on a bench almost dozing. He jumped up when he saw me and shook off his sleepiness. "Well?" he asked. "How did you like it?"

I told him that it was a lovely experience and I could see why my mother enjoyed it so much. "I could have one of those baths every day," I said.

He slapped me on the back jovially and told me that I was truly my mother's son.

I smiled at his words and told him, "I wish that I could commission a sculpture of her face like you have, father."

"That will not be necessary, Zaki. I will give the mold to one of the artists and they will make it with plaster. Once it dries, you will have it."

I thanked him, excited that I would receive such a gift.

"Do you feel hot or cold now?" he asked me.

I told him that I was comfortable and that the mint leaves had left me with a cool sensation. Every draft of air that hit me caused me to feel a soothing coolness upon my skin. It was a feeling I could get used to and I could see why he used mint in the summer.

We talked about dreaming after that. I asked him for any advice that he could give me so that I could have success in my homework.

"The best way to start anything is to make up your whole mind to do it. Any vacillation, on your part, will have the effect of hindering you. If you tell yourself to look at your hands, but also think that you would like to have a dream about a beautiful woman or other worldly wishes, you will be stopped in your tracks. Your aim must not be divided; it must be true like an arrow."

It did not sound like easy advice to follow. Of late, I had noticed my thoughts and they were all over the place, rarely settling on anything. To hold only one thought was difficult even though it sounded simple. It seemed that the simple things were the difficult ones. My father's expression was very intent, as if he was willing me to understand his words and find comprehension in them. It felt hopeless. I swallowed loudly.

"Look, Zaki. All of this is very new to you, but it will come to you. Perhaps it will come to you slowly or all at once, but it will come. You do not notice that there has already been a big change in you. I have noticed something very heartening to me. Your conversation is expanding along with your view of the world. In days, you have metamorphosed into a person whom one can have meaningful words with."

I looked at him in surprise. "Really?"

"Yes, really. I am astounded by your progress. You do not stumble as often as you used to when unfamiliar subjects are broached. Your questions are not the basic questions of children any longer. You are learning to think and it comes naturally to you, it does not seem to strain your concentration as it once did. Do you need to pee?"

I told him that I didn't need to.

Come," he said as he led me down the hall.

Suddenly he came up behind me and pushed me towards the wall, grasping hold of my hands and positioning them flat on the wall. With his knees, he kept my legs away from the wall. He got behind me and screamed in my ears to look at my hands. I thought I would faint from the fright. My father had never hit me or treated me roughly. To hear him yelling in my ears completely shocked me out of my wits.

"Look at them. Look at your hands, Zaki. Do you see them? There they are in front of you to look at. Look at your hands." He removed his hands from mine and grasped my shoulders. "Look at them, Zaki. Command yourself to look at them tonight while you are in a dream. Say it out loud, Zaki."

"I will look at my hands in my dream," I managed to mutter.

"Know it and then say it, Zaki. Say it with force."

We stayed there until I said it in such a tone that even I was convinced that I would see my hands in my dream. He told me to shut my eyes and said that he would walk me to my room. He urged me to repeat to myself that I would look at my hands and to acquiesce to his guidance and not to worry about obstacles, that he would lead me to my room and that I was in no danger of stumbling. I had no choice. In silence, he led me to the room at the end of the courtyard and to the edge of my mat. I felt around and, eyes closed, positioned myself on the soft bedding.

He told me that he would stay until I fell asleep and that I should not open my eyes. I heard the rumbling of Chahal as she settled down near me.

"She will keep you safe during the night," he said. "Don't open your eyes. Keep on repeating to yourself that you will see your hands. Let your body relax and let sleep claim you, my son. You will soon dream and in that dream, you will see your hands."

"Thank you for my bath and for my mother's face."

"Shush," he softly whispered. "You are most welcome. Now sleep well."

I easily drifted off.

In my dream, crowds of strangely turbaned people were milling around me in an outdoor marketplace. It was filled with the sounds of barter and informal commerce. The sun shone high overhead. I wandered around gawking at the citizens of the peculiar place for a short while. I knew that they were not from my tribe. Then, I realized that I was in a dream and remembered what I had to do. I stopped in mid-step and ceased looking around. I lifted my hands, palms upward, and held them away from my body. I gazed intently at them, looking at them in wonder. I was dreaming and I had done what I set out to do. What a feeling.

The sun hid and everything darkened.

The marketplace disappeared.

Blackness enveloped me.

I found myself in what appeared to be a dark cavern. Suddenly, long hideous masks loomed above me, surrounding me in a circle. They were red, black, and white. The mask faces were static, but the eyes had a malevolent intelligence peering from them, looking down upon me.

I was horrified. "Wake up. Wake up. Wake up," I commanded myself.

Abruptly, I was blown backwards by a strong sucking wind that lifted me off my feet. The masked beings moved as if to stop me.

Seconds later, I woke up on my mat. I was in my room at my home, but it did not occur to me that I was somewhere different from where I had fallen asleep. I exhaled loudly in relief.

"I'm here. I'm back."

I got up from my bedding and walked over to a small window ledge that was near the corner of the room. I looked around for Chahal, but did not see her. Shaking my head at Chahal's abandonment, I tried to look out the window that overlooked the grounds, but the curtain stymied my vision. I lifted the filmy cloth and looked out. The shade of a wild dog jumped from shadow to shadow beneath the trees outside. It turned to look at me. My eyes widened in panic.

"I'm not awake! Wake up. Wake up. Wake up," I cried.

Again, I woke up. Now I was back at my father's house. Frightened, I curled up into a fetal position and drew the covers about me. Chahal watched me with her ears pulled back tight against her head. I tentatively reached over to her and was relieved that she was real and solid. She relaxed and soon closed her eyes. I let out a relieved sigh as I closed my eyes.

The next morning, I woke up and found that Chahal was nowhere around. I figured that she must have gone off to hunt. Then I remembered that I had recently learned that her "hunting" sometimes involved going to people's houses and cadging food from her admirers.

After visiting the room for men, I went to my father's dining area. Servants had laid out platters as if for a troop.

My father looked down at the array and chuckled. "I think they've overestimated your appetite, Zaki."

There was no way that I could eat even a tenth of what had been put out. "Why did they serve so much food?"

"I let them know that you would be eating here this morning and didn't know what you liked for breakfast, so I think they are testing you to see what your preferences are. Next time, they will plan things out a bit better, I hope. Still, you're a growing boy, not some gluttonous sow."

"This is excessive. Don't you think it would have been better to wait for me to awaken and then ask me what I like?"

"Yes, but it's too late for that option. Did you dream of your hands or not?" he asked.

I nodded and was about to tell him what happened when he clapped loudly, twice. A scribe, a chubby young man with a round face, entered the room. My father gave him orders to fetch the Cabicacmotz and Ahtoobalvar immediately.

"You should hear what happened, father. It was most strange," I said after the scribe left.

"I will hear your story as soon as your teachers arrive. Can you hold the memory of the event longer?"

I told him that I would probably remember it for the rest of my life. It was curious because the memory I had felt like a regular memory. It was not as ephemeral as memories of dreams usually were. Often they vanish from one's mind a few moments after waking. The dream was even more memorable than regular recollections of everyday events. It had a dark intensity to it that did not allow me to shake it off and forget it.

"Very good," he said. "Let us begin to eat."

We scooped some food onto our trays and began to eat. The food was quite delicious. There were some dishes with unusual spices. I asked him what they were and he sent for the cooks to be fetched.

When they arrived, they seemed wary, as if they suspected that they were about to hear complaints. One was a middle-aged cadaverous man who looked like he had not eaten in forty years. He nervously hopped from foot to foot. The other was tall with a rounded paunch and he moved like a tortoise, slow and cautiously. Their eyes darted around the table and over our trays, registering what had been eaten and what had been ignored or rejected.

I complimented them on their food and their faces lit up with gladness. I told them that I had a sister who enjoyed experimenting with various spices and questioned them about the inch long aromatic green rods I had found. They were a new taste for me and I found that they gave a pleasing flavor to the shredded meat.

They told me what it was and offered to send some home with me along with a plant to give Maricua. That way, she could always have it at hand. I thanked them and they left.

"You have made their day, Zaki," my father said. "They are bored cooking solely for me. I should praise their creations more. I don't want them to feel unappreciated."

"This really was one of the best breakfasts I've ever had. It must be dangerous to be the king. You could get too used to eating like that."

He chuckled softly. "I know. That is why they usually have orders to provide simple breakfasts of fruits and dried meats for me. When they heard that we had a guest, and that it was you, they got a bit excited and took the opportunity to get creative."

Chahal sauntered in then and plopped herself down near the door to the courtyard. A moment later, a manservant led Ahtoobalvar and the Cabicacmotz into the room. They greeted us and then sat down at the table. Servants brought them trays and my father urged them to help themselves to the food.

"What happened here, Alomi?" Ahtoobalvar asked. "Did you also send out invitations to the Knights Peccary?"

Credulous, I asked, "Are there really peccary knights?"

They all laughed.

"I'm afraid not, Zaki," the Cabicacmotz dryly said. "They died off quite a long time ago and no one wanted to take their place. They had a tendency for getting picked off by hungry farmers. It's a shame, really, since they made excellent eavesdroppers because no one takes notice of animals. Until they get hungry, of course. Who knew farmers could be so bloodthirsty and cruel to such docile creatures?"

We all laughed at that. I would have to be more careful; it shamed me to realize how gullible I was. I resolved to learn more of the different elements of our society.

My father explained that the cooks were taking advantage of having an extra mouth to feed and went overboard with the choices.

"I will have to commend and reward my scribe for being so efficient," my father said. "I did not expect the two of you to arrive so quickly."

Both men looked questioningly at my father.

"Scribe? What scribe?" asked Ahtoobalvar. "Did you send us a message?"

My father stared at him with his mouth open. "How did you know I sent for you to come then?"

"I didn't. I thought Zaki sent her to fetch me."

"Who?" my father asked.

"Chahal, of course," Ahtoobalvar said. "She showed up when I was with the Cabicacmotz and practically forced us to follow her here. She was most adamant."

I looked at her. She yawned and began licking her paws, ignoring us.

"Then where in the world is my scribe?"

"Is everyone sure that she is really a cat?" Ahtoobalvar asked. "She seems to know a bit more than she would if she was a mundane creature."

Everyone shrugged at that. Then Ahtoobalvar shrugged too and refilled his tray.

"I presume you have a success to share with us then, Zaki," the Cabicacmotz said.

"Um, maybe." I said. "I don't really know if I did it right, though." I told them every detail of my dream. "That's what happened."

"Things went well for you. Very well. Great, in fact. Your first time out and you were able to escape your body," Ahtoobalvar said.

A smile began to spread on my face.

"There is only one problem, though," he added.

I grimaced at his words and began to rub my knees.

"Do you know why things became scary and out of control?"

I shook my head and shrugged.

"This being your first time, you were only supposed to look at your hands for a few moments. Later on, you need to look at your hands and then look back at your dream. When you kept staring at your hands... I even suspect that you gazed at them. You brought in your everyday awareness into the dreamlands and the scary things that rule dreams came out to get a good look at who had escaped their control. The trick is to become mindful in the false world of dreams and not let the inhabitants realize that anything special is among them. They are the enemies of humanity and they seek to keep us unaware and in their power."

"Oh. I had been afraid that the Creator didn't like what I was doing and decided to punish me."

"Don't be stupid. It is nothing like that. The Creator wants us to be awake and aware. That is why we are teaching you all of this." Ahtoobalvar huffed out a breath and then looked back at me, as if to make sure that I had not taken his chiding too seriously. "Look, you did something unusual in their world and that alarmed them. They are great performers. Nightly, they arrange theatrical productions for mankind. Like all illusionists, they prefer that you believe their illusions. If you had merely been a normal dreamer who had momentarily become aware, they would have pretended that everything was normal, waiting until you began dreaming again."

"They really watch for people to start dreaming again?" I asked.

"Yes. They would have waited until you slipped back under their illusion. A sly tactic of theirs is to offer you food or drink. Then, if you accept it, you lose your dreaming control. You are lost." His eyes moved to a corner of the room and his eyes lost focus. "When you get older, they will offer you other things."

"Like what?"

Ahtoobalvar opened his mouth and then seemed to catch himself before he answered, shaking his head. "Never mind that, you will find that out later. You showed strength and they came out to inspect you. Now they know who you are and that you know how to escape from them."

"I don't know how to do that."

"Yes you do, because you did just that."

We all sat in silence for a few minutes.

The Cabicacmotz finally broke the silence. "I wonder why the black stone didn't help him out more." He flung a hand out as if to indicate that it was as useful to question the wind about that fact and said, "Or maybe it did help. Who knows?"

My father's face became ashen and he slapped himself on the forehead. "Burning suns!" he exclaimed. "I forgot all about that blasted stone when I sent him off to bed."

The Cabicacmotz asked him to describe what had happened before I went off to sleep and my father recounted how he had helped me focus on my dreaming task.

The three of them laughed at the fact that their own dreaming teachers had performed the same techniques for helping them on their first try. They talked about how they had afterwards done the same thing themselves when they had to remind themselves to look at their hands in dreaming before going off to sleep.

The Cabicacmotz mentioned that separate dreaming teachers would be necessary for Hac and Cham if they had not been able to perform the exercise on their own. Ahtoobalvar was unconvinced and told the Cabicacmotz that he would go to their homes that night if necessary, or mine if they were to stay there instead.

They returned to the subject of my dreaming and the Cabicacmotz said that it was not up to my father to remind me of my duties. He told me that it was up to me to protect myself and be ever mindful to wear my navel stone.

"I want a belt made for him immediately," my father said. "Also, I want to commission Zotabah to make a necklace of the black discs for him. Please take care of that today. It would please me if his two little friends also received pendants of the stone, just in case. For now, though, he should tie a cloth about his waist to keep the stone in place. Go and do that now, son."

Ahtoobalvar stood up with me and told me that he would help me wrap the cloth around my middle. He spoke to one of the servants and directed him to bring us a long cloth or kidskin. The man returned with both items and we went to the little room I used.

He looked around the room, seemingly pleased with my accommodations.

I told him that the room was a bit small for my tastes.

He clucked his tongue and said, "No. A small room is perfect for now. If it were too large, it would be more difficult for you to remember and hold in your mind. This room needs to become saturated with you and you need to become saturated with it. Eventually, this will be a location that your dreamer will go to. You need to keep things simple for now, you are a beginner."

He asked me to get the stone from my pouch and to nestle it in my navel.

I took off my tunic, so that I only wore a loincloth, and placed the stone in my bellybutton. He wrapped the soft leather around my waist, advising me to let him know if it was too tight or if the stone felt like it was slipping from its place. I let him know that it felt fine. Then he looped the cloth a few times around me and tied it off.

I put on my tunic again and we went back to where my father and the Cabicacmotz were. They both gave Ahtoobalvar questioning looks and he nodded at them and told them that the stone was securely in place.

"I was going to have Zaki accompany me today to get used to the duties I perform, but getting those things taken care of are more important. Perhaps after everything is done and he gets measured for the belt, he can come back and see me," my father said.

We all said goodbye to my father and then we left.

The Cabicacmotz told me that we should pick up Hac and Cham so that they could also get measured for belts. I was excited to see where they lived and eagerly agreed that they should come.

When we were a short ways from my father's estate, we came upon the scribe who had been sent to find Ahtoobalvar and the Cabicacmotz. He was out of breath and sweating profusely. When he saw us, his faced paled and he leaned himself against a retaining wall.

"Where were you?" the man asked. It appeared that he was about to cry.

"The cat found us first," Ahtoobalvar said.

Tears pooled in the man's eyes. "I am going to be dismissed for failing in my duty," the man blubbered. "I am new to my position."

The Cabicacmotz assured him that he was not at fault. Only when he promised to accompany the man to see my father did he calm down. The three of us stayed outside while he went back to the house with the scribe.

When he returned, I asked him why the man was fearful of my father. It bothered me to think that my father's workers thought him an ogre and feared him.

He laughed and said, "The Naualalom is no beast. He is a fine and good man. The scribe is merely new to his post and is awed to be serving the king. He does not know your father well enough, yet. Because he has been selected to serve the king, he believes that his work must be impeccable and that any failure, even when it is outside of his control, constitutes a grave and irreversible error. This is not so. Your father is fair and just. The most he would do is to give him a firm talking to, nothing more. If he was stealing from your father, or from the tribe, that would be a different story, of course."

I tried to imagine what the man had felt. I was accustomed to being around my father and my status was high because of my birth, so it was difficult to imagine myself having to please persons in power, to be in a weak position. One must feel lost and with no control, I concluded, if one had to depend on another's whims.

In silence, we walked for a long time. Walking past many farms, I felt that my feet would come off if we went farther. Even Ahtoobalvar complained about the distance. It was amazing to me that they could live so far away. At first, I was interested to see their home, but my curiosity had passed and now it was an annoying inconvenience.

We passed through a grove of shady trees and found Hac and Cham dozing beneath one of the trees. The Cabicacmotz told me that it was very fortunate that they were there, since their home was still far away. My mouth dropped open in surprise. He shrugged and told me that their parents chose the farm because it was at the edge of the wilderness. I asked him why they did that and he told me that some people preferred quiet lives away from cities and that his own home was even farther away. I resolved that I would never allow him to convince me to visit him.

"No doubt these two could have been helping around the farm, but they probably told their parents that they had school to attend to, and look at them," he said as he kicked the bottoms of their sandals to awaken them. "Wake up, idlers," he yelled.

Hac and Cham jumped up and tried to make sense of their surroundings. Their eyes got big and wide when they saw the Cabicacmotz and Ahtoobalvar. They tried to pretend they were fully awake, when it was clear that they were still groggy. Then they tried to speak, but they were incoherent and didn't seem able to concentrate on their words, losing the thread of what they were saying in mid-sentence.

"All right. All right. We were asleep," Cham cried.

"I think that is more than obvious," said Ahtoobalvar. "Fortunately, you have saved us a trip out to your parent's farm. We will have to come up with a better way to retrieve you. This is the last time I am walking all of the way out here to fetch you shiftless buffoons. You need quarters closer to the citadel proper." He turned towards the citadel and began walking away. He looked back and became visibly annoyed when he saw that the two boys were not follow-ing him. "Get over here. We have places to go. You cannot expect your teachers to lead you by the hand every mo-ment of the day. Hurry. You all need belts." He forced the brothers to march ahead of us with the promise of a kick if they did not keep a steady pace. "I'm afraid you'll find some bushes to snooze under if we let you trail this little parade."

A little while later, I tried to start a conversation with the boys. "Were either of you able to find your hands last night?" I asked.

Quickly, Ahtoobalvar slapped me on the stomach with the back of his hand as he gave me a hard look and mouthed the word, "No."

The boys turned around and told me that they hadn't had any luck. They hadn't seen Ahtoobalvar slap me.

The Cabicacmotz said, "What a coincidence, neither did Zaki here."

I almost protested, but Ahtoobalvar caught my attention and stared into my eyes as he gave a slight shake of his head. It was such a minimal movement, that the boys did not catch it.

"It was harder to do than we expected," said Hac. "Neither of us could remember to do it while we were asleep. I don't know what we're going to do."

"This little conversation is no reason to stop walking boys," Ahtoobalvar told them. "Let's pick up the pace. I'll keep you company up there and give you a few dreaming pointers while I make sure you aren't dragging your feet." He walked to them and they all started walking briskly in front of us.

The Cabicacmotz turned to me and said, "Let us stay a bit farther behind them. You should become aware of a few things. Do not ask the boys about their progress. That is a proper question from a teacher, but not from a fellow student. You have experienced a success and would like to share your victory with your friends, but you must not do so."

"Why?" I asked.

"Because not every person does well with competition, no matter how friendly it is. In some people, it spurs them on, but in others, it only serves to retard their progress and make them feel inadequate. Do not do that to them. If the three of you are to learn with Ahtoobalvar, you will all have to keep your advances secret from each other until he decides that you may discuss them. This is why I wanted each of you to have separate teachers. It would have made lies and secrets unnecessary. No doubt, from now on, he will speak with each of you separately. No two people develop at the same rate. Remember my words; do not discuss dreaming with them."

We sped up our walk a bit so that we were right behind Ahtoobalvar and the boys.

I heard Ahtoobalvar say, "Tonight, you can sleep at Zaki's house and I will help each of you prepare yourselves for dreaming. While I'm busy with you two, the Cabicacmotz can help Zaki. Someone needs to shake up that slacker so that he can finally get some serious dreaming done." He turned around and winked at me.

Both boys laughed at his words.

I was happy to hear that the boys were going to spend the night at my house again.

After that, the six of us went first to the leatherworkers and ordered belts. The Cabicacmotz insisted to the merchant that we needed the belts immediately. The man was glad for the business, but told us that we would have to come back later to pick up the belts since he didn't have any that would fit us. He said that they would have to trim down a few that were for women.

Each of us protested loudly that we didn't want to wear anything that was meant for women. The man patiently explained that all belts were the same, except that the belts for women were smaller. Since we were even smaller than women were, he would have to shave down the dimensions before we could use them to keep navel stones in place.

That appeased us.

We left and went to Zotabah's shop. Chahal waited out on the street. I suspected that she knew there were dogs in there. I didn't know if she smelled them or if she knew because she had visited the store in the past. I suspected the latter, mostly.

There, we commissioned a necklace for me that was made out of discs of the black stone. He assured me that he would make me one that was comfortable and sturdy enough to withstand everything that a young man could put it through. I couldn't imagine what he thought I would be doing with it, but I believed him.

"He's not going to use it as a swing, Zotabah," the Cabicacmotz said.

Zotabah blushed and said, "I know that. It's because males tend to treat jewelry with less care than the more delicate sex does."

Ahtoobalvar cleared his throat. "Speaking of women, Zotabah, I think you should contract a woman to help you with the dust in this place," he said as he coughed weakly. "It will spruce up the store and attract more customers."

Zotabah said, "Right now, I have more than enough work. It seems that everybody's coming in."

"That's why you need someone to take care of the little things. You shouldn't have to concern yourself with meaningless details like sweeping and cleaning." Again, he coughed, only now with a bit more force.

Zotabah put his lips out like a duck and nodded his head. "Perhaps you are right. I should find someone to help me. I'm too busy for those types of things. But who?"

Ahtoobalvar pretended to think and snapped the fingers of his left hand, saying, "I know precisely the soul to help you around here. I'm going to send her by. When should she come? Is tomorrow too late for you or do you think you'd need her today?"

Zotabah seemed bewildered and said that tomorrow would be fine. Then he asked us if we needed anything else. The Cabicacmotz told him that he would like to have two pendants, for Hac and Cham, made out of the black stone. He told him that they should not show the triangles in the rock and that raw and unpolished bits of the stone would do.

"Well, we don't want them cutting themselves on the edges," Zotabah said. "Let me bring some out so you can see." He turned away and went to the shelves.

The Cabicacmotz raised his eyebrows at Ahtoobalvar. Ahtoobalvar smiled back with a smug expression and nodded conspiratorially at him.

Zotabah came back and showed us some bits that had been lightly polished so that the rough edges were no longer a problem. He described how he would wrap them to hold them in place and fashion a loop for them so they could be hung at the end of a leather string. He told us that, since we were males and active, leather strings would suit us better than something made from silver or gold, as well as being cheaper.

The Cabicacmotz agreed and told him to charge the king's account. Zotabah seemed a bit unsure about doing that and the Cabicacmotz put his mind at ease with the statement, "If you don't send him the account, he will think me remiss in my duties. Since he charged me with this task, he will be most disturbed if he does not receive word from you that it was carried out. That is why you must send him the bill immediately."

Zotabah agreed to do so and said that there were many accounts that he had to send out bills for. He said that he would take the accounts to the runners and have them take care of them.

Runners were young men who lent themselves out. They ran errands and ferried messages all over the city and frequently beyond. They were known to be expensive, but were confidential and extremely reliable. Reportedly, a guild ran them and arranged schedules for their services. They were called runners because they always ran with their messages, never walking.

"Sure you could do that, Zotabah, but that seems to me to be a duty more proper for an apprentice. Certainly, apprentices are paid for any services they render, but they are much cheaper than the runners are. Why go to them if you have an apprentice right here? Hac should be in charge of doing that for you. Besides, it will give him the opportunity to learn the city and get to know where everything is," the Cabicacmotz told him.

Zotabah gave him a doubtful look and said, "I don't know. I think that it's not right to make an apprentice do things like that. Shouldn't I only make him study and learn from me? If he goes running around doing my errands, he won't learn anything about stones. He didn't get an omen for the purpose of doing my chores for me."

The Cabicacmotz answered him in a smooth voice, "Teaching should take into account the student's needs and need not be confined to one subject matter. Your student here is a farm boy who is still illiterate and who doesn't know the city. He can learn those things from you. He is also shy and reserved. He should become more

357

accustomed to dealing with people. He is also a growing boy who needs exercise. What better way to get some than while he learns to navigate the city streets and helps you in your business? He will also be learning how to conduct a successful business. You have more to teach than simply stones, Zotabah. Indeed, you have much to offer a young and eager mind like Hac's."

Zotabah nodded and tapped his finger against his lip, thinking about what the Cabicacmotz had said. "You know, I never thought about it that way. That will be good. He will also earn some income, as well. It will be modest, but it will be enough for a student. Do you think I should have him sweep also?"

Ahtoobalvar quickly answered, saying, "Certainly not. That is women's work. That would be an abuse of your position as his teacher. The other things are acceptable and right, but not when it comes to tasks that are more fitting for women."

Shrugging in embarrassment, Zotabah said, "I guess you are right. When should I ask Hac to begin?"

"Why not right now?" the Cabicacmotz said in answer as he lightly pushed Hac towards Zotabah.

Hac seemed very happy that he was going to begin working with Zotabah.

We left them there and went out onto the street. Chahal stood and rejoined our group. I didn't know how she managed, but she ignored us even as she was a part of us. She emitted feelings of disdain and anger, at having been left outside, towards us. No one seemed to notice it but me.

Cham seemed annoyed that his brother was no longer with us. He said, "Oh, that is great. Hac will have riches while

I get nothing. How come I don't get to be someone's apprentice?"

"You can be mine," Ahtoobalvar told him. "I can always use some help in my shops and workshop. You will have to be careful, though; hardened clay cannot be treated roughly or carelessly."

"Really? Do you think I will be good at something like that?"

"I think it will be necessary for you to become good at it. Your subjects are difficult and they all seem to involve action. You need something to balance the warrior and I can think of no better balance than art and beauty."

"When can we start?" Cham asked him.

"Right now," Ahtoobalvar said. "I'll show you one of my shops and then we can go back to my workshop."

The Cabicacmotz told Cham to return to my house for supper. He also told him that he and I would be picking up the leather belts for the three of us.

We left them and walked towards the leatherworker's shop. There, we picked up the belts and carried them home in nets. After we had dropped off the belts at home, we went to my father's court.

When we were almost there, the Cabicacmotz said, "It is good and wise of your father to want you to become accustomed to the duties he performs. You should consider yourself his apprentice and, thus, an integral part of his court."

"When are we going to have lessons with you again?" I asked him. "I thought that our class would be meeting at least every other night."

"Normally that would be so, but things are in flux now because of Parutzya's and Carumo's news. We are having a short sabbatical until we decide what to do. Until then, the students will be meeting with their other teachers."

"How will they know when to see them? Is there a specific schedule to follow?"

"They will know when they are summoned by them. The teacher will send a summons to the student when it comes time to give them a lesson."

"How come I haven't received any, yet?"

"You have. Tomorrow you are to see the Balam Ch'ab."

"Why didn't you tell me before?" I complained.

"I am telling you now. Besides, I didn't want you to become nervous about it like you are now."

"I'm not nervous," I lied. Merely hearing the man's title gave me chills. His demonstration was still clear in my mind. The man was fearsome. Even when he was a man, his eyes were the eyes of a jaguar, surveying everything before it and assessing it like a hunter or a predator. To add to my worries, I feared that I would never be able to become like him and the man would hold me in scorn. I had no confidence that I would ever be able to accomplish what he showed me in that tent. It must have taken great skill in magic and I felt that it was of a dark quality. I was terrified.

He rolled his eyes and said, "Fine, you are not nervous. Now, let us go. We have to see what is going on at the court. They are discussing various strategies to deal with the news the spies brought us." He sighed loudly and checked my appearance. Seemingly satisfied, he told me that I should seat myself beside my father, to his right, while the Cabicacmotz would sit beside me. I should not speak. If there was a question that I wanted to ask, I was to ask him in a quiet whisper.

I asked him if there were any other things, which I should keep in mind, regarding the protocol of the court.

He thought for long moments and finally said, "Do not express surprise, approval, or disapproval at the suggestions of your father's advisors. Right now, everyone is tossing around ideas and making suggestions. To hinder that process with expressions of judgment are counterproductive. Speak only if your father or I ask you to, for now. Do you understand?"

I nodded and told him I did.

We entered the cave.

Part Four

False Gods

Guards stood near the cavern entrance, escaping the sun by standing in the shade of the rock. They nodded as we passed. Their eyes betrayed a flicker of nervousness when they saw Chahal.

After the sweltering humidity of the day, it was cool and refreshing inside the moist dampness of the cave's entrance. We walked upward for twenty paces and then the floor began to slope downward. Torches lined the walls of the narrow hall. The slope steepened and took us down into an enormous cavern filled with pillars of mineral deposit. Torches also lined the walls, but their light did not reach the ceiling, leaving it in a deep black gloom. It always put me on edge.

When I was younger, I believed that the darkness was the home to gigantic carnivorous bats. I would run through the cave, trusting that I was finally safe if I reached the corridor leading to my father's court. I restrained myself from breaking into a sprint solely because the Cabicac-motz was with me and I didn't want to embarrass myself.

The cavern was used for large congregations and tribal ceremonies when the protocols called for them to be conducted underground. I had never seen it used in ceremonies, but I had occasionally come by when there were criminal proceedings to be seen. Those days were popular among the tribe and they attracted crowds.

We walked to the left along one of the many corridors, following the blue rope. Other corridors had differently colored ropes. There were six others. I didn't know where the other ropes led. I had been warned, since I was able to walk, not to enter any of them under threat of a harsh spanking.

My senses barely registered the slight slope to the floor. When we had walked about fifty paces, I looked back to where we had entered and saw the inky blackness of the larger cave as a small sphere way down below. We kept on going for a while. There were a few other smaller caves along the way. Usually, they were lit up, but today they were not. The whole place was quiet and seemed deserted. The dark rooms made me nervous and reminded me of the dark cavern ceiling below. It was not difficult to imagine monstrous bats in the other caves and I kept on looking back to make sure that something didn't peek out from the darkness after we walked past those rooms.

"Does the dark frighten you, Zaki?" the Cabicacmotz asked.

His question made me jump. I had been concentrating on my fears and his voice startled me. "Only here," I replied.

"I don't appreciate caves, either. That is why I am hardly ever here. Even the large cavern upsets me. It always seems that there is an ominous feeling of silent danger. It might only be my imagination, of course. I prefer to see sky above me."

It surprised me to hear my feelings so finely echoed in his words. I told him about my childhood fear of bats living in the darkness.

What he said did not put my fears at an end. "There are bats in some sections. Workers clear out the guano every morning. Then it is distributed to the farms.

"Do you mean that I am eating food that gets covered in bat droppings?

"It is mixed with water and other materials before it is put on the plants, Zaki. It is only to help them grow. It is a fertilizer. Besides, it is not as if the food is not washed before getting to you."

First, my water might be contaminated with pee and now my food might have bat poop on it. If I could, I would have never eaten again.

We had to drop our disturbing conversation because already we could hear the drone of voices coming from the throne room.

The room was filled with men and women. Despite the coolness of being deep within the cave, the room was a bit uncomfortable because of all of the people's bodies. When I first walked in, I thought I would faint. The air was heavy and stifling.

The crowd quickly opened up for Chahal, allowing us an open path to the throne.

Chahal plopped herself before my father, not even greeting him. It was silly to expect otherwise from a wild being, but her rudeness mortified me. She looked down on the congregants and then began grooming herself as if she was in the town. She was a spectacle, especially when she lifted up one of her legs and began licking the base of her tail.

Everybody laughed and I felt my face redden. I quickly seated myself on the platform at my father's feet and looked down at the ground. The Cabicacmotz sat next to me exactly where he said he would. I was glad not to have come here alone.

My father put his hand on my shoulder and squeezed it. When I looked up, he gave me a wink.

The laughter at Chahal's antics did have one benefit; it lifted the mood of the room. Before, it had seemed that the atmosphere was charged with an oppressive gloom. I didn't know what they had been discussing beforehand, but it didn't seem that many people felt optimistic.

"Continue with your report, Carumo," my father said.

"We were able to witness a battle," Carumo said. He and Parutzya stood before the platform, with their backs to it, facing the crowd.

"How? Where were you?" many voices asked, interrupting his story.

Parutzya answered, "We were above the battle site, hidden in a cave covered with brush. We had the view of eagles, but we were not too high above. We saw clearly."

That satisfied the crowd.

Carumo continued with their story, "The warriors of the tribe who were eventually defeated came onto the battlefield. There was a distance between them and the victors, the dark Toltecs. It was, approximately, one twelfth of a league. The vanquished wore the typical regalia. The others were covered in red. They had even painted their faces with it. We did not understand why, but later we did. They were in red to identify them as coming from the dark ones. When the doomed tribe fought them, the reds fought well, but they did not put much effort into it, they seemed weary almost. The warriors, at that point, were only armed with knives, clubs, and short war lances. When everyone was engaged, the true fighters came in. They came silently and wore clothing that blended in with the earth. The warriors were caught unawares. We saw how the reds were used as decoys to engage their opponents and trap their attention. Meanwhile, a cruel snare was placed around them. There must have been two-hundred hidden warriors, in all. The reds were only there as decoys, they were a sacrifice. The other tribe's warriors never had a chance for they surround-ed them. Then they let fly arrows, darts, and thrown spears. The most terrible point came when their spear throwers were sent in."

In a voice of complete outrage, a man cried, "But those are not weapons for war!"

"No, they are not," Carumo agreed. "They are the weapons of hunters and that is how they defeated those brave warriors. They cut them down and hunted them as if they were mere animals. I have never seen such dishonor done on the battlefield. All in silence. They were implacable foes and the warriors fell. Some men lived and they were bound and taken away."

I had heard tales of war from warriors in the forums where such men congregated. War always sounded dreadful, but I couldn't help but think that those dark Toltecs had come up with a shrewd technique for ensuring their victory.

What Carumo said next completely sickened me and stopped me from considering their methods clever. "Some of the men continued to resist even after they were bound. They were castrated on the spot. After that, no more men resisted."

An old woman asked, "I need to know what they did with the cut off members."

Why would she need to know such a thing? How macabre.

"They were placed in sacks and taken with them."

The old woman looked down at the ground, in thought.

After that, a man asked, "What about the wounded survivors?"

"If the wounds were incapacitating or crippling, both sides were systematically dispatched by a blow to the head with a heavy club. Only those who could walk unaided were not killed. Then all clothing that was stained with blood was removed from the bodies and placed in sacks as well," Carumo said as he looked at the old woman who was curious about such hideous details.

I quietly asked the Cabicacmotz about the old woman and her deranged questions. He told me that the woman was an expert in detecting and counteracting black magic. I wanted to ask why the dark Toltecs had taken the blood, but the conversation in the room distracted me.

"Why were the reds also dispatched, if they were fighting along with them?"

"They had served their purpose, it seems," answered Parutzya.

"Are the survivors forced to fight later battles painted in red?" a man asked.

"Yes. The survivors are made to fight battles some time after they are taken. We were unable to determine how long they are held before being forced to fight."

"How do they ensure that they do not fight against their captors in these battles?"

Parutzya answered, "After the hunters come in, there are slavers who are in charge of relieving the reds of their weapons, whenever feasible. Otherwise, the slavers wait until after the battle. Also, the archers can take them down at any time necessary during the battle. These men have no other choice. Their villages and cities have been burned to the ground and their people are forced to work as slaves on farms or in the caves. Any family they have is held hostage to ensure their continued obedience. We believe that later on, after proving their submission, they are assimilated into the society. At a very low status, of course, but still absorbed into it."

"That is monstrous," a man said, and everyone agreed with him.

Carumo went into a long account of the tribe's metalwork, which further horrified everyone. Unfortunately, neither he nor Parutzya were able to give more details of what the metal might be or how it was made.

My father asked, "Do we have any good news?"

No one said anything.

Finally, the Cabicacmotz made a statement that lifted everyone's spirits, although I didn't understand it. "Still, they fight like men and not like gods. They use weapons of matter. There is no deity in their work that I can see."

"But didn't the dark priest tell the spies that their gods had revealed to them the secret of their metals?" one man asked.

"Revelations about physical matter rarely come from the Creator, especially when it involves unjust warfare. I think we are looking at information that comes from Xibalba. Nothing tastes as sweet to them as despair, pain, and fear. Those dark Toltecs are keeping them well fed. Still, I say, there is nothing of genius in their works. These are shocking events, but ultimately they are mundane actions. Our foes have not reached true genius or godhood, nor are they working under the auspices of the Creator because their very acts are an insult to the heavens."

"Do you think they can be beaten?" a man asked the Cabicacmotz.

"No stronghold is truly invulnerable. One needs to know whether to use subterfuge or force. It depends on using the right tools. Therefore, yes, I do. Here, we must use both subterfuge and force. We need to surround the enemy and stand united with others. We know that we have a moral obligation to place them in check because they are our own. We have allowed a menace out into the world and it is destroying everything in its path... Anyway, we see what we have to do. We must do to them what they do to the tribes they slaughter out on those fields. We must surround them so they cannot move. Their empire must be halted and suffocated."

"Do you think, Cabicacmotz, that we must kill them all?" someone asked.

He only shrugged.

"Does anyone have word from our envoys or returning ambassadors?" my father asked the crowd.

A small man answered, "The ambassadors are traveling back to us, safely so far. Most of the envoys are soon to arrive at their destinations."

"Why are we making our ambassadors return and merely sending them envoys as replacements?" I whispered to the Cabicacmotz.

"These envoys are specially trained in war and its arts. If our assistance is needed in such matters, a normal ambassador is unskilled and inferior to an envoy of war. An ambassador is a polite representative of our tribe and often a lubricant for commerce." He cupped his hands around my ears and whispered, "Also, ambassadors tend to come from ranking families. If there is warfare, no one wants them to be caught up in it or killed. Cherished members of those families cannot be left unprotected and vulnerable. The families are under your father's rule, but still he needs them and their support as well. They can provide many fighting men, should he require them."

A heavy woman at the back of the room asked a question that surprised everyone, "Would anyone care to shed any light on why the pochtecas have been rounded up and placed in homes within our fair city? They are under guard, but still they are here."

The Cabicacmotz looked at my father and they shared a loaded look. Finally, both men nodded.

"We are interested in taking over the pochteca's routes and using them as emissaries to the farther kingdoms, especially those who are closest to the dark Toltecs and in the most danger," my father said.

There was a collective gasp from the assembled.

One man shouted, "What possible purpose can be served from allying ourselves with pochteca filth?"

My father made a hand motion indicating that either Parutzya or Carumo should answer the man's question. They suddenly seemed nervous.

Parutzya took a deep breath and said, "Our time with the pochtecas has not been easy. It is a rough and difficult life. Nevertheless, it has not been hard because of the pochtecas themselves. The danger comes from thieves and bandits on the routes. We have found the pochtecas to be honest working folk who simply enjoy the nomadic life. They like travel and observing the different customs that they encounter. The people are kind and good-hearted. In fact, although they are not particularly religious, they do believe that there is a Creator, who stands above all, so they are not godless heathens. They welcomed us when we first joined them and took care to show us how to travel safely, conduct business, and how to do a number of necessary tasks."

"How did you join them at all?" an old man asked them.

"We pretended to be travelers who were searching for a good home. We told them that we had lost our families in a forest fire, that many of our people had perished, and that the survivors had gone in different directions. They treated us as orphans and have been a great help to us. They were generous with us and never took offense when we made profits that would have gone to them had we not been there. These people might not have our specific beliefs, but we see our beliefs reflected in their actions. It is instinctual with them; they naturally act with honor and prize goodness."

"Can you tell us more about their society and its structure?" my father asked. I could tell that he already knew the answers, but wished others to hear it.

Carumo told us that the pochtecas had five mercantile townships of moderate size. All traveling pochtecas visited each town on their journeys in order to replenish their goods, if necessary, and to deliver raw materials to the craftsmen. "It is very odd," he said. "The pochtecas are uninterested in the accumulation of wealth. They only seek to gain enough to keep their artisans with the proper materials. Their craftsmen and artisans live only to create works of art. There are so many jewelers that their raw materials are difficult to transport because of the weight. When itinerant pochtecas become too aged to roam the routes, they are given modest but comfortable residences in one of the towns as a reward for their many years of service. From then on, they provide small services to the craftsmen as long as they are able to do so. The towns are close-knit and friendly. They treat each other as family. Individuals who have been elected into service provide their leadership. It is a strange system. No one family is exalted. Everyone is considered equal, whether they mold gold or sweep floors. They are most unusual in that regard. Although they are artisans and salesmen, they deeply enjoy philosophy and learning anything they are able to. They are a wealth of information when it comes to the customs and beliefs of the different tribes and kingdoms. We believe they are an untapped resource and that they would be eager to learn our ways."

"Interesting," a man said. "I had been led to believe that they were merely sneaky merchants who only cared to cheat us out of our jade."

All laughed.

Parutzya and Carumo laughed as well. Then Parutzya took something small out of her satchel and held it up. "Your jade receives the care of the pochteca carvers after it leaves your hands. Here is an example of their work. Please pass it around the room."

She handed it to my father who then handed it to me. It was a small carving of a head with thick lips and a head-dress. The workmanship was very fine and detailed. It impressed me. I then passed it to the Cabicacmotz.

Everyone who saw it commented favorably about it.

The Cabicacmotz spoke, "We are contemplating adopting these people, the pochtecas. We wish to form a deep alliance with them and to initiate them into our ways."

"For what purpose?" a man asked him. "I can see that they are fine craftsmen, but that should not be our sole reason. We also have good artisans. We could compete favorably with them and not lose any face."

"We do not need to compete with them. You are right that it is not the sole reason. The true reason is that we have examined them and found them to be honorable persons. What they have that we do not have is license to roam. They are more or less welcomed anywhere. They can enter freely where we cannot. We wish to teach them the secrets of the twins and to have them carry our teachings far and wide," the Cabicacmotz told the man.

Most of the people in the room were outraged to hear that and many began to shout that we should do no such thing. My father and the Cabicacmotz were silent until the people finished expressing their disapproval of the plan.

A woman with a mean look said, "We have already unleashed a menace to the land and you wish to unleash an even worse one upon it? Who is to say that they will use such a secret only for good things? What if the dark ones learn of it?"

"The dark ones do not know of it already. Even if they did, they could not use it. We have found that only those with a clean heart are able to produce the spirit in the first place. The division in our tribe came when we refused to worship the false god, Tohil. It was only a mortal who had been transformed by drinking from the Red River of Xibalba. When we destroyed the false one, many left and continued to worship him, even though he no longer was. They are stunted in their spiritual growth, so they cannot advance as we have. No one who sacrifices others to demons may accomplish what we have. It is antithetical. Note this, when we become double, we cannot do everything that we please. It is still subject to the will of the Creator. The last time I became double, I tried to feed starving people in a faraway land and was unable to do it. Not because I didn't have enough power, but because my will was shot down from above."

I had no idea about what he was talking about.

"Your words have validity," the mean-looking woman answered, "but we do not know everything about the double. This information might fall into the hands of those who have an incentive to warp it and abuse it. Everything has a dark side and I fear that these dark Toltecs will delve into its secrets and discover it. Especially if they have friends below who can help them unravel it."

"I propose that we refrain from calling them Toltecs at all," one man said. "Can't we simply call them the dark ones?"

Everyone agreed to this. It disgusted everyone to think that those people were any relation to us and sought whatever distance they could find, even if it was only a semantic distance. It was an ugly situation.

The Cabicacmotz asked the mean-looking woman to come up with safeguards to protect the secret of the twins from finding its way into the wrong hands. She did not appear happy about that and seemed like she was going to continue arguing against the pochtecas being inducted into the tribe.

I secretly agreed with her. My hypocrisy knew no bounds, since I was half-foreign. The problem was also that the pochtecas were looked down upon as being a people with no land or nobility. Because they were made up of individuals who had left their tribes or who were alone in the world, it appeared that they had no loyalties. Their only unifying trait was an incurable wanderlust that they all had. Later on, I came to like their worldview, but at the time, I was unable to conquer the rumors and stereotypes surrounding them that had been ingrained in me since I was young.

"If we absorb the pochtecas and send them as our emissaries, why is that better than sending ambassadors bearing gifts?"

"Because our ambassadors will not know the particular rituals that each kingdom considers polite and appropriate. We could waste years overcoming petty social blunders that the pochtecas would not make. The advantage is that they are a free people whose only connection is to trade. They are neutral and are accepted as such. They are natural ambassadors," the Cabicacmotz said.

"If they consider themselves to be neutral and free, in a way, why would they agree to become a part of us?" one man asked.

Carumo answered before the Cabicacmotz could and said, "We don't. We merely hope, at this point. We think they might agree if given a compelling reason, a reason that speaks to the heart of them. We have found them to be good people who are committed to righteousness, justice, and the principles of light. In fact, they regularly weed out individuals who do not conform to those ideals. I believe that if they are allowed their autonomy they will agree, but I am not sure. Absorption into the tribe is more for our own people. Our people must learn to consider them as worthy individuals. They should not treat them as walking trash. We talk of the brotherhood of knowledge very easily, now we must put it into practice. These people are ripe for knowledge. Already they have made discoveries on their own. They are slowly building a body of knowledge and have also rejected destructive paths."

A man interrupted and asked, "What have they rejected, then?"

Carumo counted off their exemplary qualities on his fingers. "They have rejected human sacrifice because they deduced that the Creator gave life and they are not the ones to take it away. They have rejected the indiscriminate use of perception altering plants because they do not like dependency on anything. In fact, they find that they interfere with their ability to think clearly and only use them sparingly. They have also rejected witchcraft because they firmly believe that a person's freewill should not be tampered with and that it is the only thing that humans truly own. Something we discovered, which surprised us was that they are pacifists who abhor violence. I can give examples of their worthiness all day if necessary."

I had not noticed him before, but the Tzuhunik raised his arm to speak and said, "I see that their spiritual traits are in conformance with ours. I am satisfied with that. Their mundane qualities are also desirable. They are expert at dealing with people and their artisanship is rarely equaled. What concerns me is that we have infiltrated their group and it is known to harbor spies from other tribes, as well. What are we doing about pochtecas that aren't really pochtecas?"

The Cabicacmotz said, "We have already identified a couple who are actually spies. They have been sequestered and have only been told that they are being held because we plan to try Carumo and Parutzya in criminal proceedings. They are being subjected to mind readers. They come from a tribe that is approximately 200 leagues to the east and south of us. We are beginning to suspect that they were problematical members of a royal family who were sent on a fool's errand to get them out of the way, but we are still unsure about that. They believe that they were sent to bring back information about precious resources in gems and metals. We might use them to open avenues of communication with their tribe."

"And what do you plan to do to prevent the pochtecas from being used as a haven for spies in the future? I realize this is premature, but it is important to plan ahead in such matters," the Tzuhunik said. "Also, I would welcome the opportunity to question those spies. It interests me that they are so far from home."

"We will arrange that for you, Tzuhunik. As to the other problem, we are putting our best seers to the task of identifying how many spies are traveling under the wings of the pochtecas. Then we plan to individually test all of them." The Cabicacmotz smiled towards Parutzya and Carumo. "It is also a worthwhile exercise for the mind to consider that there might be many such spies who come to like the pochtecas and their life enough to switch loyalties. Their outlook on life is such that they are able to convert others to their ways of thinking. We might be able to capitalize on that, as well."

Parutzya smiled and said, "We are not planning to become pochtecas, Carumo and I, we have merely judged them and not found them wanting. We feel that this will be a natural brotherhood."

A woman near the front remarked, "If all this comes to pass, there is one group who will not play along with it. The Chuchmox will never agree to divulge their secrets to the false Chuchmox of other tribes."

I saw the old woman, who asked about the ghastly details, purse her mouth and roll her eyes at the woman's words.

My father said, "We can worry about that later. Besides, the Chuchmox are reasonable women, they can be convinced."

One man exploded with laughter and soon everybody joined in.

When my father finished laughing, he said, "As I said, we will worry about that particular problem later."

"What is our ultimate goal in this?" an old man in the back of the room asked.

The Cabicacmotz said, "In the short term, we seek to end the reign of the dark ones. Our ultimate goal must be more abstract. It is to establish an empire of wisdom. We must form a brotherhood, which is committed to the principles of light and goodness, with the other tribes. That is our true goal. This empire must fight against Xibalba and all that it stands for."

The old man responded, "Then we will attract students from all of the tribes whom we will train in our arts and instruct on how to be moral beings upon this earth. I believe that I like this goal. We have been too isolated and have not shared our knowledge, as we should have. Now we will."

Somehow, everyone finally seemed to agree. Everybody filed out of the room, chatting amiably as they left.

When only the four of us were left, I asked them who Tohil was. It intrigued me that we had once been fooled into worshipping a false god and I wanted to know the particulars about it.

The guards emerged from their hiding spots behind the curtains, at that point. They seemed a bit tired and hot. It was easier to breathe in the room after everybody had left, but it was still uncomfortable. Being behind a tapestry for such a long time could not have been too enjoyable.

My father answered me, saying, "I think your question would be better answered outside of a cave and under the protection of the sun, I think."

I gave him a dubious look and said, "I'd also like to get out of this hot room, father, but I'm not going to get scared of the dark from a story."

He raised his eyebrows at me and said, "You haven't heard the story yet, then. The sun is a great protector."

He gave a look to the Cabicacmotz who nodded solemnly in response.

"Let us have some lunch as I tell you a scary story," my father told me.

We left the caverns and went to my father's home. Servants prepared a picnic for us under the shade of a ceiba tree. Each of us was able to have a backrest because of the tree's accommodating trunk system, which flowed outward at ground level.

"So is anyone going to tell me about this false god?" I asked.

My father mumbled around his food and pointed at the Cabicacmotz, indicating that he should start the story.

The Cabicacmotz told me that when the experiment at Tulan was at its peak, right before the speech of all the tribes involved had been scrambled, the tribes found three statues that held spirit familiars. At first, the tribes were content with the idols, believing them to be gifts from the Creator. Mistakenly, they believed that any wondrous occurrence was the work of the divine. When Tulan failed, darkness spread upon the earth. The sun, moon, and stars were not visible. When all became darkness, the idols became as boys, real people with magnificent powers. It also became cold, snowing and hailing. Our tribe had light, fire. It had been provided by Tohil when we needed it. It is said that he spun in his sandal so rapidly that flames appeared. All other tribes wanted our light. We would have given it to them, but a Xibalban appeared and told our tribe to ask for tribute for our god. We were fooled into this because the Xibalban told us that he was a messenger from those who had made us."

"How did you know that he was from Xibalba?" I asked.

"We know now. Despite all of our knowledge, at the time, we were still foolish and stupid. We speak now in retrospect, of course. The being that appeared had wings like a bat and the milk white skin of the Xibalbans. Believe me, now we are very familiar with those beings. We will not make that mistake ever again."

"What were the tribes supposed to give the god?"

"Heart sacrifice."

It shamed me that my people had been so bestially stupid. "Why would a god ask for death from those it has supposedly created?"

"Exactly."

The Cabicacmotz added some weird facts. "Something must have gone wrong with the experiment at Tulan because everything went dark after they did something. The problem is that we don't know what they did specifically. When darkness descended upon the world, horrors accompanied it. Things from the dark. Things that did not have a way into this world until the dark provided a path. The whole world was covered in darkness. We think that the underworld opened up and when light did not keep it down in its hole, it came up and walked the earth as it did in its own level. It was then free to ascend the levels. That is when the gods came to life, the false ones. Since it was dark, the false ones were able to move about freely. They weren't stuck inside stones or statues; they were unfettered and free. They also had unbelievable power. The tribe was in awe of them."

"Why did they want people's hearts?" I asked.

"They wanted the blood," my father told me.

"What for?"

"They drank it," he said.

My thinking was very clear and I was able to follow their words with an incredible acuity. "Blood is forbidden to be ingested. And why would something that has created something need what it has created as sustenance?"

My father and the Cabicacmotz looked at each other in surprise at my words and then began to chuckle softly as if sharing a secret.

"Good thinking," my father said. "You are most sharp to-day. I told you that you had changed. All you needed was to be forced to think and now your mind is taking well to the exercise. Anyway, a real deity would need no such thing. A real deity would also not fail to follow its own commands. As I said, they were false gods."

"How were they gotten rid of?" It frightened me to think that they could return.

"When the light returned to the earth, the sun shone up-on everything. They were turned back to stone. All of the original animals were also turned to stone. If you remember, the Zaki Coxol, the White Sparkstriker, took all of the animals who had turned to stone away and hid them. He did not take the stones of the false gods. He left them."

I waited for one of them to continue the story, but they were silent. I motioned with my hand to urge them to go on. They looked at each other and seemed hesitant to continue.

Finally, my father said, "They might have been restrained within the stones, but they still had power. They were able to come out during the day in spirit form and they continued to give instructions to the tribe. They always were ones to come up with rules and regulations."

"Why would they do that? Make laws."

"Because they love to constrain man. We have laws that come from the Creator. Laws that make sense. Laws that are written into our very cells. We are not to murder, lie, cheat, steal, and a host of other laws, which are for our good. They are natural within us. Burdening us with a host of petty little regulations has no other purpose than to cause us to fail. And then when we fail, and we inevitably will because they are inane rules, they mop up our grief, despair, and remorse."

"What? How?"

"It is their true sustenance. They are the inverse of real gods. What they crave is the darkness of man. Everything in the worlds is a cycle or a chain. We eat animals that eat the grass, which soaks up the water and the sun to survive. We don't know how they do it exactly, but they do. It is a chain of events. With the Xibalbans, we do not know the mechanics of how they truly feed, but we do know that that is what they thrive on."

The Cabicacmotz said, "Think about it this way. In man, we become stronger when we receive positive remarks about our actions. For children and normal persons, this is a necessary ingredient. Some exceptional individuals do not need such things because they have evolved and they receive the positive remarks from honestly evaluating themselves. They need no one. They judge themselves. On the other side are those we call dark sorcerers. They strive to keep others down and they do it by attacking their foes with negativity and criticism. They seek to kill the spirit of man. Often they do not know it, but they are the emissaries of Xibalba. Sometimes they are unwitting, other times they know exactly what they are. They will not survive what comes after death. The dark sorcerers also, like the Xibalbans, their true masters, often work in concert with each other. They choose a lone soul to attack and they mercilessly try to bring them down. Beware of those who conspire with others to harm someone. In that situation, the only person who has a chance is the person being attacked. That person, if they are strong, will withstand the abuse and use it to help clear themselves of anything negative within them. When the person reaches the sublime state of perfection, the actions of the dark sorcerers bears fruit because the lone person forgives them. Precisely what they did not want, but they cannot help themselves. They are like caimans laying in wait in the waters, attacking their prey in concert. Despite all of their efforts, when the person being attacked succeeds in forgiving them, that person receives a jolt of energy that is unimaginable in its magnitude, and they use it to transport themselves into the heavens. Many times, they come back with stories of glory, but sadly, few believe them. Remember this in your interactions with others, Zaki; the evil and the weak need a pack behind them. Only the truly strong can stand alone."

Every word was entering me like a thunderbolt. I could feel its truth in every inch of my being. I had people like that around me and they were my half-brothers and half-sisters. Maricua was excluded, of course. All of my life, they had tried to make me feel worthless and alone. What a treasure.

My realizations were sidetracked when my father continued talking. He said, "To bring us back to the subject of the false gods, though, when they were on earth, they wanted blood and despair. We found that it made them stronger."

"So they had bodies?"

"Certainly. They were not like bodies that were still human, though."

"What are you saying?"

"I am saying that they were no longer what you or I would call human any longer."

"They were once human, these false gods?"

"They were. The thing is that they drank from the Red River of Xibalba."

I reeled. I didn't want to think that people would do such a thing and then conspire against other humans to steal their lives. I said, "I still don't understand how they can gain strength from despair."

In an angry tone, the Cabicacmotz said, "Don't try to play stupid, Zaki. Inside, you know that such a thing is possible. When a person is in the throes of despair and grief, snakes happen along and use their tongues to taste the air.

They use it somehow to drink in those terrible emotions. Pay closer attention to the world around you. I asked you to identify animals and beings, which live for the night, and there is a prime example. A snake is the representative symbol of the underworld. It might use the sun to warm itself, but it is still a creature of darkness. Watch the world. Everything has an abstract food. When a house contains someone who is approaching death, flies and rats converge."

"If the Xibalbans somehow use what is negative, what then does the Creator live off of from us?"

The Cabicacmotz smiled then and said, "Nothing. The Creator, the one true God needs nothing, but he is pleased when we surpass the tests of this world. There are powers, which are from the above, which are nourished from us. They say that when men reach the sublime state, the winged creatures of heaven will nest upon them. They do not hurt the person. The heavens rejoice when man's emotions emanate purity, justice, and righteousness."

"What are the tests of this world?" I asked.

My father laid his hand on my shoulder and said, "There are so many, Zaki, that we would be here for years explaining them all. They can usually be identified by a close self-examination. There are many pitfalls. I will rattle off a few. Failure to notice the truth is one. We love to make conjectures about things and we fail to reach the ends of logic about certain things."

"Like about what?"

"Some people like to say that animals, such as dogs, can only experience the present. This is a lie or else the animal would not learn from its mistakes. It needs memory.

When a pet has fouled the house, it knows that it has not acted right for a long time. When you show the dog their mess, they know they did it even though many hours have passed. Those who like to make specious pronouncements speak with great assurance and certainty about their words, but they are merely that. They fail to see the whole process. They do not take it the extra step and evaluate all of the permutations of possibility. They stop when they find something that sounds good to them. Don't speak idly. When you speak with certainty in your voice, make sure that it is true certainty you hold and not just hollow speak without anything to back it up. Besides, we have been able to evaluate exactly what animals remember and experience because we corroborate things. Either we transform ourselves into certain animals and experience it that way or we ask the animals themselves."

Already I had seen people of genius transform themselves, so that was not a great revelation to me. To hear that we could communicate with animals captivated my interest. "I can talk to animals? Can I talk to Chahal?"

My father chuckled and said, "You can talk to them, of course, but would you be able to comprehend their replies? There's the trick. Unfortunately, for now, you will be unable to do so until your naual emerges. Your own genius must come out. You are on your way. Dreaming will bring it out or another way will. Do I have to stress to you the importance of bringing yourself to a state of perfection in your thoughts, emotions, deeds, and speech?"

It was disappointing to hear, but I already knew that something like that could not come easily or casually. I shook my head to let him know that I understood.

The Cabicacmotz added, "Another thing to remember about our plight as humans is that homogeneity is not a good thing to have. A group mind indicates that something other than us is in charge. Beware of homogeneity masked behind goodness. Especially that. Some people like to think that they are good only because they have the outward appearances down pat. They speak the same way, smile the same way, and they behave in the same way. They constantly mention the Creator to remind the onlooker that they are pious. The time spent speaking those words would be better spent ridding themselves of their feelings of superiority and their false piety. Their homogeneity is often accompanied with a gossipy tongue that is used to converse with others like themselves about the failings and shortcomings of others. They like to think that they are better than others are because they judge that their set of beliefs is true or better in some way. Often, they are people who have never even been to the heavens. If they had, they would know that their behavior is detrimental to themselves and those around them. Truly, it is the most pernicious homogeneity because it caters to our personal feelings of being special and better than others."

Continuing, he said, "There is also a homogeneity of evil and it hides behind a laxness in one's self-examination. They tell themselves that what they think and feel is the natural state of humanity and that everyone is the same way. Those are lies. Certain groups have distinguishing features. You must learn to recognize them. For example, loose women have a wild look in their eyes and a bold salaciousness. All women like that look at potential lovers in the same manner and mood; there is homogeneity. Their boldness is not the assuredness of women like the Chuchmox whose confidence comes from within. Instead, they think that they can do whatever they like and bed whatever man comes along with impunity. Watch people, Zaki, and you will learn a great deal."

"I thought that problems like that did not happen in our tribe. I thought we were all wise. How can things like that happen here when you've told me that the lords of the life force were performing grand undertakings?"

They looked at me as if I was delirious or stupid.

My father said, "Not everyone in our tribe is a genius or a lord of the life force, Zaki. Many people are stunted in their growth. In a tribe of this size, not everyone can be at a level that we can respect. Do you have any idea how many people we count as ours? The numbers are staggering; I can assure you. Look around and watch, as the Cabicac-motz advises. You have half-siblings who delight in torment-ing you and making you feel worthless, and they have the advantage of nobility. No, not everyone in the tribe is as good as we would like him or her to be. There is jealousy, pettiness, vice and things we would rather not even men-tion. The fact that we are tribesmen does not insulate us from stupidity and weakness. It is a battle that we must wage every moment of every day. Xibalba always waits and it caters to our basest desires. You have already learned about the false mind of man that was imposed upon him from down below. Either you can revel in the confines of that mind or you can fight against it and exer-cise your own which is much better and flexible. The naual, your genius, can only emerge when that false mind is rendered inactive. Banish it now."

His words were forcing me to think about the circumstances of my life and my shortcomings. It made me extremely uncomfortable. It was the way my father spoke and his authoritative tone that made me feel that darts were piercing me. I wished to return to the easy to manage topic of others, so I directed the conversation back to the women. "Do you kill the women who are like that, also?" I asked.

"Certainly not. What they have is fixable. We do other things to correct the problem."

"Like what?" I asked. It was heartening to hear that they were not killed because of their sexual weaknesses.

He told me that women like that were sent to the Chuchmox for instruction. I asked him if the Chuchmox were composed of women like that. There was a wicked thought in my mind that I would be able to learn all other sorts of things from the Chuchmox. He quickly disabused me of any such thoughts.

With a laugh, my father said, "I wouldn't dare ever suggest such a thing to a Chuchmox. I recommend that you do not, either. Protect yourself from a harsh whipping at the hands of those manly women."

Despite the kind words of the first Chuchmox I had met, my father's advice scared me. I feared them and worried about learning from them. Later on, I would learn that the Chuchmox were not manly women, rather they were sexless.

He told me that if the promiscuous woman was married, the marriage was invalidated because of the woman's adultery. The marital property was severed and the woman's holdings were kept in trust. The woman's head was shaved and she was sent to the Chuchmox for a period of three years. During that time, she learned to conduct herself with decorum and dignity. At the end of the period, she could return to the society under a different name. Then she was watched for two years where her every move was watched and evaluated to make sure that she did not return to her old ways. If she was successfully rehabilitated, she was allowed to remarry, her properties were returned to her, and she was free to live her life. If she was still promiscuous, her head was shaved again and she returned to the Chuchmox for an indefinite period.

"What difference would it make to send her to the Chuchmox to live? Wouldn't the women see men anyway around the city?"

That caused them both to burst out in laughter.

The Cabicacmotz said, "The Chuchmox sometimes lead normal lives as city women, but most opt to live at one of their fortresses. No men are allowed usually, unless they are to learn from the Chuchmox or are invited for a specific purpose. There is no romance or sexuality to be found there. Any women that are like that are kept away from the students, far away. They are not ones to put up with impropriety. When you go there, don't even imagine such things."

We had strayed so far off course that I was mystified at how the conversation had turned to such matters. It seemed that every discussion was destined to stray off of the path, like river waters during flood season. To bring us back to the subject of the false gods, I told them, "The conversation is interesting and I will have to think about all of it some more, but not now, please. I would like to know how the false gods came to be. Did they just appear one day?"

"You will have to do much more than merely think about what we are telling you, Zaki, you are expected to put our words into practice in your own life," my father said to me. "Still, I understand your curiosity about the supposed gods, so I will tell you more about them." He took a deep breath before continuing. "We do not know exactly how they came to be, but we have our suspicions. When the tribes were doing what they did in Tulan, we believe that they opened a rift into the underworld. That rift probably swallowed up some people and they entered bodily into Xibalba. To spend any time in that place is dreadful. A moment can seem like an eternity. If people were sucked down into that world, they probably came to one of the two rivers and drank from them. There is no other way for that to have happened. Then they found their way back to the surface and established themselves as gods. That whole world is one of power and to bring that dark power up to our level can be devastating to the inhabitants of our world. Luckily, the sun came and shone upon the world or we would never have been able to defeat them. They commanded that much power."

"Did these false gods have names?" I asked them.

"Their names were Tohil, Auilix, and Hacauitz."

"How were they defeated?"

"When the sun came," my father replied. "As I said, they were diminished, but still powerful. During the day, they could only roam with spirit bodies. When night came, they were in their own bodies and they were unstoppable. Remember, we are speaking of people who drank from the

Red River of Xibalba. They had a terrible thirst for the blood of mankind; they lived off it. At first, they asked for the blood of creatures like deer, but they soon tired of it and asked for the blood of man."

"Why didn't they ask for that to begin with?"

"Because they still had a shred of humanity in them, is my guess. That quickly wore off, though. Also, the true Xibalban who appeared to our forefathers specified that these gods would be best served with our blood."

"If they drank from the rivers, father, wouldn't they have been considered true Xibalbans at that point?"

"No. They were only a hybrid of the races. They were born as men and then when they drank from the Red River, they were defeated by Xibalba and their souls were forfeit to that realm. To drink from that river is to be beaten by Xibalba."

"So how were they defeated? We keep on straying off of that subject," I complained.

"Well, the daylight helped us. The stones were their bodies, which had been petrified by the sun. They had established a priesthood that cared for them and protected them during the day. Those men were called the Ahtohil. Our tribe was disgusted with what was happening because they knew that eventually they would be called upon to give their blood. The gods were unquenchable in their thirst. In consequence, the tribe conspired against Tohil and his companions. During the day, they drugged the Ahtohil and found the stones housing the dark ones. They tore them apart and carried their parts far and away, in separation. They had also killed every Ahtohil they found, but some got away."

"Where did they hide them?"

"They took them to many places. I only know of one."

"Where is that?"

"It is far away in a place called Concealment Canyon."

"Do you mean that it is in a cave?"

"No, Zaki. I said that it was a canyon, not a cavern. It is a clever name because it can never be mistaken with other canyons. It has a different configuration than other canyons. The most vital parts of the stones were hidden in plain sight to ensure that they were never allowed to return to Xibalba and the darkness. There, they might return to power. We feared that. Anyway, the canyon is a common target when the spirit is released from the body. Everyone is tasked with searching for the vital stone parts of Auilix and ensuring that they are still in their place. Let me describe the place so that one day you might help us make sure that it is safe. As I mentioned, it is a clever name because it perfectly describes where it is. There is a strip of rock, which connects the two top portions of the canyon. One can walk upon it. Almost underneath there, Auilix is hidden on a ledge above a river. No regular man can find it, only seers can see it clearly or those whom the seer reveals it to. We left a group of tribesmen in the area to protect it, but we still look to make sure that it is secure."

"Do you think that they are still to be feared?"

"No, I think that we took care of them very well. The danger comes from those people who somehow enter Xibalba through dreaming and partake of the rivers. We must always be on alert against that possibility. If that occurs, we would again have to dispatch false gods who seek to establish themselves over us. We can never allow any Xibalban to hold dominion over the earth."

The Tzuhunik walked into the garden and joined us.

He did not greet anyone, he merely said, "I think you should all know that the Etamanel Evan plans on coming over tonight to visit Zaki and Cham. He heard that Cham was staying over tonight and decided to come. I will stay. He is not to be trusted with the young men."

"Come and sit, Tzuhunik," my father said. "We were discussing one of your favorite subjects, the false gods."

The Tzuhunik swallowed loudly. I could tell that it was not truly a favorite subject for him. Perhaps he was simply knowledgeable about them, I reasoned.

My father pressed on despite the Tzuhunik's obvious discomfort. "Tell us about your weird lady friend," he said to him. To me, he said, "The Tzuhunik has encountered one of the descendants of Tohil."

This was horrifying to me. To imagine those terrible beings reproducing with women was disgusting to me. Their whole families would suffer disgrace. Shame on their male relatives, for allowing such a union. "Why would anyone allow their female kin to marry them?" I asked.

All of the men exchanged a snicker. My father told me that I was jumping to conclusions. He told me that any family would welcome the introduction of a "god" into their number, but that the reproduction they utilized was completely nonsexual and did not require marriage to make it come about. They snickered again for some reason.

"The false ones convinced the populace that they were gods. The people had never seen such wonders," the Tzuhunik said. "From heaven come miracles, from earth heroic feats, and from Xibalba comes magic. The damnation of our ancestors was the inability to gauge where the wonders came from."

"Oh, stop boring us, Tzuhunik," my father complained as he slapped his thigh. "Tell him about the woman. Now there's a story you don't want to miss, Zaki." He impatiently waved his hands towards himself as if he was calling the Tzuhunik's story to him.

The Tzuhunik grimaced and said, "What would you like to know, Zaki?"

I thought for a moment and asked, "Are there really descendants of those false gods? Those who drink the blood of humans for sustenance?"

"Ah, the blood. What makes you think that there is only one kind of dark god? If you had stopped at the first question, the answer would be truer than if you add the second question." He looked at my mystified expression and said, "There is more than one kind."

"Really? How do you know?" I asked him.

"We occasionally come across them."

"What happened?"

"Nothing."

"What do you mean by nothing? Something must have happened."

"We found that once we double up, we cannot cross the divide which separates us. We cannot cross into their type of existence and they are barred from ours."

"How? Why?" I asked.

"With the blood ones, we might momentarily succumb to their allure, but fate steps in. It is a repulsion of such force that we cannot hide it from them. They retreat. They find that we become dangerous to them and step out of the arena. They cannot follow us onto our path because they have succumbed to one of the two big prohibitions of our plane, drinking from the rivers."

I did not understand him. I was not even able to follow his reasoning to any degree.

He tried to get up to leave or walk around and I found that I could not bear for him to leave without explaining things to my satisfaction. I stopped him from leaving. "Wait," I said as I touched his arm. "Tell me about what happened to you."

He gave me a sad smile and said, "It was a woman. It's always a woman, isn't it? I was having continual thoughts, in my youth, about those beings. I was around ten suns older than you were, though. I began having dreams of a woman with silky ringlets. We met for years in dreams. It was a love so real that I could feel her soft caresses. I wanted more and called out to her for months urging her to make herself known to me. This calling out was in dreams and in waking life. I told her to meet me at a gathering that I was going to in the lands of another tribe. I promised her that she would not be rejected, that I would love her no matter what. I believed that I could join her. I told myself that I would. I didn't want to end up old and frail."

"Do you mean that they do not age?" I asked.

"They stay the same age as when they first take the blood, whether they are five years old or a hundred."

"And then what?" I asked after he paused for a long minute of thought. I was anxious to hear the rest and he sat there looking unhappy.

"She showed up," he finally said. "The night before, I had felt her watching me. I walked through the streets of that city and beckoned her to show herself. She did not appear to me alone or in a cunning fashion. The next day, it was in the afternoon, but indoors, mind you... When our group was arriving at the meeting hall, she stood there and introduced herself to me as one of the hostesses to our group. How she arranged that, I have no idea. She even told me the name she would like to be called. It was different from the name I knew her as. I felt that I was in a dream and smiled at her in wonder. Then I felt something so unnatural, that my momentary happiness disappeared. She was the exact same form that she was in dreams, but there was a wrongness to her being. She watched me as I felt this and the look of hope that she had gotten when I first smiled at her went away. She moved away from me, pretending that nothing was wrong and treated me as she did every other person in that hall. She tried to make me jealous by flirting with another man. Also, and this is another oddity we were unaware of, she made a point of eating nuts and drinking water where I could see her, as if to confuse me as to what she was."

"Really, she could eat? Do you mean that they can survive on other substances besides blood?"

"Yes, although I do not know if they can sustain themselves in such manner. I have no idea if she had to vomit later or not, but I stayed indoors for the whole time, past sunset, and she did not leave the hall for a moment. I know because I watched her out of the corner of my eye. Maybe they can eat some raw foods, at least. Who knows? All I know is that she ate nuts, and possibly some berries, and that she drank water. I definitely saw her swallow. It was one of the few times that I allowed myself to look directly at her."

"So then what happened?"

"I avoided her for the rest of the night. I even felt that she was unattractive. Nothing could have been further from the truth, mind you, she is a beautiful woman. She read my mind as I had those thoughts and I felt her sadness. I endured her long glances and the thorough reading of my mind. I was in pieces. I told myself endlessly that there were no such things as the children of Tohil, even though I had one right in front of me. I vacillated between belief and disbelief. My confusion was so great that it felt like a daydream. Then I left. Later on in the evening, as I was walking back to the inn I was staying at, I felt her scrutiny. I even invited her back for another try and I was only greeted with her absence and the maddening knowledge that I had given up the chance at immortality. I was young and stupid. To become like her is to give up true immortality."

"So you don't know that she was like Tohil," I protested. "You don't have any proof. She might have merely been some hostess with a common face who liked a foreigner. After all, she was out and about in the daytime and munching on snacks."

"No, Zaki. No. I have watched her hunt, since then. She looks the same, all these years later. I know how to watch her without the comfort of my warm body. As for the daylight, the hall windows were open towards the east and the day was overcast. Therefore, they must have a tolerance for the sun or can tolerate it if they are not directly in it. The other times I have seen those types have been at night and they refused to answer my questions about their limitations when I asked."

"Then, why didn't she give you another try?"

"We can feel harmony with them only in dreaming, where they cannot harm our physical bodies. Once we embark on the road that we are taking, nothing can divert us. We are pledged to that path. Fate itself will step in and right any misstep into their direction. I was not in control of my emotions and thoughts. Despite my decision to welcome her into my life and join her, I could not. Something outside of myself governed me. The children of Tohil are confined to their dreams and bodies. Their spirits are locked into the matrix of their very cells. They cannot divide, so they are confined to Earth and its nether regions. I had already performed the operation of the double, so I was steered back onto the paths that lead into the heavens. The revulsion I felt towards her was unmistakable, I could not breach its hold, even though I tried to feel love and kindness towards her. They do not see us in that way. I have had conversations with others of her kind. They see us as objects of fascination. They do not find us repulsive or wrong. They want what we have and try to bask in our glow. Maybe you have not noticed, but we shine. The light we reflect is warm and soothing. You are on our road and already shine, as do your little friends. Some day you will shine like the sun itself."

"I haven't seen any sign of people liking me for no apparent reason. In fact, I feel, most times, like how she must have felt." It was true; I felt that I repulsed people.

"People have their own worries. Some see, most do not. Don't worry about regular people. They might feel that you are different, but it is not an unnatural difference, such as what I am talking about with the descendants of Tohil. With you, it is not dark. In fact, they see the light in you and it is frightening to them. Don't worry about it. The beings like her are aware of what we are and realize that they have made the wrong decision and that it is an irrevocable one."

"What do you mean?"

'The moment she first drank the blood of whoever turned her, she was doomed, confined to this world and its lower regions."

"You mean Xibalba, right? Then why could she meet you in dreams?"

"We may not drink blood. It is forbidden. She willingly took a drink, from a descendant of one who had drank from the actual Red River, Tohil or one of his cohorts. Once that is done, the spirit adheres to the body and its rules. Their consciousness, dream body or spirit... Actually, I am unsure what to call it with them. Anyway, it may roam through the dreamlands, but it is not an exalted existence there. One is largely confined to worlds that do not have the reliability that this reality has. It is not a stable universe in that direction. Thus, you have a spirit which clings to matter, producing a more durable and strong body. It is similar to what we do. Once we place our spirit into our dreamer or into our bodies, we are almost unstoppable. The spirit is a dynamic force, but to be effective and truly used to its maximum, it needs to be joined with the dreamer or the body purposely. Therein lies the problem, they cannot perform the maneuver of uniting their spirit with their dreamer; the spirit is locked into the body. The blood drinkers have a limited ability outside of their bodies, so they can interact in dreams with other beings or undergo out-of-body experiences, but they cannot command the same kind of power that they have in waking reality. They cannot break free. They are stuck at a level of power that only an imbecile would be satisfied with. They see the limitless possibilities open to us and are curious about us; they want to learn how to do it. The problem is that they can't. They are bound. It is like the fool who bargains with his soul. Doomed to a hell, unable to get free and escape because he has willingly given up his one method of getting out of there, his spirit. Yes, it is a vehicle."

"But when their spirits return to their bodies, aren't they uniting all three then? Why wouldn't they then be said to have united them? Wouldn't three be better than two would? That confuses me."

He smiled. "I don't want to give you the real answer. This is something that you should ponder for yourself. I will tell you that it is possible and occasionally happens to regular people who must perform incredible feats to save a loved one or a child. Go from there and do some thinking."

That did require some serious contemplation on my part. I would have to think about it later because as I was considering his words, he interrupted my thoughts.

"Always keep in mind that those beings command great physical strength, Zaki. Don't ever think that you can use one as an experiment. Even though we can protect ourselves from them, we cannot force them into anything. They have free will. We cannot become monsters by denying any person, born as a human, that right."

"I have no intention to, but if they are so strong why can't they force us to go with them?"

"Are you dense? We do not fit nicely into the category of normal humans. We are an evolved category. You weren't listening when I said that we could protect ourselves from them," he complained. "Our bodies know what to do to protect us. They will immediately transport us out of there, if there is such an immediate threat. It is not the normal threat of an earthly death, which is natural and acceptable to the spirit, but a destiny-shattering death. Our spirits know what to do. Either we get out of there safely or we would annihilate the being who was trying to drag us into the same pit they are stuck in."

"You mean that we would win?"

"If we do not experience divine intervention, our spirits will do the job. Legend says that the Creator made us in the image of himself. Our spirit is the aspect of ourselves, which is made in his image, not these weak physical forms. The spirit is eternal and our piece of the divine. Consider that."

"We become immortal when we become double?"

"No, I did not mean that. What we do have is incredible strength in that form. A body, as strong as theirs is, cannot begin to match it for durability. We cannot be killed in that form unless the spirit is added to the physical body and not the dreamer. We are corporeal then, not so with the coupling of the dreamer. There, with the dreamer, we can withstand any physical attack. They are at a disadvantage. They can be killed. Then they will be forced to endure the rest of existence without even a body. That is a miserable state, especially given the strength and vigor that they enjoy while in their bodies. That is part of the allure of the person who is adept at utilizing the double. The blood drinkers see us and come to the realization that they are now the ones at a disadvantage; they are not the most powerful creatures in the world. They know that they must retain their bodies if they want to stay strong. Therefore, they are not going to put themselves in jeopardy with us. If we are in that other form, one's wish is one's command. What you will shall be, absent divine decrees to the contrary, of course."

"Divine decrees?"

"Yes. The Creator has a sort of denying power over what we do while in that form. One cannot stand there and perform vast miracles that are not in the plan. One time, the Cabicacmotz tried to feed a whole nation of hungry children and wasn't allowed."

I remembered the Cabicacmotz mentioning that and wanted to question him about it, but feared that the conversation would veer off in another new tangent and that we would never find where we had left off. "Okay, back to the children of Tohil. Why are the people who can attain the double so alluring to them if they know that they are in a dangerous situation?"

"Many reasons," the Tzuhunik said. "With some, it could simply be them finding themselves in the same situation a human finds themselves in with them, the appeal and beauty of danger. A jaguar in the jungle has a commanding majesty that is hypnotic. Perhaps they see some of that in us. More probable, though, they are trying to do what they can to get out of the situation they find themselves in. They see more power and want it. Do not succumb to the temptation to judge them too harshly, Zaki. They are doomed to an existence of being tied to their bodies. That does not mean that, come the end of time, things will stay the same. The Creator might allow them to return to the fold, having learned their lesson. I don't know what he will do. Another possibility is that some might be able to see how much better things can be and merely want to experience it secondhand. They watch and listen, trying to learn how to do it. When they can't, they must be satisfied with the dregs of the experience, our memories of divinity."

"You make it sound so unattractive," I complained. "These are tales from my childhood that I thought were only meant to scare me, yet somehow I wanted them to be real. Now that I know it's real, I regret that it is. Does that make sense to you?"

"Yes. Everything about those beings is regrettable. You are looking at only one type though."

"What do you mean?"

"Consider the tale of the twins, Zaki. The first test that a man has to pass in Xibalba is when he comes to the two rivers. One is Red River and it is composed of blood. The other is White River and it is composed of pus. Xibalba is the place of testing. Both sets of twins successfully passed those two tests. The first testing is to refrain from drinking the blood from Red River. The next is to refrain from drinking pus from the White River. It states that to succumb to those rivers is to be already defeated by Xibalba. It is a trial of endurance and will."

I nodded and said, "Have you ever come across the ones who drank from the White River?"

"Yes. I have come across those. They are very hard to catch, not that you would ever want to, but, yes, they are out there. They are much paler than the ones who drink blood, but can pass as regular humans without notice. The seer experiences an even deeper revulsion towards them. Their temptation lies further within the reaches of Xibalba. It is a closer step to hell. The blood ones are closer to our world, so they do not repel us as much."

"Why is that? Is it because of what they drink?"

"Maybe that's part of it. Remember what I said about the drinking of blood being proscribed. Seers have looked into the matter and have concluded that the life is, indeed, in the blood. With the White River folks, the death is in the pus. If the life force is contained in the blood and used as a supply of energy, the inverse can also be true. The force of death can also be used as a source of sustenance."

"How can they get their energy that way? It must be really hard to find enough, ugh, juice."

"I'd rather not talk about that. We know that those folks are doomed, in a similar way that the blood ones are."

"Why do you mean?"

"They are both bound to their bodies and confined to this world and under it, they cannot break free. One is bound through a consequence of misusing the life force, the other of misusing the death force. The rivers travel in opposite directions, but they are still found in the same world as each other. Those rivers are possibly found in some limbo world even. We do not know exactly how a rift was made into Xibalba that time in Tulan, but we should all be glad that we have not been able to replicate it or make it again. Anyway, it takes a deliberate act to ensure its irrevocability. A thought of doing it is not enough, neither a wish nor a mere dream. It must be performed voluntarily."

"Where do we travel? Is it the same road?" I asked.

"We travel over those rivers. We walk a tightrope upwards to heaven."

"Where is this place located in respect to our path?"

"Xibalba is always below us. We do our utmost to ensure that no one opens a rift into that hellish world. Some may find a way in through who knows what means. If they wind up in there, though, it doesn't matter if a person falls to the left or to the right, either fall lands in the same place, so it is only a matter of what kind of hell they experience if they fail."

"Why, in the world, would someone drink blood to quench their thirst?"

"It has a double meaning, like a lot of the things we deal with. In heaven, there are two rivers also, milk and honey. In Xibalba, it is blood and pus. It also may be a thirst of a different kind, possibly, that is meant," he replied. "To misuse the life force, by drinking blood, is a temptation to some. They steal life, in order to cheat death. Only later do they discover that they would have been better off if they had just died. Its members are alluring and sensual to regular people who fear death."

"To misuse the force of death, by ingesting it and living off of it is a specialized taste," he continued. "It takes a very weak individual to want such a devastating power. Others of their kind led the blood ones to that life. With the pus, though, it is a solitary temptation. Often, they are sorcerers who are attracted to that realm. They must manage to locate the actual White River. Thus, their fewer numbers. It is the temptation of commanding terrifying power. Regular people are repulsed by them. The pus drinkers do not bask in the adoration of their fans. They don't have any. They, too, would have been better off dead, but the time has passed for such decisions and they are stuck with it. It is a lonely existence that makes them despise and fear the world even more than before. Love and affection are only available to them from beings who do not fear them and that is hard to find because they are associated intimately with death. They are horrible beings, especially spiritually."

"Why's that?"

"Because a person who feels powerless and ridden upon can best be tempted by a fierce and real power. They have more power than the blood ones since the life force is confined and finite within a person's blood. The death force, on the other hand, is vast and encompassing. Anyway, those people are angry at the world to begin with, usually. It takes a lot of abuse to make one susceptible to being tempted by such a disgusting act. They are, thankfully, much rarer."

The Cabicacmotz interrupted, saying, "I must add something... Store my words; don't think about them now. Those who drink from the Red River lock their bodies with their spirits. Those who drink from the White River lock their bodies with their dreamer. They both view the world primarily through the eyes of the body. I apologize, please go on, Tzuhunik."

The Tzuhunik nodded, but did not say anything more.

I thought about what the Cabicacmotz had said. I was powerfully enthralled with the idea of the people who were from the White River. Childhood tales of terror had inured me to the idea of blood drinkers, but the pus drinkers were a new horror for me and I was fascinated. "If they have more power than the blood ones, why don't they seek us out or challenge us or try to conquer the world?" I questioned.

"Because they know that we get our energy from a much greater source," the Tzuhunik said. "To avoid being defeated by those rivers requires that we respect the force of life and the force of death. We do not misuse them. The temptation to fear death or to fear life is not a problem for us. Therefore, we are not defeated. We may not always be able to pull off what we will, but if our plans coincide with the Creator's, then we can. To get one's sustenance from him means better energy all around. Life force and death force? He is master of them both, since he created them in the first place."

"The flow of the rivers is different," he added. "The River of Blood seeks to flow upwards towards life, the other down into the abyss, the land of the dead. It is rare when a pus drinker seeks us out. Either they are confused or they have realized that they are condemned and seek to reverse the process, but that is rare for them to realize."

"To answer your second question, they cannot conquer the world by sheer force; they could not even master their own base motives, which led them into the hell they are in now. No, they would be destroyed immediately. Mankind would rise up and overcome them. They are strong, but they cannot withstand everything we can throw at them. They can be killed. That is their weakness; they must sustain their bodies for however long they can. It is better to be on the world rather than in its depths. No one wants to end up in Xibalba. Therefore, they take the measure of secrecy to hide from mankind, which has the means and the impetus to destroy them, in order to keep their bodies safe and whole. If they lose the body, it's an automatic passage to hell, a land of horror where they no longer have command as they did here on earth."

"But if the blood ones steal the life force from people and kill them, then what do the White River ones do? Do they also kill?"

"What they do is even more horrible. Their touch keeps death at bay, but it does not heal. Only the blood ones can perform that wonder, but they do not often do it because secrecy keeps them from being hunted. The pus ones would not even want to heal the person. They stave off death for a while, prolonging the misery and despair of a person who needs to be touched by death. The dying or injured need to be released from this world and death performs that function normally. They step in and separate the person from the forces that can alleviate their suffering. It is an interloper, a parasite. When the body of the human can no longer supply their needs, when it is too weak to give them pus or the misery they love, they leave. They do not bother to kill; it is assured. That, to me, is more horrible than killing a person and depriving them of a normal life. To deprive a person of death is much worse. Now do you see why they disgust me?"

"That is appalling. Do we ever have to see them or get to, somehow, stop them?"

"We occasionally move in and place death back where it should be. With the blood ones, the process is so quick that we simply could not stop it altogether. It has its role in the world now, it seems. With the pus ones, we are alerted to an ongoing and lengthy affair of evil. We sense when it is going on and often find ourselves witnessing the abuse without consciously willing ourselves there. It is as if we are the healers or the guards of the populace. Then we kick them out, allowing death to perform its mercy."

"I thought that you had said that the White River ones were difficult to find. Didn't you say that?" I asked.

"Yes, I did, but I should have qualified it with the words 'when they are not conducting their despicable acts'. They act like normal men and women, but are much paler. They ingest something that does not lend them any color, after all. One can sometimes find them in the fields of quarantine, operating in places where there is isolation and insufficient supervision of the suffering. They often break into places like that to feed. I have seen them, many times, posing as patients. It's sickening. The problem with finding them and identifying them is that they look exactly like regular people when they are hiding amongst the populace. When they feed, they can become wraithlike beings. They are, at times, partly incorporeal."

"But don't they need their bodies to do their work?"

"I would think so, but I have seen it. To my reasoning, there must be some aspect of the process that is easier performed as a ghastly specter. I suspect that it is when they feed upon the despair of the person. When they feed upon the liquids, they need the body, but the dessert probably needs a ghost shape to enjoy. I also think that they may utilize the ghost shape when they do not feel like being part of the crowd. I think that they can become vaporous for periods of time. I don't know enough about them to be sure, but I suspect that they have strange powers at their command since they are tied to their dreamer, which belongs to the realm of magic. In any case, they need the pus, but could probably get by without the misery. The thing is that they would never give that up. Thus you have a powerful being that can elude capture more easily than the blood ones can, since they can become mist, unless they are exposed to the sun."

"So they can't ever go out in the sun?" I asked.

"Correct. We are still unsure about the blood ones because of what I saw, but I know for sure that the pus ones cannot abide the sun in any measure. The pus ones can hide better, though, since they can mist into hard to reach places."

"Can those ever do their nasty work on us, I mean you?"

"Never count yourself out of our number, Zaki. To answer your question, I have never seen it happen. I believe that we require a more personal version of death, one that does not allow interlopers. People like us have a cordial relationship with death. Some of us can even see and converse with our deaths."

"Have you?"

"Yes. I believe that you will too, if blood counts for anything," he said as he looked over at my father and the Cabicacmotz.

"Let's go back," I said. "If I met a woman descendant of Tohil, she would not be enticing to me?"

"You would rather vomit than let her touch you. You will not find beauty and sensuality in her embrace; you would find ugliness and a feeling of being unclean. It is an overpowering response to finding yourself before one. You will not be different. You might feel pity towards them and regret that you could not free them from the quicksand, but you will feel the wrongness of them and your very spirit will recoil. We are incompatible. We are like travelers who meet at an inn. One needs to go east and the other needs to go west. Neither can change the mind of the other and cause them to travel the same path, there is only the moment of intersection. You will remember them because they are unique, but we can find no peace in their arms."

I was rapt. The tales told to children were supposedly true. It was incredible to me, but I disbelieved it all, yet believed it at the same time. It was like being divided in two.

I wanted to question them about other stories I had heard which were horrifying, but I first wanted to clear up a few points. "So it was meaningless to destroy Tohil, Auilix and Hacauitz, if their offspring are still here."

"No, Zaki," the Cabicacmotz said. "It was vitally important to eliminate them. There would be more of those creatures here if we had not done so. They would be legion. In addition, if the false gods were still around, no human would be free. They drank from the actual Red River. They were almost unstoppable because of that and because they were probably also gifted seers who fell into Xibalba when the rift opened in Tulan. No, their loss is truly our great gain. No man on this earth would be free of their terrible yoke if they had not been destroyed. Their offspring are nothing in comparison to them. We can pick them off at our leisure unless they reproduce too often and that will not happen. They are usually secretive and they fear the dwindling of their food source. Many have opted to only feed from animals, so with some we have no legitimate quarrel."

"What weapons were used to destroy Tohil and his companions?"

My father answered my question. He said, "You do understand, Zaki, that none of us were actually there, right? This all happened many years before any of us here were born into the world. We are telling you the accounts of what those brave men and women did. To be fair, each of us probably asked our teachers the same questions you are now asking. Anyway, when they had located the lairs of those false gods, they were in a cave. Some had to battle the spirit forms of those beings while others dragged their stones out into the daylight. Many perished, so powerful were the false ones even without actual bodies. Their repertoire of magic was chilling and utterly stupendous. Remember what the Tzuhunik told you, Xibalba is the source of all magic. Those beings had a direct connection to it. Putting the stones directly into the light of the sun greatly diminished their strength and they were then unable to project their spirits away from the stones. Still, when the tribe got the stone statues of the false gods into the sun, they found that they were impervious to weapons. Flint would not work against them. Neither would obsidian. Finally, enraged at being so close to the goal, of ridding the world of such an evil, one man raged and wept at his impotence. He struck out with his hands against the statues. He wore rings of gold and golden bracelets. Amazingly, those things damaged the statues as easily as obsidian knives upon flesh. Our warriors armed only with jewelry were able to destroy those beings and sever their parts. That was their end. That is why we favor the yellow metal, which is so abundant in our land. The Creator knew we would need it and bestowed it upon us. It is the metal of heaven and of the sun."

The Tzuhunik added, "It is important to wear gold. It even follows one in dreaming."

He had succeeded in confusing me. I asked him to clarify his words.

He said, "If you wear gold and fall asleep, both your dreamer and your spirit will also wear the item. Therefore, it has an esoteric function that few other substances have."

I asked him to tell me what other things also did that. He told me that it was a dreaming experiment that everyone had to perform and that he couldn't deprive me of my task by telling me.

My father chided me for asking improper questions, saying, "This is work that every student must do on their own. We tell you about many things, but you must corroborate them and put them into practice for yourself. Otherwise they will not have any force in your own life, Zaki."

I wanted to protest that my question had been innocent and that I had not known that it was improper to ask about that, but the guards came walking up then. In their midst they had the Etamanel Evan.

"Is this how you treat your guests now, Naualalom?" he asked. He was clearly put out at being surrounded by guards and treated with suspicion. One of the guards held him by the upper arm. He fidgeted and pulled himself out of the guard's hold. It made me laugh. He reminded me of an infant peccary, which did not wish to be held and squirmed in protest.

No one else laughed, but I could tell that everyone was amused.

My father said to him, "Guests approach a servant and wait to be announced to the master of the house. They do not presume to walk in whenever they feel the whim. This is not the marketplace where anyone can walk wherever they like. It is my home."

The Etamanel Evan pointed at the Cabicacmotz and the Tzuhunik and said, "They do. I have seen them."

My father softly shook his head in negation. He said, 'The Cabicacmotz is my personal advisor as well as being a member of my family. He is always welcome as if this was his own home. The Tzuhunik is a close friend of mine since our own schooling with the former Cabicacmotz, yet he always presents himself to my manservant. There have been times when I have been occupied and he has had to wait. He does not sneak over walls and hide behind trees like a beast of prey, lying in wait for the perfect moment to pounce on his quarry." He raised an eyebrow as if he was inviting the Etamanel Evan to deny his accusations.

I looked at the Etamanel Evan with worry. He was flustered and seemed to have gravy stains all over the front of his muslin robes. His eyes were glassy and red, making me wonder if the guards had roughed him up enough to make him cry. I felt sorry for him. He was not as polished as the other men were and acted more as a child would than an adult. I could not really understand why my father and the others did not want me around him. He seemed harmless.

"If I come onto your properties uninvited, Naualalom, it is because I have a student who is not being allowed to learn from me as the omens dictated. I am forced to resort to subterfuge in order to even see him."

417

The Cabicacmotz stood and said, "You can see him any time you like. The Tzuhunik is to be there also. You were informed of this."

"Why am I not allowed to see my student without a chaperone? Is it because he is the prince?"

"You are no longer to see any of your students without a chaperone, Etamanel," my father told him. "After the conduct of your students at the festival, you and your school are required to undergo a period of evaluation and supervision."

This was news to me. They had told me that the Eta-manel's weed was injurious to my will, but had failed to tell me that there was an actual incident involving the man or his students. I wondered what had happened.

"Those were trumped-up charges of misconduct. My boys, by chance, happened to fall on the Chuchmox' tent. They weren't trying to see those women undressing."

The Tzuhunik rolled his eyes and dryly said, "Oh, of course not. Moreover, we can also suppose that when one of them squeezed the breast of one of the Chuchmox that he was also not trying to do so. How is the young man after that, by the way?"

This was too good to miss. I was so glad that I was there to hear about it.

The Etamanel Evan blushed and mumbled something about the boy recovering and that he still had to sleep on his stomach as his back was still covered with unguents.

"Your failure to properly supervise your students and instill in them morals and a sense of decorum led to the young man's injuries, Etamanel," my father said. "You are to blame for what happened to him. If you had not been blasted out of your gourd, you would have watched your students and brought them into line. Instead, you let them run around like inebriated monkeys and they angered the Chuchmox. The boy's back would not be sliced to ribbons from the whipping the Chuchmox gave him and you would be allowed to see your students without a chaperone. Frankly, I don't see the situation changing anytime soon. Look at you, you are dirty and unkempt, even on the day you strive to see the prince at my home."

"No. I am just free from any thoughts about my personal appearance. It is to all of your discredit that you cling to such foolishness," the Etamanel Evan countered.

"You know that is not so, Etamanel. It merely sounds good to you. Your lack of thoughts about your appearance stems from laziness, not from freedom. It does not reflect inner order, it reflects disorder, and you know it. For years, you have been smoking as much of the weed as you please and have allowed yourself to become indulgent and unused to functioning without it. You have failed in your duties to your students. Instead of providing them with an extra avenue of perception and a cushion for their other educational responsibilities, you have given them a crutch, a vice. They are now crippled in their development."

"I gave them happiness," the Etamanel Evan protested. "I taught them about the weed as fate told me to. It is a plant of happiness."

"Your responsibility as a teacher was not fulfilled, Etamanel. There is nothing wrong with happiness, but it cannot be had at the exclusion of all else, especially duty. People cannot smoke the weed as often as they like and be capable of learning everything they should from their other teachers. It interferes with that. They have not learned restraint from your teachings. What appears harmless is actually not so. Your students behave as if they can do as they please and that nothing dangerous can happen to them. The Chuchmox are nothing to play with and your students behaved as if they were foreign whores. We have done the only thing we could do in these circumstances. Be thankful that you have not been stripped of your position entirely," my father said.

The Etamanel Evan did not say anything in his defense; he only hung his head and looked at the ground. It was very uncomfortable because no one said anything or tried to change the subject. My father's words hung in the air, reminding everyone of the failings of the man with the weed.

After a while, the Tzuhunik took the Etamanel Evan to the side and appeared to comfort him. I could not hear what they were talking about. Finally, the Etamanel nodded and looked over at me. It was the first time he had looked me in the eye since he first arrived. It was difficult for me to meet his eyes, I felt embarrassed for him. He grimaced and shrugged, somehow conveying to me the regret he felt at my having heard him be rebuked before everyone.

They walked back to where I sat.

In a soft voice, the Etamanel Evan told me that he had discussed me with the Tzuhunik. They had agreed, he said, that it was time for me to, once again, smoke the weed.

I looked over at my father and the Cabicacmotz. Father shrugged and the Cabicacmotz said, "When a teacher is telling you to do something, it is considered improper to look to your other teachers for permission, Zaki. You are to accompany the Tzuhunik and the Etamanel Evan as they have decided."

I looked around for Chahal and saw her sleeping against another portion of the tree's trunk. I hissed for her and she immediately woke up. She looked at me and got up to follow us.

A jaguar roared. Everyone became alert and tensed with attention. I knew the roar did not come from Chahal because it occurred while I was watching her.

"I disagree with you, Cabi." A man's voice suddenly said.

I looked and it was the Balam Ch'ab. Everyone looked surprised that he had arrived. It was clear that he was not invited, yet no one moved to eject him from the premises.

"Tomorrow, this boy is to see me and learn. I cannot have him lethargic. He needs to be alert and mentally quick. If he smokes that tonight, he will not be in any shape to do what is asked of him. I don't like this aspect of his education, but I yield to the omen, as I am required to. I will not object if he takes the weed on the day when he returns from my lands. Will that be acceptable, Etamanel?"

The Etamanel Evan swallowed loudly and nodded.

Everyone stood around and looked at each other, no one spoke. The silence was strained and discomfiting.

The Tzuhunik took the Etamanel Evan's arm and said, "If we are not going to be working, we should leave." They left without another word.

When I looked back at the Balam Ch'ab, I saw that he was staring at me. His eyes didn't blink. It was unnerving. I looked to my father and the Cabicacmotz. They avoided my eyes. I could tell that they were pretending not to notice that I was looking at them.

"Let us take a walk," the Balam Ch'ab said. He began walking into the darkness of the trees. "Come along", he urged when he saw that I was not yet following him.

I followed, not knowing if I should speak. Part of me wanted to engage him in conversation in order to convert him into a friendlier being. The rational part of me decided that I should keep my mouth closed.

When he walked, the ponytail on top of his head bobbed. It seemed jaunty to me. His steps were silent, yet firm. I marveled at his ability to avoid the dry leaves. There were many, so it mystified me that he was able to keep his steps from finding them. His head appeared to be up. Not once did I catch him looking down.

There was a terrible ringing in my ears. I almost reached up to cover my ears, until I realized that it was an internal phenomenon.

He asked, "Where is your cat?"

"She is pacing us to our left," I said, without thinking.

He stopped and said. "Quickly. Where is your sense of self?"

I told him.

"Good," he said. "Now you know. I know that place. One feels a sense of balance there. You can now move your sense of self to that place when you need to feel the world around you. You sense it about you. Remember the position."

I stammered a reply, something about not having known where Chahal actually was when he asked. I let him know that I had spoken without thinking.

"Don't argue with me, Zaki. She is to our left. I can feel her, too. Remember that specific location when you need to know the surroundings. Sometimes our bodies know what to do. It is when we try to understand it rationally that we have trouble. That is why it is important to be quick. Catch yourself when you find that you are successful when doing something naturally."

My thinking was muddled. My thoughts jumped around, albeit sluggishly. I gauged where my sense of self was and it was in the same place. Although I found him fearsome and difficult to talk to, I told him what I was experiencing.

He laughed and said, "You have to shift the sense of self away from where it is at now. How can you pay attention to my words when the world around you is inundating you with information? You cannot." He regarded me, tilting his head. "You can try to do the shifting yourself, but I don't recommend it. At this point in your training, it would be better only to make observations. We will continue to converse about things. When you find that you are easily following my words, then become aware of where the sense of self resides. Understand?"

I nodded and told him I would remember to do that.

He seemed dubious when he heard my words. He said, "Maybe we should have a little chat about what you were talking about with the men."

"What had we been talking about?"

"The false gods." He took a deep breath and seemed nervous. "It is not my wish to upset you, but sometimes people take those stories a bit too literally."

"Are you saying that those were lies?"

"When people believe what they say, we can conclude that they are incorrect, misled or gullible. A lie is a purposeful untruth. That is not what we are dealing with here."

"What about the Tzuhunik's story?" I asked. "You weren't there when he told his tale about the hostess blood drinker."

"I am one of the patrols for your father's estates. I was there, even if you did not see me. As for the Tzuhunik's story, I am not in the custom of believing things I cannot verify for myself."

"What about the Creator?" I asked.

"He is different."

I asked him whether he had ever seen him.

He told me that he hadn't.

"Why should that be different from the other stories?"

"Some stories are not stories. Some stories are accounts of people's journeys into the heavens."

"What's the difference?"

He shrugged and said, "Do you believe in the Creator, Zaki?"

I told him that I did, but that sometimes my faith was shaken with reality. There were things I felt that didn't jibe with my definition of him.

"What kinds of things?"

"My mother died before I was able to know her. Also, there are some who murder. How can an all-powerful Creator allow something like that?"

"No one knows when he will require us to go up and meet with him. The human body is fragile. With murderers, that is a different story. All of us have freewill. It is what separates us from angels, who do not always have that. They are fixed, many times. We are free; that is the second of our gifts from him. The first is the gift of his spirit. We must always search for him. I have not had any luck, yet. Perhaps you will be different. But, I can assure you that you will never find him if you want him to conform to your definition."

"What do you mean?"

"I mean that if you search for the Creator, you may get lucky. If you are after the all-powerful puppet-master of the universe, though, you will not find him because he doesn't exist."

"I'm not searching for the puppet-master," I protested.

"Yes, you are. You want a god who will protect you from others who are exercising their freewill. You despise the idea of freewill. Every person claims to love their freewill, but that is a lie. Most, actually, would prefer freedom from choice, at least, freedom from the choice of others. Come to terms with the knowledge that in this world, everything is permitted, but not everything is sanctioned by the Creator. We can do anything we please, but that does not make it right. In this world, savagery is possible, but so also is great good. It is as if he has given us autonomy to see what we make of it. Perhaps only through self-governance can we understand his governance."

His words shocked me. They were the words of the pious, of a man who truly thought about our fate as men in a world that could be cruel and uncertain. I wasn't in the mood to discuss such things. I found the topic boring and wanted to change the subject.

"Why shouldn't I believe that there were blood drinkers?"

"I'm not saying that there are none. I'm saying that I have never seen any, so I neither believe nor disbelieve. I have found it to be a good tenet for this plane. With the heavens, I accept what sounds right to me, the same with the below. For this world, I will believe things with certainty when I see them. Also, I have it on good authority that that little bit about the gold cutting through the false ones was an embellishment on the part of storytellers who wanted to share knowledge about gold's more useful attributes."

"How do you know that for sure?" I asked.

He gave me a look that made me feel gullible and foolish. "The Ahtzic Uinac is my father. He has revealed certain twists... That part is complicated and I won't discuss the circumstances. Be wise. The storytellers don't always believe their own stories, it seems. If those creatures were such a threat, do you believe that our storytellers would fail to give us the key to their destruction? Also, if they claim to have destroyed all three false gods, why is the dreaming populace only asked to watch the remains in only one location? Shouldn't there be many sites of vigilance? It doesn't make sense and no one wants to hear about it. I have tried to bring up the subject with many learned people of our tribe. Perhaps they never existed and the story is a cover for something else entirely. Maybe they only rid us of one of those blood drinkers and want to hide that from us, or it happened so long ago that no one knows what really happened. I honestly don't know."

I was having a difficult time figuring him out. What he talked about didn't sound like what I expected a formidable warrior to talk about. I expected him to be silent and mysterious. Alternatively, I would not have been surprised to hear him regale me with battle stories. This was mildly disorienting and unanticipated by me.

"In case you have not noticed, I am not an advocate of the use of plants," he said, changing the subject without warning. "People take all sorts of things and feel that they have received great revelations. Who knows if what they have learned has any use? Any attempts to replicate their results are in vain because the plants carry the user to the point of success too quickly. The person cannot remember how to get to that point without utilizing the plant again. Beware of shortcuts; sometimes there is a great toll to pay, especially bodily. Don't expect any shortcuts with what I teach you. Every gain will be difficult to attain, but it will be all yours. It will be the product of your own efforts and work. You will know every step necessary. The way will not be hazy or unclear; you will know it as you know the lines on your palm."

"Are you saying that the Tzuhunik mistook what he saw because he uses plants?"

"No, Zaki, I didn't say that. I will admit that the fact that he is a plant user makes me more skeptical about what he says. Among the users, he is more reliable than others are. I respect that he only uses them when he has to. It would be better, of course, not to ever need them. That is a vain hope."

I did not believe that plants were foolish to use. Naively, I still thought that medicinal and perception-altering plants were equal, if not synonymous. To my credit, though, no longer did I confuse or equate them with herbs used in the preparation of foods. I expressed my belief that plants were of great use and that they provided excellent healing medicines and salves for the tribe.

He laughed and told me that they were not the same. He said that the benefits of medicinal plants were usually subtle and slow. He told me to remember how quickly the seven-pronged leaf had worked on my perception. "The advantage of plants like that is that they work quickly upon you. The disadvantage is exactly the same. Without a scribe, there is no possibility of you remembering everything you realized, experienced, or thought about."

"I don't get that impression from the Tzuhunik," I said. "I get the feeling that he always knows what's going on. There's something very somber about him; the man has probably never had an irrelevant moment. I was afraid to laugh around him."

The Balam Ch'ab chuckled at my words and nodded. "It's true that I don't approve of plant use, but that man does fall outside of the scope of my judgments for those very reasons and for one other reason that he told me about."

I asked him what that reason was.

He said, "I've mentioned that plants get you from your everyday awareness to another point of reality so quickly that you can never hope to get there again without the help of the plant. The Tzuhunik has my respect because he has noticed a very important point in the whole process." He sighed loudly and walked away, shaking his head. He turned back to me and said, "To tell you the truth, we had an argument about this very thing and he pointed out something surprisingly basic to me. What he told me was that he agreed with my reasons for disliking plants, but he defended them because of one single reason. Here it is... Plants might get one to another point of reality too fast for one to learn how to do it, but that is not the true role of plants, it is only one of their drawbacks. Their real role is to provide the possibility of another point of reality."

I scrunched up my face trying to understand what he was telling me. As was typical, his words had washed right over me. These past days had forced me to abandon my usual state of being, the mindless state where I never had to think or pay close attention to anything. The complexity of all these conversations was wearying to me and I was physically tired. I wanted to sleep. I wanted to be a child again and not have to think about such weird things. I missed the days when life was undemanding and everything in my world had a simple explanation. Would I ever have such peace again? The Balam Ch'ab's voice brought me out of my thoughts.

"Do you see, Zaki? Without plants, man might never conceive that there are other possibilities of being. That is why we need plants. Not because they carry us from everyday reality to extraordinary reality, but because we could never conceive that those states of extraordinary reality even exist, on our own. That is their gift. Possibility."

He shook his head again, roughly, as if he could not believe his own words. "I never thought I would ever be the defender of plants, I can tell you that. Let us leave this topic, though, I did not ask you to walk with me in order to discuss plants."

"Then, what did you wish to talk about?" I asked.

"There are some things that I wish to know the answers to and I believe that you have them."

He could not have surprised me more. Even though I was technically a man, I was untried and still felt like a child.

It mystified me that he could want to know something that I knew. I told him that I would gladly tell him what he wanted to know, if I knew it.

"I see many natural jaguars in the jungle, as you might have guessed. The females periodically go into heat. Chahal has never been in estrus, to my knowledge. Do you know why she has not?"

"What is estrus?"

He rolled his eyes and gave a loud sigh. I knew I had disappointed him somehow, but I could not answer his question if I did not understand his wording.

"Estrus, or heat, is when the female enters a fertile period in her reproductive cycle and seeks males in which to mate with, so she can have little jaguars. Chahal has never been fertile. We would have smelled it on her."

A look of horror crossed my face as I considered the possibilities.

Again, he rolled his eyes. He said, "Real jaguars avoid us. We do not mingle in any way. Remember that. Don't bother trying to seek friends or allies among them. They know we are men and not true jaguars."

I just looked at him. Chahal would never avoid me, I believed. Perhaps she really was different from others of her kind. I always thought of her as a domesticated wild animal, but I never forgot that she was one. We never played rough and I kept away from her claws and teeth. It was a wary trust that I had for her. She was not a perfect pet, but she was mine and I loved her. His words made me worry about her. She might even be ill. I wondered aloud if I should take her to one of the healers of animals.

He told me that I should not worry, that he would have smelled any disease upon her. He assured me that she was healthy, otherwise.

I asked him if he had ever observed Chahal interacting with any other jaguars and he told me that he had not. "It is not something to be concerned with, Zaki. She might not know any others. All of them are solitary beings, except during the mating cycle. In addition, the fact that we roam the jungles helps ensure that they do not enter our territories. It is not unusual that none of us would have seen her with any of her kind because they simply do not come here."

"What else did you wish to ask me?" I asked him.

He waved aside my question and told me not to ask because the questions were dependent on my answer to his question about Chahal's heat cycle. After a few moments, he admitted that there were other questions, but that they would be better learned during my training.

"Are there any questions you have for me?" he asked.

I told him that I was curious to know how many Jaguar Knights played on the bateh team, the Jaguars, and why they had the same name.

"Bateh teams are often named after mighty beasts. It is a way of somehow invoking the spirit of the animal or its great qualities; it is a form of hoping. It might work for teams that have exceptional talents, but I have seen untalented teams that were called Jaguars and the name didn't help them play any better. So no, there is no connection between the team and the group. There are five of my men on the bateh team. A few play for the Eagles."

"So the team and the group are completely distinct," I said.

"That is correct. There is some overlap in exercises or philosophy, of course, but that could be said of almost any group when compared with another."

I asked him to spell out any commonalities that I could understand.

He told me that both groups fought against death and worked to abolish it.

My mouth dropped open and I asked, "So you can come back to life too?"

A look of consternation crossed his face and he sighed loudly. "Death is a greater foe than our insistence on looking like ourselves. It is not a common victory, Zaki. It is not a simple affair, it takes great energy and will to accomplish. Only a true adept can ever hope to defeat death, and sometimes not even those reach that pinnacle."

I told him that after watching the game during the festival, I had been under the impression that our people knew how to accomplish it.

"Accomplishing it and abolishing it are two different things. Accomplishing it alone, without anyone else's intent, is very different from what you saw at the game. What you saw there was the realization of the intent of every one of the lords of the life force. It was not a solitary feat by the captain of the Pumas, everyone pitched in. He would have died like anyone else if he had not had help. I only know of three men in our tribe who are able to resurrect themselves on their own."

"Who?"

"Your father, the Cabicacmotz, and me. Imagine..."

"Wow," I cried. "You can do that?" I had thought that he had been avoiding my question before, so I had not pressed him to answer me, believing that he was embarrassed by his inability to accomplish the miracle.

He ignored me and continued, "Realize this, Zaki, you are learning from people who others would love to learn from. You cannot possibly fathom how fortunate you are. You are my only student. We received a few omens from other boys, but they will be receiving instruction from my other men. Your father, obviously, will not have any other apprentices. Neither will the Cabicacmotz."

"The Cabicacmotz is in charge of the training of all of the boys," I countered.

"None will be receiving his personal attention as you will. He is your uncle and now he will be your brother-in-law, as well. It is as if you cannot fight your fate. Everything is dropping into place like stones in a barrier, trapping you inside. I find this all very strange. Something is happening, but I am unable to figure out what it is, yet."

"Would it be better if one of your men taught me, instead of you?"

"No. The omen was clear to me. I pretended that we were willing to let you go, but that was not the truth."

"You lied?"

He laughed at my expression and said, "It was bluster and only performed for a specific purpose. The purpose was to teach you that it is unwise to insult those whom you do not know, that you should guard your tongue, and that you should assess situations more prudently. They were words used to convey a message other than what was actually said. You believe it is a lie now, but the Cabicacmotz understood my aim and recognized it for what it was. It was a dance of words. They are the preliminary words that men speak to each other. The next time you observe men, notice that the meanings of their words are obscured at their greeting if they are taking the measure of each other."

I nodded, even though I knew that I would probably not remember to do so.

The left side of his mouth curled up in a smile and he chuckled to himself. He pointed at me and said, "Now, that was a lie."

I apologized and told him that I would try to be a better student.

He laughed and told me that trifling lies did not concern him. That because of his accusation now, I would remember to pay attention to what was the underlying truth in certain conversations. He added that women did such things as well and urged me to take notice of the hidden meanings within conversations that seemed polite or perfunctory. "Don't rely on the actual words to determine the intentions of people. Listen with that other part of you that knew where Chahal was."

"Do I have to place my sense of self in the same place?"

"No, it is similar, but not exact. The proper method for such an exercise is to have the intent to become aware of the intentions behind words. The body will follow your command. Once you feel that, then gauge where the self resides. You will have to do it many times to learn how to do it. Then you move on to the corroboration. At that point, you need to have a guide who will verify that your conclusions are correct and true. Without that corroboration, you might fall prey to the suspicion that you are imagining things and that it is all lies or madness."

He looked towards my father's residence and announced that Hac and Cham had arrived and were waiting for me in one of the outer courtyards. "It is time to head back. Remember to get a good night's rest tonight. You will need it. For me, I have to patrol your father's lands until the moon is between the zenith and the horizon."

He then ran into the trees without a farewell.

When I walked back, I caught glimpses of Chahal pacing me in her easy lope. I switched my attention to the walk ahead of me in order to test out the Balam Ch'ab's advice and soon I was feeling her location without the use of my eyes. As I felt her steps, I also became aware that there was another big cat pacing me, only it was to my other side. I almost tripped over my own feet when I realized that it was the Balam Ch'ab.

They escorted me home, a vigilant and swift guard.

Then I took my rest.

Part Five

The Balam Ch'ab &

The Chuchmox

I stood upon one of the temple roofs with the Cabicac-motz and Chahal, in the early morning. The jungle canopy to the east shaded the barren floor of the complex. The temple tops glinted with a golden hue as if tears of a god had just dripped on them from above. Soon they would come alive like fire.

From our vantage point, we could see the tents of the newly arrived pochtecas who camped in the fields before the jungle. Chuchmox were at their posts, reclined like statues while they kept watch over our lands. Their bright clothing, reflecting their directions, stood out in the shad-owed gloom.

I was so nervous that my bowels felt loose. Once again, I questioned the Cabicacmotz about why I had to go and see the Balam Ch'ab. The question never changed and the answer never did, either.

"You must go because a pebble lodged in the heel of your sandal."

I considered it the feeblest of omens. Unfortunately, the Balam Ch'ab was the first in his group to see the omen. How I wished the pebble had made me walk on the heels of my feet.

Last night, when he had spoken to me at my father's compound, he did his best to put me at ease, yet I found him too sober and pious. He spoke of many things and I felt defenseless against his use of words and logic.

The Cabicacmotz pulled my attentions back to the temple top. He pointed to a parade of figures in the distance. "Look now; there is the Balam Ch'ab's father, the Ahtzic Uinac, the master storyteller."

I saw a palanquin carried by eight men in the group and asked him what it was. Palanquins were seldom used and usually only by visiting royal women. My father had an entourage of guards, but it was his custom to walk in the open.

"The Ahtzic Uinac is a frail and elderly man. He would not be able to get around at times, but for his attendants. To accompany you to see the Balam Ch'ab is beyond his abilities. The training home is deep in the jungle."

"Why does he need to come along? I do not want to force a man out of his sickbed to walk into the jungle with me. Why can't you walk me there?"

The Cabicacmotz looked at me as if I was a fool. After a moment, his face softened and he said, "I forget you are young, Zaki. You never learned how things proceed formally. This is the story-master's duty. That man has enough will to get out of bed to accompany a prince to his first lesson with his own son, the great Balam Ch'ab. He would never pass along this duty, not even to his named successor. So be polite and listen to everything he says. His story will hold lessons for you regarding the changing of a man into a jaguar."

He climbed down from the roof of the altar and helped me down.

When I was halfway down the temple, I noticed that he was almost to the base and said, "Uncle, wait for me."

He looked back with a frown and sat to wait for me. When I reached him, he patted the step he was sitting on to invite me to sit with him. I did. He said, "Zaki, I have been remiss in teaching you formal manners. I told you not to refer to me as your uncle because you would inadvertently do so in front of your fellow students. I am the Cabicac-motz, the blazing star from the Pleiades; refer to me by my title." He jutted his chin towards the slow moving group we were to meet. "Only call that man Ahtzic Uinac. His time is near; give him the tribute of his title. Do not refer to him in the honorifics of polite social speech. Only use the formal Ahtzic Uinac. We become our titles. If you do otherwise, you deny him the power of his office and you will diminish his story. In addition, to do otherwise is disrespectful. Do the same with the Balam Ch'ab."

I was not going to call the Balam Ch'ab anything else. I appreciated the advice. Anything that kept me out of trouble with the man was a worthy activity in my eyes. I nodded and told him that I would do so.

We waited for the palanquin, while we stood before the temple. Pale green cloths, that fluttered in the early breeze, covered the compartment. I could see that the men chosen to uphold it were all of the same height and build to ensure a smooth ride for the one traveling. When it neared, I heard a man laughing behind the canopy cloths. "What a memory you have, Cabicacmotz."

"T a kazah r a vach (*lower your eyes*), and bow your head briefly, Zaki," the Cabicacmotz whispered to me.

I did what he asked when the child of innocence, Tukumux, parted the curtains to reveal a wizened man with a long white braid. Age and sun wrinkled his face, but still his eyes were sharp and bright.

The old man smiled at me and motioned me with his hand to come closer. "Come, come," he said. "Let me see you, young prince."

The closer I came to the palanquin, the more I could smell jasmine. At its threshold, I saw that bits of the vine were scattered around the man. Underneath was the smell of age. Not yet was it the scent, which signals the approach of death.

Again, I did what the Cabicacmotz had told me to do. The Ahtzic Uinac imitated my movements, then touched my cheek. His hand was cold and dry, yet soft like a scholar's palm. "You favor your mother," he said and looked towards the Cabicacmotz. "Perhaps you will even sprout hair upon your chin like this one did. I see he has tired of using unguents to remove it."

Unlike the men of my tribe, the Cabicacmotz had a small beard that he kept trimmed close to his face. In the sunlight, it was almost golden, marking him as foreign.

The men exchanged polite words until the Ahtzic Uinac clapped his hands lightly and Tukumux pinned the curtains of the palanquin back. The other attendants set the story-master down and rubbed their hands. Two fresh attendants took hold of the rear bars and lifted them up. In the compartment, he stretched his legs and rested them against a foot brace. He seemed to be leaning back when they began dragging the palanquin towards the jungle. "Come, young man. We are off to see my son."

We left the Cabicacmotz behind. Chahal walked next to Tukumux with his hand on her neck. I should not have been surprised; my cat had many friendships that I was only now learning she had.

"You come from an esteemed line, Zaki," the Ahtzic Uinac said. "Your father, mother, and uncle have the blood of genius. To assure succession, it is necessary for kings to have more than one wife. In that manner, your uncle can further combine his blood with your father's blood. Much is expected of you and any offspring he and your sister, Maricua, produce."

I merely nodded and refrained from subjecting him to my opinions.

"When I was a young boy, I watched the famed building engineer, Puch'um Maram, build the temple you and the Cabicacmotz descended."

His statement excited me. Never had I seen the building of one of the great temples. Even now, in such an early generation, myths guarded the secrets to the building of the temples.

The architects and masons were a close-lipped group and deliberately restricted knowledge of proper construction. If someone hoped to learn anything, he had to ask the men who built roofs. The two groups were always at odds and despised each other. The roofers wanted no part in secrets and refused to help the others give themselves airs. I asked him to tell me how they built the temples.

He smiled and said, "In the most obvious way. They used canals and sand."

"Sand? For what?"

"Think about this. Dragging a large stone with a rope across the ground is another matter entirely from lifting that same stone up steep and narrow steps. Why did you think that the temple complex was so devoid of any greenery? We are on the same level as the jungle, but the jungle is verdant and fertile. Life blooms easily in its soil. Here, it is the barren sand of wastelands and deserts because we see the deep sand, which the temple builders dug up to assist them in their works. They spread it around the construction site and the job was easier for them."

I told him about a game I played with, when I was a young child, which consisted of small blocks of stone. I often built pyramids with them.

"But did your temples have rooms inside?"

"Only on the topmost level, like these do, did I include rooms." I always believed that I had built accurate and perfectly formed temples.

He leaned out towards me, beyond the shade of his canopy and whispered, "These do have rooms inside." He chuckled softly and leaned back when he saw my eyes widen.

Now it was my turn to lean towards him. "What do you mean, Ahtzic Uinac?" I said in a low voice. "Do you mean that they are hollow inside?"

He grimaced and tilted his head side to side as if unsure how to answer my question. "Not completely. Some only have a small room and some have more." He raised his eyebrows and jutted out his bottom lip. "What do you think about that?"

I was amazed because there were no indications that they were not solid. They had no openings. "What did they put in there? Are they tombs?"

"No, they are not tombs. We utilize the temporary tombs for seven days on the topmost level before removing the sarcophagus. After that, we transfer the body to the earth or to flame. Your question would be more apt if you asked me about what they put in there now."

My speech stuttered when I asked him.

"Two or three priests or acolytes are always at attention within each opening. When they hear a particular noise from their comrades, they push the stone outward and other attendants push the stone back in."

His statements confounded me. I looked at the temples in fascination. The knowledge that people were in there in the darkness filled me with horror. "What do they do in there?"

"Indeed, that is the question." His lip curled up in disgust. "Beware of those who call themselves solely by the name of Balam."

"Do you mean that I should be scared of your son and the Cabicacmotz?" My body was in a state of alarm and the heat of the day could not take away the goose bumps on my arms and neck.

"No. No. I do not mean that. My son is the Balam Ch'ab. The Cabicacmotz plays with the Balami, the Jaguars. No. They are both honorable men and you have nothing to fear from them. No. I mean the priests who call themselves only by the unadorned title of Balam."

I did not know what to say. Never had I spoken to one of the temple priests. Many times, I had seen them in the marketplace or around the temples. They always wore black and seemed somber and unapproachable. My father disliked them and refused to take any for an advisor. Because of that, there had never been any opportunity for me to meet any of them. From what I had heard, my father was not the only one who disliked them.

We were at the entrance to the pathway into the jungle. The two attendants gently set the palanquin on the ground while eight men prepared to carry it back up. No longer could they drag the conveyance. Level earth was behind us.

Although our society expected and often forced individuals to conform, there was a deep appreciation for the different and the unusual. Occasionally children were born with deformities or imperfections. In modern times, surgery is often used to eliminate any indication that the child was born different. Such a thing would have been unthinkable and odious to us. We celebrated it and expected much of those who were born different if their intellects were undiminished.

Dwarfism, in particular, was a fortunate occurrence. The birth of a dwarf was a marvelous omen of luck for the whole tribe. The Zaki Coxol, the White Sparkstriker, was a famous dwarf in our oral history who had the ability to see into the future.

These were not things to be ashamed of; physical manifestations outside of the norm decreed that power touched the child. The name Jaguar Paw or a similar name was common for children born with a clubfoot or malformed hand. Everyone considered the blind, deaf and mute special, especially in esoteric ways because they sensed the world through alternate means. Those who had what is now termed Down's syndrome or other forms of mental retardation were valued workers because of their sweet manners, ability to focus on detail, and their honor regarding the keeping of secrets. These people taught diplomacy to our outgoing ambassadors, such was their renown for courteousness. We called them the children of innocence.

Their schooling was more fluid than ours was. Often it would take time to see what their particular strengths were, and then they trained their talent.

Each member of the tribe who was born different was in the thick of things. We discovered many unknown talents that man was capable of through them. We did not marginalize and relegate them to sanitariums or the inside of the parental home. The different did not face contempt or pity; they were simply another member of the tribe. Never did our society engender in them the bitterness that can only adequately express itself through sarcasm.

I asked the Ahtzic Uinac for leave to speak with Tukumux.

To address or speak to a lord's guards was impermissible; to do so was the same as attempting to ingratiate oneself to them in order to divide their loyalty from their lord. Should danger strike, a guard's personal feelings must not prevent him from protecting his master first.

To speak to a servant was a minor impropriety. Many heated quarrels occurred involving particularly clever servants being enticed away to other houses. The rule for guards extended to servants when the person was in new circumstances as I was.

The Ahtzic Uinac told me that Tukumux was not truly his servant and that he was only accompanying them because he was going to introduce him to friends of his who were weavers and traders.

Chahal ran off into the trees after I indicated to her that she should hunt. Tukumux seemed sad to see her go. I had to explain to him that these were her hunting lands. I also told him that I wondered why he was going to see the weavers.

"I did a bad thing, they told me," he said.

This took me aback because there was not a mean-spirited bone in him. I asked him what he did.

"I did something and I made your sister cry," he told me.

"To Maricua? Why?"

"No, not Maricua. Marilya. I ruined her hair for the wedding feast."

Pain shot through my chest. No one invited me to the celebration. Marilya was the second eldest daughter of my father. She was as beautiful outside as she was horrid on the inside. She was a viper disguised to look like a woman. I felt pity for the unfortunate prince she was to marry. A daily beating from Maricua was a kinder fate.

I could easily imagine why Tukumux was in the middle of things. Tukumux might have been a child of innocence, yet he was a genius when it came to spatial puzzles or problems. He could look at a braided hairstyle and understand its intricacies, at a glance. Because of this, his services were in demand by the women of the city. One woman would wear the exclusive hairdo that a personal servant of hers devised. Then other women would become envious and hire Tukumux to replicate it for them. He made enough jade and gold to provide for himself and his parents and keep them all in comfort.

In general, the braiders of hair were our confessors. They provided that spiritual comfort while they helped people keep their hair tidy and presentable; it was an esteemed and well regarded profession whose practitioners were trusted for their silence. Indeed, they swore oaths of secrecy before they could perform their duties.

Tukumux was not a proper confessor, no child of innocence could be. To tarnish the purity or naiveté of these children was a serious transgression. The elders allowed the women to employ him for braiding, but they could not burden him with their moral dilemmas or divulge their sins to him.

I asked him what he had done to ruin Marilya's wedding feast while I silently prayed for him to receive eternal blessings.

"I thought she would be happy. She was marrying the eastern prince and his hair is new. You know how the women love the new hair," he said between sobs.

He spoke the truth. The eastern tribe's prince had an unusual hairstyle when compared to those of our men and women. He had bangs above his eyebrows and his hair did not even reach his shoulder. Instead, it was a rounded shape. Our tribe wore their hair long and braided. The farm workers would shear the hair above their ears to the nape of their necks, but they were another matter.

"I gave her front hair like his," Tukumux said.

I laughed with delight. I knew I should not, but Marilya had never spoken one kind word to me. Like her mother and the rest of my father's wives, she would escort my other half-brothers and sisters away when I was around. They learned to avoid and hate me for no reason.

"The Ahtzic Uinac says I should have another job."

"Maybe, I think I need to go back and talk to him again."

When I returned to the story-master's side, he asked me if I agreed that Tukumux would do well at weaving. I told him that it was likely since he excelled at understanding plaits in hair.

"Yes, I also think so. His role is too uncertain with the women. What will he do if they tire of him or a better braider comes along? He takes care of his parents. He should learn a new trade that he can turn to if things go badly for him."

"Do you think it will?"

"Who can know? The women will probably avoid him until Marilya leaves to go to the east with her husband. Afterwards, they will probably shower him with gifts," he said with a knowing grin. "She is a difficult woman to like, Zaki."

Without preamble, he began speaking about our ancestors. "Legend tells us that the first humans were four men: True Jaguar (Iquibalam), Jaguar Night (Balam Aqab), Jaguar of the Precious Tribe (Balam Quitze), and Black Tailless One (Mahohkutihax). These men were almost like gods upon the earth, so great was their knowledge and vision. They would see and they would know. They could see the planets with their eyes. When they spoke to their makers, their speech was clear. They understood. Be aware that the legends also tell us that there was more than one creator involved in the making of man. When they saw how perfect the vision of man was, they discussed it amongst themselves and decided that man's vision should not be so acute. They decided to diminish it. To accomplish this, they divided man in three. When he was body, spirit and dreamer, his sight was imperfect. The spirit received the greater part of vision, the body another part and the dreamer received the rest, which was the least of all."

"The four men went out into the world remembering how wonderful their sight had been. They knew something limited them, but they knew not what. They tried everything in their power to regain their sight."

"Since the jaguar was the most dangerous predator on earth, they deduced that its sight must be the greatest among the animals. They attempted to transform themselves into jaguars in order to benefit from its greater sight."

"Understand that the life of man had not yet been made finite. Later the powers would correct this, but these men had incredible amounts of time to experiment with to learn to see properly again. They discovered four ways to increase their sight. Never was it the same, but they discovered the secret to becoming jaguars. They learned to become jaguars by forming and utilizing their double. Each man became a jaguar double through a different method than the others. Thus, there are four ways to reach it."

The Ahtzic Uinac looked around, stopping his story. He told me that we would stop for a time to allow the men to rest and that he would continue his tale later.

For a while, we had been hearing the sound of water. Now it was very loud and close. We entered into a small green clearing with a small cataract. Chahal was waiting for us there, daintily picking at a rabbit she had run down. The pool underneath the fall was clean and bluish and it was a welcome sight because of the long walk in the heat. After they had set the palanquin down, most of the attendants and I went to the water's edge to drink. Tukumux carried a gourd, dipped it into the pool, and then took it to the Ahtzic Uinac, who stayed seated on his cushions.

When everyone had drank enough water, half of the men jumped in. Tukumux and I were the last ones in, preferring to enter it slowly. All of us swam around and relaxed in silence, avoiding each other's eyes. I do not know if the Ahtzic Uinac's retainers would have spoken among themselves if we had not been there, but I suspected they would not have. They seemed comfortable with the silence. Tukumux was not. Several times, I had to stop him from speaking to the men. A while later, the men left the pool to replace the guards around the story-master and the rest jumped in.

Once we were on our way, the Ahtzic Uinac resumed his tale. "Each of the four men is the grandfather of a lineage. The line consists of men who attain the jaguar double through the same means he used.

Abruptly, he changed the topic. "Have you learned the hidden meaning to the name the Chuchmox call themselves?" he asked.

I told him that I knew about their name.

"Very well, the first of these lineages is that of Iquibalam. We tell outsiders that his name is True Jaguar, but his real name is Dream Jaguar, Ichiq Balam. He reached his knowledge through dreaming."

"Next, we have Balam Aqab, Jaguar Night. To us, he is Balam Q'abar, Drunken Jaguar. He attained knowledge through intoxication. The intoxication can be from any substance except the mushroom because of the next lineage."

"Then there is Jaguar Quitze, Jaguar of the Precious Tribe. He is Balam Aqoz, Mushroom Jaguar. The mushroom, which gives man visions, was his means to obtaining his knowledge."

"Finally, there is Mahohkutihax, the Black Tailless One. His true name is Mahohcuatah, Lord Who Gathers His Twin. His means was his will."

"When any man attempts to transform himself into another being, one of these methods will be his means to achieving it. No one knows beforehand what method will work for him." He looked me over and said, "Right now, we can probably exclude the mushroom since none of the omens at the festival indicated that you should learn about the mushroom. More likely one of the other methods will work. You are learning dreaming, you are ingesting the weed, and my son and the Cabicacmotz will show you how to tune your will. Your use of the seven-pronged weed will hinder their efforts, but it is still a possibility. Of course, if none of these other methods work, you will be compelled to use the mushroom."

"Are you saying that the Balam Ch'ab will only teach me to become a jaguar through the method of Mahoh-cuatah?"

The Ahtzic Uinac placed his chin in his palm and thought for a few moments. "Yes, that is what I am saying. Do not worry, though, his methods will prepare you well to become a jaguar no matter which lineage you eventually fall in to. Not all of his men are of his same line. He is simply the leader of the Jaguar Knights. The men who can trans-form into jaguars are the Balam Qotih, the Double Jaguars, regardless of which lineage they come from. All such men are required to work as Jaguar Knights. The means are not important, the result is. The exercises he will make you perform will affect your thoughts while under the weed and they will be memorable enough that you will recall them in your dreaming. We are all interested in seeing which line-age will claim you."

"If the Balam Ch'ab belongs to the lineage of Mahoh-cuatah, the line that uses the will, why then was he spotted and with a tail?" I asked.

He laughed at my question, as if it was the question of a young child. "That was how the grandfather of the lineage appeared when he formed his double. Individuality comes into play, though, so it does not mean that his whole line will be the same way. When a man uses the will to change, he must keep in mind all of the qualities of the jaguar. Perhaps the loveliness of the dark jaguar enchanted him. Personally, I believe that he chose it because it requires less thought and he would not have to use extra energy in willing his spots into existence. The same thing probably happened with his tail, he did not consider it worthy of the energy it took to form it. Our Jaguar Knights have come very far in their art since those days."

The trees gave way and before us was a wall of stone, taller than the height of a man. We walked a little ways and saw the Balam Ch'ab seated on top of it. I could not understand why we did not meet him at the gate proper. He looked me in the eye and nodded. He did not smile or welcome me. He reached behind him and lifted a rickety wooden ladder, placing it on the other side of the wall. Then he climbed down.

"Go into the training camp and wait for me," he told me.

"I must greet my father and see him off."

Chahal leaped up to the rounded top of the wall. She growled when she slipped and lost her footing before vanishing behind the wall.

I said goodbye to the Ahtzic Uinac and Tukumux. Then I climbed into the camp.

When I reached the top of the Balam Ch'ab's wall, I almost fell and could understand why Chahal growled. There were patches of a slippery substance on the rounded top. With care, I flipped my body over it to position myself for the climb down the other side, where another ladder awaited me. The uppermost stone was a sand colored marble, in the shape of half cylinders, which matched the rock under it. It was slick and smooth.

Once I was inside the camp, I smelled my hands. They were greasy and smelled like smoked animal; it was lard. Either the Jaguar Knights were messy eaters or they took irritating measures to make their camp difficult to enter. The height of the wall was well over a man's height, but someone could climb over it with assistance. The lard was merely an annoyance. I could not imagine that it would impose much of an impediment.

The training camp had fooled my eyes from the outside. Inside, I could not see the other side of the camp. The area I was in was broad with a worn perimeter path inside the wall. Beyond were footpaths through gardens leading to a trio of wooden huts. Behind the huts were trees and bushes. I could not see Chahal, yet knew that she was exploring the camp beyond the bushes.

The Balam Ch'ab caught me laughing and asked me why. I told him that, beyond the wall, the place appeared to house nobles, but inside it seemed that it housed peons.

The nobility often used walls of stone to indicate their territory, as well as for their housing. They would never accept homes made of trees. For a roof, it was acceptable, for a dwelling, it was not.

He looked at the huts and told me that they only housed the finest men and women, adding that the vast majority were from the noble classes.

"Women visit their men in the training camp? How can you allow that?"

The Balam Ch'ab raised his eyebrows and blinked a few times as if unsure what to say. He smirked and seemed about to say something when he burst out with a deep snort and began laughing. "What do you think we are doing out here, Zaki, running a house of prostitution? Do not tell me that you did not know that some of our knights could be women."

I protested that I had not known and that it was un-thinkable that they allowed women to become warriors and killers. Women should stay at home cooking, cleaning, and raising children, I told him. Underneath my words was the belief that women were not strong enough. I believed men should protect them and shelter them away from the realities of war. "Why are we burdening them with such awfulness and strife, don't they do enough?"

The Balam Ch'ab doubled over and clutched his sides. His braid danced along his back like an agitated snake.

Irritated that he was laughing at me, I stressed my points over again.

Laughing, he laid face down on the grass with his hands stretched to the sides.

I ended my argument with the words, "Once I am king, no longer will the women have to do these dreadful things."

"Oh, please stop."

I saw that tears were running from his eyes. Aggravated that he did not give my arguments the attention they deserved, I walked away and stared at the wall. When I was there for a short time, I realized, with wonder, that I was no longer nervous around the Balam Ch'ab and that I had argued with him. A cold feeling overtook me; it dispelled the heat I felt when I voiced my beliefs in anger. Now I felt exposed and foolish, and began worrying that the Balam Ch'ab would punish me somehow. I turned around to see where he was.

He sat up and brushed dirt from his palms. He looked over to where I was and motioned me to return and sit with him.

When I was before him, I began to apologize for my outburst, but he stopped me.

"Quiet yourself and sit down. Do not say another word or I will begin laughing again." He waited for me to sit in front of him and told me that he had not laughed that hard in many years. He even thanked me.

Before he could stop me, I told him that I did not recognize myself and that I was not usually argumentative.

Stopping my apology with a wave of his hand, he said, "That is your reaction to stressful or difficult circumstances. Do not bother apologizing. You were unafraid and you thought clearly about your arguments. That is a good quality for a jaguar knight. I am pleased. Only afterward did you worry about your actions. In the fury of the moment, you are no coward, no matter how wrong you are"

I slouched with relief. As soon as I relaxed, I noticed that I had been clutching all of my muscles, especially those in my buttocks.

"We do have to clear a few things up before we begin, though," he said. "We use huts here because we are in the jungle and many creatures live in it. Occasionally, if we are not vigilant, we must set fire to the huts and build new ones. We could not easily clean stone buildings with fire."

Mice infested the huts a few years back, he told me, and several knights and students died because of them. It was after a long rainy season, when the trees were particularly fruitful. Because of the abundance of food, the mice bred more profusely. They spread and began looking for hiding places and food. They chanced upon the training camp. Since the presence of the knights kept natural predators away, especially jaguars, the mice quickly reproduced and nested in the walls and roofs of the huts. The droppings were everywhere. No one noticed since the dirt floor was dark in color. The mice were stealthy and would hide or be still when people were about.

"Many breathed in that filth and died. We thought they only had minor fevers, but within days, they were dead."

"How did you realize what was wrong or know how to fix it?"

"We called in the healers. They could not overcome it because it killed so rapidly. The Cabicacmotz came after they were baffled and saw into the problem. He also gave us the solution. Fortunately, we noticed quickly that those who slept in the huts were the ones who fell ill. Not one of those people were old or infirm, Zaki. We burned the huts and they scorched the earth when they fell. Fire kills, but it also cleanses."

I asked him whether the original huts were stone and he told me that they were not because the outer wall made it too difficult to bring in stones.

"Why do you not use the main entrance?"

"There is no entrance to the camp. Either one enters it as a jaguar would or one is provided with a ladder as you were today."

"Can you not cut a hole for stone to be brought in, then?"

He looked at me with disgust. "The wall is our most splendid tool for teaching the steps of the jaguar. We would never mutilate it for a mere luxury."

I decided not to ask any further questions when I heard the acid in his voice.

"Come. We have sat for long enough," he said. "I will show you where to leave your satchel and where you will sleep." He walked to the smallest hut and I followed.

My spirits sank when I saw the crude lodgings and the hammock where I was to sleep. A thought occurred to me when I remembered my father's preference for hammocks.

"Was my father a Jaguar Knight?"

The Balam Ch'ab smiled with delight and said, "He trained here, but he cannot be a knight."

It hurt me to ask, but I finally said, "Was he unable to transform himself?"

He shook his head. "Of course he could turn himself into a jaguar, Zaki. He is a talented and capable man. Never think otherwise. He cannot be a mere knight simply because he is the king who commands us."

"Take off your clothes and remove your stone," he ordered me.

I protested, telling him that I did not wish to take a nap and that Zotabah, Ahtoobalvar and the Cabicacmotz demanded that I always wear my navel stone, even to sleep.

"You are mistaken if you think I will let you take a nap so soon. It is time for work. I am going to show you the wall." He looked me over, focusing on my necklace. "Don't worry about the navel stone, Zaki. The necklace will suffice to keep you safe. This way you will not lose your stone or ruin your belt. Now, remove your clothes while I fetch you a proper training garment."

He left me in the hut. I took off my tunic and removed the leather belt that now kept my navel stone in place. Afterwards, I stored the belt and stone in my satchel and threw it onto the hammock. His story made me paranoid about vermin. A few moments later, he peered in and handed me a leather thong that tied on either side of my hips. With chagrin, I put it on and emerged from the hut. The crotch area was too thick and unwieldy; it hindered my gait. I complained that it made me walk like a monkey.

I stopped complaining when I looked up and saw that he was wearing an identical thong. He did not walk funny while wearing it and seemed comfortable. It looked well worn and discolored.

"Make sure that your sides are tightly tied," he said as he walked to the largest hut. "This is what we wear for the wall. The wide crotch is used because no one wants their privates to fall out while they straddle the wall."

The hut was a few times larger than mine was and it was as austere. There were a few more hammocks and some trunks of trees for seating.

Near the entrance, there was a large clay vat of lard. He directed me to apply the lard to my leathers, thighs, stomach, and chest area. When he saw that I was being sparse applying the lard to my groin, he told me that I would be uncomfortable until the lard seeped into the leather and made it supple. After hearing that, I slapped it on as thick as I could. I sniffed myself and knew I smelled like a roasted animal.

The Balam Ch'ab deftly applied his own lard and then dipped his hands in a vat of talc. He told me to do the same, telling me that the talc would soak up the oil on my hands and make them less slippery.

When we reached the stone wall, he told me to stay on the ground while he demonstrated what he wished me to do. He climbed the ladder and straddled the wall.

"The first step to becoming a jaguar is to learn to move like one," he said. "The jaguar is a being composed of balanced sides. Its sense of self is located primarily upon its spine at the base of its head and its awareness switches from the left to the right side alternatively. The eyes connect to the shoulders. You will see."

"When the jaguar runs, it hunts prey. He is a creature of efficiency and purpose. His focus is on what he must do. If stalking, he creeps. When chasing, he runs. His shoulders lead his forward movement and his sense of self confines itself to the tight wire of his spine. Usually the sense of self is where his skull meets his neck, but it can be anywhere. He is balance incarnate and can easily switch his awareness from the right to the left. With that, he maintains balance. That movement is connected to his shoulders and eyes. Remember that the sense of self is separate from awareness."

His words confused me and I began to ask him to explain.

The Balam Ch'ab told me that only action could resolve my questions and he demonstrated the actions I should perform on the wall. "For now, you must tuck your feet behind you, so they rest on the wall." He pulled his legs up and rested the front of his feet on the rounded edge, soles to the sky. What I thought was a carved line of adornment in the wall was a ridge that was three hand lengths from the top of the wall. The Balam Ch'ab put his hands on the line and pulled himself forward, going counterclockwise on the wall.

I ran along the perimeter path beside him while he used his hands to pull and slide himself along the wall. The training camp was enormous. We passed a stream twice that flowed in and out of the camp through a shallow hole in the wall. The rest was trees, pasture and gardens. It resembled the estate I shared with Maricua, my sister.

When the Balam Ch'ab completed his circuit around the camp, he did not appear out of breath. His ride ended at the other side of the ladder. I was anxious to get up and try it. I waited for him to climb back down.

Instead, he sat up and said, "One of the most important things for the transformation is the knowledge of where the jaguar's sense of self resides. As men, we feel that our sense of self is often dependent upon a line that is vertical. We are upright beings. The jaguar is not, it is a horizontal creature. It parallels the ground. We are earth to sky; he is earth to earth in forward motion."

He climbed down from the ladder and came to where I stood. "All right, Zaki. You need to get up there and position yourself the same as I showed you. Remember to tuck your feet up on the back."

I climbed the ladder as quickly as possible and positioned myself. It was a relief to discover that the line for the hands was at a comfortable distance for me. He decided that I needed to apply some lard to the front of my feet to avoid blisters. From a small pouch hanging from the ladder, he found some lard and applied it to the tops of my feet. I was ready to go and almost pushed off, when he grabbed my ankle and held me there.

I wanted to get going, but he wanted to bore me with more talk about the jaguar's sense of self.

He crouched down, resting on his haunches, and drew a straight dotted line in the sand of the perimeter walk. There was an arrow at one point. Next, he drew an inverted arrow, a vee, whose point originated midway along the dotted line. The ends of the vee extended a small bit from the end of the line with the arrow. Then he drew small arrows on the ends of each arm of the new vee.

He stood up, brushing dirt from his hands. With his toe, he pointed at the dotted line and said, "This is the spine and tail of the jaguar." The arrow indicated the advancing movement of the jaguar. The vee was a difficult concept for me to grasp.

"Always, the two separate lines of the vee flow from the origin of the spine," the Balam Ch'ab said. "Physically, they attach to the shoulders of the jaguar. The jaguar leads with its shoulders. Watch Chahal sometime and you will see the truth of my words. Even when she walks in that languid way of hers, she leads with her shoulders. The head may be in front, but it still follows the shoulders. It is secondary. The difficult thing is to keep in mind that the awareness attaches to the movement of the shoulders and alternates with the shoulders. Right, front and back while the left does the same. The sense of self shifts slightly, though not as largely as the sense of awareness shifts. Its sense of self will feel as though it is moving in a small half circle. It will not be the wide swings, as it is with its awareness. Its forward motion balances at the spine. When the cat runs, the balance can be anywhere along the spine."

I pretended to know what he meant since I was restless and eager to push off. I nodded with a serious look on my face as if I was weighing his words, when all I could think of was the fast ride he took upon the wall and how it looked like incredible fun.

"The jaguar's sense of self is parallel to the ground and is always at the level of his spine. It moves forward and back along that level. Lateral movement is confined to that small half-moon shape I just mentioned. A man's sense of self can be anywhere and strives to go up as far as it can. The jaguar's strives to move forward. Our natural inclination is to move upwards, the jaguar's is to go forward."

I wanted to put a stop to his explanations and said, "I'm having a bit of trouble imagining what you said. Maybe I have to feel it while I am moving."

He gave me a sly half smile and said, "Perhaps. One final piece of advice: imagine that your hands are claws while you use them to grasp hold of the ridges along the wall." Pulling the ladder away from the wall, he nodded to grant me permission to leave.

Without waiting for him to change his mind, I grabbed hold of the ridged line and pulled myself forward.

I zoomed on that wall. With the lard lubricating me, I was able to reach speeds that I found incredible. The more momentum I gained the less effort it took to move faster. Several times, I almost slipped from the wall and had to unhook my feet to balance myself. There is something magical about speed. It somehow unleashes the elation we hold inside of us. Decorum demands a great price from us, it requires us to subdue our delight and only evidence it with a smile. Nothing held me back when I was on that wall. I whooped and yelled my happiness without a care about how I looked.

After my fifth circuit around the camp, the tips of my fingers hurt. When I was close to where the Balam Ch'ab sat waiting for me, I felt a familiar stickiness on my hands. I did not dare look to check, but I knew that my fingers were bleeding.

The Balam Ch'ab stood up and came to where I waited for him, still atop the wall. He glanced at my hands and said, "Come. We must clean them and apply a salve to them. I tried to stop you after your third run, but there was no stopping you, boy." He replaced the ladder in front of me and urged me to climb down.

I tried to move forward. My body did not wish to cooperate. My feet, hooked at the ankles, felt weighted and glued together. The muscles of my thighs refused to unclench and did not ease enough for me to move them. Even my hands froze in a clawing grip. "Balam Ch'ab, I cannot move. Something is wrong with me."

"Nothing is wrong with you, Zaki, except that you enjoy excess. You pretended not to see me trying to stop you and that is your own fault. This occurred because you over exerted yourself on the wall. You are in fine company, I suppose, because it happens to almost every student."

He came over to me and unhooked my ankles, leaving them to rest on the top of the wall. Then he took my clawed left hand in his, wrenched my fingers into a natural position, and massaged them. Next, he climbed the ladder and straddled the wall. He did the same to my right hand. He directed me to let my hands and legs hang down the wall to get the blood flowing to them.

I did as he told me and experienced the painful prickling of renewed circulation.

When he saw the faces I made, he told me to swing my arms and legs back and forth to relieve the sensations. After a while, I was able to make my way to the ladder and begin climbing down. If he had not assisted me, I would have slipped because I was still clumsy and stiff.

As soon as I was on the ground, I looked down at my bloody hands. A few of my nails had split and the skin on the tips of my fingers was raw and red.

We walked to the stream in the camp and he told me to leave them in the flowing water for a while. The cool water felt good on my wounds. The ride on the wall removed most of the lard on me, but there was still a bit on me. The Balam Ch'ab told me to sit in the stream and use a sea sponge that he packed with sand from the bottom of the stream to rub off the rest of the lard. I removed the thong and did so.

When I got out of the water, I almost dried my fingers in my hair, but he admonished me and told me to let them dry naturally because it was more sanitary. There were some aloe plants around and he cut off a leaf, removing the thorny edges with his knife. I squeezed the leaf and rubbed the sticky gel into my fingers.

We then went to the large hut and he opened a covered gourd filled with a green salve and handed me a large flat brush. I had to dip the brush in the salve and paint my body with the salve, except my face, groin, and feet. The salve irritated some cuts I had, but soon turned cool and numbed my muscles. Then I put my tunic back on.

The Balam Ch'ab settled down on a hammock and told me to do the same. I took the one next to his and kept my eyes on the thatched roof.

He told me that it was common for new students to feel worn out after a few circuits along the wall. "Most of them do not overdo it as much as you did, though. After the third round, they are usually too tired to continue. The wall looks easy, but it is hard on the hands and the need to maintain balance demands watchfulness. This creates a tension of the body that is difficult to sustain."

We were through with the wall for the day, he said, because my hands needed time to adjust and that eventually I would notice that the tips of my fingers developed protective calluses that would let me ride the wall for longer periods.

"Did you notice where your sense of self was on your ride?" he asked.

I told him that the wall was so exhilarating that I thought of nothing else.

"That is a pity," he said. "I hoped that you would keep my words in mind. I cannot blame you, though. We do not have such devices in the city. It is only natural that you would drop all thoughts."

Sleepiness was overtaking me even though it was early in the day. I nodded at his words and decided to look over at him to see if he saw me nod. He reclined on his hammock staring at the ceiling as I had. He nodded to himself as if he had seen my nod.

"Before you fall asleep, Zaki, I wish to ask you about the story my father, the Ahtzic Uinac, told you. What did he say?"

I told him about the four lineages as best I could.

"I suspected something like that would occur," he said.

I did not understand and asked him to explain.

"My father is old. I fear he tires of telling stories. Lately, he prefers to tell unvarnished truths without the cushion of formal tales. The proper method would have been for him to have one of his apprentices accompany you and whisper in your ear as he speaks his tale. He must have purposely left the apprentice behind. That way, he could reveal the hidden truths within the story himself." He sighed. "I have not decided whether it is a result of dementia or determination. I should not interfere."

I did not want to appear callous by not saying anything, yet I did not really know what to say to him. After a brief time, I said, "Then it must be determination, Balam Ch'ab, because he was quick and clear in his conversation. He was kind enough to teach me about several things. His eyes were not the dull eyes of an old man; they were as shiny as an eagle's eyes and seemed to notice everything. Tukumux was with us because your father worried about him. He was taking him to some weavers to learn a new trade. You are lucky to be able to claim him as your father. He is kind and intelligent."

My words must have relieved him because he smiled.

After that, we both fell asleep for a time.

We woke up later in the afternoon when the shadows covered the camp.

We sat on the grass with our backs against some squat stones. The remains of the stew and fruits we ate for dinner were next to us on the grass.

"Balam Ch'ab, how does riding the wall help one turn into a jaguar?"

"One must acquaint oneself with the different parts that compose the jaguar. One part involves the outer physical-ness, feeling the shape and skin of the cat and still another part involves knowing the sensations that occur within the jaguar. Your voice must even become that of the jaguar... for who ever heard of a jaguar speaking as a man? Only the man speaks as a man. The jaguar rolls his growls and his audible vocabulary is singular. Unlike man, he does not engage in idle chatter. Everything the jaguar voices is to be listened to. His inner voice is harder still for it is composed of assurance and power. His demeanor is one of watchfulness coupled with the assuredness of triumph should battle be called for."

He stood up then and began pacing around me aim-lessly, caught up in his thoughts. "All of this is difficult to explain because you do not yet have the proper back-ground to appreciate my words or put them into context within your own life. You have never bothered to feel how your skin feels wrapped around your muscles or even observed your breath as it flows in and out of you, have you?"

With great embarrassment, I softly shook my head to indicate that I had not done any of those things. Truly, they had never occurred to me.

Still pacing around, he grabbed his lower lip, doubling it down the center as he thought. "Right now, your lessons with the Cabicacmotz are suspended until things settle a bit with the pochtecas and the visiting tribes, but soon he will have to address these deficiencies. Or someone else will have to." He sighed loudly, "Since I have noticed, I must correct it. It is imperative that you notice everything about you, Zaki. Feel which parts of your head are virtually hairless and which are hirsute. Go on now, feel."

His demand sounded silly to me, but I complied. I felt the smooth curve of my cheek, without the benefit of my hands, and then I felt the fuzzy covered feeling of my scalp. From my scalp, I could only feel a short distance before the feeling diminished and vanished. It was as if my hair no longer connected to me the farther it was from my head. He made me feel the parts with my hands and forearms. Then I repeated the exercise without hands again.

After that, he made me observe how it felt when I swallowed and how often, how my heart felt beating inside my chest and its rhythm, and the sensation of sitting on grass.

He told me that I was to watch myself carefully to observe what I felt, sensed, heard, saw, and imagined. I complained that such activities would consume my days and force me into inactivity or useless introspection.

"If you think you can come into the camp and ride the wall without any other work on your part, you are fantasizing. I would have no qualms throwing a recalcitrant student out, especially one who will never work as a Jaguar Knight. Your being here is a gift to you, not me. I will tell you that any undertaking in your schooling is a battle and no battle has ever resulted in triumph without the proper groundwork and knowledge. You are the base in all of this and you will get nowhere without knowing everything about yourself because the task is to become a jaguar. How can you transform into something if you do not even know how the original being works and feels? You. When you have to know and keep in mind everything about the secondary being, the jaguar? It cannot be done."

Feeling lazy after our dinner and not finding work attractive then, I was trying to find a way out of further work, despite his threats to expel me from his teachings. "I know myself, Balam Ch'ab. I know that I will become so immersed in observing myself that I will be unable to step out of my house."

"You barely know yourself, Zaki. You have not even begun to look beneath the surface of your personality and faults. No one can do this work for you; you must do it. I have only called your attention to your physical feelings and they are so foreign to you that they seem to be arcane facets of life. What will you do when you must move your awareness or sense of self to other locations to change into the jaguar? Do you realize that you must view your place on this earth from another perspective than your own? When your sensibilities must be those of the jaguar and not those of a human prince? The only way I know of to buttress you for that shock is for you to know yourself."

"I am going to tell you things, which you must hear, about becoming a jaguar. I will be as precise as possible and you must not interrupt me. I know I have been speaking for a long time. I have an ability to do so even though I do not have the knack to be a storyteller," he said and shrugged disinterestedly.

"I am the leader of the Jaguar Knights as well as the leader for those who are in Mahohcuatah's left lineage. Because you are also a dreaming student, you have already heard about the dreamer, the body, and the spirit. Man goes in a circle, one could say. His dreamer is associated with his left and his spirit is considered his right."

He saw my look of bewilderment and asked me why.

"Do you mean that the Chuchmox, since they are women of the left, have to do with the dreamer?"

"Not necessarily. We are merely talking about associations, not definitions."

"Then it has nothing to do with the actual physical locations of the dreamer and the spirit?"

"To speak about such things is too tricky," he replied. "To say that one or the other is the definite location might ruin a student. Not everyone is the same. In one person, the locations might be accurate, yet in another be reversed. Only you can make that determination along the way. With the Chuchmox, their deliberate shift towards the left with their awareness also shifts and alters the locations of their dreamers and spirits."

I expressed my dissatisfaction at not finding out where the other two bodies were.

"The best thing to do is not worry about any of this. Accept the designated associations, arbitrary though they might be, and remember that they are only used to make talking about them or instruction easier. Don't try to tie down what is not physical in such a way. What is amorphous is changeable and might be on the left, the right, before, or behind, as it sees fit. To expect the dreamer and the spirit to respect our desires regarding where they should be is hopeless. Enough of this, Zaki, we are getting bogged down with tripe."

"To continue... I belong to Mahohcuatah's lineage, so my training involved honing my will and learning to see. This seeing is specialized because it involves seeing energy that is invisible because this energy it is not composed of matter. One approaches the dreamer while one is in the body. Having the dreamer's sight be secondary to those of the physical body is a good trait for the Jaguar Knights. To have the dreamer be the primary eyesight is dangerous because those will have bad eyesight and attack any living things before them. We have some of those. They have their uses."

I raised my eyes at this to show how bad an idea I thought that was.

He caught my expression, shrugged, and looked somewhat sheepish as he said, "I know. It sounds absurd, but those men must work as Jaguar Knights because they have learned how to become jaguars. We must waste nothing, especially genius. First, we tried only using them on one night, but they decimated the animal life and we never allowed it again. Now we are able to control them better. Do not ask me how, but it involves bringing in the spirit-jaguars. I will discuss that later with you."

"To belong to my lineage, you must have great will and be able to see energy. I would prefer that you quickly grasp the ability to see energy so we will tackle that the next time you come. It is something that should be done during the day, when one is at the beginning." He had an after-thought and corrected himself. "Is it true that the Etamanel Evan placed a woman on your belly to help you see the lights in the sky?"

I nodded.

"Do not think for a moment that the technique belongs to the seven-pronged. It belongs to mankind itself. Here is what I want from you Zaki, perform that exercise every afternoon or morning. Try to do it when the sun is halfway to its zenith or the horizon. Given your propensity to gaze to excess, have a guard or Chahal with you as the others have commanded."

"The second part of turning into a jaguar, for those of my line, is to know themselves so completely that they begin by feeling their body and one by one replacing each quality with the corresponding quality that the jaguar has. You feel your breathing and you replace it with the type of breath that the jaguar breathes. You run down your inventory of how the jaguar differs and put it into practice, leaving behind your humanity, yet retaining your intellect. In addition, the more one does it, the easier it gets. It becomes second nature and men transform immediately by will, they know that state so completely. Otherwise you would have sat in the tent for a great while at the festival."

I recalled my time at the Festival of Adults where, before my eyes, the Balam Ch'ab disrobed one moment and became a jaguar the next.

"If you are taking the path of Mahohcuatah, you must keep this in mind. If you take the path of the dreamer, these techniques will show your dreamer the way into that particular sensitivity of being. If intoxicated, you will perform these actions in your mind and you will relive them and find a way to make them a reality. I cannot speak to you of the mushroom because those men are few and I am not one of them. There is something wild and fluid about those men. Personally, I find them rather terrifying because I cannot fathom what they know for they have summoned order from chaos itself, I believe. Likewise do I feel about dreamers because I have never much liked dreaming." He opened his arms to indicate the realm around us. "This is my place and where I have influence. Do you have any questions?"

"If you belong to the left part of Mahohcuatah's line, who composes the right line and why?"

A wry look passed over his face and vanished. "You have pre-empted my later explanation of the spirit-jaguars being paired with dreamer-jaguars, but I will answer you anyway as the night is early." He took a deep breath before he said, "Well, the right and left are predilections like all others and they are not permanent. One day, I might choose the right, but for now, I am more comfortable going left to the side of my dreamer. When that day comes, I must relinquish my leadership of the Mahohcuatah line of body-jaguars and become a novice among the spirit-jaguars. I would still be the leader of the Jaguar Knights, but my individual path would be changed."

"What is the difference?" I asked.

"Purity of spirit, basically. A man's spirit may reject him if it finds him unworthy. The man must be a paragon of virtue. The spirit enables man to climb to the heavens, therefore miracles manifest for the spirit. Since this is a physical change, the spirit-jaguar must bring the miraculous down to earth, but he cannot enter heaven in that state because he is bound with a body of his own choosing and not the Creator's."

"When the body-jaguar is made with the dreamer, the man has chosen a body whose realm is that of earth and the underworld. The realm of the underworld is one of magic and wonders. I long to combine my body with that of the spirit, but I realize that my post might require me to kill a man and my spirit will not allow itself to be tainted in such a manner."

"Why then must the spirit-jaguars accompany the jaguar-dreamers who cannot see well and are dangerous?"

"Because they can reverse the mistakes of their charges and bring the dead back to life. Indeed, that belongs to the miraculous. To countermand death is a divine gift. Magic is useful, but miracles are manifestations of heaven upon earth."

"But wouldn't you be able to do it, since you can come back from death, like my father and uncle?"

"Your question is more complex than it seems and would require a lecture about energy and other matters. Let us leave that topic for another day."

"Be careful, Zaki, that you do not get lost in our taxonomy of terms, many overlap. There are four lineages, but we often refer to those in them by the terms body-jaguar, spirit-jaguar and dream-jaguar. These terms do not refer to any one lineage; they are merely convenient ways of looking at things. Body-jaguar refers to when the body combines with the dreamer, yet the eyes of the body are dominant. A spirit-jaguar means that the spirit is used, in any combination. Even if the eyes of the body are the primary ones, the spirit has so much power that the combination is called a spirit-jaguar. A dream jaguar results when the governing sight is that of the dreamer and the secondary sight is that of the body. All of these permutations can be found within the lineages."

He looked up at the stars and said, "It grows late. Go to your hammock and sleep. Apply more aloe to your fingers before you go to take your rest."

The Balam Ch'ab stood up and went to the large hut. When I went into the small hut, I saw that Chahal was already there, asleep under my hammock. Sleep came easily.

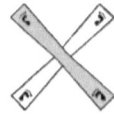

The next morning, the Balam Ch'ab sent me home with Chahal.

When we neared my home, I found the Tzuhunik and the Etamanel Evan exchanging words with a group of the Chuchmox.

"There he is," said one of the women when she saw me.

Women crowded me, demanding that I go with them to their underground citadel.

The Tzuhunik, trailed by the Etamanel Evan, stepped forward. "You women have no legitimate claim to Zaki. Last night it was agreed between the Cabicacmotz, the king, and the Balam Ch'ab that Zaki would have a lesson with us. We must not fight among ourselves like this."

The last thing I wanted to do was spend time with anyone, except Hac and Cham. Maricua or the servants probably made a meal for me and it waited for me while the adults argued back and forth.

One of the women pushed the Etamanel Evan after he accidentally stepped on her foot. His face paled as hers reddened. Soon they would come to blows and he clearly could not match her ferocity.

"Stop," a matronly woman cried, when it appeared a melee was at hand. The woman's eyes were out of focus, as if her thoughts turned inwards. "The Paqal Paray has decreed that the men should be allowed to accompany the boy to the citadel. He can take his lesson with them while he learns from us."

The Tzuhunik readily agreed, stating that it was an intelligent compromise. The Etamanel Evan seemed both relieved and frightened.

I could not believe how quickly the situation settled. When I told the women that still crowded me that I needed to go home to Maricua and a meal, they told me that Maricua knew I would not be home today and that they had food. Without giving me time to protest, someone put a hand on my back to move me forward. I turned to see who it was and saw it was the Tzuhunik.

"Be quiet and move. Don't argue with the women," he said. "We go as they say."

Chahal roared a growl and a path opened up for her through the crowd. I expected to see the women scared of Chahal or scream as she approached them, but instead they acted as if nothing was wrong and that there was no danger. A moment later, Chahal was walking at my side.

We arrived at the foot of a large hill that was west of the citadel proper. Everyone knew the hill because the sun set behind it every day. What few knew was that it was the home of the Chuchmox, the female sentries. Underneath the great mound was an underground cavern system that hid these women.

We veered towards the southern ridge of the hill. At a juncture between two boulders, they turned into a short canyon. The canyon was devoid of life except for a cactus draped with long weeds. Behind the weeds was a jagged narrow entrance. We filed in and the women in front of me lit torches and small gourds to fill our path with light.

Winding halls of rock led through the system. A woman in the back, who wore a long skirt, instantly obscured the sandy ground where we passed. In that way, we left no trace. Dark pathways were constantly around us. I could not figure out how the women were able to direct us through the maze. Almost immediately, I lost my bearings. No longer could I discern where east and west were.

The Tzuhunik walked behind me. I heard him mutter to the Etamanel Evan that we were going in circles. I tried to remember the cavern walls around me to see if he was right, but the darkness prevented me from noticing features of the rock.

A short while later, no longer were the two men behind me. Instead, a trio of young women walked behind me. Someone, I realized, diverted them to different sections of the underground.

Moment by moment, my anxiety grew. The darkness in the passageways seemed to peer at me. My old fears, about the giant bats that dwell in caves, made me feel as if my heart was being compressed into a small cage. I told myself not to worry as I placed my hand on Chahal's neck. I calmed down when I realized she had no fear of the cave.

"Where are my other teachers?" I asked. The stale air of the mound thinned my voice and the rock absorbed the excess sound, causing my voice to sound hollow and dead.

"They are being shown their quarters for the evenings to come."

This alarmed me more than anything else could. I could tolerate the idea that we would spend a night here, but more than that I could not bear. How horrible it must be, I thought, to live in darkness and not see the sun and breathe the clean air of the surface.

A few women behind me giggled, as if they heard my thoughts. Those giggles more than anything caused me to have an attack of nerves so severe that my thinking became disordered and frenetic. I walked without noticing anything around me as I tried to reorder my thoughts.

Soon I became angry at being forced to come here. The women around me looked like leering demons in the flickering flames. Their faces looked like skulls when the lights hit them, especially when it blackened their eyes and under eye areas. They were callous and rude, I thought, to listen in to my personal thoughts.

An old woman walking next to me said, "No thoughts are ever private, young prince. Ideas are communal and are shared by everyone, whether you like it or not."

I turned towards her to argue when I realized who she was. To my horror, I knew the woman.

At the war council of my father, she was the one who wanted to know what the dark ones did with the body parts of the vanquished warriors. The Cabicacmotz told me that she was an expert in matters of black magic and rituals.

"When will we stop?" I asked.

"When you accept that you are here until we give you leave to go," she answered.

"How did you divert the Tzuhunik and the Etamanel Evan? They were right behind me."

"We took them away when they suffered moments of distraction at the same time you did. That is the time to perform such maneuvers. Men do not realize how attuned women are to them. We can sense distraction like a jaguar smells fear."

"Like a dog that takes advantage of his master's moment of daydreaming and eats a turd when he's not paying attention," one of the young women behind me said.

"You are not helping, Kaq Lez. Stay silent. No more colorful examples."

I glanced behind me and saw who Kaq Lez was. She was a pretty girl with a grin on her face. When she saw me looking back at her, she turned to me and made a face that destroyed her appearance of prettiness. She put the oil lamp to her chest, so the light cast ghastly shadows on her face. Then she narrowed her eyes and stuck out her front teeth in a bucktoothed grin as she nodded.

The old woman turned around and before she finished turning, Kaq Lez lifted the lamp back up and put on a blank look.

The old woman sighed and shook her head. "Every sun, the girls seem to act younger and younger." She looked over at me and said, "I know who you are, Zaki. Why do you not know who I am?"

"You have not told me," I said.

"A great advantage can be had if one knows who is speaking. If you do not know, ask. There is no sense in your learning the art of governance if you do not take into account the personalities and specialties of the members of council. Governance is not a cold art, it is a breathing and living one which remains fluid and ever-changing because it involves humans," she said. "What kinds of people, do you suppose, your father consults?"

I thought back to my day at court, when I heard the hideous reports of the spies. All of my teachers seemed to be there. Now I knew who she was.

"You must be the Paqal Paray, then."

"Ah, good. I am glad to see that my brother's son is not a dull-witted fool."

"You are my aunt?" I asked.

"Not by blood, Zaki. I refer to your father as my brother because...well, we came into our power at the same time. We are cohorts."

One of the girls said, "Silence. We approach."

The air in the warren slowly grew colder the farther we walked. We entered what must have been a large cave. The firelight failed to illuminate anything other than our faces. I could not gauge the dimensions of the section we were in because immediately the lead woman took a sharp turn down a corridor and we followed her. Soon I began to hear a deep humming sound reverberating through the cave.

We emerged into a long cavern and stood on the shore of a swift underground river. The women stayed silent and rebuffed my attempts to ask them about the emergent point of the river. We walked over a short sturdy bridge and stopped for a brief rest while some of the women removed the bridge and hid it behind some boulders. They refused to talk about that also.

Another woman took over the lead and guided us to the left. She led us to a small corridor and we continued. No longer were the women silent; they chattered excitedly among themselves. I could not see why they seemed happy, but I was glad they were no longer soundless. The silence made me feel that they were leading me to my doom. This felt more normal and natural.

I asked the Paqal Paray the reason for the silence. She told me that the areas we were silent in were areas where sound easily traveled and that they kept the silence because they did not want anyone realizing that they were here. I expressed the opinion that no one could follow them through such an intricate maze.

"A good tracker could tell we were there and read our path as easily as a scribe can read the stones. Don't underestimate the skills of other men or allow yourself to be lulled into thinking they share your inexperience with the underground."

I decided to stay silent after her gentle rebukes.

Finally, we emerged into an enormous cavern filled with torches. The smell of cooking saturated the air and I felt my mouth fill with saliva as the scent overtook me. Several groups of women had fires going.

The Paqal Paray led us to a small group and we sat in a semicircle around a fire. I could feel eyes on me and I turned around. Kaq Lez was behind my right shoulder. She laughed when I caught her watching me. I could see her more clearly than I had in the cave and was surprised to find that she appeared to be close to my age yet younger. In the tunnels, she looked older, like a maiden. Now she was a girl. I wanted to know who she was and to which family she belonged. Most of all, I wanted to know what she was doing with the Chuchmox.

Before I could talk to her, my attention was pulled away. A woman served me two large pieces of fish wrapped in fried corn patties. Everyone around me received food and we ate in silence, watching the fire and hearing the murmur of the other women in the cave.

When we finished, the Paqal Paray directed a lithe, athletic woman to show me my quarters. I asked the woman to tell me her name. She avoided my question by providing details about the layout of the cavern system and particulars about bathing and other hygienic matters I was supposed to obey while visiting them.

We reached a long dark corridor and walked down it a short distance, after she lit a torch from a sconce at its entrance. There seemed to be rooms along the corridor.

Cloth covered some openings and others were filled with a dark chill. She told me that the ones with cloths at the openings were rooms that were in use.

Halfway down the hall, she walked into one of the dark rooms. Her torch revealed a large bare cave with a pallet stacked with folded cloths and blankets. The walls were uneven and curved. She placed her torch into a sconce near the entryway, telling me that was where I should keep it.

"You must always place your torch where the holder is because all of these rooms have emergency exits," she said. "Come stand here, near the door, and tell me where the second opening is, young boy."

I did as she asked and was unable to see any other entry point into the cave. A feeling of frustration filled me. So far, these women confounded me and it was clear that they were not fools. If they said there was another opening, there must be one. I could not see it as I walked further into the room and glanced back at her.

She seemed pleased and nodded.

I walked to the end of the room, where the pallet was. Glancing to my left, I saw an opening leading into black nothingness. My mouth opened wide with delight as the optical illusion vanished. It seemed like magic, but it was simply a practical matter. The left side of the wall curved, hiding the second entrance within the gloom of shadow. If one stood at the main entry, it was impossible to see. In the low light, I tried to find tool marks or any indicators that this was a planned aspect of the cave.

The woman took the torch from the wall and walked to where I was. She noticed me examining the walls and asked me what I was looking for. I told her and she laughed.

"You will find nothing, for this room is the first we found that had the special way out. Nature formed it this way; it is the template for all other rooms of the Chuchmox. Once we saw how beneficial and tactical this particular cave was, we used it to mold the other rooms into its equal. We take pride in our caves and moldings, but perhaps in them you will see signs of tools having been used for our constructs. From now on, whenever you stay here, this will be your sleeping room. Your cat is still in the larger cave, but she will find her way here for this is also the room she stays in when she visits."

I was ready to ask her about Chahal's stays here and she shushed me.

She held the torch to light up the shadowy corner. I could see a small triangle of space where one could hide. At the corner, a crude rope ladder went up into darkness.

The woman brushed past me, went to the ladder, and told me to climb up behind her as she ascended. She held the torch high above her head and away from the ladder. I had a difficult time climbing up behind her because the ropes would sway and shake along with her efforts.

When my head emerged, at the next level, she took me by the elbow to help me climb up into the upper cave. Her torch barely penetrated the stifling darkness around us. Beside her was a large clay vat. Dipping her fingers into it, she showed me that black ash filled it.

"This is one of our most closely held secrets, young prince. Should our cavern citadel ever be breached from the inside, this is how we will survive. I will tell you the things you should remember. After you climb up, draw the ladder up behind you to keep invaders from following you. Don't take the time to unfasten the ladder from where it is secured. If they are crafty enough, they can still shimmy up the tunnel, the walls are close enough together to allow that. Second, if they follow you, do this. Cover yourself quickly with the ash so you blend into the darkness and extinguish your light or place it so you are in shadow and wait for them. Third, bash them on the head when they emerge. There are many clubs lying around here," she said as she used the torch to show the ground around us. There weren't as many clubs as I expected to see, but they were there.

"What then?"

"Then you make your way to the exit tunnels on the hill and go to the outside. After that, you should run or hide as fast as you can. If our caves are invaded, the Chuchmox will fight until darkness covers the sky. Then we will make our escape. It would be useless to be cut down in the open daylight. We wait for night. Then you will be very glad for the vat of ashes outside of each escape hole."

"Are you going to show me the way to the surface?"

"Certainly."

She led me around a small maze in the upper level, which had such a low ceiling that I often had to crouch. It was simple for me as a boy, but it would be hard for a grown man; he would have to crawl at particularly low sections. The woman merely bent at the waist and passed through. I was delighted to realize that smaller people would have the advantage here.

"Whatever you do boy, never take the left path in the upper levels, where we are now. If you will notice, we have taken the right hand path at every juncture. Always remember that. The left hand paths are sabotaged. They are deadly and filled with traps."

A short time later, we could smell and feel fresh open air. We emerged into a broad cave that had a wide opening to the west. Hanging vines covered most of the opening, but I could still see the sun as it set.

I asked her if we could stay to watch the sun set. She looked bored with the idea, but allowed me to stay and watch as the sun abandoned the world to illuminate the land of the shadows. I sat behind the vines and saw the blazing orb dip. Clouds lit up with its golds and reds, heralding the coming of darkness with their brilliance. They mixed with the greens of the vines. I felt my eyes close with sleepiness as the colors mingled behind my eyelids.

A slap on the face brought me out of my slumber. The woman was standing above me with a look of fright. Regret flashed across her face. I reasoned that she was scared because she remembered that I was the prince. No doubt, she realized that she could be in trouble with my father. Her slap had only startled me; I felt no pain where she hit me. I told her not to worry about it and that I would not tell.

She shook her head and told me that she did what she had to do because I refused to wake up. I glanced at the sky and saw that it was full dark now.

"I can see why everyone is worried about you. They think that one of these times you will not awaken. I am only glad you did not disappear also. I hear that happens to you too," she said as she shuddered. "Don't worry about not telling anyone, I plan on telling the Paqal Paray exactly what I was forced to do. I should have realized when I saw you gazing at the dying sun."

Now I was the one worried. I didn't want anyone hearing about how a woman slapped me simply because she had a difficult time awakening me. I did not believe a word about my supposed disappearance while gazing. To me, I fell asleep, nothing more.

"I was not gazing," I argued. "I was enjoying the sunset and simply fell asleep."

She snorted like a man and put her hands on her hips, "I refuse to discuss this. Let us go."

Setting a brisk pace, she led me back to my room and then back to the larger cavern. From afar, I could see where the others waited for us around the fire.

As I was walking and weaving my way through the cave behind my guide, someone pinched my side. I turned to see Cham grinning at me. Hac was with him and greeted me. The woman turned around and rolled her eyes before leaving me with my friends.

Cham immediately began talking. "Let me tell you about my day, Zaki. You will never believe it. I had the most frightful time. All day long, I have spent with my face in the hands of teachers, behind a curtain of pelts. They would teach me that silence is useful to the assassin, but that it is less useful to the warrior. Timing is crucial. If an opponent is in the process of being attacked from behind, while facing you, one should refocus his attention back to you in order to mask the sounds of the back stabber," Cham said as he pantomimed a maniac stabbing someone and the other actions that he described. "Once he is weakened, a killing blow is delivered with more focus on defensive moves than one would ordinarily utilize. You might as well be invisible, if you can remain in your opponent's blind spots. They taught us about periphery vision, Zaki."

Cham explained what periphery vision was while Hac added details to help me understand the concept. I asked Hac if he had attended Cham's lessons.

"No. But we walked quite a ways here and he told me about what happened to him," he explained.

"I have never been so afraid for my life, Zaki," Cham said as he grabbed my arm.

"Having to maintain eye contact with a teacher sounds like a truly miserable way to pass the day. I would have been terrified," I said.

Cham released my arm and looked at me with his mouth hanging open. "I told you I was in fear for my life, not because I was pissing in my panties because I had to face another man, but because they were dropping boulders from the cliff right next to where we were standing! My teachers would force me to not be petrified or distracted and let me tell you something, Zaki."

"What?" I said quietly, shy that I had mentioned a fear he didn't share.

"Moments are eternities within themselves. Time is big. We merely speed it up," he said, wide-eyed and dazed.

Cham's words rattled me in a visceral way. My thoughts were too dull and slow to comprehend fully Cham's words, yet my body knew and was disquiet and alarmed.

The Cabicacmotz came up to us and placed his hand around my shoulder. "I'm afraid it is time for you boys to join us around the fire," he said.

"But I didn't get a chance to tell him how to know if plants are ailing before they show physical symptoms," Hac protested.

My uncle led us away quickly without giving me a chance to reply to Hac's request. When we neared the others, I saw that the Tzuhunik and the Etamanel Evan were there as well. The Etamanel Evan looked completely ill at ease, while the Tzuhunik was engaging in an animated discussion with the Paqal Paray.

The Paqal Paray abruptly stopped speaking when we joined them and sat. Leaving us no time to adjust or greet those who sat near us, she began, "All that glitters is reflected light. Our light source, the sun, emits too much light for us to use directly without the assistance of making the light bounce. That bounding light can be utilized much as we use springing traps. The held down branch whips upward when you cut the vine holding it. The branch is the reflected light. The vine is your own attention. The knife, which cuts the vine, is your will."

"What is the bending of the branch?" I asked.

The Paqal Paray laughed. "The branch signifies the light of the sun catching something shiny upon the ground. Do not worry about my examples; they are not exact. This is simply a manner of speaking to acquaint you with the concept of harnessing the glitter."

"What does the vine mean again, Zaki?" Cham asked me in a whisper.

I was about to shrug when the Paqal Paray continued, "When light is reflected, there is movement in the light's path of innumerable small strands and bits of light. It moves in one general direction or path before the light expands outward, depending upon where the original light falls upon it."

Hac nodded. Both Cham and I were both confused, judging by Cham's face.

Hac asked, "Why is the light in bits rather than how it is when it is in the sky?"

It amazed me that Hac knew about the threads of light in the sky. Only Cham and I were students of the Etamanel.

I whispered to Cham and asked him about Hac. He told me that Hac had always seen the lights in the sky and that he had taught him how to see them.

Our attention returned to the Paqal Paray and I heard her say, "Only original light can emit the continuity of threads. Once its path is broken, as it is with reflected light, we are able to catch its secondary beginnings. Also, that which we see is spreading from a smaller base and we see that it expands in an inverted triangular shape," she said as she brought her wrists together while angling her palms and fingers outward.

Fortunately, I understood her last words.

"Your words intrigue me, Paqal Paray," said Hac. "I have seen this triangle in reflected light when there is enough darkness to contrast it. Do you mean that we can utilize this upward thrust of the light if we attach our attention to it? Thereby utilizing the bounce of original light, catching it somehow?"

I looked over at Cham and realized that we were the stupid ones in this lesson. As if to prove my point, the Paqal Paray shared a glance with the Cabicacmotz that conveyed her pleasure at Hac's intellect or ability to follow her words. For a moment, I felt the edge of jealousy within me until I saw Hac's earnest face. He did not know that he impressed anybody; he only wanted to comprehend her words, nothing more.

Then I truly understood what Cham had said when he told me that Hac was good. My small friend was incapable of guile or pride.

"Yes," she said. "This is what is taught when gazing at glitter. Do not mistake it for that which scintillates. That which scintillates is elusive and quick. This occurs when gold dust is scattered in a sunbeam, when fog is pierced by light, and when steam catches the light from a fire."

I felt embarrassment for Cham when he asked, "Are those the only instances where things scintillate?" I thought it was clear that she was only citing examples.

Instead of scoffing, the Paqal Paray kindly answered, "No. There are other times when scintillation occurs. You should record instances in your scroll, should you chance upon them. To gaze upon that which scintillates is an advanced technique because its instances are elusive and speedy, but you should be mindful of it. Perhaps you will chance upon an occurrence which is best suited for you, that does not occur to your teacher."

"Are you saying that you will not be our teacher?" I asked.

All of the women around us laughed at my words. I wished I had not opened my mouth.

The Paqal Paray answered me after she finished giggling with the woman next to her. "Trust a future king to want to know where each person belongs. No, we have different strengths and we do not take individual students. If a person needs to learn gazing at shiny stones under the water, we will find many who excel at said feat and have them teach him. Perhaps one will give him the words he understands."

The Cabicacmotz then stood and told us to rise. When Hac stood, he told him, "No, you will spend the rest of the evening with the Paqal Paray. You may only leave her side when she grants you leave." Hac sat down with a smile on his face, seemingly glad about the arrangement.

I heard her tell Hac, "To quicken will and bring fruition to the past, place stones on your left side. It is a beacon, that marks the path energy must take."

Feeling as if we had been found wanting, yet glad that we could get up and do something else, we left. The Cabicacmotz eased our entrance into different groups among the sentries. We carried on numerous conversations with the women. During the course of the evening, Cham and I were separated.

Later on in the night, while a sentry spoke to me about gazing techniques for soft shadows, I began nodding off to sleep. The Cabicacmotz shook me and told me that it was time for me to sleep.

He was correct; I felt like a somnambulist. My thoughts were scattered and barely able to do more than pass lightly over any one thought. My peripheral vision had narrowed to such an extent that it seemed as if I was seeing everything around me from the bottom of a well. Nausea overtook me when I stood and I almost fell to my knees. Jerking me up by my armpit, the Cabicacmotz grabbed me by my braid and forced me to look at the ceiling of the cavern, with my head tilted back as far as it could, until the nausea passed. Then he made me go into an enclosure sectioned off by low boulders near the back of the cave. He placed my feet upwards against the cave wall as I lay on my back with my butt near the base.

When I next became conscious, I realized that I had fallen asleep. Something tickled at my awareness, awakening me further, yet I was asleep lying on my stomach, unable to move. Although my eyes were closed, I could see or somehow sense my surroundings visually.

Suddenly, someone grabbed me by the scruff of the neck and pulled me out of my body. Without thought, I jostled myself out of its grasp and willed myself to my body. How I was able to move like that, I do not know. It was instinctive. The only thing I knew was that I was in peril and that whatever or whoever snatched me away had evil intentions.

I tried to reenter my body, to no avail. I was hovering over it and some force caused me to connect with it only at my stomach. The rest of me whirled clockwise so that my physical head was to my left and my feet were to my right. I remember crying and praying to the Creator to help me back into my body.

No answer came to my pleas.

The entity that attacked me grabbed the back of my neck again, succeeding in tearing me away completely from my body. It took me to a place I never believed in, the place of dread. My unknown captor, holding me by the scruff, transported me straight into Xibalba, into the home of a lord.

We arrived at a dark cave, illumined by ambient red light. No light source was visible, yet I was able to see clearly.

I knew horror as I looked around. On a stone dais, a demon lord reclined against a stone back ledge, gracefully lounging as if waiting for me. A small smile played across its face when I met its gaze.

The Xibalban lord's eyes were like rubies glinting in the sun. White was its flesh, like a membrane over spoiled milk or infected pus. Black vertical stripes in the form of sigiled stars adorned its skin from head to toe.

My attention shifted to a tall robed being behind the lord. A cowl covered its face. It held a sharp handled instrument with a curved blade, similar to that which we used to cut maize from the fields. The robed Xibalban had no markings upon its hands.

Bound in a chair before the cowled Xibalban, sat a man. The demon grabbed hold of the man's hair and pulled his head back to expose his throat. The man cried and yelled for mercy. Immediately, the demon took the blade and sliced it back and forth along the man's bared throat. I heard the wet gurgling of the man and then I experienced something without parallel, something extraordinary. I heard as demons do.

This was music and sustenance. Despair, horror, and anguish were the food of Xibalba, as was its music. The man's emotions flooded the room like the aroma of cooking flesh. I sensed the ecstasy and satiation of the lord from this feast of pain and knew great fear.

Wide eyed with terror, I looked again at the lord to see him reclined on his dais. Its eyes looked behind me, at the being that held me, and it nodded once.

Still held and carried about like a lifeless puppet, I was unable to prevent being carried towards the Xibalban lord and forced to my knees before it. Horrified, I gazed up at the lord to see another small smile move across its mouth.

The being behind me took hold of my head and made me look at the sigils upon the lord's skin. A voice, which was not a voice, told me to memorize the markings and to count their number. I saw the way the black lines faded to grey underneath its white flesh, as if its skin was a thin veneer covering a deep well of black corruption. The lines did not intersect, yet they formed stars with six points. The voice also told me to summon the Xibalban, by using the pattern of his sigils, into my world. Dark and profane knowledge filled me as to how to complete such a feat. When I attempted to tell myself that I would never summon the demon lord, the being that held me shook me.

In our culture, many families of means had leather strips made up in the style of a loosely bound book. Leather was a necessity and meat was not always plentiful. Most often, these books were connected with cloth strips. Those with leather connecting the pages often remained forever in the same position when the leather dried out completely and hardened.

The Xibalban lord opened one such book, perused it for a moment, and hung it on one side, forcing the slats horizontal to the floor. I noticed that it had leather binds holding both sides of its pages. The being behind me turned me to a wall. From there I saw the shine upon the leather glittering on the wall.

To say that speech occurred is insufficient and incorrect. I received a communication of knowledge from the lord. Through him, I learned what the Chuchmox knew; they knew how to transfer their whole consciousness to the left side of their bodies. It was a physical knowing, almost akin to a feeling.

With that knowledge, I performed the act and received a pleased feeling from the Xibalban. Nevertheless, I was unable to switch back to normalcy and could not even remember how it felt.

My eyes reverted to the shine of the book playing on the wall. I tried to experience my consciousness on my right and jumped to it. Then I slowly expanded to the left while retaining my hold upon the right. After that tentative brush, I released my hold upon the right and bounced completely into the left again.

Something which was outside of me, although I didn't know if any of those in the room were its source, told me to perform the maneuvers while looking at the light play upon the wall.

When I did this, I saw that the swing of the book caused it to appear as if it was bouncing upon the wall, upwards and downwards. The book created the illusion that the world around me was in a constant flux of repetitive motion. I watched that for what seemed like a long time.

Eventually, the being holding my neck shook me from the sight of a dancing world. It turned me around to an empty cave of stone. All three beings were gone.

The same being, which told me to look at the wall, advised me to remember what I witnessed. While it transported me into nothingness, before the obscuring dark fell, I held on viciously to my memory. I was even able to carry it into the reality of my night in the cave of the Chuchmox.

When I returned to my body, I found myself inside the enclosure huddled against the rock face in the position of a babe. Sitting up, I saw my necklace strewn across the floor, pieces of flat black rock crumbled. My navel stone was no longer in my belly button and had rolled a short distance away, intact. I grabbed it off the floor, stood, and looked around the cavern for my uncle. Finally, I saw where he was and went to him.

After I told my tale to the Paqal Paray and the Cabicacmotz, they marched everyone out of the caverns, into the dawn. I hadn't known I was gone for a full night.

None of the women complained, but I could tell that they were frightened and exasperated at having to leave their abode.

When I asked the Cabicacmotz why we had to leave, he looked upon me with disbelief. "Zaki," he said. "An emissary of Xibalba has entered the sacred caves of the women. We must cleanse the cave of its presence."

He explained how people would saturate the air, with the intent to cleanse, with smoke of a powerful plant. Afterwards, they would wash as much of the walls that they could and cleanse all of their belongings in the subterranean river.

"Needless to say, you are no longer welcome to sleep within their caves."

I felt rejected and conveyed my sadness at not being able to learn with them.

"They are not rejecting you, you little fool. They are merely avoiding a lot of unnecessary labor and busywork. Hardly anyone enjoys cleaning. No, from now on you will be taught gazing while out of caves. The other option is to watch you every moment and not permit you to fall asleep.

They will choose the easier option until we eliminate the threat."

"How will you eliminate the threat?"

With a sad grimace, he told me that they might not be able to and that my only recourse was to learn as much as I could, as quickly as I was able.

When I asked him why, he said, "The only thing that will place you beyond their reach is the third body."

We stood there for a long while, watching the last of the women file out of the cave.

He said, "Nephew, you now know much about those creatures. They shared their techniques and knowledge with you. Do you wish to call upon them as they requested?"

I could hear the apprehension in his voice and feel his hope that I would not.

With full sincerity, I answered, "No, my uncle. They must never be brought here." I now knew the true adversaries of man and I resolved never to seek them and, if I could, to educate others of their danger.

Nodding, he put his arm around my shoulder and led me towards the path.

Epilogue

Those were the first days of my instruction in the esoteric arts of my people. I do not know if the people of today will want to hear about what people from such a long time ago thought about and acted upon. Perhaps I fool myself and this is only my way of confessing my life because no one braids my hair for me any longer.

It is my hope that my words will comfort those who seek knowledge and reveal what mankind has forgotten. Something strange is going on all around us and few seem cognizant of it.

As we immerse ourselves in daily life and dogmatically hold its view, we push aside the mysterious and the arcane. We hide behind the belief that every odd feeling or thing can be explained away by chemical reactions in the brain. Such a belief is the sorcery of today and its only use is to keep us trapped in a world of boredom and uncompromising rigidness. Yet it is not a strong enough sorcery to banish truly the inexplicable. It is only a panacea, something to soothe the reason.

I wish to tell more of what happened to me in my early education, but perhaps fate will step in and silence me somehow. I wish to be able to continue even to the point of relating how the teachings manifested in my experiences.

Those who seek truth should remember to polish their spirit by purifying their thoughts, hone their physical body by performing good deeds and exercise their dreamer so that it is aware and only engages in acts that are in keeping with their bodies and spirits. The rest will come naturally.

I believe I have given the seeker of wisdom enough to begin and perhaps that will be enough to turn the tide. Prepare yourselves, for the enemies of mankind are already engaged in battle against us. My choice is to fight.

Accompany me and accept the birthright of man, the twin.

Acknowledgments

This book was begun in 1997 and has gone through various changes and numerous drafts. My gratitude to the many reviewers consulted throughout this process. Thank you to my literary manager, Dr. Kenneth J. Atchity, and to his staff for putting up with my weirdness and frequent disappearances. Thanks also to Lisa Cerasoli for the book design and David Angsten for the cover...cover painting by the author. Any mistakes made are mine. As for the content within, I thank J for the retrieval at the Immigration Clinic in South Bend, Indiana, my enemies for the opportunities they have unwittingly provided to me, the Popol Vuh as translated by Dennis Tedlock, and the Quiche-English Dictionary by Munro A. Edmonson. Any others I've missed, you also have my thanks. To the man with long gray hair and a hat, my hat goes off to you as well!